HEART

A BALLSY BOYS PRODUCTION BOOK 3

K.M. NEUHOLD
NORA PHOENIX

Heart (Ballsy Boys Book Three) by K.M. Neuhold and Nora Phoenix

Copyright ©2018 K.M. Neuhold and Nora Phoenix

Cover design: K.M. Neuhold

Editing: Rebecca J. Cartee at Editing by Rebecca

All rights reserved. No part of this story may be used, reproduced, or transmitted in any form by any means without the written permission of the copyright holder, except in case of brief quotations and embodied within critical reviews and articles.

This is a work of fiction. Names, characters, places, and incidents either are the products of the author's imagination or are used fictitiously. Any resemblance to actual persons, living or dead, businesses, companies, events, or locales is entirely coincidental. The use of any real company and/or product names is for literary effect only. All other trademarks and copyrights are the property of their respective owners.

This book contains sexually explicit material which is suitable only for mature readers.

❦ Created with Vellum

1

MASON

My fingers fly over the keys of my laptop, the code starting to blur in front of my burning eyes. My typing doesn't falter as I try to blink the tiredness away. A few stray tears escape, my eyes clearly making a desperate attempt to re-lubricate after hours spent staring at the screen with very little blinking. It's starting to feel like there's sand behind my eyelids, but I don't want to stop until I've finished a few more lines of code.

My eyes aren't the only thing getting tired and sore. My wrists and back ache, but it's nothing I'm not used to. Our ancestors worked to become upright, and we thank them by spending our lives hunched over our computers.

As I finish the last line I wanted to get in, I lean back against my couch cushion and push my glasses to the top of my head, rubbing my hands over my eyes. The tears are doing nothing to help the burning, but I'm sure only getting my eyes off a screen for a while tonight will help with that. Not that it's likely to happen. What would I even do other than sit in front of my computer or boot up my video games?

I glance at my phone, sitting on the coffee table, right by

where I have my feet propped up. I *could* text Heart and see what he's up to tonight. But I highly doubt he's free on a Saturday night. Not that I have the first clue *what* he could be up to on a Saturday night. What do normal people do? Probably go to the club and find someone to hook up with? Drink with friends and then find someone to hook up with? It seems like that's how most single people who aren't freaks like me spend their weekends.

Whatever Heart is up to, I'm sure he's having too much fun to want to be bothered by me.

The shrill sound of my door buzzer makes me jump, nearly toppling my laptop onto the floor. Who would be stopping by here at eleven on a Saturday night? My heart hammers as I close my laptop and set it aside. It couldn't be Brad, could it? He'd stopped by a few times since we broke up, but it had been at least a month now since he'd bothered.

I don't know why I wasted time with a fucking loser like you anyway. An echo of his words pricks at my skin and makes my stomach roil.

I stand on shaky legs and go to the door.

"Hello?" I say after pressing down on the intercom button.

"Hey, man." My best friend—Troy's—voice crackles through the speaker, and I breathe a sigh of relief. I buzz him up and then open the door a crack before going back over to the couch. Leaning back against the cushion again, I tug each of my fingers to crack the knuckles and then crack my wrists as well.

"I recognize that look. How many hours have you been coding today?" Troy asks, stepping inside and closing the door behind himself.

"Not that many," I lie, and he fixes me with a look that

tells me he isn't buying it. "Like thirteen, I think. I took a break to eat something around seven, though."

"It's a Saturday night, what are you doing sitting here all alone?" he asks while heading to my fridge and pulling out a couple of beers. I shake my head and wave my hand to let him know I don't want one and Troy rolls his eyes. "Have a drink or I'm dragging you out of the house to socialize with strangers."

I cringe at the threat and sigh in defeat.

What the fuck is wrong with you? All you want to do is sit in your apartment all alone. It's like you're not even fucking human. Brad's words twist my gut, just like they did the first time he said them to me.

"Mase, I'm not trying to be a dick. I'm sorry," Troy says, hovering in the kitchen like he can't decide if he should just put the drinks back and let me be or keep trying to push me out of my comfort zone.

"You're fine, just bring me a drink." I wave him over, and he smiles, passing me one of the beers when he reaches me. "Where's Rebel tonight?"

Troy and Rebel started dating a few months ago, and now it's rare for me to see one without the other, with the exception of when Troy and I are working on the mobile game we developed. Even then, if it's marketing related, Rebel's there. The man knows how to market, which I'm sure is part of the reason he was promoted to a behind the scenes role at the Ballsy Boys porn studio.

"He's out with the guys. I was going to tag along, but then I decided I'd rather come hang out with you. It's been ages since we've just chilled."

I nod and take a sip of my beer, casting around for something to add.

"You want to play video games?" I offer, and Troy smiles.

"Duh."

I laugh and set up a new game I'd gotten a review copy of a few days ago. I didn't start a review blog to get free early copies of games, but it's a definite perk.

For a while, we fall into a comfortable silence as we play and drink. That's what I like about Troy: he gets this part of me. I'm not so sure he—or anyone else—could understand most of me, but it's nice to have this at least. I'm lucky Troy decided to take me under his wing and make me his friend. He's the first person in my life who's bothered, and I had no idea what I was missing until I had Troy and Heart as friends.

"How are things going with you and Heart?" Troy asks.

"What do you mean?" I don't take my eyes off the screen as my character wrestles a multi-legged beast. "We're friends, we hang out and stuff."

Troy introduced me to Heart when he and Rebel started hanging out. Heart works at Ballsy Boys with Rebel and that's something I try really hard not to think about because we're friends.

"Is that seriously all it is? I introduced you guys so he could help you gain confidence between the sheets. Are you telling me you two have never fooled around?" he presses.

I don't know why I ever bothered with you. It would be one thing if you were good in bed, but all you do is lie there like a dead fish.

I feel my face heating, both at Troy's implication and Brad's words in my memory. Troy really thought Heart and I had been... Oh god, is that what all of them think? Is that what all their friends picture when I show up to hang around? That Heart and I are...

"No," I reply emphatically. "*Nothing* like that is going on.

I happen to like being friends with Heart, and there's no way *that* wouldn't ruin it."

God, Brad was right. I can't even say the words, let alone think them. Of course I'm not any good at the actual act.

"Okay, if not Heart, then what about someone else?"

"What?"

"You dropped douchebag Brad *months* ago. It's time you get back out there."

"Why? I've been thinking about it, and I don't see why people put so much emphasis on dating. I'm perfectly happy alone. I'm happier even than I was when he and I were dating. I don't need a boyfriend."

"You're happier without Brad because he was the fucking worst. The right person would be better, make you feel better."

"Not everyone gets a fairytale ending like you and Rebel," I sigh.

"Not if they don't *try*," Troy insists. "Look, I get how scary dating is. If anyone understands the desire to stay single, it's me. But I'm telling you, the right guy is out there for you if you're open to finding him."

"How is that not fairytale bullshit?" I challenge. "Look, I'll think about it if you promise to drop it," I lie. I don't want to think about dating. All I want to think about is finishing my dual degree in programming and graphic design and get hired by a top game design company.

"I'll drop it *for now*. But don't think I'm not going to drag your ass out to the club soon to at least window shop."

I roll my eyes and bite my lip against a smile. He may be a pain in my ass, but Troy is a good friend.

Even after the subject is dropped, I can't keep my mind from wandering back to Heart now and then throughout the rest of the night. There's no way he'd want to teach me how to be better in bed. He's sexy and confident, everything I'm not. I'm sure he has *more* than enough partners to keep him entertained without some loser like me begging him to fix whatever's broken with me.

Troy leaves around one in the morning, and I realize as I'm getting ready for bed that I have a text from Heart asking if I want to come over and hang out tomorrow…or later today, I guess. I respond in the affirmative and then crawl into bed, trying hard not to think about everything Troy said tonight.

I SHIFT BACK and forth on my feet and glance between Heart's door and the stairway I just came from. I'm here too early. I knew I should've waited until later in the day to come over to Heart's to hang out.

Stupid, stupid.

Brad always said I had zero social graces. Yet another thing he was right about. I don't know how to be normal. Even when I'm trying to prove to myself that he was wrong when he called me boring, I still manage to do it in the most awkward possible way.

I hear Heart on the other side of the door moving around. *Oh, shit.* Heart said he wanted to hang out today, and I was stupid enough to show up way too early and now I'm ruining his whole morning.

I push my glasses farther up my slightly sweaty nose and shuffle my feet toward the stairwell, trying to decide if I should just leave. *But, he already knows I'm here.* It would be equally as awkward for me to leave now.

I cringe and clench my fists a few times to try to calm my nerves. Just as I'm about to turn and make a run for it—

deciding I can just make up an excuse later—the door swings open. My mouth gapes as Heart stands in the open doorway in nothing but a pair of skimpy briefs, his tattooed skin on full display and a noticeable bulge in the front of his underwear.

"Mason," Heart greets me with a smile, but he seems slightly out of breath in nothing but his underwear.

"I'm sorry; I'm too early," I apologize, biting down on my bottom lip.

"No, you're fine," he assures me, leaning against the door frame and letting his gaze flit over me quickly. *Did he just check me out?*

I shake that thought off. Of course, he didn't check me out. I'm me and he's...well, he's a gorgeous porn star.

The pit of my stomach tightens, and my cock thickens against my thigh. I know exactly what Heart looks like in the throes of passion, and that's something you just shouldn't know about a friend. In my defense, I've made a real effort not to jerk off to Heart's videos since we've started hanging out. Even if he always was my favorite...and maybe I slip up sometimes and enjoy one, even though I know I shouldn't.

"Sorry, I'm kind of just waking up. I was out late last night," Heart explains as he steps aside to let me in. I blush at the implication of Heart's *late night*, then hate myself for it. Brad was so right: I'm a total prude. But I'm hanging out with a porn star; I should get association points or something, right?

I follow Heart in and he heads over to his dresser beside his bed, pulling open the top drawer.

"Oh no, it's not like that," he assures me as he grabs a pair of jeans and white t-shirt from his dresser, pulling them on and then plopping down on his couch. I follow suit.

"Why not? I mean, you're hot and obviously...*that* stuff isn't a big deal for you..."

Heart chuckles and nods. "Yeah. It's complicated, though. Plus, I don't know, sometimes casual sex gets pretty boring, but I don't really do relationships." Heart's smile falters, and a hint of sadness peeks out from behind his happy mask.

"Same," I commiserate.

"At least there's always Xbox and jerking off," Heart adds with a cheeky smirk before handing me an Xbox controller from the table next to the couch.

I'm not a huge fan of shooters, but I can certainly hold my own with casual to moderate gamers. After all, videogames are my life.

I may not understand people very well, but coding I get. Designing I totally get. Creating a game works out both sides of my brain, the analytical side needed for the programming and the creative side coming into play with the art design.

Brad was never supportive. He said I lived in a fantasy world and that I'd rather play video games than have sex. He was right.

My mind travels back to my chat with Troy last night and the way he implied everyone assumed I was hooking up with Heart. Had Heart heard the other guys gossiping about us? Does he know why Troy introduced us to begin with?

"You got really quiet; are you having fun?" Heart checks as he blows the head off one of my soldiers.

"Yeah, just thinking."

"Care to share with the class?"

"Um..." I bite my lip, keeping my gaze trained on the television where I'm lining up a sniper shot on one of his guys. "It's kind of personal."

"You don't have to share if you don't want, just thought I'd offer. I'm a good listener, and we are friends or whatever."

Friends. Yeah, I guess we are. I never had many friends growing up, what with my dazzling social graces and all. But over the past six months or so, I've gotten close to Troy, and he introduced me to Heart. Two close friends may seem like a small number to a lot of people, but it's two more than I've ever had in my entire life.

"Do you know why Troy wanted you to meet me?" I ask, trying to swallow around my dry throat.

"No, I thought Rebel invited me to dinner that day to be polite and that you and I just happened to meet. Was it a set up?"

"Kind of," I admit, chancing a glance out of the corner of my eye at Heart. He's focused on the television and too beautiful to be real. "Okay, don't get weirded out or anything if I tell you?"

"I doubt anything you could possibly say would weird me out."

"Ugh, fine, the thing is I confided in Troy that my ex said I was really boring in bed. I think he was hoping you would *help* me."

Heart stills beside me, and seconds later, I can feel his eyes on me. I grip the controller harder, cursing myself for opening this can of worms. What was I thinking?

I startle when Heart's hand comes to rest on my knee, and finally I chance a look at him. He's smiling. I don't think it's a teasing smile; it looks too gentle for that.

"Is that what *you* want? Do you want me to help you spice up your bedroom moves?"

A little squeak escapes me, and I feel my face and neck

flame, my sweaty hands white knuckling the Xbox controller. "I don't...uh...I don't really know. No?"

Heart's hand on my knee squeezes gently, and he scoots a little closer. "Why don't you think about it? You don't have to answer now."

"Is...uh...is that something *you* would want? I mean, look at you, you could have anyone. I'm just ugh. There wouldn't even be anything in it for you."

"First of all, you are not *ugh*, you're *mmmm*," Heart purrs, and I feel my blush deepen. "Keep that straight. And, secondly, it just so happens that I think there's something very sexy with a little student/teacher role play. It would be hot to draw you out of your shell and teach you a thing or two."

My hands start to tremble, and I feel my heart going wild again. "I'll think about it," I croak.

Heart can't be serious, can he? Maybe he's just messing with me or teasing me. It wouldn't be the first time a guy pretended to be interested in me as a joke.

The conversation drops, and we return to playing.

The rest of the afternoon is spent on various games, and eventually we order a pizza. I don't know why it surprises me to realize Heart is just a regular guy. For some reason I thought he'd be on a different plane, being a gorgeous, confident porn star and all. And I start to wonder if it would be so bad to take Heart up on his offer after all.

2

LUCKY

It's already been a long day, and my shirt is sticking to my back in the sweltering heat, but I can't go home just yet. I have one more check up on the client, and all I can do is hope that my gut feeling about him is wrong. He's been my client for about four months now, and so far, he seems to toe the line. He's answered every question I've asked him, has shown me proof of gainful employment, he's not been seen with any of his former associates, and yet I have the feeling he's keeping something from me.

I can't explain it, this sixth sense I have, but I guess it's what my boss calls my radar. She says it's one of the things that makes me such a good parole officer. Maybe, but it's also one of the things that can make my job complicated. Like in this case, anyone else would've been content with the information provided, but no, I can't let it go. This tingle down my spine, this churning in my stomach every time I meet with this guy, everything tells me something is off. And I can't let that go.

It's why a find myself at the end of a long, hot, busy day on my way for a surprise visit to the cheap motel he's staying in after his release from prison. I'm allowed to do these, obviously. And it's not like I don't do them with anyone else. I do, but usually not when there has been zero indication that one is necessary. In this case, I have nothing else to go on but my intuition, which is telling me to keep digging.

The fact that I'm single only plays into me being a workaholic. Most of my coworkers have a family to get home to, so they'll think twice before taking on more hours. Me, I have no one waiting for me, so I can work as many hours as I want to.

I hope to have that too, someday soon, someone will be waiting for me. Hookups have never been my thing, but lately, I've become even more reluctant to engage in those one-night stands. They're too messy for me, too disruptive in my life and my routines. I want something a little more permanent. Someone a little more permanent, I should say. Someday...

I park my car two blocks away from the motel, not because I don't want to be seen anywhere near it, but because all the parking spots are taken, as usual. This is not the best part of town, which is why, as always, I am grateful for the fact that I drive a company car and not my own.

There are a few men hanging around outside near the entrance to the motel, and I give them a short nod as I walk inside. Usually, I report myself to the front desk, as is custom, but in this case, I really want my arrival to be a surprise. In case Jake has some kind of arrangement with the front desk, I don't want them to announce my presence and give him the opportunity to hide anything.

So, I simply walk up to his room, take a deep breath, and knock forcefully on the door. It only takes seconds before the door is yanked open, and I come face-to-face with my client, a six-foot-seven former basketball prodigy who got addicted to painkillers and then started selling them to support his habit. He's still young enough to turn his life around after a short stint in prison, and I really hope he will.

However, a quick peek over his shoulder into the room makes it crystal clear that my gut feeling was spot on.

"Jake," I say, my stomach sinking. "Unannounced house visit. Can I come in, please?"

This is not a question that has any other answer but "yes" and we both know it. Still, Jake hesitates.

"Anything you want to tell me, Jake?" I ask.

He sighs and drops his shoulders. "I don't know what to say. Busted, I guess." He opens the door wide to let me in, and I get a better look at the twenty or so small plastic bags lined up on the table. There is also a wide variety of pharmacy bottles, and it doesn't take a genius to figure out what he's doing. I close the door behind me and turn around to face him.

"This doesn't look good," I tell him. "Can you give me any other explanation for this other than the fact that you're dealing again?"

He shakes his head, his shoulders dropping even lower. He's twenty-eight years old, and he's about to go to prison for the second time, and this time the judge won't be so lenient on him. Violating your parole conditions is one thing but violating them by committing the exact same crime you got sentenced for before, that's not good.

"I have to call the cops, Jake. Before I do that, can you at least tell me what happened?"

He lowers his long frame into a chair that looks like a kid's chair with him in it. "I was determined to change my life, you know," he says. "All these guys in prison who'd been there a few times, they told me how hard it was to make a fresh start, to catch a break as a convicted felon. I believed them, but at the same time I thought it would be different for me. After all, I don't come from a crime background, and it's not like I've been surrounded by gangs or friends who were involved in shit like this my whole life. I come from a nice, white, middle-class suburban family. I just got sucked into this because of that stupid injury I had and that addiction I never was able to kick."

His story is a familiar one, one that I have heard a lot from clients like him. They think it will be different for them because of their skin color or their background or the type of crime they committed. They don't understand that being a felon is hard no matter what your skin color is. That being said, non-white clients face even more hurdles when they try to rebuild their lives. Go figure.

"But you managed to get that job as a dishwasher, correct?" I ask.

"I did, but do you know how much I make there? Or rather I should say, how little? It pays eleven bucks an hour, man. There's no way I can live on that."

"We talked about this, Jake. You knew it was going to be rough for the first few years, until you had proven to potential employers you were a changed man. That restaurant is known for giving felons a chance, and you said you were interested in the industry, so if you had stayed there, they would've given you a chance to climb up the ladder. You could've made a career there."

Jake shakes his head. "Man, even the cooks there make practically nothing," he says. "In five years, I still wouldn't have made enough to be able to live the kind of life I want."

And there it is, the reason why so many of my clients fall back into their old lives. It's hard to adjust your life to the financial reality of having a real-life job, instead of making quick and fast money the illegal way. Whatever Jake was dealing paid well, and he could afford a life of going out for dinner, partying with his friends, buying presents for girlfriends and whatnot. And now that that money is gone and he has to make do on minimum wage like so many other people, he can't make the transition to a life that simple, without those luxuries.

I get it, and it's why I talk about this with my clients so much, especially in the first few weeks. It pisses me off that despite that, Jake still made the choice that money was more important than his future. I get so frustrated with choices like this because I want better for them. Jake is not a bad guy, not by any standard. He just sucks at making the right choices.

"Well, I could point out that even if you had been living on minimum wage five years from now, you would at least be a free man, but I guess that's a moot point by now. I'm sorry, Jake. I had hoped better for you."

Jake is quiet for a bit before he answers. "Yeah, I am sorry to. But mostly disappointed in myself. I really thought I would be better, that I would not go down this road again. I guess I wasn't as strong as I thought I was."

I take my phone out of my pocket to call it in to the cops. They'll have to collect the evidence against him and arrest him, of course. At least he didn't try to blame it on someone else. Or, the absolute most horrific cliché clients keep trying to feed me: this is not what it looks like. He's owning up to his mistakes, so maybe that means there's hope for him after all.

"It's not about being strong enough, Jake. It's about building habits every day that take you closer to your goal of the kind of life you want. And even now, it's not too late for you. You can still turn your life around; it's just gonna take longer than you may have wanted."

He sends me a sad smile. "You know, Mr. Stone, one of the things I appreciate most about you is your relentless optimism. You gave me some really good advice along the way. I just wish I had listened to you."

I sigh with a sad smile, not feeling the optimism at all. "So do I."

The calls to the cops is quick, as they know me, and a few minutes later they show up to collect Jake and the evidence. I shake his hand before they handcuff him and put him in the squad car. One of the cops slaps me on my back. "Tough call, man."

"Yeah, I know," I say. "I hate doing this."

The guy's eyes are warm as he meets mine. "I know it's horribly trite, but it's true. You can't save them all. At least, that's what I tell myself when my efforts fail. We try our best, you know? That's all we can do."

I think about his words as I drive home. He's right, of course. It's one of the things you learn in a job like mine or like his. We can't save them all. But I can damn well try. And defeats like today, losing a client like Jake, it hurts. I know it's not my fault. I know it was his choice to do this, but I still take it hard. It's not that I blame myself, but incidents like this do make me wonder if my approach is the right one.

I have a long list of clients I am responsible for right now, and I know that statistically, I will lose a few more of them to their old lives. So no, I can't save them all. But there's a few I will have to work harder for, to make sure they stay on the right side of the law. There's a few that I refuse to lose.

And at the very top of that list is a foul-mouthed, tatted up bad boy who stubbornly refuses to vacate my dreams. And oh, the dreams are sweet. And sexy. No wonder, since they're fueled by the overabundance of videos of him on the Internet...and on my computer.

Some days, I wish I had never met him, because he's becoming an addiction unlike anything I've ever experienced before. But other days, I am grateful that I'm responsible for him, at least professionally. Because I will fight for him. I will do whatever I can to make sure he turns his life around.

And I'll be damned if I lose *him*.

3
HEART

I let out a long sigh as I lazily wipe the cum off my stomach. Damn, that was a good one. I re-watched my first shoot with Rebel, and it had me spurting all over myself. Hot damn. That guy not only has a perfect cock, but he can work it, too. He fucked me into next week in our shoot, and my ass hurt for a few days after, but I'd do it again in a heartbeat if he'd let me.

Fat chance of that, though, now that the guy has gone all lovey-dovey with his boyfriend. Not that I can blame him. Troy is fucking gorgeous, and the two of them pretty much set the room on fire every time they are together. It's kinda nauseating, really.

I drop the tissue on the floor, where they join an empty pizza box, a few days' worth of microwave meals, and a stack of unidentified trash. I really need to clean up a little, if only because I promised Mason we could hang out later today. Poor kid has no idea of the total pig that I am, and while I'm sure he'll discover soon enough, I can leave him blissfully naive a little longer. I don't, like, go all out domestic before he comes, but I do take out the trash at least.

A forceful knock on my door has my heart skipping a beat. Oh, fucking hell. I don't need to see who it is. I know. The number of people who have my address is limited, and the number of people who will show up unannounced is even less. Someone must've let him in downstairs...

Mr. Stone. It has been three whole weeks since the last house visit, and the guy obviously takes his job highly serious, so I guess I was due another visit. Well, he's in for a treat considering the state of my apartment.

I pull my boxers up and debate throwing on a shirt, then decide against it. Any chance I get to rile the man, I'll take it. And so I throw open the door, wearing nothing but the tight, pink boxers I did a shoot for last week. They look damn good on me, stretching tight around my ass and my package. Let's see if Mr. Stone agrees...

"Hello, Mr. Stone," I say, my voice a tad huskier than usual.

His dark green eyes drop down for just a second before they're firmly focused on my face again. I can't suppress my smile. That's more of a reaction than I've gotten out of him so far. He's a little ice cube, Mr. Stone, but I'll manage to melt him someday.

"Gunner," he says, his face all cool and detached again.

God, it's so strange to hear my official first name out of someone's mouth. Very few people call me that anymore, except for him, of course. And the people at my work. No, not the Ballsy Boys. My *other* work, the one I have to show up at every Saturday for at least another six months.

I put a hand on my hip and tighten my abdominal muscles. Trust me, I know how to work this body. "I assume you wanna come in and hang out?"

His face remains carefully blank, but his eyes give him away. They flicker downward, to my cock and then back up again, and his Adam's apple bobs as he swallows. Oh, Mr. Stone *likes* what he sees.

"I'd prefer you put on some clothes first."

Ha! I knew it. This guy is totally gay. I suspected from the moment we met since his eyes widened ever so slightly when he saw me, but so far, he's been damn hard to read. This statement says a lot, though.

I lean back against the door post, stretch my arms above my head and take my time to yawn. "Does it bother you that I'm not wearing much?"

I look at him from underneath my lashes, but his face doesn't show a reaction. It seems he has himself in a tight grip again.

"I figured you'd be more comfortable inviting me in if you were wearing clothes."

My grin broadens because he just painted himself into a corner. "Dude, I fuck guys for a living. This doesn't bother me at all, so come on in."

I throw the door wide open and turn around, leaving him little choice but follow me inside. I cringe a little as I witness the state of my studio but hide my discomfort quickly. This is not a guy I want to be too honest and vulnerable with. I sweep a pile of clothes off the couch onto the floor so Stone has a place to sit, and then I drop down on my bed again, with my back against the wall.

Stone carefully closes the door behind him, his face hardening as he sees the mess.

"The maid called in sick," I say.

He grimaces, though I'm not sure if that's because of the chaos or my spectacularly lame joke, and steps over all kinds of shit to lower himself on the couch. "Do you have any guns or illegal substances on the premises?"

I scoff. "Premises? It's a studio, dude. Where the fuck would I hide anything?"

He sighs and folds his hands, sitting ramrod straight on the couch. "Gunner, we've talked about this before. You need to address me as 'Mr. Stone'. Your lack of respect for my position as shown in your state of undress and your language is disconcerting and doesn't reflect well on your attitude toward your rehabilitation. If I were you, I would try and curb your affinity for curse words. They won't help you with reintegrating into society."

Mr. Stone. If there ever was a man aptly named, it's him. He's a living, breathing piece of stone. Unflappable. Emotionless. Unmoving. What I wouldn't give to see this guy lose his composure for a second. God, it would be worth all the trouble I'd get into, seriously.

"At my current job, fuck is a perfectly acceptable word. As a matter of fact, it's the one-word summary of my job description. How's that for reintegration and rehabilitation?"

Another sigh. "I've expressed my displeasure with your chosen profession on previous occasions. Holding company with people like *that* will not help you find a respectable place in society, Gunner."

I jump up from the bed before realizing it, my fists clenched. "You do not get to judge them, you hear me? Not when I was turned down for every single job I applied for because of my record. They're the ones who took me in, accepted me. Hell, they're my friends, and you do not get to spew your sanctimonious, judgmental shit all over them!"

For the first time, there's emotion on his face, but it's not what I was expecting. There's a hint of a smile on his lips, and for the life of me, I don't understand why. He should be furious with me, so why is he amused?

"There's that infamous temper I was warned about. I was wondering what I'd have to do to get you to drop the cool act and show me your true colors."

My mouth drops slightly open. "You were baiting me? Why the fuck would you do that?"

"Isn't that what you've been doing to me from the first time we met? Provoking me with your attitude, your words, and even your sexuality? Hell, you're walking around in your damn underwear, hoping to get a rise out of me."

I blink. It's like Stone has been replaced with another guy that looks exactly the same but acts completely different. What the hell? Has he been playing me this whole time? Why?

"I'm... I don't know what you mean," I offer lamely.

He scoffs. "Don't play dumb now. You're better than that."

"All right, I *was* baiting you, okay?" I grab a shirt from the pile of clothes on the floor and pull it on, then drag on a pair of shorts. "There, happy now?"

The man's expression is unreadable. "Happy is still a ways off, but you being dressed is a good start." He leans forward on the couch, his eyes piercing. "Look, you're gonna be stuck with me for a whole year...and even more if I don't sign off on your successful reentry into society. The longer you resist my efforts to help you, the longer this process will take. Your parole does not end until I say so."

"I thought it was for a definitive period of one year," I mumble.

"Not if I advise against ending it. And I will if you don't start working *with* me instead of goading me and resisting my every effort to help you."

He's got me by the balls, and we both know it. The thing is, as much as I bitch to myself about him, Stone isn't that bad. I could do worse. A lot worse. I only have to think back to some of the guards to remind myself how much worse things could get.

"What do you want from me?" I ask.

He leans back in the couch, his face surprisingly friendly. "Tell me about your week. What did you do?"

4

MASON

I walk through the door of my studio apartment and toss my backpack on the floor. Being around people all day never fails to drain my energy. All I want is to retreat to my solitude and recharge my batteries, so I can do it all over tomorrow.

I kick my shoes off and flop down on my couch, my phone in my hand. I spend a few minutes checking the download figures for my and Troy's game and then browse the social media sites Rebel helped up set up for marketing. It holds little interest, and after a few minutes, I find myself scrolling through my bookmarks to find one of my gamer forums to check out. When I scroll past BallsyBoys.com on my bookmark list, I pause.

One thing I never considered when I started hanging out with Heart, and getting to know Rebel better, was how much of an effect getting to know porn stars would have on my jerk off habits. I used to pull up these porn sites without a second thought and take care of business. Now, they're people, and it feels weird as hell.

However, my dick doesn't seem to be getting the weird

factor today. A few weeks ago, Heart mentioned he did a shoot where he tried out different anal vibrators. My cock thickens at the memory of the way his eyes rolled back and the little smile on his lips when he talked about the shoot. I'd gone home that night and jerked off three times imagining Heart fucking himself with different vibrators.

I wonder if that video is up yet. I unzip my pants to make room for my growing erection. Reaching into my boxers, I lazily stroke myself to full hardness, and then I click on the link before I can talk myself out of it.

There it is, right at the top of the suggested videos list. *Heart Tries Out Some New Toys.* My breath hitches at the thumbnail image—Heart's famous 'O' face. It's why the viewers love him so much, the way he bites his lip, his eyes rolling back when he comes. It's like he's being utterly tortured by the vastness of the pleasure of his orgasm.

My cock throbs in my hand, encouraging me to click on the video.

"Hey guys," Heart greets the camera with his friendly smile. He's sitting on a bed in nothing but a pair of royal blue boxers. The colorful ink covering his arms, hands, and chest holds my attention for more than a few seconds. My favorite is the rose on the side of his neck. It flutters with his pulse and calls out to be licked and bitten.

My own thoughts surprise me. I don't usually take it upon myself to lick or bite anything in bed. With Brad I just tried to make the right faces and noises and hoped he was having a good time. Spoiler alert, he wasn't. Not that I don't enjoy sex, it's just... Okay, yeah, I don't like sex that much. It's too stressful. I'd rather jerk off on my own because there's no one to try to impress, no judgment, no anxiety.

"I have a few toys I'm going to try out today, so this should be fun," Heart says on screen, picking up a box and talking

about the promotional details of the product. Then he unboxes it and pulls out an egg-shaped toy and a remote control.

I wiggle my pants and underwear farther down and watch as he teases the toy along his already dark, dripping erection, testing out the different vibration speeds.

I lick my lips and watch as a dribble of clear precum drips from his tip. He settles back and bends his knees, slipping the toy between his ass cheeks to tease his hole. He moans, and the camera pans up to his face, capturing the pink flush in his cheeks and the way his lips are parted to allow panting breaths passage into and out of his lungs.

"Yeah, this one is good," he says breathlessly. *"Really good."*

His eyelids close and another moan falls from his lips. My cock aches as I stroke myself slower than I really want to. I don't want to finish too fast and miss the rest of the video.

"Better try the next one or this will be over too quickly," Heart echoes my own thoughts, turning off the vibrator and setting it aside with shaking hands. He fumbles with opening the next box, his cock flexing against his stomach, his balls high and tight.

The next toy he pulls out is long and thin with a number of ridges. It's curved near the top so it'll hit his prostate perfectly. I shiver with anticipation, squeezing the base of my cock to slow things down.

By the time he's lying back again, Heart has his breathing more under control. He's back from the edge, but I have a feeling this toy is going to take him right back there quick as hell.

The camera is tight on his hole as he eases the toy inside. There's a keening cry, and his hips flex. The camera pulls out, the angle still from between his legs, and you can see his toes curl as his cock heaves again against his stomach.

"Oh fuck," I gasp, reaching for my balls and tugging them hard to pull myself back from the cusp of orgasm.

"I'm almost afraid I'll come as soon as I turn on the vibration," Heart laughs, his voice husky and his chest rising and falling rapidly again.

He presses the button on the base of the toy and gasps. His toes curl harder, and his muscles tense as he fights against the threatening orgasm.

"Oh shit, fuck," I moan, unable to keep myself from stroking faster now.

My eyes are glued to the screen as Heart hits the button again, increasing the tempo of the vibrations, and he groans, his hips thrusting involuntarily. His jaw clenches and a near sob tears from his throat.

"Oh god, I can't..." he whines and then moans from deep in his chest. His cock throbs angry red, every vein prominent and pulsing.

"Yes, oh god, please come," I beg, so close to letting go.

"Ungh-ahhhhhh."

"Ohhhh!" My cock gives a hard pulse before exploding at the same time Heart does on screen. Steaks of thick, white cum paint his chest, just as my own does until I'm breathless and my cock is softening in my hand.

Heart gives the camera a lazy smile. *"I'd say that one is a definite winner. Let's see what else we have to play with."*

I close the video before he can grab the next toy, feeling a little guilty for coming so hard to a video of my friend getting off. But also, unable to feel too bad for it because holy hell, was that hot.

I take a minute or so to catch my breath, and then I kick my pants the rest of the way off and make my way to my bathroom to clean up. As I wipe the globs of cum off my skin with a damp washcloth, I wonder what Heart would think if he knew I watched his videos. Would he think it's weird? He *is* a porn star; he obviously knows people watch his videos.

I can't imagine what that must be like, knowing anyone on the street might know what you look like when you get off. I shudder in horror at the thought. I think that's part of what makes sex so uncomfortable for me; I spend most of my time worrying that I'm making stupid faces or embarrassing noises to enjoy any of it.

Once I'm clean, I grab my pants off the floor by the couch and pull them back on. Then I plop down and pick my phone back up. I haven't called my dad in a while; it might be good to check in. God knows he won't be the one to call me.

I hit the call button, and the phone rings a few times before he answers.

"Hello?" He sounds confused that someone is calling him. I'm sure it's been weeks since his phone rang last, likely the last time I called actually. He's one of the last few people alive who has a landline instead of a cell phone and no caller ID at that.

"Hi, Dad, it's Mason."

"Mason, how are you?" he asks. "Still enjoying the big city?" The way he says *big city* sounds like something filthy, and I chuckle to myself.

When I told him I was moving to LA for school and would likely stay in the city if I got hired by one of the game developers in the area after finishing my degree, he supported me, but I could tell he didn't understand it. *Cities are full of too many people; I prefer the peace and quiet*, was what he said when I told him.

"I'm good. Can't say I *love* the city itself, but I've been making friends recently, and school is going well. I designed a mobile game with a new friend and downloads aren't doing too bad on that, so it should look good on my resume when I graduate."

"Mobile game, what's that?"

I snort and shake my head. "It's a game people download to play on their cell phone," I explain.

"Oh, that's nice." I can tell he's still confused, but I appreciate the effort. "You always were good at all that technology stuff. I can't even program my VCR."

Yes, my dad still has a VCR. Don't even get me started. I was extremely grateful that he was always willing to buy me computers and things to work on as a kid. I needed one for homeschooling when I was young anyway, but he was always willing to shell out money for all the different programs I asked for as I learned to program and later when I got interested in design.

For me, homeschooling was a blessing and a curse. I had a lot of time to focus on my hobbies since I always finished my work at record speed. But the social part...yeah, I think it's pretty obvious how I fared on that front.

"How have you been, Dad? Anything new? Getting out at all?"

"I don't need to get out. I have everything I need right here. I go out to drop off the furniture I make at the consignment shop and to buy groceries. I don't need anything else."

"I just worry about you is all."

"I keep telling you, you don't need to worry about me. You're too young to spend your time concerning yourself with your old man. You should be out dating and enjoying yourself."

Oh my god, why is everyone so obsessed with me

dating? "Not so sure dating is for me, Dad. You got by just fine all these years. Why can't I?"

"The last thing you want to do is be like me, son."

"You're a good person and a good dad. There are worse people I could aspire to be like," I point out.

"Like I said, you're young. Don't resign yourself to being alone forever just yet."

"Okay, Dad," I agree reluctantly. "I suppose I should let you get back to work, huh?"

"Yeah, the stain on my table should be about ready for a second coat," he agrees.

"Maybe I'll come visit sometime soon?" I offer. He lives just over the border to Utah, about a five-hour drive. Just far enough that it's kind of a pain to visit, but not so far that I can avoid feeling guilty about not going home more often.

"You know you're welcome any time you like."

"Love you, Dad."

"You too, Mason. Take care."

I hang up and lie back on the couch, grabbing my laptop and bringing it with me. Time to sink into my work for a while.

5

LUCKY

When I find myself checking the clock for the fifth time in twenty minutes to see if it's ten o'clock yet, I realize I have a serious problem. A five-foot ten size problem covered in sexy tattoos, to be more precise. Gunner Harris, aka Heart. The boy—well, technically at twenty-two, he's a man and not a boy—is everything I should stay away from. Too young, way too damn sexy, a fucking porn star, and not in the last place, a client.

He's a *client*.

It's what I've been telling myself since the second those impossible gorgeous eyes of his focused on mine. They're not green and not blue, they're both, with some golden flecks thrown in for extra effect.

It's like his face and his body and his whole appearance: it shouldn't work, this mish-mashed combination of sharp angles and smooth skin, of full lips and those colorful tats, of this tight body with the impossible round ass. But it does. Oh, god, does it ever.

He's invaded my dreams, this man who oozes sex out of

every pore in his skin. I cannot stop thinking about him, and it's unhealthy. It's sick. And the fact that there are videos of him online, beautifully shot videos where he...

Dammit, I'm hard all over again. What the fuck is wrong with me? I'm thirty-three years old. I'm a Marine Corps veteran who has fought and survived two tours. I'm an experienced parole officer. And yet this man, this twenty-two-year-old boy, has me all twisted up inside. He's a client, but he's making me feel like a sex-crazed teenager.

Can't say I appreciate feeling like this.

"Lucky, your ten o'clock is here," Sasha, the front office girl, calls out.

I sigh. I had better keep this professional. Hopefully my cock is reading that memo, too, because sweet fuck, it's still hard. Luckily, I'm wearing a dark blue polo shirt that covers my groin.

"Thanks!" I call out to Sasha.

Heart—I really shouldn't think of him by his porn name, should I?—is sitting in the waiting room, his Converse-clad foot tapping impatiently. I've rarely seen him sit completely still. There's always some part of him moving: his fingers, his foot, his lips. It accentuates the fluid moves of his body. Everything he does is graceful, and it fucking annoys me. Probably because it's so damn sexy.

"Mr. Harris," I say, keeping my voice as cool as I can.

His head shoots up, and that damn smile is on his lips, the one that says he knows exactly what I'm thinking, that he can see right through me.

"Mr. Stone," he fires back.

I jerk my head to indicate that he should follow me, and I lead him into my office, which is a fancy name for a glorified cubicle. I take my place at my desk chair, and he drapes himself in the folding chair across from me.

"How have you been?" I ask with equal amounts of obligation and true interest.

"Fine."

I hope we're not back to the monosyllabic answers he gave before we had our little tête-à-tête last week, because that was like pulling teeth. But I need to get the required stuff out of the way first before I can dig deeper. "Have you been in contact with any known criminal elements this week?"

He shakes his head.

"Verbal answers, Gunner. You should know the drill by now."

He smirks. "I do, but I like it when you get all displeased."

I bite back a sigh. He's in a defiant mood, it seems. He can't ever see how much he gets to me. That would be like giving this kid a weapon. And we both know he'd use it. "Stick to the rules, please."

"No."

My eyes widen for a second before I realize he's answering my previous question about contact with felons. Little smart ass. "Have you used any drugs, including weed?"

"No."

"Have you had any alcohol or been to an establishment where alcohol is being sold?"

"No."

"Have you traveled outside the state of California?"

"No."

"What activities have you performed this week to ensure gainful employment?"

He quirks his left eyebrow. "You really wanna know what activities I performed this week at my job? Well, I rimmed this guy—"

"Knock it off."

He shrugs. "You asked."

"I wasn't asking for details about a shoot you did." I try to make my tone as stern as possible.

His right eyebrow joins his left. "You asked me about my job, didn't you? That's my job, you know. Fucking men. Getting fucked."

He's. Killing. Me. As if I needed even more mental images of him with... No, not going there. Absolutely, definitely not going there.

I've never been more thankful for my poker face. At least, I hope I still have one, because he can't know how much he affects me. "There's no need to be crass, Gunner."

His face darkens. "I hate that name," he says.

"Why?"

He slouches in his chair. "It was my father's name. Or rather, his rank."

This, of course, was not in his file. His rather impressive file, I might add. "He was a gunnery sergeant in the Marines?" I ask, 'cause that's the only rank that would fit the name.

"Yeah. Killed in action in Afghanistan. Good riddance."

I frown. "That's a pretty harsh statement."

His eyes drop to the *Semper Fi* tat on my right arm, and then his face distorts into a sneer of derision. "Should've known you'd take his side. You guys always stick together, right? God forbid you'd actually turn against a brother, even when he's a total asshole."

There's so much venom in his voice I almost recoil. What the hell happened to him? Or to his dad? "I'm not choosing anyone's side, Gunner. I was merely pointing out that it's a pretty harsh thing to say to be glad someone got killed. I lost friends over there, you know."

He makes an angry gesture with his hand. "This is not about you or your friends, so don't take it personal. I have every right to be glad my father got killed, because it saved me from having to kill him instead."

His words echo between us, and his face tightens as he realizes what he just said—and to whom he said it.

"You can't make statements like that to me, Gunner. You know I have to report this, and if I do and someone interprets it the wrong way, your ass will be sent back to jail."

There's a flash of something in his eyes before he covers it up, though he's still radiating pure anger. "You gotta do what you gotta do. I'm not taking it back, 'cause it's the fucking truth. And for the love of everything holy, will you please stop calling me Gunner?"

"What would you like me to call you?" I know what he's gonna say, but I need him to say it anyways.

"Heart. Call me Heart."

I sigh. "Are you sure it's a smart idea to be so open about your career in the adult entertainment industry?"

He leans forward in his chair, his mouth pulling up in a sexy smile. "You can't even say it, can you? It's called porn, Lucky. Gay porn."

"Don't call me Lucky. I'm Mr. Stone to you."

"Don't change the topic...Mr. Stone. And it's colloquially referred to as gay porn, not the adult entertainment industry."

He's pushing my buttons, and I have to force myself not to react. "Whatever you call it, it's not a job that will help you reintegrate into society. If you want to make better choices—"

"I'm not interested in your Hallmark power of positive thinking BS," he cuts me off.

I sigh. "Don't you want a real job at some point?"

"What I do is a real job. Trust me, porn is hard work, and I'm earning every penny of it. Besides, I'm damn good at it... as I'm sure you know."

I gently shake my head, ignoring his little challenge to get me to admit I've seen his videos. Which I have, but torture couldn't get me to confess that. "Why are you making everything in your life about sex?"

Heart's tapping foot comes to a sudden stillness as he looks straight into my eyes. "Because it is, and it has been for a long time. It's all people want from me. Sex. And don't you dare claim you're different, because I'm not fucking blind. You try to be professional, but you want just the same as everyone else."

I release a slow breath. I don't know how he spotted it, but maybe I haven't been hiding it as well as I thought. Now I have no choice but to admit the truth, because lying would permanently damage the already fragile relationship I have with him. A *working* relationship, obviously, not the other kind, which would be impossible.

"I don't want to be attracted to you," I say softly.

"Join the fucking club. Nobody wants me for anything else but sex, and I've stopped believing people who say differently. The last guy I believed when he told me he loved me got me sent to jail for three years for something I didn't do. So you can take your judgmental attitude, Mr. Stone, and shove it up your ass."

Before I know it, he's out the door. I lean back in my chair, pissed at myself beyond words. I fucked up big-time. Heart was absolutely right. Who am I to judge him for the choices he's making when I haven't taken the time to understand how he got to where he is?

I know I tend to be black-and-white in my thinking. Morally rigid, a date once accused me of being when I objected to him downloading illegal software. I still don't think what he did was right, but maybe he did have a point that I could try harder to put myself in someone else's shoes. I do tend to dole out snap judgments...and while it's often necessary in my job, that doesn't mean it's a good thing as a human being.

I have no right to judge Heart for how he's rebuilding his life, especially since he's not violating his parole in any way. I should be applauding him, not criticizing him. If I want to have even the slightest chance of helping him, I have to do better than this.

And I've had many clients who claimed they were innocent, framed. But I've never had one I want to believe as desperately as Heart.

6

HEART

I storm out of Lucky's office, pissed as hell at myself for letting him get to me. So what if he wants to fuck me? Everyone else does. And why on earth I blurted out that shit about Terry, I'll never know. It's not going to make one damn bit of difference to tell Lucky or anyone else that I was set up. I was convicted for it, that's all that matters. That's the black mark I'll wear for the rest of my life.

I check the time and realize I need to get my ass over to the studio before I'm late for filming today.

Ever since Rebel started doing behind the scenes work, he's been shaking up the shoots a lot with some fresh ideas to bring in new viewers and to excite our long-time subscribers. One of his big ideas has been what he calls *boyfriend scenes.* Boyfriend scenes require acting, since we have characters and lines, and the idea is that rather than some of the dirty, kinky scenes, these ones are sweet and intimate. Boyfriend shoots require a lot of slow kissing and tender words.

When Rebel first told us about it, I laughed to myself when Tank cringed. Tank is a big, gruff guy and the last person you'd associate with sweet or slow in any sense. Rebel rushed to assure him that he wasn't going to have *everyone* doing these scenes, but that they would be carefully paired.

This is the first boyfriend shoot I've been scheduled for and, if I'm being honest, I'm a little nervous. I pull up at the studio and notice Pixie's little beater Honda already there. Kudos to Rebel's decision on this one because if I had to pick anyone to do one of these scenes with, I would've chosen Pixie.

Pixie is newer to Ballsy Boys, just like me. And he's one of the sweetest little twinks I've ever met. I've done a few scenes with Pixie, and I've always enjoyed filming with him. He's professional and enthusiastic, and he's a greedy bottom, which is always fun.

I head inside and straight for the set. Normally, I'd hit the locker room first thing, but this shoot doesn't require much prep since we don't have costumes or anything this time. I looked over the script, and the idea is that Pixie and I are boyfriends who decided to spice things up by filming a little video. I've gotta give it to Rebel; it's a great idea.

I find Pixie lounging on the large bed in the middle of the set for today. He's in nothing but a pair of pink briefs, his hair styled to look messy. He's talking to the big boss, Bear, and both are smiling. It almost seems like Pixie is flirting, but I'm a little too far away to hear what he's saying that's making Bear blush and shake his head.

I tilt my head a little and take the two of them in. Bear is about forty and he's a total silver fox. When I first started, I looked up some old videos Bear did back in his twenties; he was hot on camera. And, he runs a top rate operation here.

I was a little nervous about getting into porn, having heard some horror stories from guys working for different studios. Not that I didn't live through worse as a teen, doing my best to get by on the streets. But I knew as soon as I met Bear that things at Ballsy Boys were all above board. He has a lot of respect for us, he pays us fairly, and he never expects us to do anything we're uncomfortable with. He's a good boss, and it's nice seeing him smile.

"Hey, Heart," Pixie calls out, waving me over. "Are you ready to be my boyfriend for the day?"

"You know it, sweet thing. Come here and give me a little sugar." I pucker up, and Pixie happily crawls across the bed and plants a kiss against my lips with a loud smack.

"You guys ready to get to work?" Rebel asks, appearing behind Bear.

"I'm always ready," I assure him with a wink. "Just give us two minutes to get camera ready."

I step off to one side and strip down, then I climb onto the bed beside Pixie. He slips out of his underwear as well, and then the awkward moment of *getting ready* ensues. It's one of those not so glamorous parts of porn no one talks about, but it's not like we show up to set with erections solid enough to pound nails. My cock is just slightly plumped but certainly not camera ready yet, and Pixie is even less there than I am.

"Can you kiss me a little?" Pixie asks with a quiet shyness that's just *so* Pixie. He licks his pretty pink lips, and I smile at him.

"Of course. Come here, sweetness."

Pixie's kisses are just as sweet as the rest of him, perfect and soft as he slides his tongue against mine, and our lips move in tandem. I can feel my dick stirring, and his seems to be doing the same, bumping against my hip as it swells.

Our kisses are warm and nice, but unfortunately not more than that. I'm glad there's nothing more in the touches

Pixie and I often share casually both on and off camera. As nice as it would be coming home to him at the end of the day and curling up in bed together, I'm not what he needs. I'm not what anyone needs, and no way in hell am I ever trusting anyone with my heart again.

Pixie pulls his mouth away from me with a little wet noise, and he smiles at me with puffy lips.

"That's better," he says, reaching down and giving his now hard cock a slow stroke.

"Much," I agree, pressing one more quick kiss to his lips before signaling to Rebel that we're ready to go.

We take a few seconds to make sure we're arranged for the best visual impact with our legs tangled and our bodies pressed close, our cocks sandwiched between our bodies. And then we wait for the camera framing check.

"Good to go whenever you're ready," Rebel calls.

I take a deep breath and slip into character. Cupping the back of Pixie's head, I pull him into a hot, slow kiss. I open my mouth wide as I push my tongue between Pixie's lips, making sure it looks good for the camera. These kisses are different than the ones before the camera was rolling. These kisses are all about exaggerated tonguing and angling our faces so the camera can catch all the action. When Pixie whimpers and grinds his erection against my stomach, I pull back from the kiss to deliver the lines Rebel gave me.

"This is going to be so hot to have on film. Do you think you'll watch it later when I'm not home and jerk off to it?"

"Yeah," Pixie answers in a breathy voice. "I can't wait to see how sexy you look when you make me come."

I roll Pixie onto his back and kiss along his neck, and he makes cute little gasps and moans for the camera.

"I love you," Pixie whimpers, and for a second I freeze, my whole body feeling like I touched a live wire.

I know this is all part of the scene, that Pixie's just playing a part. The script says I'm supposed to say it back, but I can't seem to force the words out. Those are words I haven't said in years. And the last time I said them, they blew up in my face.

I promised myself the day I was sentenced to three years in jail that I'd never say those words again, never let myself feel them again. Loving someone makes you too vulnerable to any way they might decide to hurt you. Never again.

"You too," I murmur against Pixie's chest. That has to be close enough for the scene because that's as close as I'm going to manage.

Pixie doesn't seem to mind my variation from the script. He just reaches down and threads his fingers through my hair while I continue licking and kissing his chest.

"Flip over, baby, I want to taste your ass."

I sit back to let Pixie wiggle out from under me. He gets on his hands and knees, and I move into position for the best camera angles. I spread his cheeks and snake my tongue along his crease and then tease his hole.

Pixie whimpers and flexes his hips. The kid is damn good, this is going to look great on camera.

It doesn't take long for his hole to soften under my ministrations. I'm sure he prepped beforehand, but I spend a good few minutes making it look good and having fun licking and sucking his tight little pucker. I love sex, and I love eating ass, so this really isn't a hardship for me to spend my afternoon with my face between Pixie's ass cheeks.

This particular scene isn't planned for anything more than rimming and jerking off, so once I'm sure we've got some good footage, I reach between Pixie's legs and run my fingers along his smooth balls and up his slender shaft.

"Your tongue feels so good. Please make me come," Pixie pants in a perfect breathy voice.

I wrap my fist around his cock and stroke him, while I fuck my tongue in and out of his tight hole. His legs start to tremble as he squirms and moans. I slide my free hand over his ass and into his crease. I slip two fingers inside and work them until I find his prostate. Pixie tenses, and I continue to lick his rim and play with my fingers in his hole.

It only takes a minute before he's spurting his cum all over my hand and the bed sheets. I jerk him through his orgasm, and when his muscles relax, I sit back and grab my cock, jerking hard and fast until I'm shooting onto his ass and back.

I lick up the mess afterward and kiss along his shoulders tenderly before nuzzling his ear and then kissing his lips softly.

"Cut," Rebel calls out. "That was incredible. Our viewers are going to love that. Hell, I think Bear is sporting wood over here after that scene."

I chuckle, and Pixie reaches for a blanket to cover up. He always seems to get a little shy once a shoot ends. I grab his underwear and pass them over, along with a towel, so he can get cleaned up.

"Thanks, Pix; that was fun."

"Yeah," he nods and blushes.

"All right, unless you need anything else, Rebel, I'm going to hit the showers and head out."

"You're good. Thanks, man."

7

MASON

I'm right in the middle of a boss battle with Black Dragon Kalameet in Dark Souls when my door buzzer starts going off.

"Hold on," I mutter to myself, since whoever is at my door obviously can't hear me.

My stomach pitches, wondering if it might be Heart stopping by. After the awkward conversation at his place the other day, I've been a little slower to respond to his texts... Okay, I've been outright ignoring him.

The words *You Died* flash across the screen, and I curse under my breath as I toss my controller onto the couch. I cross the room in two strides and press down on the intercom button.

"Who is it?"

"How many late-night callers do you have, dude?" my best friend, Troy, crackles back.

I roll my eyes and push the button to unlock the outside door, and then I unlock my apartment door and head back to the couch. A minute later, Troy and his boyfriend, Rebel, are walking through the door like they own the place. I've always wondered what it must be like to feel so comfortable in any space other than my own well-kept bubble.

"Get dressed, we're going out," Troy declares.

"What? It's ten thirty at night," I complain, settling deeper into my couch.

God, you're so boring. Don't you ever want to do anything fun? Brad's voice echoes in my ears.

"On a Friday, ten thirty means the night is just getting started. Come on, Grandpa. Your mourning period over what's his nuts is over; it's time to get back up on the horse-sized cock."

Heat rushes into my cheeks. "Maybe I already have," I bluff.

Troy stops and studies me for a second. "You haven't," he declares after a few seconds. "Do you need help picking something to wear?"

I consider protesting some more, but one look at Rebel and Troy standing shoulder to shoulder with their arms crossed over their chests and I know I'm going out tonight whether I like it or not.

"I can do it myself. Give me twenty minutes," I grumble.

I can hear Troy helping himself to my PS4 before I close my bedroom door behind me. My stomach knots as I stand in front of my closet staring at my plain, boring clothes. I don't have anything flashy or eye catching to wear to a club, because the only time I ever went was with Brad. And god forbid any other man at the club look at me with Brad around. After two fist fights with innocent bystanders, I decided to stop going out altogether. Brad had seemed equal parts annoyed and relieved when I stopped joining him every Friday night at Bottoms Up.

A soft knock at my bedroom door makes me jump.

"I'm not ready," I call out, hoping the plaintive edge in my voice isn't as obvious to Troy as it is to me.

"Mind if I come in?" It's Rebel, not Troy.

"Um...sure."

Rebel steps in and offers me a reassuring smile. "I know Troy is a bulldozer when he makes up his mind about something, but we're really not going to force you to go if you don't want to."

"I know. I think I want to go," I admit. "I'm not ready for a hookup, but I want to go and see what the scene looks like through a single man's eyes. I just need to figure out what to wear."

"Want some help?" he offers.

"I guess. There's not much to work with, just plain shirts and jeans."

"That's okay," Rebel assures me. "If you want sparkles and fishnets, we can make that happen next time. But if you're worried about being generally alluring, I think playing up your whole cute nerd look is the way to go." Rebel pulls out a t-shirt with Super Mario on it and tosses it at me, followed by my nicest pair of jeans. "Wear these and skip the underwear, and you'll be golden."

"Really?" I ask, eyeing the clothes. This isn't what Brad would've told me to wear to the club.

"Trust me." Rebel offers me a wink and then slips back out of my room.

I change into the clothes he suggested and finger comb my wild curls. *You might be halfway attractive if you tried at all.* My chest deflates a little, and I tear my gaze from the mirror.

I'm not sure how long it takes us to get to the club with LA-traffic on a Friday night, but when we arrive, there's a line down the street to get in.

"Oh man, we're never getting in," I complain.

"There are certain perks to being a porn star," Rebel tells me with a smirk.

I trail behind Troy and Rebel, who head straight for the bouncer, hand in hand.

"If it isn't my favorite porn star," the bulky man greets Rebel with a fist bump. "The rest of your crew coming tonight?"

"Not that I know of, but you know Brewer, you can't keep him out of the club."

"Oh, I know Brewer all right," the bouncer agrees with familiarity and longing in his tone. "Have a good time, bro. Put in a good word with Heart for me, yeah?"

Rebel chuckles. "I'll see what I can do."

I eye the bouncer as I pass, trying to imagine the brute with Heart. Irritation flares in my chest for reasons unknown to me. Heart can fool around with anyone he wants.

The club music is an assault on my ears when we step inside. I forgot how much I hate this part of going out—people packed wall to wall, music so loud you can't hear yourself think, flashing lights. It's like being in a nightmare, or hell, or a hellish nightmare.

As I look around, my brain starts constructing an idea of a hell realm I could design in a game that would be similar to this. It would be unique from versions of hell that are usually portrayed, more of a hell party but overwhelming enough to make battling a demon in the midst of it a new challenge. I pull out my phone and start making notes so I won't forget this idea later.

"No design notes," Troy admonishes, tugging my phone out of my hands. "You can have this back after you've had a drink and talked to *at least* one hot, available man."

I sigh in defeat as Troy shoves my phone into his pocket. I gaze longingly at Troy and Rebel's hands clasped together. They're a real couple, in it together. I don't see how I'll ever have someone who loves and respects me the way those two do.

"I'm going to get a drink," I concede, pointing in the direction of the bar.

"We'll be dancing, have fun." Troy winks at me and then drags his man into the crowded dance floor.

My skin prickles at the touch of what feels like a million strangers as I push my way up to the bar. I breathe in through my nose and out through my mouth slowly, trying to keep my heartbeat from getting too high, my anxiety levels from peaking.

When I finally reach the bar top, I order a vodka and sprite. With my drink in hand, I go in search of a quiet corner to hide out in for a while. I'll have a drink or two, and Troy will be too distracted by Rebel to realize I didn't attempt to awkwardly flirt with men who could never possibly want me anyway.

With my back pressed to a wall and a nice little bubble of personal space, I let my gaze wander around the club. It's so easy for everyone else to meet someone and charm them, to dance and flirt, to take a stranger home and simply *enjoy* yourself. My heart is thundering with anxiety just imagining it.

It's like you're from another fucking planet. Why can't you just be normal? I gulp down my drink, desperately wanting to chase Brad's voice out of my head.

"Hey."

I startle at the husky voice in my ear. My glass slips from my fingers, and I hold my breath waiting to see if it'll shatter. By some miracle, it doesn't, but the remainder of my drink does end up all over the floor.

The man who surprised me bends down to grab my glass, quickly scooping the stray ice cubes back into it. I take a few seconds to appreciate his broad shoulders and the oddly sexy back of his head before he stands back up. My face is flaming, and I wonder if I run away in shame now if it'll be less embarrassing than facing whoever made the mistake of trying to talk to me.

My head is down when my glass is thrust back toward me. I force an appreciative smile and pull my head up, braced to see amused pity on the man's face. I draw in a sharp breath at the dark hair and eyes and broad jaw of a man who is so far out of my league it's pathetic.

"Um, h-hi," I stutter, my face getting impossibly hotter.

"I'm sorry I scared you, let me get you a new drink."

"Oh, that's okay," I try to wave him off and end up sloshing a few of the ice cubes out of my recovered glass.

"I insist," he says, and a crooked smile appears on his lips, making my stomach swoop.

"Uh...o..." I clear my throat. "Okay."

"What are you drinking?"

"Vodka and sprite."

He takes the glass from me. "Wait here?"

I nod a little too enthusiastically and then sag against the wall when he's gone. I push my glasses up and run my hands over my face. Why am I such a fucking spaz? My dork scores just went up to about a million.

That thought pings an idea in my head—a game where the Player Character is a total awkward nerd, and the player has to navigate high school, trying to raise his social standing or find other ways of making friends. My fingers twitch for my phone to make the notes for it, and I curse when I find my pocket empty. If I forget this idea before Troy gives me my phone back, I'm going to murder him.

It's not long before the guy returns with a fresh drink, and I have the urge to curl up in a hole again.

"Here you go." He hands me the drink. "My name is Lucky, by the way."

"Thanks," I mutter, lifting it immediately to my lips. "Mason," I say belatedly as I realize giving my name as well would be the normal thing to do.

"Sorry again for scaring you."

"It's okay. I'm just jumpy, not your fault."

"The club not really your scene?" Lucky guesses.

I snort a laugh. "How could you tell?" I ask sarcastically. "Was it my Nintendo t-shirt? Or maybe the way I'm pressed so hard against the wall it's like I'm trying to disappear?"

"Little bit of both," Lucky agrees with good humor. "For what it's worth, I think your shirt suits you. Nerds are in these days, so you might as well lean into it."

"Yeah, that's what my friend Rebel said," I agree, still skeptical of the idea. Even if nerds *are* in, there are a lot of guys better looking and less awkward than I am. "I'd rather *lean into it* by being back at home playing video games tonight."

Lucky's eyes light up. "What do you like to play?"

"Oh, uh..." My face heats again. *Real smooth, you've got a hot guy talking to you and you're going to nerd out all over him.* "I don't really know," I mutter.

"Oh," Lucky's face falls. "I know I'm a little late to the party, but I'm obsessed with *The Last of Us*."

"Seriously?"

"Yeah, the story is incredible, and the game play is flawless."

"Yeah, it is," I agree with a relieved smile. "I'm playing

Dark Souls right now, but I like a lot of different games. I just got a review copy of a new game that's based around Norse mythology; it's really awesome."

"A review copy?"

"Oh yeah, I...uh...I have a game review blog."

"That's awesome. I know most gamers look down on mobile games, but have you played *Break-up Artist*? It's actually a lot of fun, and the gameplay is a lot better than what you'd normally find in a mobile game. Plus, none of the microtransaction bullshit."

"Yeah, um..." I bite down on my bottom lip, torn between being pleased and embarrassed by his inadvertent praise of my work. "That's my game actually. Well, not *just* my game. My best friend, Troy, and I developed it."

"Seriously? That's amazing."

I blush and take a sip of my drink to hide my pleased smile.

"It's not that amazing. That game was easy to put together; it's really basic."

Lucky steps a little closer, his smile warm and his body radiating all kinds of heat, tempting me to sway closer to him. He opens his mouth, and my heart hammers, wondering what he's going to say next. Before I can find out, his mouth snaps closed and he frowns. He reaches into his pocket and reads something off his phone screen.

"Dammit. I have a work emergency thing; I have to go."

"Oh." My shoulders sag.

A work emergency on a Saturday night? What is he, a surgeon? More likely it's his way of getting out of here before I get any ideas about his attention.

"It was nice getting to chat with you," Lucky says, giving what looks like a genuine smile. "Do you think I could get your number?"

The surprise must show on my face because he chuckles at me as he holds his phone out toward me hopefully.

"Um...yeah...sure." I grab the phone and nearly drop it, my hands are shaking so badly. It takes me a few tries to get my name and number entered in correctly thanks to my nerves, but when I manage it, Lucky is smiling.

"Awesome, I'll see you around," he says, pocketing his phone and leaving me staring after him in surprise.

My stomach is still fluttering as he walks away. Could he have really had a work emergency? I suppose it's for the best either way. Where would that have gone if he hadn't left? Certainly not back to my place or his. That route would only lead to embarrassment.

But what if he actually calls or texts me? We'll go on a date and then...what? I'll disappoint him in bed and that'll be that. Maybe I really should take Heart up on his offer. If it *was* a real offer. That way, if I ever do find someone who's miraculously interested in me, I'll know I won't disappoint them in bed.

"There you are," Troy says, coming out of the crowd with Rebel on his heels. "Have you been hiding over here all alone this whole time?"

"I had a drink and talked to someone."

"Really?" Troy asks in surprise. "Was he hot?"

I feel a new blush in my cheeks and I smile. "Yeah he was really hot. But he had a work emergency so he had to go."

"Bummer. But at least you took the first step. You'll get 'em next time."

I nod. "Can I have my phone back?"

Troy reaches into his pocket and hands it over. I quickly type out my notes for the other game idea I had. Then, with shaking fingers, I pull up the text stream from Heart.

Heart: Just saw a rock shaped like a dick lol

Heart: I'm stuck on this Halo boss, do you think you could give me some pointers?

Heart: Are you ignoring me?

Heart: Oh my god, you're totally ignoring me

Heart: Is this about the sex thing?

BEFORE I CAN CHICKEN OUT, I send him a new message.

Mason: Sorry, I was being weird and felt awkward about the whole sex thing. But, if you were serious about helping me, I think I'd like to do that

I HOLD MY BREATH, instantly wishing I could call the text back before Heart can read it. The little dots show up, telling me he's typing, and I feel like I might pass out. He's going to tell me he was just kidding or that he changed his mind after he thought about it more. I've ruined our friendship.

Heart: Absolutely! This is going to be fun ;) Hang out Sunday so you can help me with this damn Halo boss and then we can talk more about this?

Mason: sounds good

8

LUCKY

The air is already zinging with heat as I step outside at nine. The clear blue skies tempt me to head to the beach instead, but I don't allow myself to be persuaded. Sure, it's Saturday and as such, it's technically my day off, but as a parole officer, the occasional weekend work is expected, of course. Plus, I take my work very seriously.

At least, that's what I tell myself as I get in my car to drive over to the senior center where Heart is doing his community service every Saturday. He's been working there for three months now, and he hasn't missed a day yet. Moreover, his supervisor at the center is raving about him, quite the contrast from the what-the-hell-were-you-thinking email he sent me after I showed up with Heart. I know he doesn't exactly look like a boy scout, but that email was a bit...harsh. I'm grateful Heart has managed to prove him wrong.

It does make it harder for me to come up with a valid reason to visit him at the center. Again. If there were issues or complaints, I could use those as an excuse, but I don't have anything else other than that I want to see him. Which is bad news on every possible level.

The Ballsy Boys released a new video yesterday of Heart and that little twink Pixie. That boy is cute as a button, especially compared to the bad-boy vibe Heart gives off, but I swear, I wanted to smack him for that convincing job acting like he's in love with Heart… Like, for real, swat him away like an annoying bug. What the fuck is wrong with me?

When the hell did I change from a rational, reasonably put-together adult into this obsessed fan? God, it's like I'm turning into some fucked-up stalker. I hardly even recognize myself. Hell, I changed my shirt twice this morning. Twice. For a man who owns the grand total of three different color shirts—black, dark blue, and gray—that's quite the feat. He's got me twisted like a pretzel, and I don't know what to do.

Even more since I met that cute nerd, Mason, at the club yesterday. He's very much my type with him being all awkward and flustered. I could totally see myself dating him, building a relationship with him. He pushes all those protective buttons in me…unlike a certain porn star.

Ugh, why doesn't even the exciting prospect of a date with sweet and nerdy Mason completely eradicate Heart from my brain? He's like a fucking addiction.

Granted, I've acknowledged the problem, so that's a good first step. Every change starts with recognizing where you are…and then expressing where you want to go. Where I am is halfway infatuated with a kid over ten years my junior who has a rap sheet. That, I can acknowledge.

The problem is the next step, realizing where I want to go. See, that's where it gets fucked up. Because as much as my brain knows I should turn the car around and head to the beach on this glorious Saturday, my heart insists we're heading exactly where we want to be. And dammit, it's right.

I sigh as I turn into the parking lot of the senior center. I'm so screwed.

"Good morning, Mr. Stone," Jerry, Heart's supervisor, greets me as I step into his office.

"Good morning. I'm here to check in on Gunner."

Jerry nods. "Sure thing. He's assisting with clean up in the dining room. The residents have just finished breakfast. Do you know where it is?"

The slightly patronizing tone this man uses grates, but I ignore my urge to inform him I could find my way in the dark using only the stars to navigate, so I merely nod.

In the dining room, I find Heart spraying a table and wiping it down with a cloth. He's dressed in unflattering, drab brown scrubs, but even in those he looks hot. It's such a different picture than how he usually is that I blink twice.

"Have you finished yet, Mrs. Roberts?" he calls out to a lady sitting at the end of the table.

"It's too hard for me to chew," she says in an apologetic tone.

Heart hasn't seen me yet, and I study him as his face breaks open in a soft smile. "Did they forget to cut off the crust for you again? Let me help you."

He walks over and carefully cuts the bread into tiny little bites. Using a fork, he feeds her a bite. "Is that better?"

She nods as she puts her frail hand on his, and the contrast between her pale, wrinkly skin and his colorful tattoos couldn't be bigger. "Thank you, Gunner."

He smiles at her. "Remember what I asked you to call me?"

Her face wrinkles even more as she clearly tries to

remember, but then it lights up. "Right, I forgot. Thank you, Heart."

"You're welcome, Mrs. Roberts. Now, I'm gonna clean the other tables, but you call out if you need help, okay?"

He turns around and spots me, and something flashes over his face before he pulls down the mask I'm all too familiar with. What will it take for him to smile at me the way he just smiled at that woman? So carefree and...sweet?

"Mr. Stone," he says, sashaying over. "To what do I owe the pleasure of your company?"

"Just checking in with you," I say, forcing my face to stay neutral.

He crosses his arms. "You certainly take your job seriously."

The implicit challenge is as clear as the sky outside. I sigh, my shoulders sagging a little. Why am I even trying to keep up the pretense? He knows better and dammit, so do I.

"I do," I say, and it's all I can offer him.

"We have to stop meeting like this," he says, the corner of his mouth pulling up in that lopsided smile that always makes my stomach do weird things.

"It's the only way we *can* meet," I say before thinking better of it. This boy, no, this man, has got me feeling things I shouldn't feel and, as a result, saying shit I should not be revealing. To him least of all.

Heart's sexy grin falters as he realizes I'm sharing more than I intended. "Lucky..." he says, his voice husky.

I can't do this. I'm risking everything.

"I need to go," I say and I'm already walking away from him when I hear something. It only takes me a second to realize what it is. The sound of someone frantically trying to get our attention because she can't breathe. Mrs. Roberts is choking, her hands slapping the table, then pointing toward her throat.

Heart and I run toward her at the same time. When we reach her, she's turning blue, and I can see she's about to pass out.

"We need to do the Heimlich," Heart shouts, and I nod, realizing even in the midst of panic that I'm amazed he knows this.

"You do it," I tell him, not wanting to take over from him.

He hesitates less than a second. "No. I can't."

There's no more time to argue, so I bend her over first, smacking her solidly between her shoulder blades, then again when nothing happens. She needs a full Heimlich. Oh, god. I've practiced this in training, but that was ages ago. I try to remember the rules.

I lift her up under her arms, her body going slack in my grip. "Dammit, Heart, help me," I snap.

He helps me keep her upright. "Bend her body over a little. Now hold her so she doesn't fall."

I curl my arms around her waist, then make my right hand into a fist, circling it with my left hand. Right below the ribcage, I remember, and I feel until I think I found the right spot. Then I pull with all my might, inward and upward, once more when she doesn't respond. Suddenly, she coughs and spits something out. With a wheeze, she draws in a desperate breath.

"Check her mouth to see if it's clear," I tell Heart.

With more gentleness than I expected, he opens her mouth and looks inside, then feels around with his fingers. "It's empty now."

I can hear her breathe, the frantic breaths of someone who came too close to not being able to breathe. I remember the feeling after running out of oxygen once on a dive.

"I think she's okay, but call in a nurse or doctor or whatever," I say.

Heart nods, then speeds to a red button on the wall as I gently lower Mrs. Roberts to the floor. Her pale blue eyes flutter, then look at me. "Who..." Her voice comes out a croak, and she clears her throat.

"It's okay, ma'am. Don't force it. I'm Lucky Stone, a... friend of Heart's." I grab a napkin to wipe a bit of saliva from her chin. "Can you breathe okay now?"

She nods.

Footsteps come running and seconds later, two nurses kneel beside me. "What happened?" one asks.

"She was choking, so we had to do the Heimlich. I think she's okay, but you'd better check her breathing."

The other nurse quickly checks with her stethoscope, then nods. "Breath sounds are good and equal. How are you feeling, Mrs. Roberts?"

"Okay. I couldn't breathe."

"I know," the nurse says. "We're gonna get you back to your room, okay?" She looks at me. "I'm sorry, you look familiar, but I can't place you. Are you her family?"

"No. I'm a friend of Heart's. Gunner," I add when she looks at me quizzically. I don't know how many people here know his background, but I'm not ratting him out.

Understanding dawns in her eyes, and her face hardens. "Right, *him*. It's a good thing you were here, then, otherwise she would have died."

If I hadn't been watching Heart—who's been standing aside all this time—I would've missed the way he cringed at her words. That old saying about sticks and stones proves to be bullshit once again, because that casual remark hurt him deeper than a stab wound.

I open my mouth to defend him, but Heart subtly shakes his head, so I close it again. We watch in silence as the two nurses lift the elderly lady back in her wheelchair, then roll her to her room.

"Why didn't you do the maneuver?" I ask Heart when they're gone.

"Because if something had gone wrong, if she had died, they could've brought murder charges against me...and no one would've believed I was innocent."

He says it co casually, so matter-of-factly that the impact of his words is even bigger. And I wish I could assure him he's wrong, but I can't. He's not. Once people know you're a felon, they never look at you the same again. I'm not speaking from personal experience, of course, but it's what my clients keep telling me. People don't see a person anymore. They see a felon, a crime, a rap sheet.

"I'm sorry," I tell him. "I know that sounds empty, but I mean it."

He studies me for a few seconds, then nods. "Thank you. I appreciate you not feeding me some bullshit about how I'm wrong."

"I wish you were, but sadly, you're right."

He drags his hand through his hair with a tired gesture. "It's all they see, you know? The tattoos, the bad boy, the criminal...the porn star, in some cases."

I could argue that he owes the last bit to his own choices, but I don't. As he rightly pointed out to me before, it's not like he has a ton of career options. Not with his criminal record hanging over him like a dark cloud, in all likelihood for the rest of his life.

"I'm sorry they're not willing to look deeper," I offer.

He shrugs. "It's not like there's much more for them to discover other than my body…"

Again, the casual way in which he says it breaks my heart just a little. What happened to him that he believes he's worthless outside of sex?

"It's not how I see you," I say, and his head shoots up, his eyes darkening.

"It's not? Then what do you see when you look at me… Mr. Stone?"

Has my name ever sounded that sexy? I doubt it, just as I doubt I've ever gotten hard before from someone merely using it. But it's what he wants, what he's counting on, to have this effect on me. It's all he knows: sex. So I can't let it be just that, especially because it's not.

Sure, I'd like nothing more than to bend him over that big table right there and fuck the living daylights out of him, but I won't. I can't, but even if I could, he needs more, even if he doesn't realize it. He deserves more. And fuck it all to hell and back, I want more too.

"What I see when I look at you is trouble…trouble with a capital T. Now I have to decide how much trouble I'm willing to be in when it comes to you."

9

HEART

I wipe down my counter and glance around my place to check if I missed any little messes. Waking up early to clean my apartment doesn't have anything to do with the text Mason sent me Friday night. It needed to be cleaned anyway. So what if Mason wants to take our friendship to a different level? I'm a porn star, *casual sex* is my middle name. Besides, this isn't even like it's sex for the sake of sex. He needs help and who better than me? This is practically a public service. I should get a gold medal or some shit for teaching Mason how to suck a cock.

I snort a laugh at myself and toss the rag I used to wipe down the counter into my laundry hamper then glance at the clock. It's already eleven, I would've thought Mason would be here by now. Unless...maybe he changed his mind? It's possible he was drunk Friday night or something and woke up regretting ever sending that text.

That thought leaves me feeling oddly hollow. Not that I care about having sex with Mason. He's my friend, and sex is easy to come by.

My mind flashes to Lucky's disapproving expression that

he gets whenever the subject of my career or casual sex life comes up. He definitely wouldn't be for me *corrupting* Mason. Not that it's any of his business. He's my PO, not the sex police. Hmm...that would be kind of a kinky role play though, and I bet Lucky would be a natural at playing the part. My cock starts to harden, and I reach into my jeans to rearrange it, cursing myself for thinking about Lucky that way.

The events from yesterday assault my mind and just like that my erection is no longer a problem. As annoyed as I was at Lucky checking up on me, I'm glad he was there. If he hadn't been, poor Mrs. Roberts would've... I shudder and shake off the thought.

Too bad Lucky is so sure I'll never *reintegrate into society*, what with being a sex crazed porn star and all. Fuck him. Huh, I wonder if he's a top or bottom...

The shrill sound of my door buzzer yanks me from my thoughts and sets my heart racing surprisingly fast. Seriously, it's just Mason, no big deal. Mason can't make me nervous; he's like a puppy with big feet he can't help tripping over.

I walk over and press the intercom button. "Mase?"

"Uh...yeah..." he replies.

I hit the button to unlock the front door and then crack my door open before heading over to the couch and grabbing my phone to make it look like I've been chilling on the couch rather than cleaning all morning. Again, not really sure why I feel the need to play it cool with Mason, but it's easier to not look too deeply into any of this. Maybe I slept funny or something.

Mason's footsteps in the hallway sound hesitant—like he's considering turning around and leaving before he's even made it inside. He totally regrets that text Friday night.

I stay still and quiet on the couch, waiting for him to come to me so I don't make him even more nervous.

When the door finally creaks open, I can't keep the relieved smile off my face.

"Hey, man," I greet with a nod.

"Hey," he replies breathlessly, and my mind wanders down the path of wondering what *I* could do to make him sound that way. What would he *let* me do is the bigger question.

I set my phone down and grab my Xbox controller off the coffee table, sitting up and patting the seat next to me. Mason hesitates for a second, but when I hold out my extra controller to him, his shoulders sag as some of his tension eases, and he joins me on the couch.

"Why don't you show me the boss you can't beat," he suggests, and I happily comply. Once he's in his comfort zone, we can talk about that text.

The hours slip away as we play video games together, and by the mid-afternoon I can tell Mason isn't even thinking about the sex issue.

"You hungry or anything?" I ask after a kick ass round of *Call of Duty*.

"I could eat," Mason agrees with a shrug.

"Cool, I'll order a pizza."

I use my phone to order, and out of the corner of my eye, I catch Mason smiling and tapping away on his phone as well. An odd feeling of irritation settles over my skin. Is he texting someone? Is that why he suddenly wanted sex pointers? To impress some new guy he met? I don't know why those thoughts send my heart pounding furiously.

"Texting someone?" I ask in a would-be casual voice. Mason winces, and I realize I didn't play it as cool as I was hoping.

"No." He sets his phone down, his posture stiff and a frown on his lips.

"You can," I hurry to assure him. "I was just being nosy." It's not entirely true, but it's easier than whatever confusing thing I was feeling a few seconds ago.

Mason blows out a long breath and gives me a shaky smile. "Sorry, my ex used to get all…" He waves his hand like I'm supposed to guess the rest of it, and from what little I've heard about Douchebag Brad, I get the picture.

"Really, I didn't mean to sound like a dick. I was only curious because you don't usually text anyone when we hang out."

"I wasn't texting anyone. I had an idea for a game so I was just making some quick notes so I wouldn't forget."

"What was the idea?"

"It's stupid," he waves me off.

"Dude, I'm sure it's not stupid."

"It's a game where you play a pizza delivery person, but then I thought there would be all kinds of things to navigate through to get your pizza to the customer on time, like car chases and stuff," Mason explains, looking wary but excited.

"That sounds awesome. I'd play that," I tell him. He blushes and shakes his head a little before dipping his chin to hide his smile. "So, elephant in the room…that text Friday night?"

Mason's cheeks go from a pink tinge to bright red in seconds flat.

"Yeah…*that*." He clears his throat and shifts on the couch, carefully avoiding my gaze. "We don't have to do that. I'm sure you'd rather fool around with guys who know what they're doing."

I snort and shake my head, reaching out and putting a hand on Mason's knee. "I get plenty of sex with experienced men. I think it would be fun to help you up your skills. But if you're uncomfortable, we won't do it."

"It's not that." He squirms in his spot again, looking around my apartment like there are endless fascinating things to hold his attention. "I don't really like sex, so it would be kind of a waste anyway. Why get good at something I don't even want to do? I'm fine being single the rest of my life."

"You don't *like* sex?" I ask, unable to hide my surprise at that statement. I've heard of people who aren't particularly interested in sex, obviously. But not *liking* sex? That's a new one. "How many people have you had sex with?"

He doesn't answer at first, instead getting up and walking to my kitchen to fill a glass with water. He stands with his back to me and I have to resist the urge to go to him and give him a reassuring hug.

"Just one," he admits after several long minutes.

"Douchebag Brad is the only person you've had sex with?"

He sets the glass down on the counter and finally turns to face me again. "Yup," he confirms. "I know, there must be something wrong with me."

"Sweetie, there's nothing wrong with you. You dated a guy who wasn't nice to you and being berated doesn't make a lot of people feel very inspired to get down and dirty between the sheets."

Mason lets out a long breath. "I guess I didn't think of it that way. I mean, he wasn't that mean at first. I was really nervous since I hadn't been with anyone else, hadn't even kissed anyone, and he was okay for a while."

"You haven't even kissed anyone else?" My heart hurts a little at that. I get up off the couch and move to stand in front of Mason. We're about the same height, so when I tilt his chin off his chest, his eyes meet mine steadily. "Do you mind if I kiss you? I can't stand that the only person you've kissed was that horrible to you."

His lips part on a sweet little surprised gasp, and one of his shoulders offers a weak shrug. I brush my thumb over Mason's soft bottom lip, and his eyes widen, his pupils dilating.

"Do you *want* me to kiss you?" I check again, not satisfied with the unenthusiastic response. It would hardly make anything better to force a kiss on him to counteract the issue.

"Yes," he whispers.

I move my hand from his chin to the back of his neck, and I take another careful step forward so we're chest to chest. His pink tongue darts out to wet his lips, his chest rising and falling rapidly against mine. And then, to my surprise, he surges forward and presses his mouth to mine.

I smile against his lips as he moves them clumsily but eagerly. His nose bumps mine, and our teeth clack once or twice before he seems to get his nerves under control, and the kiss evens out into a gentle rhythm. Mason's hands tremble as he grabs onto the front of my shirt, and then his tongue finds its way into my mouth.

He moans as I suck his tongue and then slide my own against his in the hot confines of my mouth. His fingers tighten around the fabric of my shirt and his erection bumps against my hip, heating my blood and making me want to move things along a lot quicker than I should.

The extra little something that was missing the other day when I was kissing Pixie on set is here now with Mason. It's a warm little flutter in my stomach, an ache in my chest pulling me closer to Mason every second. I haven't felt anything like this since...actually, I don't think I've *ever* felt anything like this.

I drag my lips away from his, panic snaking through my chest. Mason's panting breaths cool the moisture on my lips with heavy puffs. His eyes are still closed, and his lips are swollen and wet from our kiss. An odd sense of pride snakes through my chest, distracting me from my momentary panic.

"Was that..." he starts, his eyes fluttering open. "Was that okay? I know I'm not the best kisser..."

I cut him off with a quick peck on the lips, and then I press my own erection against him. "Does it feel like I have any complaints?" I challenge with a raised eyebrow.

He shakes his head and smiles. "But, if you're supposed to teach me to be better...what could I improve on?"

"I can teach you some techniques, but *better* is subjective. What I like in a kiss is different than what someone else might like. You were eager and that's hot. As far as technique? That comes with getting used to kissing someone and learning what they like."

"Oh," Mason's face falls. "I never really got better with Brad. He said I slobbered like a golden retriever when I kissed."

Rage spikes in my chest at the sad way Mason recounts his ex. "Brad was an asshole," I declare simply. "Tell you what? We have half an hour until the pizza gets here, why don't we snuggle up on the couch and get a little more kissing practice in?"

Mason's breath catches, and he nods eagerly, warming my chest and the pit of my stomach. I can't erase all the awful things Brad said and did to him, but maybe I can show Mason what sex can be like with someone who cares about his pleasure.

I take Mason's hand and tug him to the couch. I sit down, and Mason looks a little lost, trying to figure out where he should sit, so I help him out by grabbing him around the middle and dragging him onto my lap, his legs straddling me on either side.

"How's this?" I check once he's in place.

"Good," he answers, licking his lips again and running his hands over my chest absently. "I want to try the thing like how you sucked on my tongue," he says, and I chuckle.

"Anything you want," I assure him, dragging him in for another round of wet, hot kisses.

I wonder what Lucky kisses like. He seems like the take charge type. That thought sends a delighted shiver down my spine. It's easy to picture Lucky grabbing my hair and yanking me into a bruising kiss.

I shake the image off and focus on Mason. It's not fair to him for me to think about someone else while making out with him. Mason's a nice kisser too now that his nerves are ebbing. More than nice—sweet, eager, *hot*. He whimpers against my lips, licking at my lip ring, and my cock throbs. Yeah, helping Mason out is *definitely* not a hardship.

10

MASON

My fingers trace my lips, remembering the way Heart's mouth felt against mine. That was *nothing* like anything I ever felt with Brad. With Brad it was all stress and usually insults if I didn't do something the way he wanted. But with Heart...it felt nice. It felt like how it was probably supposed to feel.

For some reason, my mind wanders to the man at the bar—*Lucky*. I wonder how he kisses. Nice like Heart? Nicer? Hotter? More aggressive like Brad? Would he be patient like Heart? Probably not, most people aren't. Which is why I need Heart to teach me how to be good at all this stuff. He can make sure my skills are up to scratch before I kiss someone else again. Plus, Heart is *really* fun to kiss. My stomach flutters remembering the way it felt to have Heart's hands and lips all over me. Well, not *all* over me. Maybe next time. My whole body heats at the image.

My phone vibrates on the couch next to me, and I reach for it absently, still imagining what it would be like to have Heart's lips *everywhere*.

Unknown: Hey

Mason: Who is this?
Unknown: It's Lucky. We met at the club Friday. I was really handsome and charming?

I CHUCKLE, and my stomach does a funny little flip. He's really texting me after I made such an ass of myself?
Mason: Oh yeah, hey. I'm surprised you're texting me
Lucky: Why are you surprised?

I GROAN AT MYSELF. Lack of confidence is *not* sexy. *Way to already mess this up, Mason,* I chide myself.
Mason: Just because you had to leave so fast. I hope everything was ok with work?
Lucky: Yeah, that happens sometimes unfortunately. I was wondering if you'd want to grab a bite together?

MY HEART HAMMERS in my chest. He wants to grab a bite? Like a date? What about Heart? I know we're not dating or anything, but is whatever we're doing supposed to be exclusive? Not that we've done anything more than kiss, but there was the implication of more to come. Not to mention, it's not exactly exclusive anyway since he's a porn star, but outside of that are we not supposed to hook up with other people? Is that what Lucky even means? Maybe he just wants to hang out and talk about video games and stuff. Maybe he wants to be friends like how I'm friends with Troy and Heart...well, maybe not like how I'm friends with Heart.
Mason: Like a date?
Lucky: Yeah, if you're up for it.

· · ·

Dang, okay, I need to figure out the protocol here before I mess things up. My hands shake as I pull up a new message for Heart, but my hands are shaking too badly to manage to type it out, so instead I hit the call button.

"Hey, what's up?" he answers after the second ring.

"I have like a weird question."

Heart's warm chuckle gives me goosebumps and makes my shaking hands worse as I clutch my phone harder in an effort not to drop it.

"You sound nervous. Is it a sex question?"

"Kind of. The thing is, Friday night I went to Bottoms Up with Troy, and I met this guy."

"Ooo, this is getting interesting quickly. Was he hot?"

I let out a shaky laugh. "Yeah, like crazy hot. We talked for a few minutes, but then he had to leave for some work emergency, and I kind of figured that was a polite way of blowing me off. But he did ask for my number, and now he's just texted me," I confess.

"That's awesome," Heart says. "If your question whether you should hit that, I think you already know the answer."

"I just wasn't sure if...you know, after the other day...I mean, you and I..."

There's a long pause, and I pull the phone away from my ear to make sure we haven't been disconnected. When Heart speaks again, there's a slight strain to his voice I'm not used to hearing.

"Babe, listen to me; you and I are friends. There's no reason going on a date has to change anything about our arrangement unless you want it to."

"So you and I aren't like exclusive or anything?" I check.

There's another long pause on the other end of the phone.

"Mason, I really like you as a person, so I'm going to tell

you something. I've been really hurt before and because of that, there's absolutely zero chance I'm going to date anyone ever again. You and I are going to have some fun, and I'll make sure you're confident when the time comes to jump into bed with this hottie or the next one who comes along. And then you and I will go back to just being friends. Okay?"

My heart sinks a little. This isn't news. I mean, I didn't know for sure that Heart *never* wanted to date anyone, but he definitely gave off that vibe so it's not surprising to hear. This means I can accept the date with Lucky. So why do I feel bummed about it?

"That's great. I guess I'll tell this guy that I'll go on a date with him."

"Can't wait to hear all about it. I've gotta get on set, so I'll talk to you later."

"Later."

I take a deep breath to try to calm my shaking fingers and manage to type a reply to Lucky.

Mason: Yeah, that sounds great

Lucky: Awesome. You had me nervous for a second with how long it took to respond. I thought you were trying to think of a way to tell me to fuck off.

Mason: No, I just had a call from a friend. But I'd love to go on a date.

Lucky: How's Friday at six sound? I'll pick you up?

Mason: Perfect

I SET MY PHONE DOWN, and an excited squeal escapes me. Aside from Brad, I've never had a date. And Lucky is about a billion times more attractive than Brad. Not to mention, Lucky is an *adult*. He has a job that's important enough to warrant emergencies. Oh god, that means I need to figure out something to wear that won't make me look like a nerdy kid.

I get up and go to my closet to see if I have anything remotely suitable for a real date with an actual adult. I flip past all my graphic tees and find a few button-up shirts that I absolutely hate, and that's literally it. Ugh, this is why never dating again seemed like such a good idea. If I stay home every weekend alone and spend my time playing video games and jerking off to porn, there's no stress, no opportunity to make an idiot of myself. Once you start adding extra people to your life, everything becomes so much more complicated.

11

HEART

Hot water cascades over my face until I tilt my head back and run my hands through my hair. There's nothing like a shower after working up a sweat on set. People often ask what the worst thing about prison is and to me it was a toss-up between the food and the communal showers. Although the beds really sucked too. It was all shitty, to be honest. But the first thing I did when I got out was take a scalding hot, forty-five-minute shower.

I rinse the last of the soap from my body, and then I shut off the water. I pull back the curtain and grumble when I realize I forgot to grab a towel. Nudity obviously isn't a big concern here, but it's chilly back here, and I don't relish walking around soaking wet, all the way to the lockers to grab a towel.

Like a little wish granting sprite, Pixie saunters over with a towel in his outstretched hand.

"I noticed you didn't have a towel."

"Thanks, Pix." I take the towel and drop a quick kiss on his cheek.

I dry off and then sling the towel over my shoulder and head to my locker to get dressed. Pixie seems to have left, but Campy is still there. Come to think of it, I'm not sure what Pixie was even doing hanging around today. As far as I know, he didn't have any filming scheduled.

Campy glances over at me and then averts his gaze quickly.

"Look all you want, you just had your cock up my ass."

He chuckles and tugs his pants up. "This is a weird job, right?"

"I guess so," I shrug.

I've never made money from anything other than sex, so for me it's not so strange. But I guess I can see where other people might feel uncomfortable sometimes. I pull my clothes out and start putting them on, watching Campy dress as well and realizing how little I know about him.

"Hey, you wouldn't want to grab lunch or anything, would you?"

He looks surprised by my offer, his eyebrows scrunching and his lips parting. "Uh...um...yeah, sure."

We finish dressing and head out.

"This is going to sound odd after we just spent the morning fucking, but I don't think you and I have ever had a one-on-one conversation."

"Huh, yeah I guess not. You don't make it to a lot of the events we have to do, and I don't come out for a lot of the socializing, so I guess it makes sense."

We decide on the Mexican place we all love right down the street from Ballsy. As soon as we're seated, I wonder if this was a mistake. I can't ask someone to hang out to get to know them better when there's so much of my past I'm not willing to share.

"I'm surprised you're not hanging out with Mason this afternoon. You two have been joined at the hip for months it seems," Campy says, and my gut twists.

Ever since Mason got that date for this weekend, I've been feeling...weird. It's a hot, uncomfortable feeling in the pit of my stomach I just can't place.

For some reason I'm not just obsessing about Mason's date, but it has me wondering if Lucky dates. If I had to guess, I'd say he's not a hookup guy. But is he single or does he have a partner? Is he as uptight in a relationship as he comes off, or does he have a softer side? And why the fuck am I thinking about Lucky's love life? At least I can explain my obsession with Mason's date as concern for my sweet, fragile friend.

"Yeah, he's got class and then he said he has some coding to work on this afternoon."

Campy nods and shoves a salsa-covered chip in his mouth.

"How's it going with your new roommate? Decent guy so far?"

A light blush creeps into Campy's cheeks. "Yeah, he's cool," he answers gruffly. "Tank and Brewer's scene the other day was pretty intense, huh?" he segues.

"Yeah, I'm not surprised it nearly crashed the server with all the views. Who would've guessed those two would have so much chemistry?"

"I think it's a fine line between love and hate kind of a thing. I bet they've wanted each other all along but couldn't admit it until Rebel put them together and the sparks flew. Watch, they'll be dating and declaring their love any day now."

"Yeah, I could see that," I agree.

"That would be three of us paired off. Think Pixie will be next after that?" he muses.

"Well, it sure as shit won't be me," I vow. "I don't do relationships, they're nothing but trouble and heartache."

"Yeah, I don't have time to date. Plus..."

"Plus what?"

Campy turns his head away quickly, a look of panic on his face for a few seconds before he schools his features. "Nothing, I didn't mean to say that."

"No worries." Who am I to begrudge a man his secrets?

All this talk of dating has my stomach doing that horrible twisting thing again. For some reason, all I want is to find Mason and prove to myself that his going on a date with someone doesn't change anything.

We stay on easy topics the rest of the meal—movies, books, the other guys. And when we finish eating, my one-track mind is still stuck on Mason.

Heart: I know you're busy, but mind if I swing by for a few?

Mason: yeah, sure. I'm already making myself cross-eyed with code, a short break couldn't hurt

MY STOMACH UNKNOTS A FRACTION, and when I part from Campy, I head toward Mason's apartment instead of my own.

After he buzzes me in, I jog up the stairs and find his door slightly ajar like usual. I push it open and stand for a second, caught in the strangely appealing sight of Mason's face fixed in rapt concentration, his fingers flying over the computer keys. The tip of his tongue is sticking out between his teeth, and his curly hair is sticking up everywhere, reminding me of how he looked after we fooled around the other day.

I kick off my shoes and shut the door behind me. Mason finally looks up from his computer, and the lines in his forehead smooth out as he smiles.

"Hey." He sets his computer on the coffee table, and before I can think about it, I'm on him.

I grab his legs and swing them up onto the couch and then blanket his body with mine. He gasps in surprise but his smile doesn't wane.

"What are you—"

I cut his question off with my lips. It only takes him a second to catch up with my intention, and his tongue darts out to lick my lip ring. I take the opportunity to shove my tongue into his mouth, licking and sucking, savoring his flavor on my tongue. His body is warm and pliant under mine, making my dick hard as granite as I swallow all of his whimpers and moans. I'm tempted to make my way south and suck something else instead of his tongue.

There haven't been many sexual encounters in my life that were for no reason other than *wanting*, but Mason makes me crave it, and that's scary as fuck.

I yank my lips from his, my heart hammering and too many emotions swirling through me.

"I can't hang around; I just wanted to stop over and say hi on my way home," I explain as I heave myself off him.

"Oh...um, okay. Did I do something or...?"

"Not a chance, you're perfect," I assure him with one more quick peck on his now damp lips. "Let's hang out this weekend. You free Friday night?"

Mason pales a little and squirms in his seat. "That's when I have that date I mentioned."

My damn stomach does the irritating twisting thing

once more, and I force a smile. "Of course. Well, call me and tell me how it goes, and we'll hang out next week, okay?"

"Yeah," he agrees eagerly.

"Have fun, and if this guy isn't nice to you, tell me so I can tear off his dick and choke him with it."

He giggles and nods. "Thanks, Heart."

"Any time, babe."

12

MASON

I stand in front of my closet hyperventilating. I knew three days ago I had nothing to wear on this date, but I pushed that issue aside, and figured it would somehow all magically work out on Friday. Well, it's Friday, and I still have nothing to wear on a date with a sexy, mature adult like Lucky.

I grab my phone and hit dial as the panic rises inside me.

"Hey man, what's up?" Troy asks happily when he answers.

"What's up? You pushed me to date, and now I'm having a meltdown, that's what's up."

"You have a date?" Troy, of course, completely misses the point of my call. "With Heart?"

"No, not with Heart," I huff.

"Oh, I thought you guys were hooking up now."

"We are, but he's not who my date is with. Can we please focus on the problem?"

"You're hooking up with Heart and dating someone

else?" Troy verifies, and I cringe a little at how...*slutty* that sounds. "Way to go Mase! Damn, I didn't think you had it in you to play the field like that. I'm honestly proud."

"Great, thank you, bro hugs all around. But I have a huge problem."

"What's the problem?"

"I don't have anything to wear. Lucky is like a *real* adult. I'm sure he's going to take me somewhere nice, and all I have to wear is graphic tees. I'm going to look like a child."

"Breathe, I've got you covered," he reassures me in a soothing voice. "What time is your date?"

"Six."

"Plenty of time. Hang tight, I've got help on the way."

"Thank you, seriously so much."

"No problem. I expect all the juicy details tomorrow by the way. Oh, dude, if you're dating two guys you should totally try to negotiate a three-way."

"Oh my god, I can't even handle pleasing one guy in bed, no way in hell am I going to try for two," I mutter, ignoring the spike of heat that goes through me at the image of Heart and Lucky both naked and hard, kissing me, touching me, *wanting* me.

Troy chuckles. "Try to relax and have a good time. Dating should be fun, and if this guy says one damn thing to you the way Brad used to, I'm going to lay him out."

"Got it, thanks," I say with a smile before hanging up. I don't know how I got lucky enough to have Troy as a best friend, but he kind of makes up for having such a shitty first boyfriend.

Half an hour later, my door buzzer goes off, and I rush to let up Troy or whoever he sent over to help me. I open the door and wait, feeling completely idiotic for needing help picking out clothes for a date. I'm surprised when Pixie comes into view with his arms full of bags.

I haven't gotten to know Pixie well, but his sweet smile puts me instantly at ease the way most people fail to do. He has something shimmery on his cheeks and his eyelids sparkle in the hallway lights. Even weighed down with bags, he's somehow graceful in his movements as he approaches.

"Fashion help has arrived," he declares when he reaches my door. I bite my lip as I take in the rest of Pixie's outfit—tight, low rise jeans that may or may not have come from the women's section and a tank top with some sort of bedazzling on the front.

"Um, I'm not sure..."

"Oh hush, I'm not going to dress you like me. It takes an expert to pull this off." He flails one of his bag-laden arms. "We need to get to work; we're short on time."

"We have two hours still," I say, stepping back to let Pixie in.

"I know, I really wish I'd known sooner. But the show must go on." He drops the bags next to the couch and then turns around and looks at me with a critical gaze. "Do you know where he's taking you?"

"No, just a restaurant. But he's mature and really adult, so I need to look nice."

"Sexy, adult outfit coming right up," he declares, rummaging through the bags and pulling out numerous items to toss on the couch. "Strip down to your underwear for me?"

I gape at him. He wants me to get practically naked right here in broad daylight? Scrawny body and all?

"I...uh..."

"I really don't care what you look like naked. I see naked men all day, every day. Plus, you're not my type, no matter what you look like under your clothes, so there's nothing to feel weird about."

That calms my nerves a little so I make quick work of my clothes before I can overthink it any more. He's right, this isn't sexual so there's no reason to feel weird about it.

"What's your type?" I ask out of curiosity as he ponders the clothes he brought.

Pixie stops sorting and shoots me a wicked smile over his shoulder. "You really want to know?" he asks, and I shrug and then nod. "Daddies."

"Daddies?" I ask, certain I heard him wrong.

"Oh yeah. There's nothing like a big, broad, hairy man with just a bit of gray in his hair. A man who can be gentle or rough when the moment calls for it. A man who has his shit together and wants to take care of his boy."

His voice is wistful, and for a moment, I can imagine the appeal in that sort of thing, even if I know that certainly isn't for me.

Pixie sighs as he trails off and returns to sifting through the clothes while I stand in the living room in nothing but my red briefs and a pair of socks. He turns around, and his eyes fall to my underwear.

"Oh no, you can't wear those," Pixie declares, setting down the clothes he has in his hands and returning to the bags. "Here, take these."

A pair of black underwear comes flying at me from over his shoulder. I catch them and hold them up to examine.

"How are these different than what I'm wearing?"

"They're Andrew Christians."

"Why would I want to wear someone else's underwear?" I ask, having no idea who Andrew Whoever is anyway.

Pixie giggles at me and picks up the rest of the clothes he's chosen. "Oh sweetie, I don't even have time to explain how adorably clueless that was. Those are fresh underwear, never worn by anyone. Put them on, and then get dressed in the rest of these."

He hands me the clothes and then turns around so I can change. The outfit he picked is simple and perfect—a pair of nice jeans and a light blue polo.

"Can I turn around yet?" he asks anxiously.

"Yeah."

His smile widens as he takes in my new look. He fiddles with the collar and straightens the hem, taking me back to when I was six, and my mom would drag me clothes shopping, always asking awkward questions about if the crotch was too tight. If I'd known then that she'd be dead by the next year, I probably wouldn't have kicked up as much of a fit.

"Perfect. You should wear more clothes like this; you look amazing."

"Thank you. Where'd you get all these clothes anyway?" I ask, realizing for the first time the sheer number of things he brought with him.

"I know someone who owns a boutique not far from here. She let me borrow these, but you have to promise not to sweat too much or spill anything on them."

"Oh shit, can I just pay for them so I don't have to stress about ruining them?"

"Yeah, that's fine. I'll return the rest of this stuff and get back to you with the cost of this outfit," Pixie agrees.

"Thanks for helping me. You've got an eye for fashion."

He lights up at that, still fiddling with the top button on the polo, trying to decide if I should leave it open or not. "Don't tell anyone, but I really want to go into fashion design."

"You'll be great at that."

"Thanks. If I can ever afford to go to school, I guess."

"Yeah," I agree. "I'm sure you'll figure it out."

After returning the rest of the clothes to the bags, he gives me a kiss on the cheek and leaves me with a promise to let me know how much I owe for the clothes.

13

LUCKY

Mason is exactly my type, I ponder as I drive over to pick him up for our first date. He's nerdy cute, adorably geeky, and so clumsy it makes me want to bubble-wrap him to keep him safe.

He's very much like my ex-boyfriend in high school, Chris. We were together for two years, but when I joined the Marines, he broke up with me. I couldn't blame him, not when I knew he'd voiced his opposition from the first time I met him. I missed him like crazy those first months, but I never regretted it.

I'd always wanted to be in the Marines, but Chris didn't want me to because "Don't Ask Don't Tell" was still in place. It wasn't repealed until my last year on duty, though my fellow Marines had known or at least suspected, and it had never been an issue. I'd looked Chris up when I got out and discovered he was happily married, so I'd let go.

Chris had been a full-blown nerd, and when I spotted Mason in the club, my heart did a little dance inside my chest, because you don't often encounter his type at a club. He'd been flustered and adorable, and I'd *had* to ask him out. I can't wait to see him again, even though the thought of Heart is constantly in the back of my mind.

But when I see Mason, dressed in a gorgeous blue shirt that brings out his eyes, all flustered and opening the door not wide enough for me to step in, my heart melts a little, and all thoughts of Heart are forgotten.

"Hi," I say when he merely looks at me, and I do a quick check to make sure I didn't spill anything on me along the way. Nope, my dark blue button-down looks fine.

He pushes his glasses back up his nose. "Hi," he says with resolve, as if he had to remind himself it's all gonna be okay.

"Are you ready to go?" I check.

"Yes, right. I'll need to...erm, let me find my keys."

I watch as he fumbles around for a bit before digging his keys out of his pocket and locking his front door.

"That color looks good on you," I compliment him once we're in the car.

"Thank you. It's...a friend of mine bought it for me. Well, he's not really a friend, more like an acquaintance, I guess, and he didn't buy it for me, but he came over to help me get dressed. Not that I can't get dressed by myself, but I don't have a sense for clothes. So he picked this for me 'cause he thought it would look good on me, I guess."

The little rambling he does betrays his nerves, and I bite back a smile. "It does look amazing on you. And I'm with you about the lack of fashion sense. My best friend Rai always jokes I'm the worst gay in the world, because I have zero fashion sense."

The way Mason's eyes trail over me, all hungry and appreciative, makes my dick stir. "You look really nice in that shirt," he says with a coy smile. "So maybe your fashion sense isn't too bad?"

I snicker. "If you ever look into my closet...and I hope we'll get to that point," I add, just so I can watch that gorgeous blush creep up on his cheeks. "You'll have to agree with me. I have shirts in three colors: black, gray, and dark blue. That's it."

"Why?" he asks, and when I look sideways, I spot a little frown between his eyebrows.

"I'm a man of routines. Maybe it's because I was in the Marines, maybe it's my personality, I don't know, but I like routines. I have a pretty busy job that demands a lot of flexibility and on-the-spot decisions, so I like to simplify where I can. I once read that President Obama only had suits in specific colors so everything would match and he never had to worry about that, which reduced his stress. I liked that concept, so I started buying only shirts in those three colors, the same type of jeans, and black socks."

"And the same color underwear, too?" he asks, then covers his mouth with his hand. "Sorry, that was... Ignore that. My filter doesn't work well when I'm nervous."

I chuckle. "Why are you nervous?"

"Because you're...you and I'm me, and I don't really understand why you asked me out?" he stutters.

"Maybe because you're super cute, exactly my type, and I want to get to know you better?"

"I'm your type?" he asks with a disbelief that informs me he didn't figure he'd ever be anyone's type. I wonder what his story is. Surely I'm not the only one who's attracted to sweet nerdy boys like him?

"Yeah, you are. And by the way, it's black."

He scrunches his nose again. "What is?"

"My underwear," I tease him, before taking pity on him. "How's the video game-designing going?"

Mason lights up. "Really well. Troy and I are meeting

with people who maybe want to sponsor our game. The Breakup Game, I mean. He's gonna do the presentation, obviously, since we both know I'd fuck that up six ways till Sunday." He laughs a little. "But he wants me there in case they have questions. He's more the technical guy, I guess, who does most of the coding, but I'm the designer, so..."

"It sounds like you guys complement each other well."

Mason nods. "We do. We're good friends, too."

"That's good, that you got both, the working relationship and the friendship."

"What do you do?"

It sounds like an obligatory question, but I think that's more his social ineptitude than lack of interest.

"I'm a parole officer," I say, inwardly waiting for the inevitable weird reaction men usually have when I mention my work. Some immediately ask for weird stories, like if I know any murderers, or if I'm scared of my clients. Other feel obligated to share their often lengthy opinion on anything related to my job, ranging from prison reform to harsher sentencing, mandatory minimums, or whatever.

"Oh," Mason says. "That seems like a hard job to me."

"It does?" I ask. He's probably thinking of dealing with murderers on a daily basis, 'cause that's where people's minds usually go. They think they couldn't handle being around someone who's guilty of a crime like that.

"Yeah. I don't know anything about it, of course, but it seems to me it's a lot of fighting red tape and people's prejudices. Like, people have all these preconceived notions about...what would you call them, felons?"

I smile a little at his answer, which shows he's trying to put himself in my place. "To me they're clients but yes, felons is what most people call them. Most of my clients are convicted felons, so..."

Mason nods. "Is it? A hard job, I mean?"

"Hmm, good question. It is, but I also find it rewarding. There's a great satisfaction in helping people create a second chance for themselves."

He's spared an answer when I park the car at the restaurant I picked, a casual Italian bistro. Considering Mason's penchant for clumsiness, I figured casual would work better than something more stylish or formal.

I get out of the car, signaling him to wait for me to open the door. I love that he obeys, his cheeks adorably flustered when I open his door and extend my hand to help him out.

"Thank you," he says, and his hand feels so perfect in mine, that I don't let go until we're inside the restaurant.

Conversation flows smoothly, though I'll admit that's because I make a real effort to keep Mason comfortable. His nerves show every now and then, but he's getting more relaxed as time passes, maybe because he feels we're having a good time?

"So, do you do this a lot? Date, I mean," he asks after we've ordered espressos for dessert. "Not that there's anything wrong with that, with dating a lot," he adds quickly.

It's a classic Mason-approach. I haven't asked about his previous boyfriends yet, but my guess is someone fucked him up good, because he's super careful in asking personal questions, as if he fears getting reamed out.

"Not much," I admit. "I've become picky, to be honest. Someone really has to strike my fancy. I've never been a one-night stand or casual hookups guy. And to be honest, I'm more interested in dating guys that are looking for a real relationship...like me."

There's that cute blush again, the one that makes me

wonder how much more I can make him blush in bed. I bet I could make him blush for hours...god, I'd love to try.

It's then that I realize he hasn't responded to my answer, not even with a "thank you" for the obvious, if indirect, compliment. Maybe he didn't pick up on it? I study him, the restless way his hands move as they play with his napkin. No, that's not it. He's nervous about something, but what? It hits me.

"How about you?" I ask, making an effort to keep my voice casual. "Do you date often?"

Yup, his blush intensifies. "No, not really," he stammers. "But..." His eyes stubbornly focus on the table as he obviously gathers courage to say whatever is on his mind.

"My ex was a real jerk, and I didn't know it, but Troy told me he was, and he's set me up with a good friend of his who's...experienced so we could be friends and maybe more, so I could practice, and he makes me feel good when we kiss?"

His breath is a desperate gasp for oxygen after this sentence that he spat out faster than I would have thought was humanly possible. But I got what he said, and my heart does a funny squeezy thing in my chest.

I don't think but reach for his hand and envelop it in mine. "I'm sorry about your ex, and I'm happy you get to experiment with someone who makes you feel good. Everyone should have at least one toe-curling kiss in their life, you know?"

The smile he sends me is the sweetest, and my heart does that squeezy thing again.

14

MASON

By the time Lucky walks me back up to my apartment, I'm torn between elation at how well our date went, and utter terror that the part where we kiss is coming up, and I might be really bad at it. Sure, kissing Heart has been nice. Okay, it was way more than nice, it's been hot as hell. But that doesn't mean I won't fuck up kissing Lucky.

With Heart, it was easier since I've known him for months, and there were no expectations. With Lucky, I feel a lot more on the spot. If I screw this up then the way we clicked over dinner, our comfortable conversations, and the way he looked at me at the restaurant will all be erased. I'll be nothing more than the guy he never calls again because I kiss like a dead fish.

"Hey." Lucky's hand brushes my shoulder as we walk up the steps to the second floor of my apartment building. "Are you okay?"

"Yeah," I try to reassure him, but it comes out as more of an embarrassing squeak. Heat rises in my face, and I try to shake off the feeling settling in my chest, but when I shake my head, I stumble on the next stair. I hold my breath as my planted foot slips out from under me and the ground rushes up to meet me.

I close my eyes and wait for the inevitable crash. But, instead of getting a face full of filthy, hallway carpet, Lucky's strong arms wrap around me.

"Whoa, that was a close one," he chuckles as my feet touch solid ground again.

His arms around my middle are warm and solid, and as if my humiliation wasn't complete, my cock starts to get hard.

"Thank you." I'm proud of how little my voice shakes when I say it. Well, at least he thinks I'm a clumsy freak now so the kiss problem is probably solved. *Way to go, dork.*

We reach the landing of the second floor, and I almost tell him that his duty of seeing me home is through. Why force him to walk down the hallway to my door when it's only going to make things more awkward? But then Lucky's large hand comes to rest on my lower back, and something about the gesture calms my nerves and propels me forward. *Heart said I was a good kisser; this will be fine.*

We reach my door, and I turn to face Lucky with my heart in my throat.

"I had a nice time; I hope we can do this again?" I cringe at my formal words and tone, but at least I managed to get them out without squeaking or tripping over my own feet again.

Lucky smiles, his teeth biting into his bottom lip, and I wonder if he's trying not to laugh at me. His hand that was on my back is now resting loosely on my waist as his eyes flick over my face.

"I had a really nice time too. It was refreshing to go on a date with a guy who's *exactly my type.*"

I blush and roll my eyes at his emphasis, but something warm settles in my stomach. There's no reason for him to go out of his way to make me feel like he's attracted to me, but he's doing it anyway.

Lucky leans forward just a fraction, the question clear on his face. I take a deep breath and ignore the nervous roll of my stomach. Then I tilt my chin up, swaying forward in invitation. He takes the hint, his lips descending on mine. It's not much like the kiss I shared with Heart, which was fast and almost frantic, although still *very nice*. And it's *really* not like any kisses with Brad.

Lucky kisses like he's trying to swallow me whole and will take all night doing it if he has to. His lips are firm and sure against mine, guiding me but not like he doesn't think I know what I'm doing, more like he knows exactly what he wants, and he's happy to show his partner how to do it. A little shiver runs along my skin as his hand tightens on my hip, and his tongue licks into my mouth.

He pulls back entirely too soon, and I nearly stumble, unconsciously chasing his lips. Lucky chuckles at me and then runs his thumb along my damp bottom lip. I risk a glance at his face and am relieved not to see any sign of disappointment there. I want to ask him if the kiss was good for him, but I remind myself once again that insecurity is *not* sexy.

"I'll call you soon," Lucky says, and as much as I want to smile and maybe say something flirty, my mouth gets the best of me.

"Is that like a way of letting me down gently or are you seriously going to call? Because I understand if this was a one-time date or whatever, I just don't want to drive myself crazy wondering. Not that I'll be sitting by my phone waiting for you to call or anyth—"

Lucky cuts me off by pressing his lips to mine one more time, this time just a quick peck against my lips, effectively derailing my rambling.

"It's not a blow-off; I *will* call you."

"Okay, cool." I'm sure it's too late to play it cool, but I try anyway, doing my best to hide the shaking in my hands as I unlock my door and step inside. Lucky waits until I'm inside before he leaves and something about that protective gesture makes me feel...*nice*.

I'm practically bouncing on my toes as I think over the evening. I can honestly and easily say I've *never* had a date like that. Not that it was a tough competition since the only date I've ever had was my first date with Brad. It was fine, he was nice enough, but it wasn't anything special, and he got pissy at the end when I wasn't ready to sleep with him. In hindsight, there were a lot of red flags with Brad, but at the time, I was just happy someone was interested in me.

I kick off my shoes and flop onto my couch with a smile on my face. Lucky is so nice and incredibly hot, I can't believe he's interested in me.

I'm not sure why I avoided mentioning Heart by name when I talked about him to Lucky. Maybe part of me thought it would be weird if Lucky recognized the name from Ballsy Boys. Not that I'd begrudge Lucky watching Heart's scenes if he has. But *knowing* it's the case would certainly have put even more pressure on my theoretical, future sexual encounters with Lucky. Best not to find out what kind of porn he likes ahead of time.

Without thinking, I pull out my phone and dial Heart's number. I'm not sure if it's weird or not, but I want to tell him that I didn't mess up the kiss.

"Hey, boo," Heart answers in a relaxed voice.

I sink deeper onto my couch and close my eyes. I can

hear Heart's TV on in the background, and it's easy to imagine I'm sitting right next to him. He'd probably reach over and run his fingers through my hair or kiss my cheek. He loves to touch; it almost seems subconscious. It weirded me out a little when we first started hanging out, but now, when I hear his voice, I crave his little touches, like a Pavlovian response.

15

HEART

I mute the television and press my phone harder to my ear. I can hear Mason breathing on the other end, and I wonder if he realizes it's been a good minute without him saying anything. He must be lost in thought. If it wasn't for the relaxed cadence of his breaths, I'd start to worry that maybe his date went badly.

"I didn't mess up the kiss," he says after another few seconds.

"Of course, you didn't." I smile and remember just a few days ago when I was the one he was locking lips with. I'm not sure what kind of stupid pills Brad was taking, but Mason is a great kisser—so sweet and eager. I reach into my pants and adjust my thickening cock. "Why don't you tell me about the whole date, then we'll get to the kiss at the end."

"It was perfect," Mason sighs, and I'm not sure if he means the date or the kiss, but I hope it's both.

He launches into the details from the beginning. Mason leaves out his date's name, and I don't ask. Some part of me doesn't want to think too hard about the guy who's going to get to enjoy all the sexy I'm helping Mason to unleash.

And I have to say, the way Mason's describing this guy, he sounds pretty great. I cringe when he mentions that the guy is a PO, but what are the odds the dude even knows Lucky? There have to be hundreds of PO's in a city as big as LA.

"I thought I ruined things at the end when I tripped up the stairs, but he didn't seem to think any less of me for being a clumsy idiot."

A laugh bubbles from my throat as I imagine poor Mason tripping over his own feet, all cute stutters and pink cheeks.

"Yeah, being okay with you being a klutz is a major requirement for dating you."

"Shut up, I'm not *that* bad," he argues, and I laugh again. "Okay, fine I am. But only when I'm nervous. I almost never drop or break anything around you anymore."

"That's true," I agree, a warm feeling settling in my chest knowing that Mason feels comfortable around me. "This guy sounds pretty great. Are you going to see him again?"

As soon as I ask, I almost wish I hadn't. If it becomes a regular thing with this guy, our hooking up is over before it even really started. Not that it's a big deal. Sex is easy to come by. So why is there disappointment settling into my chest? Maybe it's because I was looking forward to teaching Mason some things? That must be it.

"I'm not sure. I think so. I mean, he said he'd call so I guess we'll see."

"He'd be an idiot not to call you."

"That's true," Mason agrees and then lets out a surprised laugh which I join in on. I've *never* heard Mason say something positive about himself. Granted he said it in a joke-y way, but *still*.

"I'm glad it went so well. But listen, we have some stupid team building thing at the ass crack of dawn tomorrow so I'd better get to sleep. I'll talk to you later, okay?"

"Yeah. And Heart? Thanks for everything. I couldn't have...just...thank you."

"Believe me, it's my pleasure."

I hang up and toss my phone on the couch beside me. Leaning my head back, I run my hands over my face and wonder at the strange, empty feeling in the pit of my stomach. I *don't* want a boyfriend; I'm just upset that the easy friendship Mason and I are building will be disrupted by whoever this guy is he's dating now. It happened with Rebel, so why wouldn't it happen with Mason?

Maybe that's something I'll just have to get used to if I'm going to stay single forever and I am. Friends will come and go; there's no point in dwelling on the inevitable.

∽

"It's too damn early," I grumble and smack a mosquito off my arm.

"Well, you should've thought about that before Tank punched Brewer in the face," Campy jokes.

After an *incident* on set recently where Tank "accidentally" punched Brewer and then took him to the hospital, Rebel and Bear decided we needed to have some team building time off set. Last week, we were dragged to a rock climbing wall, and while that wasn't too terrible, Tank and Brewer managed to get out of it before the worst of it even started. Now we're walking through the woods at seven-thirty in the morning on a Saturday. I told Bear I'd have to be out of here by noon to get to my community service at the senior center, which means it's going to be a long-ass day.

At least Tank and Brewer aren't sniping at each other like usual. Maybe we were right all along that those two just needed to fuck out whatever their issue was so we could all have some peace.

"Oh my gosh, look at this," Pixie calls from a few feet ahead, bent over by the side of the trail. "I think this little bird fell out of its nest." He points at it, and his eyes well up, clearly on the verge of tears. "Is he going to die?"

"Let me see," Campy says, stooping down beside him with an air of authority in his tone. Does he know something about birds? Maybe he grew up on a farm or something? Come to think of it, I don't even know where Campy's from. Maybe Rebel and Bear were right about us all needing to bond with our clothes *on* for a change.

"He looks okay. He might be a little dehydrated, but Mom should be able to help him out with that. Let's put him back and let her take care of him."

"But if you touch him, won't the mom reject him?" Pixie asks as Campy scoops the little hairless thing up gently.

"That's actually a common misconception. Birds, rabbits, none of them mind if their baby has a little human stink on them. They still know it's their baby," he explains, settling the bird into the bush directly over where he fell from. "There, good as new. Mom's probably already watching, waiting for us to leave so she can come feed this little guy," he assures a still worried Pixie.

"You know a lot about animals," Pixie notes, and Campy shrugs.

"I watched a lot of Animal Channel as a kid."

The way he says it makes me think there's a lot more to it

than that. I consider pressing for more details, but if I do that, he might start asking about my past and that won't lead anywhere good.

As we hike, I have to admit, the quiet of the forest is nice. But I'm not sure how this is helping us bond. I wonder if Lucky likes hiking. Is he outdoorsy in general? Or does he prefer indoor activities? Would he be up for hanging out on the couch on a Friday night playing video games and watching movies like Mason and I do? Or is he the kind of person who wants to go out during the weekend? I'm not sure why it even matters. It's not like I'll ever hang out with Lucky socially. Who cares if he spends the weekend going to drag shows or sitting on the couch watching *Grey's Anatomy*?

And what about this guy Mason is seeing? Will Mason spend his nights gaming with this guy now and forget I ever existed?

"You okay, man?" Rebel asks.

"Hm? Oh yeah, just enjoying nature," I answer sarcastically, earning a chuckle.

"We just want you guys to be close, know you can count on each other when you need to. With new guys likely being hired soon and everything that's happened lately, it's important to know you have friends."

"Yeah," I agree, feeling a little jab in my chest.

"Troy said you and Mason are seeing each other now?"

"No," I snort. "Mason just had a hot date last night, and he's already crazy about the guy."

"Hmm," Rebel hums in understanding and irritation prickles along my skin.

"It's great, I'm happy for him." My words come out sharper, more defensive than I intend.

"Of course, you are. Mason's a good kid."

"He's the same age I am," I point out.

"You're a good kid too," Rebel teases, ruffling my hair.

"I don't know about all that," I mutter. I wonder what he'd say if he knew about my record. Or has Bear already told him? What would the rest of the guys say if they knew I'd been homeless and stupid? Would they look down on me for the things I did to survive? Is porn different than prostitution? It feels different. The things I had to do back then felt so much more desperate and sad. Working at Ballsy doesn't feel that way. I glance over at Rebel and then around at the other guys. I may not be able to tell them about my past, but I *do* see them as friends.

Up ahead, Tank and Brewer are having an argument, but for a change it seems more playful than antagonistic. Pixie is quizzing Campy on what seems to be every animal he can think of, and beside me Rebel looks happy, settled.

"Losing some of your stamina in your old age?" I can't resist teasing Bear, who's bringing up the rear of our little convoy.

Pixie snickers.

"My stamina is just fine," Bear assures me with a wry smirk.

"Good to know," I wink at him, getting a few more chuckles from the rest of the guys.

～

I sign in at the senior center right on time for my community service shift. After the incident last week, I'm a little on edge, so the first thing I do is head down to Mrs. Roberts's room to check in on her.

I knock on the door frame and then poke my head inside to find her sitting in her chair, listening to the radio and looking out the window.

"Afternoon, Mrs. Roberts."

She turns around and gives me a toothless smile. "I told you to call me Ruth," she admonishes.

When I had to sign up for my community service, I wasn't all that excited about spending my weekends with the elderly. But the more I've come to know them, the more I look forward to my shifts. They have so many incredible stories to tell. A few weeks ago, Ruth told me about being wooed by Al Capone's brother Joe back in the thirties back when Al was already in prison. She said he used to give her pantyhose, which sounded weird as hell to me, but apparently the material they were made of was too expensive during the depression for most people to afford.

"Heart, come sit and tell me about your week," she encourages, and I stifle a snicker. Yeah, definitely not going to tell sweet, old Ruth about getting reamed by Campy to collect my paycheck this week. What else did I do? Fooled around with Mason, played video games, tried not to think about my parole officer while jerking one out in the shower. I doubt she really wants to know about my week.

"It was good," I say simply. "What about you? I'm betting your life is more interesting than mine."

Ruth snorts a laugh. "If that's true I feel very sorry for you."

I pat her hand, and she launches into a story about a dispute over the television in the common room, and the woman down the hall she doesn't get along with.

"There you are," I hear from the doorway. I turn around to see Rebecca, one of the nurses, standing with her hand on her hip and a look on her face like she's smelled something foul. "I didn't think you showed up for your shift."

"I signed in," I point out, and she rolls her eyes.

"I don't have time to chase convicts all day. I have medicine to distribute and important things to do. When you get here, you report to me so I can assign a task. We've been over this before. If I have to hunt you down again, I'm just going to mark it as a missed shift."

Heat rises in my cheeks from the dressing down, and I duck my head to avoid the pitying gaze of Ruth and the glare from Rebecca.

"Sorry," I mutter. The last thing I need is a bad report being sent to Lucky. He came to check up on me when he thought everything was going well; I can only imagine how far up my ass he'll be if he thinks I'm slacking or not showing up during my assigned shifts.

"I need you to go around and change bedpans and bedding in all the resident rooms."

"Okay, I'm on it," I assure her. When she's gone, I turn back to Ruth and give her an apologetic smile. "Guess I'd better get to work. I'll stop by to chat a little more when my shift ends, that way Rebecca can't complain."

"That sounds lovely, Heart. But you don't have to spend your Saturday evening keeping an old lady company."

"Nonsense. I'll see you again in a few hours."

I do my best to avoid Rebecca and the rest of the nurses while I work. I understand why they're wary of those of us doing our community service here, but most of us are only trying to complete our requirements and get on with our lives. I wonder if the stigma of having a record will ever wash off? When I'm forty, will people still look at me and see someone who went to prison when he was just a kid? Maybe I can overshadow the stigma of prison with the stigma of being a porn star, at least that's something I choose every day.

True to my word, when I finish up my shift, I stop back at Ruth's room, and we spend an hour or so talking about nothing and everything. If I had a grandma, I'd want her to be just like Ruth. Maybe then I wouldn't have ended up on the streets after my mom died. If just one person had been around to care what happened to me, my life could've been different.

My phone pings in my pocket, and I pull it out to see a text from Mason asking if I want to hang out. A smile tugs at my lips. Maybe my life isn't *so* bad.

16

LUCKY

I grew up moving from place to place, following my father wherever he was stationed. The moment he got discharged, we moved back to LA, where my father is originally from. My mom grew up in Florida, and they met when he was stationed there. It was a classic case of love at first sight, and they got married within three months of meeting.

Their story has always sounded super romantic but, at the same time, a bit absurd to me. How the hell can you know you love someone so shortly after meeting? The older I get, the more sense it makes to me. I don't know if it's because I'm actually older, because I'm gaining more life experience, or because I'm simply changing in how I view the world, but I understand how they fell in love better now than I did when I was twenty.

Take my date with Mason, for instance. Sure, my attraction to him when I met him in the club was instant. That's easy to explain since he is absolutely my type. But *type* only gets you so far. Yet our date proved that we are a good match in other aspects as well.

Now, don't get me wrong; I'm not saying I want to marry Mason. That would be a bit ridiculous after just one meeting. But I do see myself having a future with him, even having known him for such a short time. We have enough in common to keep the conversation going, and our characters are a good match. His clumsiness is super endearing, and his hesitance and nerdy shyness gives me the warm and fuzzies. It's hard to explain, but I feel we fit together.

And I guess that's what my parents felt when they met. In their case, they had to make a quick decision because my dad was being transferred to another base, so my mom had to either marry him and follow or stay behind and run the risk of not seeing him again. So, she chose to follow him, and thirty-five years later, she has never regretted that decision, or so she keeps telling me.

No, I'm not ready to marry Mason just yet. But I do know I'll be asking him out on a second date. Soon.

Right now, I'm looking forward to finally hanging out again with my best friend Rai, who has just moved back here after breaking up with his girlfriend. I spot him as soon as I walk into the bar, his lanky frame perched on a barstool while he's chatting animatedly with the bartender, his arms and hands gesturing wildly. It is so typical for him that I can't help but smile. Man, I've missed him.

I manage to walk up without him spotting me, and then I wrap my arms around him from the back and hug him tight.

"Hey, handsome," I say. "It's been too long, bro."

He jolts in surprise, then leans back against my chest and rubs his cheek against mine, his skin smooth against my stubble. "Right back atcha, good-looking."

I let go of him, then exchange the back hug for a frontal one. "It's so damn good to see you, man."

"You too," he says, and I can hear the genuine emotion in his voice.

I sit down on the barstool next to him, and before I can say anything, he's gestured the bartender to pour me a beer as well.

"You look well," he says, then grins broadly. "Even if you still dress like shit. Dude, could you look any more boring? You do know there are more colors than black, blue, and gray, right?"

I chuckle. "Still trying to improve my fashion sense? We both know that's a lost cause."

He sighs dramatically, then rolls his eyes at me. "You really are the worst gay in the world," he repeats his often-used line.

He's not wrong, at least not in that sense. Somehow, the innate fashion sense attributed to gays has skipped me.

Talking to Rai is always so easy. I love that no matter how long we haven't seen each other, we can pick up right where we left off. This time it's been—I do a mental calculation in my head and conclude it has to be at least a year—longer than usual, but it still feels familiar. Part of that is probably because we text each other daily, so there's no need to catch up on the practical stuff.

"What the hell happened with Nicole?" I ask after a few minutes of aimless chatting, concern lacing my voice. He's been tightlipped about her in his texts, explaining to me he'd rather tell me in person.

He sends me a weak smile. "No more small talk, huh? Fair enough. It's complicated."

I sigh, thinking of Mason and Heart. "Isn't it always?"

Rai lets out a bitter laugh. "True that."

We sit for a little bit, nursing our beers, until he speaks up again. "You know I've never made a secret of the fact that

I'm bisexual, right? Nicole knew this when we started dating, because I told her on what, our second or third date? I could see things were getting serious, and I wanted her to know who I was. And she understood, which surprised me in a positive way, because I've lost potential boyfriends and girlfriends over this. Not everyone is so understanding about bisexuality."

I nod in understanding. "I know, ugh. That infernal bi-hate people can't seem to get over. Such fucking bullshit. So, what happened?"

Rai is quiet again for a long time before he answers. "I fucked up with a guy from work," he finally says, his voice barely audible over the music that's playing in the bar, and I have to lean in to hear his words.

"My boss brought in a few lawyers from a different firm to work on a big project, and I worked with this one guy, Abel, for six weeks straight. He was gay. Confidently, openly gay. And we just clicked, you know? He was smart, but we also had fun together, just joking around, the little verbal matches you know I love."

There's a wistfulness in his voice that tugs at my heartstrings. Something tells me this story does not have a happy ending, even aside from him breaking up with Nicole.

"We did really well on the case, and to celebrate that, my boss took us out for dinner. Things got a little wild, and the alcohol was flowing freely, and then Abel and I kissed."

His shoulders drop, and he's studiously staring at his hands as he continues. "We didn't just kiss. We ducked into a deserted bathroom and made out, gave each other hand jobs. I don't know which one of us regretted it more the next day, since he had a boyfriend and I had Nicole. I debated not telling her, but you know that's not me. So I confessed... And she broke up with me. I can't really blame her. She deserved better than a boyfriend who cheated on her. I just...I felt things with Abel that I hadn't felt with her in a while, and that's on me as much as it is on her. Maybe we'd grown apart, I don't know, but that's no excuse. What I did was shitty."

"What happened with Abel?" I ask, my voice as soft as his.

Rai shrugs. "He went back to his boyfriend. We texted once afterward, and he told me that his boyfriend had forgiven him, but the stipulation was that he break off contact with me. That made total sense to me, so we deleted each other's numbers, and I haven't heard from him since."

I let out a deep sigh. "I'm so sorry for you, man."

Rai steals a glance at me. "You're not upset with me?"

I frown, taken aback by the mere suggestion. "No, why would I be? You didn't cheat on me."

"No, but I did cheat. And I know how much you hate it. I was worried you'd be upset with me, for breaking your, I don't know, moral code, or something."

"Is that how you see me? As someone who would end a friendship over cheating?" I ask.

The thought doesn't sit well with me. We've been friends since high school. Did Rai really think my supposed moral code as he called it would be more important than our friendship?

"Honestly, I didn't know what to expect, Jasper."

Rai never calls me by my nickname Lucky. For him, I'll always be Jasper or Jas, and I'm wonderfully okay with that.

"You can't deny you've always been rather black-and-white in your moral judgments," Rai continues. "It's probably what makes you such a good parole officer... And I know I'm opening myself wide for sleazy lawyer jokes, but let's skip those for the moment. I think I was scared you would take Nicole's side and maybe not so much end our friendship right away but be pissed at me nonetheless for throwing away a relationship over something that was never even more than a fling, if even that."

His words sting, like salty water coming into contact with an open wound on your body. We've been friends for so long, over fifteen years, and yet Rai was worried about how I would react to this? Do I really come across *that* judgmental? I don't like this at all, and it makes me wonder if I'm really as open-minded as I've always prided myself on being.

"I'm sorry," I say. "I'm sorry about the situation with Nicole, obviously. No, I agree you can't blame her. What you did was wrong, but you know that. But I hate the idea that you were scared of how I would react toward you."

He nods then sends me a careful smile. "At the risk of pissing you off even more, but would you have reacted the same way if I hadn't been sorry? If I had tried to come up with excuses about why I cheated? Would you have felt the same then?"

I let his words roll around in my head, considering them. There's a reason Rai went to law school. Even in high school, he could out-debate every teacher we had. With him as captain, our debate team won the national championships. I've always admired that in him, the ability to tear down any argument. Now that the shoe is on the other foot, and he's using his skills to confront me with some tough questions, that admiration is laced with frustration.

Is he right? Would I have reacted differently if he hadn't regretted it? If he'd been callous and flippant about it?

Cheating has always been a black and white case for me; he's right about that. If you are in a committed, exclusive relationship with someone, you don't cheat. It's as simple as that. I know there may be extenuating circumstances or whatever, but that shit just doesn't fly with me.

My thoughts jump to Mason...and then to Heart. Mason has been honest with me about seeing someone else as well, even though he admitted they're not so much in a relationship as they are fooling around. So why don't I have an issue with that? Is it because we've only had one date and are not in a committed relationship yet? Or is it because deep down, I'm in the same position as he is, with my attraction to Heart?

Obviously, nothing has happened between Heart and me, but boy, if the situation had been different, I would've been all over him. If I had not been his parole officer and he not my client, I'm pretty sure we would've had sex weeks ago. If not sooner. Does that mean I'm somehow cheating on Mason?

God, my head is hurting from trying to work this out. And it's all moot and theoretical anyway, since Heart and I are not involved, and we will never be. Not as long as I'm his PO and he's a client. That's a crystal clear line to me, a line I will never cross. So yeah, maybe Rai is right. Maybe my moral views are pretty black and white.

"I don't know," I finally admit. "I'd like to be able to assure you I would've felt the same, but I honestly don't know."

"At least you're honest about it," Rai says. "I can appreciate that."

I take a deep breath. "Look, I get that things aren't always so easy and black-and-white as I would like them to be in a relationship. You would know that better than me, considering you're the one who's been in a committed relationship for the last couple of years. So I realize I speak from a different place. I've never been in a long-term relationship like that, but I do hope to be someday. So maybe if I am, things will change. Maybe it's something that is easy to judge when it doesn't concern you, but a hell of a lot harder when you're in the midst of it."

Rai nods. "That makes total sense. So, no boyfriend for you then?"

Now it's my time to grin. "We're not in the boyfriend stage yet, but it looks promising."

Rai's eyes light up, and he leans forward, smiling. "Oh, that sounds intriguing. Tell me more, what's he like? Where did you guys meet?"

And it's not until he asks that question that I realize I want to tell him as much about Mason as about Heart. How fucked up is that?

17

MASON

I juggle several notebooks in my arms and try to catch my laptop bag from slipping off my shoulder. I should've looped it over my neck, but I didn't think I'd have this much trouble walking the few feet to Troy's place from my car. I should've known better than that.

The bag slides down, and in my fumbled attempt to save my laptop, I end up dropping my notebooks, loose paper flying out everywhere.

"Fuck," I mutter, bending to collect my notes.

Troy's door swings open in front of me. "I can't take you anywhere," he comments with a chuckle.

I shake my head, but he's right. I'm a mess. There's no universe in which I won't screw up this meeting to get sponsors for our game. Troy kneels and helps me gather the loose paper, and once we have everything back in order, we head into his place.

"You want a drink or anything?" he offers as I sit at his kitchen table and pull out my laptop.

"I'm good, thanks."

While Troy gets something to drink, I make sure my

notes for the presentation are in order. I'm not sure why he thinks it will be a good idea for me to say anything. We'd be better off if Troy gives the whole presentation and I just sit there and do my best not to spill anything.

"Are you *sure* I should do half the presentation?" I ask Troy for the umpteenth time.

"I'm positive. I can talk about a lot of the monetary and marketing aspect, but you and I both know you're better at describing the specs and design aspects of the game. I can code, but I'm shit at explaining game design."

"I'm going to screw it up," I warn him with a sigh.

"No, you won't," he assures me. "Now, let's run through this presentation from the top to see where we need some work."

I sigh again and pull up the power point we made, sitting back to listen as Troy goes over the first half. Three hours and countless re-writes later, my stomach is grumbling, and I'm starting to get a headache.

"I'm starving; can we take a break?" Troy suggests, and I readily agree. "I'll order a pizza, and then we can get back at this after we eat."

I groan and let my head fall against the table. "Do we really even need sponsors?"

"If we want to take this game to the next level, we need sponsors. Think of how good this is going to look on our resumes. Trust me, I've been applying at game studios for months now and haven't gotten so much as a nibble yet. If we can make this game happen in a big way, it's going to be huge for both our careers."

"Yeah, okay," I agree, hating him a little for being right. This game is getting some decent downloads so far, but if we can get sponsorship, we'll be able to do a lot more with it and get more eyes on it.

Troy places the order for pizza, and we head into the living room to play video games while we wait for it to be delivered.

"How was your date?" Troy asks, and I'm glad he's focused on the game on the screen so he doesn't catch my blush.

"Good. It's been two dates now, actually."

Lucky called me a few days after our first date and invited me out for drinks at this nice little bar with live music and a really relaxed vibe. The second goodnight kiss was even better than the first, because my nerves weren't nearly as bad.

"That's it? *Good*?" Troy complains. "Tell me about the guy. What's he do? What's he look like? Does he have a huge dick?"

I sputter at the last question. "Oh my god, it was two dates. How would I know what his dick looks like?"

"Oh, my sweet summer child."

"Just because you're a slut doesn't mean all of us put out on the first date," I tease.

"Fine, but you totally *could've* put out on the second date. Besides, I'm not a slut anymore. I'm boring and settled into a committed relationship and shit," he points out.

"We're boring?" Rebel asks, coming into the living room. "Gee thanks. Maybe we should look up that cute twink, Byron, and see if he's still up for a threesome," he suggests with a smirk, sliding onto the couch on the other side of Troy and putting his feet up on the coffee table.

"Seriously?" Troy asks, looking away from the screen and giving me the perfect opportunity to annihilate his avatar.

"If you want," Rebel shrugs. "I'd hate for you to be *bored* with me."

"How could I possibly get bored with someone who rims like you do?"

"Dude," I complain, wrinkling my nose at the unwanted image.

"Don't knock it until you try it," Troy counters.

My mind conjures images from a recent Ballsy video where Heart rimmed Pixie, and my cock starts to plump in my jeans. Heart and Pixie sure looked like they were both enjoying the experience, but it *is* porn, so there's a good chance they were faking. Who really likes licking someone's ass? Plus, that must be *so* awkward to have your cheeks spread, asshole on display for someone. So why is the thought making me even harder? I shift, hoping to hide my growing bulge.

"Isn't it awkward?" I ask.

"Maybe with someone you don't know, I guess."

I nod, keeping my eyes trained on the screen. I wonder if rimming is on the list of things Heart's planning to teach me. My hole flutters at the thought. I guess if he suggests it, I'd be up for trying it.

The pizza arrives a few minutes later and we all dig in.

"Hey, you totally distracted me from getting the details on your dates," Troy realizes as we eat.

Damn, so close.

"It was fun. Lucky seems like a good guy. He's a parole officer, and he's really hot and nice. I'm not sure what he sees in me, but there's no accounting for taste, I suppose," I joke, the self-doubt niggling at my mind.

"You're a catch," Troy insists, and Rebel nods his agreement. "So, do you have another date planned?"

"Not yet, Lucky's supposed to call. I don't know what I'm going to do about Heart though if Lucky and I keep dating."

"What do you mean? Did you and Lucky already talk about being exclusive?"

"No, actually I told him about Heart, and he seemed fine with it. But it seems kind of wrong. I like Lucky, and I like Heart, isn't it shitty to lead them both on?"

"But you're not leading anyone on. Everyone is aware of everyone else and is in agreement about things being casual, right?" Troy checks, and I nod. "That's all above board."

"Yeah," I agree reluctantly. "It's just so not *me*."

"Maybe that's not the worst thing in the world. Not that you shouldn't be you. You're awesome and should totally be yourself. But sometimes it's good to step out of our comfort zone and just experience life, you know? Look at me with Rebel, if I'd stuck to my usual MO, I'd still be a lonely, miserable asshole. Now I'm a happy, committed asshole."

I snort a laugh. "I guess that makes sense."

"Of course, it makes sense; I'm a genius. Relax, have fun, and see where things go."

"Yeah, okay," I agree, feeling a little lighter after his reassurances.

"Ready to get back to this presentation?" Troy asks as we polish off the last of the pizza.

"As I'll ever be," I reply reluctantly.

After a few more hours of torture, Troy eventually agrees to call it a night. He's lighting up a joint as I head out of his place, and I shake my head, wishing I had an easy way of relaxing like he does. I'm jittery and wound tight after spending the entire day imagining giving a presentation in front of a room full of people in suits.

I don't live far from Troy so it doesn't take long to get home. I kick off my shoes and head straight for my couch to spend a few hours gaming to unwind. Before I can get a game going, my phone rings in my pocket. My heart flips, and I can't decide if I'm hoping for it to be Heart or Lucky calling. It's been a few days since my second date with Lucky, and I'm starting to doubt he's going to call, so when I see his name on the screen, I smile.

"Hey," I answer in as nonchalant a tone as possible.

"Hey," Lucky replies, his voice smooth and deep. "Sorry it took me a few days to call, I've been buried under work."

"I understand," I assure him, a smile stretching across my face. Silence stretches between us for a few seconds, and I start to wonder if there's something more I'm supposed to say. Or is it his turn to talk again? Wait, should I have tried to call *him* sooner? Am I supposed to apologize too?

"How've you been? Up to anything interesting the past few days?" he asks conversationally. There's a rustling in the background that sounds like he's getting comfortable, so I do the same, leaning back on my couch and folding my legs under myself.

"Nothing too interesting. I spent the day today working with Troy on a presentation for potential sponsors for our game. That's coming up in the next few months, and every time I think about it I want to puke," I admit. I know it seems overkill for us to spend so much time going over our presentation so far ahead of time, but Troy is indulging my need for excessive preparation.

"Yeah, public speaking is not something I'm a big fan of either," Lucky agrees.

"Really?" I can't imagine Lucky feeling nervous or panicked about anything; he seems like the type to always keep cool under pressure. Being a former Marine, I suppose that's an important quality.

"Oh yeah, public speaking and elevators are my top two fears."

"Thank you for telling me that, it makes you seem much more human."

"More human?" Lucky chuckles. "What was I before?"

"I don't know, some sort of demigod?" I smile and fiddle with a little string coming out of the arm of the couch.

"Which one?" Lucky asks with humor.

"I'm thinking Achilles, conquering hero and all. Although, I suppose even with your fear of elevators you could still be Achilles, it'll just be your Achilles heel."

Lucky barks out a laugh at that. "I'll have to watch out for being shot in the heel with an arrow then."

"Probably a good idea," I agree with mock-solemnity.

We talk for a while longer about video games we've both been playing lately and what the rest of our week looks like.

"I've had a lot of fun hanging out with you lately. Can I take you on another date this weekend?" he asks, and I do a little happy dance in my seat.

"That sounds nice," I agree, doing my best to sound indifferent.

"Great, how does Sunday sound?"

"Perfect."

"Okay, I'll text you with details later in the week," Lucky says and then pauses like he's considering his next words. "I like you, Mason. I feel like we really connect. I hope you feel the same?"

"I do," I rush to assure him.

"Good." I can hear the smile in his voice and it warms my insides. "Have a good night."

"You too."

My heart is still pounding when I hang up the phone. I don't think there's been a more perfect conversation in the history of dating.

With a happy sigh, I finally start up the game I decided

to play and spend the rest of the night alternating between thinking about when I can spend more time with Heart and what my third date with Lucky will be like, too giddy about both men to even feel guilty about how much I like both of them.

18

LUCKY

It's my day off, and I'm on my way to hang out with my brother. He's back from an eleven-month deployment overseas—the exact location unspecified, as always—and I can't wait to see him. A few years back, he bought a dilapidated house in the middle of nowhere, an hour and a half outside LA. He said he couldn't get used again to the city, that it triggered him too much. He loves the peace and quiet out here, and as I leave the hustle and bustle—and the traffic—behind me, I can't really blame him.

He's mowing his lawn as I pull up, immediately shutting off the mower as he spots me in the driveway. He's thin, thinner than I've ever seen him, and his eyes are sunken and dark. What the hell happened to him? Being an Army ranger, he usually can't tell me much anyway about his deployments, but this looks bad.

"Lucky," he says, his face breaking open in a broad smile. His arms come around me, and we hug for a good twenty seconds.

"I'm so happy to see you, Ranger," I say, my voice muffled against his shoulder. "Damn, I missed you, bro."

He slaps my back one more time, but with less force than I had expected. His body feels frail in my arms, a far cry from his usual form. I don't comment on it. He'll tell me when he's ready.

A few minutes later, we're seated on his porch in the shade, a cold beer in our hands. It's quiet here, the only sound the buzzing insects that can't even get to us because his porch has a mosquito net all around it. His garden needs a lot of work, but the butterflies don't mind the wildflowers that have popped up everywhere.

"Didn't you pay someone to mow your lawn?" I ask.

"Yeah, and he did, until I got back."

The implicit statement is clear. "How long have you been back?" I ask.

He sighs. "A month."

A month back and he still looks like this? Holy hell.

"I needed some time alone," he says.

"No apology needed. Ever."

"Thank you." He takes a swig of his beer. "How have you been?"

"Good. Busy with work. Lots of new clients."

"All work and no play?" he teases.

"I may have *played* a little as well," I say, smiling at the thought of Mason. He's so cute with that nerdy look. Then Heart pops into my head, and my smile falters.

"What's up with the frown, bro?"

"It's silly," I say, waving him off. My problems are irrelevant and inconsequential to what he's dealing with, I'm sure.

"Lucky...I could use the distraction. Talk to me about silly things, please."

My eyes find his, and it's not hard to spot the lingering nightmares. I nod. "I'm dating this super cute nerd named Mason," I say.

"Oh, a nerd. Completely your type," Ranger says.

"I know, right? He's cute as fuck, adorably clumsy, smart, and I wanna wrap him in my arms and...well, you can imagine the rest, I'm sure."

My brother grins. "I can think of a few things, yes. So, what's the problem? Is he not into you?"

"I think he is. We had a couple of dates, and they went well... I really like him. Though he's also sort of dating this other guy."

"He's a player? That doesn't sound like your type at all."

"I don't think he is. I think he got hurt in a previous relationship, and this guy is more of a friend who's helping him get over that. Like, build up his confidence again... I suspect his sexual confidence mostly."

"Okay," Ranger says slowly. "Then I'm still not seeing the problem."

I let out another sigh that seems to originate in my toes. "The problem is that there's another guy. A sexy as fuck guy, covered in tattoos, who works as a porn star...and who's a client."

Ranger plops down his beer so hard, I check to make sure he didn't shatter the glass. "Let me get this straight... You're dating two guys? And one of them is a porn star?"

He laughs, and despite his amusement over my issues, it's good to hear my brother's full laughter fill the porch.

"What the hell have you done with my straight-laced brother?" he grins.

I hold up a finger. "I've been a lot of things, but *straight* was never one of them."

He shakes his head, still smiling. "True. But seriously, how did this happen?"

"I don't know. I only met Mason recently, but I really like him. As you said, he's my type, you know? I can see myself having a future with him. But Heart, I can't get him out of my head, and I wanna know if there could be more between us as well, if it wasn't for the fact that I'm his PO..."

My voice trails off when I notice Ranger freeze. "What?"

"Heart? Your porn star client is Heart? *Ballsy Boy Heart*?"

Oh damn, I fucked up. I didn't think when I mentioned Heart's name, thus breaking confidentiality. I always call him Gunner, and the one time I don't... Usually with clients, first names are not an issue, but of course his name is anything but standard, and combined with telling Ranger he's a porn star and tatted up, it's...

"Wait? He's a *gay* porn star..."

And my older brother, my tough-as-nails, Army Ranger brother who's been to hell and back, he blushes. *Ah.* It seems I'm not the only one who fucked up.

"You're not gonna ask me the question?" he asks when I stay silent.

"You'll tell me when you're ready."

He laughs, but then his laugh transitions into a sob, followed by another one. My heart breaks as he falls apart, and all I can do is sit next to him and hold his hand as he falls to pieces. He sags out of his chair to the floor, and I let myself slide down next to him to hold him. He drops his head on my shoulder, his too-thin body violently shaking.

It takes a long time before he calms down, but I'm content to ride it out with him. I don't know what happened to him, but I can guess, and none of it is good. Crying helps, I can tell from experience, and so does talking, but I'll wait till he's ready to talk. He'll get there. I hope.

When Ranger finally speaks, his voice is hoarse and broken. "Talk to me about your men, Lucky. Tell me something sweet, something good."

I hold him close as I close my eyes and think of Heart.

"Heart is sexy as fuck, even when he doesn't mean to be. It's like everything about him draws you in. His eyes, which are a mix of colors that you can't look away from. His mouth, which curves as he smiles...and is so fucking red and sexy when he's been kissed thoroughly. Not by me, sadly...but god, his videos. His body is...perfect. He's tight and toned and strong enough to take a good pounding...or dole one out. But Ranger, he's got such a good heart. He's kind, gentle, fiercely loyal to his friends. It's what got him into trouble before...believing the best of people."

"He sounds like a good man," my brother comments.

"He is. But he's a client, and I don't know what to do... Plus, there's Mason. He's a video game designer, did I tell you that? I know you don't care much for them, but if you get the chance, check out the Break-Up Artist. It's this mobile game he developed with his best friend, and he constantly has new ideas for games. He's sweet and clumsy, and he makes me want to protect him and take care of him... and contrary to Heart, he'll actually let me."

"Sounds like you got it bad for both of them," Ranger comments after a little bit.

"I know. I do, but how is that even possible?"

Ranger chuckles. "There's this thing called threesomes. If you've ever watched porn, you should be familiar with it."

"A threesome." I scoff. "Aren't those illegal?"

"Of course not. You can't marry more than one person, but there's no law against being in a relationship with more than one person."

My brother would know, considering he managed to get a law degree somewhere along the way.

"Dude, but with my job? That would never work. Plus, the idea of Mason and Heart together is..."

I try to picture them together in my head, and much to

my surprise, they fit. Mason is all eager, plastered against Heart's body, and Heart is gentle and tender with him, taking his time to bring Mason's body alive. His cheeks are flushed, his glasses askew on his nose, his hair all messed up and sexy. Then I step into the picture, and Mason's eyes light up as he sees me. I kiss him until he runs out of breath, and his hard cock pokes me. Heart's eyes are gleaming as he watches us with pride, his lips swollen from kissing, and he drops to his knees to...

I wince as my cock swells painfully in my shorts, excited by the mental image of those two together. Who the fuck would have thought I had such a dirty mind?

"Is what?" my brother asks.

"More appealing than it should be," I say, sighing softly. It's a pipedream, this all too vivid image of the three of us, but damn, it's a good one.

19

HEART

I towel myself off in the Ballsy Boys locker room after a long day of shooting. Rebel apologized in advance for the rather strenuous scene he had planned, explaining that the two guest stars he had invited were only available today, so he couldn't spread the shoot out over two or three days as he normally would've.

When he asked me if I was okay with that, I said yes, of course. I always say yes. I am feeling it now, though. The two guys were super nice, and I'm sure the scene will turn out well, so I'm not regretting it.

Then again, I've learned that regret is a useless emotion anyway. It doesn't bring you anything. All it does is make you feel sad and guilty and stupid about the choices you made, choices that you can't change anyway. So what good does it do to have regret, other than maybe the somewhat naive belief that it will help you make better choices in the future?

I don't need to dwell much on the past to do that. I know where I fucked up, and I also know that I will never ever make that mistake again.

I'm just putting on my underwear when Rebel steps into the room. "That went well, I think. How are you feeling?"

One of the things I appreciate about Rebel is that questions like that are never a formality with him, with Bear either for that matter. The both of them are genuinely interested in us.

"It's going to take me a while to recover, as you can imagine..." I say with a smile. "Dude, when you said that guy was *hung*, you weren't kidding."

Rebel grins. "I know, right?" he says. "It looked even bigger in real life than I had imagined it from watching his videos."

"Yeah, well, I didn't have to imagine anything at all when that monster was parked up to his balls in my ass. Holy crap, I'm gonna feel that for a while."

Rebel's smile fades a little. "You're okay, though, right?" he checks.

"Sure, I'm always okay. You just may not want to schedule me for anything for, say, a week or so."

"Gotcha," Rebel says, sitting down on the bench, apparently not in a hurry to leave just yet.

I drag my shirt over my head and comb through my hair with my fingers. "Do you miss it?" I ask on impulse. "Doing scenes, I mean."

He scratches his chin. "Not really, or at least not as much as I had expected to."

"You can tell me to fuck off if you want, but I was just curious. Did you quit because of your boyfriend?" I ask.

"Oh, you can ask. I don't mind talking about this. No, I didn't quit because of Troy. I had thought about it before, because I had outgrown doing scenes myself. I really enjoy the role that I have right now, coming up with ideas for scenes and helping produce them."

I sit down on a bench across from him. "Troy didn't have an issue with you doing porn, even after you guys hooked up?"

Rebel smiles. "Dude, you have no idea how much of a problem Troy did *not* have with that. I think it actually helped him feel like what we had was casual enough for him to tolerate, commitment-phobe that he was. I'm not sure he would feel the same way right now, but he certainly doesn't have an issue with me working in porn. Hell, we watch the shoots together."

The smile breaks out on my face. "You and your boyfriend watch me get fucked? Dayum, that's some seriously fucked-up hobby you two have. Other couples do things like watch TV, you know. Or they go bowling or hiking or whatever the hell it is normal people do. They do not watch porn made by their friends together but whatever rocks your boat, I guess."

Rebel is laughing, too. Man, he is so fucking gorgeous. I know they're still getting a ton of emails from disappointed viewers hoping for Rebel to make a comeback—or at least a one-time appearance. And I can totally understand why. He's not only hot as fuck, he has a phenomenal cock, and he damn well knows how to use it. Plus, he's a genuinely nice guy, and that shows, even on camera. It's a combination that is pretty unique.

"Hey," Rebel says. "Don't knock it till you try it."

His face grows a little more serious. "It's pretty rare, you know? I've done porn for a long time, and I can tell you from experience that it's hard to combine it with a relationship. The guys I met either wanted me because I was a porn star, or they only wanted me if I stopped being one. Troy was the first who was okay with both sides of me, with both Rebel and Hendrix."

I hold up my hands. "No worries, man. I'm not even remotely interested in being in a relationship, right now, or ever, for that matter. Been there, done that, and I didn't even get the t-shirt. Let's leave it at that. Relationships are not for me."

Even as I say it, a trail of doubt sneaks into my mind. What about Mason? What if Mason wanted more than just fooling around? I shake off the thought. He doesn't. He wouldn't, not if he knew the truth about my past.

"I'm sorry," Rebel says, his tone soft. "If I may ask, and like you said, you can tell me to fuck off, but what made you decide to do porn?"

From anyone else, I would've felt this question was either impertinent or rude as fuck. With Rebel, it's different. I know he's genuinely interested. And after I asked him about him and Troy, it kind of makes sense that he would ask me a similar question. It's just that I've never talked about this with anyone, and I don't think Rebel knows my background. Bear is the only one who knows, and I don't think he would've told Rebel without my permission.

In hindsight, it would've been fine with me had Bear told Rebel, but I guess that ship sailed a long time ago. When I started working here, I had no idea of the men they were. All I knew was that I needed a job, and literally no one else would hire me; Bear seemed like a decent guy. Plus, trust me, after three years in prison, I can damn well defend myself.

But now that I've been doing it for a while that reason isn't even valid anymore. It's still there, but I've realized there's a much deeper motivation for me to do porn.

"What are the most common reasons why people do porn?" I tried to deflect his question at first.

Rebel gently shakes his head. "It's okay if you don't want to talk about this, Heart. You don't owe me an answer."

I sigh. "No, I know I don't owe you anything. It's not that I don't *want* to tell you, it's more that it's really hard for me to put it into words. I'm not much of a talker, you know?"

Rebel smiles. "You've met Troy, right? Does he strike you as the talking type?"

I chuckle. "Not exactly. So I guess you're familiar with how this works."

Rebel leans forward, placing his elbows on his knees as he gives me a warm smile. "You'll find that I'm a good listener, but only if you want me to listen to you. As I said, it's none of my business, so whatever you want or don't want to tell me is fine."

I close my eyes for a second, because it's easier to think when I feel like I'm alone, when I feel like I'm not being watched or judged.

It was one of the hardest things for me in prison, never being alone. Of course, being alone in a prison is rarely a good thing. It either means you're in solitary—which I managed to avoid, thank fuck—or you're being vulnerable to an attack of some kind. That being said, for someone who appreciates being by himself as much as I do, I struggled with the complete lack of solitude. I can't think well when I'm in the company of others.

"Have you ever had boys who did it simply because they loved porn?"

I open my eyes just as Rebel answers me. "Sure, there's been quite a few. People do this for various reasons, Heart, and enjoying sex is as valid a reason as any of the others. Are you telling me that's why you're doing it?"

I debate lying to him, but he really deserves better. "I think that's part of it, but it's a little more complicated than that. I won't bore you with the details, but I've made some pretty stupid choices in the past, choices that resulted in me having a lot of negative sexual experiences, I guess you could say. I still chose some of them, but in hindsight, they felt demeaning to me. I've come to realize doing porn makes me feel like I am once again in charge of my body, if that makes sense. Like, I am somehow reclaiming my sex life for myself, to feel good rather than used. And of course, that sounds incredibly ironic considering I got spit roasted by two dudes with massive cocks today, and my ass is still smarting like a motherfucker, but there you have it."

Rebel's eyes light up at my explanation. "But that's wonderful, Heart," he says. "I love that you experience porn like this. Especially because so many people have preconceived notions about doing porn or why porn stars are in the business, you know? Sure, there's a fair share of abuse and bullshit going on in this business, just like in any other business. And I know that some people do it for the wrong reasons, or they're forced to, or whatever happened to them in the past makes this pretty much the only option they have. But I love that you use it to empower yourself and feel good about sex again."

I hesitate before answering. "I don't want to lie to you, Rebel. I didn't have that many other options either."

Rebel gets up from his bench and extends me his hand. When I accept it, he gently pulls me in for a sweet hug. "In that case, I'm even more glad you found us. We're happy to have you, Heart. You belong with us."

20

MASON

I tug at the hem of my shirt and shift on my feet, trying to convince myself it's a good idea to go in there and go through with all of this. A couple of make-out sessions obviously didn't have a negative impact on our friendship, but if Heart wants to do more, will it change things? God, I *want* more with Heart, but it also feels like a really bad idea. There's so much to lose if things get weird with him.

On the other hand, what about my next date with Lucky? I'm sure he'll want to go further than kissing this time, and then I'll be back in the same position I was in before, having no idea how to do anything right. I need to learn. And as much as the thought terrifies me, the thought of leaving things with Heart at nothing more than some kissing feels like a painful let down. I want more with him, as much as he'll give me.

Does it make me greedy to want both Heart and Lucky so much? Troy obviously didn't think so, but this whole thing feels like it belongs in someone else's life instead of mine.

With a determined huff, I lift my fist up and rap at Heart's door and then hold my breath as his footsteps approach. I start going over in my head what I'll say when he answers. *It was a silly suggestion, can we just forget it? We're friends, and this will just complicate things. I can find plenty of guys to fool around with and improve my skills.*

The door pulls open, and all thoughts vanish from my brain as I look at Heart standing in the doorway with his signature smirk and no shirt. Why isn't he wearing a shirt? Oh god, are we going to jump right in? I can't keep my eyes from roaming greedily over the colorful ink covering his bare torso. I've never found tattoos all that appealing; I didn't understand why anyone would want to permanently mark their body. I kind of get it now.

"Hey, sorry, I spilled soda on myself like thirty seconds before you knocked at the door," he explains, stepping aside and waving me in.

"Oh, yeah, it's fine," I rush to assure him, my cheeks heating as I realize how stupid I must've looked staring at him.

He wanders over to the dresser beside his bed and pulls out a fresh shirt. I watch with disappointment as he tugs it over his head, covering all that tempting skin.

"I was thinking—"

"I'm not sure—" I cut myself off when I realize Heart started to say something at the same time. I wave for him to go ahead.

"I was thinking; I want to make sure this is fun for you, no pressure. So I found a fun game for us."

"A game?" I swallow thickly, my mind racing. Heart has a sex game he wants to play? I can barely manage not to disappoint when things are straight forward and vanilla, and he wants to play some kind of kinky sex game?

"Relax, it's nothing crazy. Just a little something to help break the tension. That is, if you still *want* to do this? Otherwise we can order food and play videogames all night like usual. I'm up for whatever."

There's no disappointment or expectation in Heart's expression. He really is okay with whatever I want to do tonight.

"No, I'm still up for it," I assure him with more confidence than I feel. Heart's smile lets me know he sees right through my façade.

"Cool, why don't we chill for a bit first? Make out a little again if you want?"

I nod in agreement. I never thought I'd say this, but I'm *really* starting to like kissing. With Brad, it always felt like kissing was just a necessary stop on the way to getting down to what he really wanted. With Heart and Lucky, kissing is about *enjoying* it. Then again, Heart's a porn star; I'm sure kissing is boring as hell for him. God, there's nothing I could do in bed that would surprise him. Actually, that thought *is* a little comforting.

"I can see you thinking from here," Heart teases, crossing from the bed to the couch and plopping down. He pats the cushion beside him and waggles his eyebrows playfully. The goofy seduction makes me laugh and drains a little of the tension from my shoulders.

I kick off my shoes and join him on the couch. I'm trying to decide exactly how close I should sit when he grabs my arm and tugs me against his side.

"Hi," I laugh awkwardly, realizing just how close we are now.

"Hi," Heart replies with a sweet smile. "Relax, I promise there's nothing for you to worry about, okay?"

I nod, and my eyes zero in on his soft, pink lips. I lean

forward and press my lips to his. There's a little zing of something in the pit of my stomach. With all the practice I've had now, I'm quicker to find a rhythm with my lips against his, our tongues hot and wet as they slide against each other. My cock aches, but neither of us make any move to do anything other than kiss. Even our hands stay respectfully well above the waist.

I drag my fingers through his hair, tugging at it to urge him closer, desperate for more of him but not ready to move on from kissing. More than this and I risk disappointing him and embarrassing myself, just like I did with Brad.

Heart kisses along my jaw and down my neck as I pant loud enough that I'm sure I'll be humiliated when I think back over this later.

"You're a fast learner," Heart notes, grazing his teeth against my Adam's apple. I let out a whimper and tug harder at his hair. "How about our game? Are you ready?"

I make a noncommittal noise that Heart takes as agreement. As soon as he pulls away, I notice my hands shaking with a mixture of nerves and being hornier than I've been in my life. His shirt tugs up just a little as he reaches for something on the little table next to the couch. I find myself fascinated with the dusting of dark hair that seems to run from his belly button downward.

Heart sits straight again and holds out his hand to me. There are two dice in his palm, but instead of dots or numbers on them, they have words on each side. I raise an eyebrow in question.

"Is this like sex D&D or something?"

Heart sputters a laugh. "No, but that would be an amazing idea. We need to invent something like that," he agrees. "It's really simple, one of these has a thing you do, and the other has a body part. So you roll both and do whatever comes up."

"Okay," I agree, licking my lips to combat my suddenly dry mouth. I hold out my hand, hoping Heart won't notice the way it's still shaking. If he notices, he doesn't comment. I shake the dice between my hands and then let them go above the coffee table. They bounce and roll for a moment, and I'm almost afraid to read what they both landed on.

"Lick stomach," Heart reads. "Good, that's an easy start."

I look at him skeptically. "I thought this was supposed to be sexy."

"It is sexy," he says, pulling his shirt over his head.

"Licking your stomach? That just seems like it would tickle and get slobber all over you. How is that sexy? I mean, the stomach isn't exactly an erogenous zone."

"Here's your first lesson, sweetie." Heart fixes me with a serious look. "*Every* part of the body can be an erogenous zone. A mistake too many people make is focusing solely on what's between the legs and forget about all the other fun ways to explore someone's body. Don't get so focused on the destination that you miss the journey."

Something inside me relaxes a fraction. When he puts it that way, it makes all the sense in the world. There's no reason to rush straight to the main event.

"Okay." I take a deep breath and take a second to look at Heart, shirtless once again. I'm not sure I would've thought of licking his stomach or, honestly, anything other than his cock if it weren't for this game. But now that I'm looking again at the colorful ink on his abdomen, the dips of his muscles, and the wiry patches of hair, it seems like a *really* good idea to lick him.

Heart lies back and crooks his finger to beckon me forward. I lean over him and brush my nose through the little bit of hair on his chest, and then I place a quick kiss just between his pecs. He hums his approval, and I kiss lower. I trade chaste kisses for open mouth kisses as I work my way over his abs. When I graze the colorful patch of wildflowers tattooed from the left side of his ribcage down to his hip, I run my tongue along them, tracing each flower and drawing moans from Heart's lips.

"Is this good?" I check, my voice husky.

"Oh yeah," Heart assures me.

"Should we, um, roll the dice again?" I ask, feeling a little more confident.

"Hm? Oh yeah," he agrees, sitting up and reaching for the dice.

Heart shakes the dice in his hands and then drops them onto the coffee table while I hold my breath. I'm not sure what I'm hoping for them to say; all I want to find out is if Heart's touch will be exciting in a way Brad's never was.

"Bite nipple," Heart reads off the dice and then turns to me with a grin. "Take your shirt off."

I cross my arms over my chest protectively.

"You're going to bite my nipple? That sounds.... that's not..."

Heart's lips press against mine, effectively silencing my protest. His lips are firm and demanding, coaxing mine to part, and then his tongue is slipping into my mouth. His hand sneaks up the front of my shirt, and I shiver at the feel of his fingers ghosting over my bare skin. My body arches closer to him without conscious effort.

When his hand reaches my chest, he circles my nipple with his index finger, and I whimper into his mouth as the sensation goes straight between my legs.

"I promise it won't hurt," Heart murmurs against my lips, and I nod my head in a trance-like way.

He reaches for the hem of my shirt and tugs it over my head. My arms go around my exposed body, and I shiver again, this time from the chill in the room and the sensation of Heart's eyes all over my skinny, pale torso.

"You're sexy," Heart says, his gaze roaming over me.

"Yeah, okay," I snort and roll my eyes.

"Take the compliment." Heart's tone holds an air of authority. He pushes on my shoulder, forcing me to lie back on the couch. "Don't think, just feel."

Easier said than done, but I do my best to follow his instructions, settling back and closing my eyes. To my surprise, Heart doesn't go right for my nipples. Instead, the first place I feel his warm lips is at the bottom of my rib cage. A ripple of unexpected pleasure runs along my skin, and my cock presses against the confines of my pants. Another kiss, this one open mouthed and right at the apex of my sternum.

I tangle my fingers in his hair, and Heart makes a sound of approval in the back of his throat. It's so different than the sounds he makes on camera, and the thought that I'm one of the few people who knows what Heart *really* sounds like makes me warm all over. Several more kisses follow, leaving wet marks all over my skin and making me harder with every passing second.

When his mouth finally brushes against my peaked nipple, I gasp as my balls tighten, and my whole body aches for more of Heart's touch. He looks up at me with a wicked smile before dragging the flat of his tongue across my nipple.

"Holy shit," I mutter, squirming under him, my breath coming out in embarrassing pants. "That's...I didn't think... oh god..." My babble cuts off when he does it again, this time ending the lick with a sharp flick from the tip of his tongue.

He moves his mouth over to my other nipple, giving it the same treatment, while using his index finger to flick the first nipple, keeping it tingling and hard. My body vibrates in anticipation. Biting my nipples sounded strange and awkward, if not a little painful, before he started. But now I'm dying to know what it will feel like.

Heart's thumb joins his forefinger, and he gently rolls my nipple between them, tugging ever so slightly. His teeth graze the other nipple, and my cock throbs. I'm too hazy with lust to feel embarrassed about rubbing myself against Heart's thigh as he plays with my nipples. With one nipple carefully between his teeth, his tongue flicks over it again. I'm squirming shamelessly against him, tugging at his hair as the words *please* and *oh god* keep falling from my lips.

Without warning, his thumb and forefinger give a hard pinch at the same time his teeth bite sharply into my sensitive, aching flesh, sending a shockwave straight through me.

"Oh fuck," I gasp, my cock giving one more hard throb before erupting. I thrust helplessly against Heart, drawing out the pleasure pounding in my veins.

Humiliation is right on the heels of the ebbing wave of my orgasm.

"Oh god, I'm so sorry." I close my eyes and wish there was somewhere to hide my face.

"What are you sorry for? That was hot as fuck," Heart says earnestly. "Look at me."

I open my eyes reluctantly and find Heart smiling at me, his lips puffy from kissing and sucking on my chest.

"You don't think I'm lame for..." I can't even bring myself to say *jizzing my pants*.

"The only thing I think is that now that I know how

much you like it, I want to play with your nipples *a lot* more. Also, that you look sexy as fuck when you come."

"Really?"

"Really," Heart assures me. "We're fooling around, coming around each other was kind of part of the deal."

"That's true," I agree, letting out a long breath. "That wasn't anything like what I did with Brad."

"I kind of figured."

"Thank you. I should, uh, probably get cleaned up."

Heart rolls off me, and I make my way to the bathroom, wincing at the way my sticky pubes tug and pull against my underwear.

Note to self, try to be naked next time that happens.

21

LUCKY

Nerves tighten my stomach, and I wipe my hands on my pants. Why am I so nervous to see him again? It's embarrassing as fuck.

Then again, so is the fact that I jacked off to his videos this morning. I promised myself I wouldn't watch them anymore, wouldn't get sucked into the deep, black hole of the Ballsy Boys website. Sure, I've had a subscription since forever, but that doesn't mean I have to look at *his* videos. There are plenty of videos on there that have nothing to do with him, so why do I keep coming back to his?

They uploaded a scene of him and Campy, pleasuring each other with some toys. I didn't even make it half way before I blew my load. The sheer look on Heart's face as he comes is enough to make me explode. He has this face, this intense look of pure pleasure he gets when he's enjoying himself. And man, the things Campy was doing to him, it was obvious Heart *was* enjoying himself.

How I wish I could see him like that, that I could bring him that pleasure. I keep telling myself that I can't, but the voice in my head that insists this attraction to Heart is insanity seems to be getting weaker and weaker. It feels like a losing battle, so what am I going to do?

I've got Mason. I like Mason. I like him a lot. Our dates have been fun and sweet and sexy, and I want to see if he and I have a future together. So why the hell can't I let go of this ridiculous and dangerous attraction to Heart?

Every time I see him, it gets deeper. And it's not just sexual. I'm admiring the hell out of him for rebuilding his life, for his strength and resilience. Plus, his sassy attitude is so freaking hot. I like everything about him...even though I shouldn't.

I see him enter the waiting room before the receptionist even calls me. I take a deep breath, then wipe my hands again, trying to will myself to relax and not show any of the turmoil that's happening inside me. He can't know. Not any more than he already does.

"Good morning, Heart," I greeted him.

"Mr. Stone," he says, managing to make my name sound sexy and lustful.

"Grab a seat. We're going to be here a while today. As you know, it's time for your formal six-month evaluation. Depending on the outcome, we may loosen some of the restrictions that are in place right now."

He nods, his face growing serious. "I assume you're going to ask me a long list of questions, so let's get started."

I speed through the usual questions first, not expecting any surprises. I've checked in with his boss, Bear, about his employment, and he's confirmed Heart has been showing up for each and every one of his shoots. He sang his praises, stressing he was reliable, hardworking, and dependable. Those may not be the first words I'd associate with working in the porn industry, but apparently Heart is doing a phenomenal job and not just on video.

I'll be the first one to admit I was hesitant that his chosen profession would work to his benefit in his rehabilitation, but it seems he's doing a great job. Bear also mentioned he's connecting well with the other boys, I guess he calls them. He's building friendships, and more than anything, that makes me happy.

Research shows that for successful reentry into society, friendships with non-criminal people are crucial. The hardest thing for felons to start a new life is the ties they still have to their old one. If you keep hanging out with the same people that got you into trouble in the first place, it's hard to make a fresh start and not be persuaded into entering that life again. That's why it makes me so happy to see Heart making different choices. There is zero evidence of him reconnecting with any of his former associates.

"So, tell me about your first six months," I say after I've ticked off the required questions. "How do you look back on this?"

Heart studies me for a few seconds before he answers. "I'm not trying to be difficult," he says, "but what exactly are you looking for? It's kind of an open question, you know."

"Well, you could tell me about how successful you think you're being in rebuilding your life. Or maybe share a little about how hard reentry into society has been for you."

Heart shrugs and slouches a little lower in his chair. "It's been okay. Pretty much what I expected after your first speech about people's opinions toward felons. I didn't expect a red carpet, so my expectations were pretty low, I'd say."

"That's a healthy place to be in," I say. "A lot of people in your position get discouraged with the less than warm reception once they're ready to pick up their life. It's not easy finding a job...or new friends."

"So you told me," Heart says, a hint of a smile playing on his lips. "Repeatedly."

I shuffle with a pen on my desk. "I'm just trying to be honest with you, to make sure you don't fall into the trap of having unrealistic expectations. I don't want you to fail."

His expression softens. "I know. And I appreciate that."

Am I finally getting through to him a little? I can only hope so. "Was it hard for you to get used to your relative freedom again after prison? I know a lot of my clients struggle with that."

Heart's answer is fast and resolute. "No. Not at all. I was too damn happy to be out."

"And do you feel you're on the right track to rehabilitate yourself? Build a new life?"

"Sure. I got no complaints."

I feel my frustration rise with his short answers. I want him to talk to me. I need him to take me into his confidence. "Come on, Heart, please. Talk to me."

He sighs with frustration, tapping his foot on the floor. "I don't understand why you want to know, why you are so interested in me. Why do you even care? You can't tell me this is just your job. If you did this with every one of your clients, you'd be burned out in no time."

I have to give him this much. If I'm asking for his trust, I have to show him more of myself as well. I close my eyes for a second, quickly weighing the possible ramifications. I'm still on the right side of the line. And I'd better make damn sure I stay there.

"You're right, Heart. I don't invest this much time in every one of my clients. I can't. You're absolutely right about that. But some of them, I just connect more with than with others. And you're one of those people I care about. I can't explain it, but can you just take my word for it? I really need to know that you're okay, that you will be okay. So please, Heart, please talk to me. Assure me that you're doing well."

His beautiful eyes are fixed on me, and he seems to search for something. Whether he has found what he's looking for or simply gives up, I don't know, but my heart leaps up in my chest when he decides to talk to me.

"I'm really okay. Moneywise, I'm fine. The shoots are paying enough to support myself and to pay all my bills without going into debt. I've even bought a piece of crap car and was able to afford the insurance, which, of course, is a lot higher considering my record."

I nod, strangely happy with what he's telling me. "That's good that you're staying out of debt. That's a huge risk factor for people like you in returning to their old life. I'm really happy to hear that." I swallow. "And you like your work with the Ballsy Boys, right?"

The look he sends me is downright sexy. "Oh, I like it very much. Do you want me to go into detail?"

I shake my head, swallowing again. "That won't be necessary, thank you. I talked to your boss, and he was very happy with your performance."

My unfortunate wording registers with me at the same time as it sinks in with Heart, and he chuckles. "I bet he is, as my performance is usually...satisfactory. I've been known to provide...happy endings," he says with a smug smile that I want to kiss off his perfect lips.

His lips... Those full lips that glisten so beautifully, all swollen and red after a scene. His lips that wrap so perfectly around a cock, all stretched, while those stunning eyes of his never leave his partners. Those lips with the lip ring that makes me want to take it between my teeth and tug it ever so gently, until he's moaning into my mouth.

I finally manage to drag my eyes away from his lips, and

I catch him staring at me, amusement dancing in his eyes. He knows exactly where my thoughts went, just now.

"I'm glad to hear your boss is happy with your work," I say lamely, not even pretending to not be embarrassed.

Silence hangs heavy between us for a little bit, and then Heart leans back in his chair. "So, did I pass the test? Are you going to recommend losing the restrictions?"

I frown, processing his words. "What restriction which you like to see gone first?" I ask.

He wags his finger at me, tsking. "Uh uh, like I'm gonna spill that. If I do that, you're going to want to know why, you'll get all suspicious again, and you'll never ever give me that freedom. I'm not stupid, you know."

I can't help but smile at his sassiness. "I never thought you were. I see no reason not to loosen the restrictions. That means that for the second half of your parole, you're allowed to leave the state of California, as long as you stay within the United States. You are now also allowed in bars and restaurants that serve alcohol, but I would advise you strongly to be careful frequenting those. You still can't drink, so if you know this is a temptation for you, I'd really advise you to stay away."

He smiles a broad, happy smile that reaches deep inside me. How I love to see him smile, to see him this happy.

"I don't drink," he says. "At all. You can rest easy there, Mr. Stone. You won't ever find me drunk."

I cock my head, surprised. "Why?"

He points toward the papers on my desk, the formal confirmation of our conversation and the new conditions of his parole. "Sign that first," he says. "And then I'll tell you."

I don't know if he does this because he's suspicious of me, scared that I will revoke the privileges I just granted him, or because he's playing with me. Maybe it gives him some kind of pleasure to be able to influence me even in a little way. Either way, I'm fine with it.

I drag the papers toward me and sign them with a big scrawl, then push them back again.

"Okay, done. Now, care to enlighten me?"

His smile tightens a little, but I can still see he's happy with the changes in his parole conditions. "My father was not just an asshole, he was also a drunk. The more he drank, the worse life got. I vowed back then that I would never touch a drop of alcohol, and I haven't. I know you are focused on my reintegration into society, as you call it, and I get that. But my life goal is not to rehabilitate myself in any way. My goal is to not become the kind of man my father was. And to tell you the truth, I'm pretty successful in that area… And to me, that's the only goal that counts."

22

MASON

Sitting on Heart's couch on a Thursday night, controllers in hand and demolished takeout littering the coffee table, feels familiar and comfortable. It's everything I've come to associate with Heart in the months I've known him. With one exception... I've been hard for an hour.

I can't stop thinking about the last time I was over when Heart licked and bit my nipples until I couldn't hold back from coming in my pants. The memory is hot as hell and also a tiny bit embarrassing, even though Heart said it wasn't anything to feel weird about. Since I got here tonight, I've been waiting for some indication that Heart wants to fool around again and so far, nothing.

Maybe he was lying last time, and he really does think I'm a total loser for jizzing my pants. That'd be a good reason not to want to mess around again. Oh god, I had one chance with him, and I blew it...literally.

"Dude, I'm kicking your ass tonight; what's the deal with that?" he asks as he blows the head off yet another one of my soldiers.

"Distracted, I guess," I shrug and lick my lips, trying not to look at Heart, sure he'll see all the desire and uncertainty written all over my face.

"I'm horny," he segues so casually I nearly drop my controller in surprise.

I whip my head around and gape at Heart, trying to figure out if he's making a joke at my expense or if he simply thinks *I'm horny* is a typical non sequitur. Or maybe this is the signal I was waiting for? Is he saying he wants to hookup again?

My distraction leaves me open for Heart to kill the last of my men and end the game in his favor.

"I...um..."

"You've had a hard-on for over an hour, so I imagine you're pretty horny too, so I'm not sure why we're ignoring the obvious."

"I wasn't sure if you wanted to...you know."

"Why wouldn't I?" Heart cocks his head and tugs his lip ring between his teeth.

I shrug again, not wanting to admit all the negative thoughts and insecurities running through me since the last time. Instead of going into all the things that would make Heart look at me with pity and concern, I climb onto his lap and flick his lip ring with my tongue.

Heart smirks at me and grabs my ass, then kisses me fiercely. My already hard cock throbs in the tight confines of my jeans as Heart's tongue coaxes mine to tangle and play, our lips sliding together with no particular urgency.

I'm struck again at the difference in kissing Heart versus Lucky. I can't really say one is *better* than the other, just very different. I love Heart's playful, hot kisses just as much as I crave Lucky's intense, claiming ones. I don't understand how I can want both men so much, but I stay up nights jerking myself off over and over to thoughts of both of them…sometimes even together—not that I'd ever admit that out loud.

"No pressure if you're not ready, but do you want to fuck me?" Heart asks after some time.

My cock jerks at the suggestion, the lust punching through me so intense I can hardly breathe. I'm not sure I've ever wanted anything more than I want Heart writhing beneath me, my cock buried deep, giving him pleasure. But I fear the actual picture would be completely different—awkward, disappointing, sexually frustrating for Heart as I blow my load within seconds.

"I haven't before," I warn, my heart pounding with a combination of anxiety and desperate need.

"I kind of figured." Heart gives me a wry smile. "If you don't want to, that's okay. I could fuck you? Or I could blow you? Hand jobs? What do you want?"

I grind my hard cock against his through our jeans. Every one of his suggestions sounds good and would come with less risk of embarrassing myself. But now that he's put the idea of topping him into my head, everything else sounds less exciting in comparison.

"What if I'm not good at it? What if I hurt you or finish too fast?"

"If it'll make you less nervous, I can prep myself and show you how so you'll know for the future. And if you finish too fast, no big deal."

He shrugs and to my surprise, I actually believe he wouldn't be bothered if I finish as soon as I get inside him. There's no judgment or expectations, just someone I trust offering me something I desperately want.

"Okay, yeah."

"Awesome, let's go over to my bed. My condoms and

lube are over there, plus sex on a couch is kind of a pain in the ass."

I climb off his lap and follow him to his bed a few feet away, shaking with nervous excitement. Precum leaks down my shaft, leaving me sticky and my underwear damp.

Heart strips and tosses his clothes onto the floor before climbing onto the bed and reaching over into his bedside table to retrieve a bottle of lube and a condom. I'm mesmerized by the sight of all of his pale, ink-covered skin on display without shame, his round, perky ass bare and within touching distance.

"This will work better if you're naked," Heart says with a wink over his shoulder as he squirts lube onto his fingers.

"Oh, yeah." I blush and tug my shirt over my head, dropping it at my feet. Next, I go for the button on my jeans. My hands are shaking badly enough that it takes me a few tries before I get them undone. My pants and underwear soon join my shirt on the floor, and just like that, I'm completely naked in Heart's apartment with him also completely naked, only inches away. *This is really happening.*

Heart is on his hands and knees on the bed, giving me an incredible view of his ass as he slips one of his slicked fingers between his cheeks. I watch mesmerized as he quickly preps himself, clearly well practiced as he adds a second and then a third finger, scissoring himself open with practiced motions.

I climb onto the bed and shuffle forward to get a better view of Heart as he preps himself. With trembling hands, I grab the globes of his ass and part them so I can watch as three of his fingers disappear into his hole over and over. His chest rises and falls with panting breaths, and the occasional moan slips from his lips. More precum trickles from my slit and runs down the length of my cock. I thrust my hips involuntarily, the tip of my cock brushing against the back of Heart's thigh and leaving him smeared with my precum.

"Put on a condom, babe. I'm about ready," he instructs in a strained voice.

I tear my gaze away from Heart's fingers in his ass and grab the condom he set on the bed. I fumble to open it, and then thank god for Troy forcing me to practice putting condoms on bananas a few weeks ago as I roll it down my length without a problem.

Heart pulls his fingers out of his hole and spreads his legs a little farther apart and then looks back at me again over his shoulder.

"You're going to do a great job; don't worry. Just start slow and I'll tell you what I need, okay?"

I nod and shuffle forward, my covered dick in my hand. I place my free hand on Heart's left ass cheek to part them a little again so I can see my target. I take a deep breath and line myself up with his hole, shiny with lube and sexy as hell.

I take my hand off my cock and press forward, but instead of pushing inside, I slip out of place and stumble a little.

"Fuck, sorry," I mutter.

"You're fine, baby, take a deep breath and try again."

I do as he says, breathing deeply and holding it for a few heartbeats before slowly releasing. Then, I grip my cock and hold it this time as I try again. This time, the tight ring of muscles just inside Heart's hole surrounds the head of my cock.

"Push just a little harder; you won't hurt me."

I push harder and feel a gentle pop as I breach the tight muscles. "Oh wow," I gasp as tight heat surrounds my cock.

I grab Heart's hips for balance as I continue to press forward, filling him slowly. When my hips are flush with his ass, I let out a breath I didn't realize I was holding. I did it; I'm inside him.

"I love that you're being considerate and gentle, but Mase, you've gotta fuck me. Please," Heart pleads in a ragged voice.

I moan at his words and flex my fingers on his hips, testing my grip before pulling almost all the way out and slamming forward again. The motion sends a zing of electricity down my spine and causes Heart to gasp loudly.

I do it again and again, picking up speed as I find my rhythm, my body moving on instinct as I rut into him wildly. The sound of flesh slapping against flesh fills the room, accompanied by our grunts and groans. The smell of sweat and sex hangs heavy in the air. I lean forward as I continue to fuck Heart hard and fast, and I lick a stripe along his spine. His skin tastes somehow both salty and sweet.

"I want to hit your prostate, how do I do that?"

"Better...it's better...oh fuck," Heart groans and tilts his head back as he tries to answer my question. The raw pleasure dripping from his tone and the fact that he can't form a complete sentence stokes my confidence in ways I never would've imagined. "Let me flip," he finally manages.

With great effort, I stop thrusting into him and manage to pull out. He lets out a huff and flops down onto the bed, face first and then rolls over onto his back. He's panting and his hair sticks to his sweaty forehead as he reaches for one of his pillows and shoves it under his ass. He waves me forward and wraps his legs around my waist.

"It'll be easier like this," he explains. I line myself up again and this time have no trouble entering him. "Oh god, right there. I won't last long like this," Heart warns.

I place my hands on either side of his head and thrust deep again. I can't manage the same pace I had in the other position but seeing Heart's face as I fuck him is *so* much better.

Heart fists his cock, his mouth falling open as he moans and gasps with each thrust of my cock inside him. His eyebrows scrunch in that way I've come to recognize after watching so many of his videos, like he's confused about how good he feels.

"Mase, I'm so close, harder, please."

I sit back and unwrap his legs from my waist, placing them on my shoulders instead and then, giving him everything I have, fuck him as hard and deep as I can manage, biting the inside of my cheek to keep myself from finishing before he does.

It's not long before he tenses, his already tight channel clamping almost painfully tight around my cock just before he coats his stomach and chest with thick streaks of cum. The pulsing of his inner muscles around my cock makes it impossible for me to hold back any longer. With a few more thrusts, my balls draw tight, and I come with a guttural cry, pumping my release into the condom.

When my muscles can't hold me up any longer, I collapse beside Heart and try to catch my breath.

"That was amazing," Heart says after a few minutes of what I assume is attempting to catch his breath as well.

"Yeah?" I check. He wouldn't just say that to be nice, right?

"Mmmm, so, so good, baby." He rolls over and snuggles close to me, smearing the cum from his stomach all over my side as well. "Shit, sorry. We could take a shower if you want."

After we just fucked, a shower shouldn't sound like a big

deal. But for some reason it sounds intimate and kind of wonderful.

"Yeah," I agree.

We lie in bed for a few more minutes before dragging ourselves to the bathroom. We lean against the sink, sharing lazy kisses while we wait for the shower to warm up. When we climb inside the shower and pull the curtain closed, in a strange way it feels like we're in our own world.

"This is nice."

"Yeah, I've never showered with anyone before," Heart muses, reaching around me to grab a bar of soap off the ledge and then using it to lather up my chest, careful to get all the dried cum off my abdomen.

"Really?"

"Yeah, it seems weird to shower with a random hookup, and my ex...well, let's just say he wasn't the intimate shower type guy."

His words hit me in the chest. He wasn't willing to share this with anyone else, but for some reason he wanted to share it with me. That means more than the sex in so many ways, but I get the feeling if I point it out, Heart will pull away. So I smile to myself and enjoy the closeness for a few minutes until we finish the shower and everything goes back to normal.

23

MASON

I'm less nervous this time as Lucky walks me upstairs after our fourth date. Don't get me wrong, my heart is still pounding, and my hands are still shaking, but I'm not tripping over myself, so it's an improvement.

"This was fun," Lucky says when we reach my door.

I nod in agreement and take a deep breath to prepare myself for what I'm about to say.

"Do you want to come inside?" I offer, my heart thundering so loudly in my ears I can barely hear my own question. You'd think after having sex with Heart a few days ago, I'd be less nervous about inviting Lucky in, but my nerves are still high. I've known and trusted Heart for a while now, but I'm still getting to know Lucky.

Lucky smiles at me and reaches for my hand, which is trembling so badly it's jangling my keys.

"Do you *want* me to come in? There's no rush, no timeline we have to stick to."

I tilt my head back so I can look into Lucky's eyes, full of kindness and concern. "I'm not ready for…um…you know.

But maybe you could come in and we could...uh...just kiss and talk?" God, I sound so lame, but Lucky smiles.

"That sounds nice."

I nod and take another breath, turning around and attempting to unlock the door. My hands are shaking too much to line the key up with the lock, and the harder I try, the more difficult it becomes until the keys tumble from my hands and land at my feet.

"Sorry," I mutter to Lucky, bending down to scoop them up. Lucky beats me to it, snatching the keys up and then putting his arm around my middle when we stand back up. His lips press against the side of my head, and his arm feels comforting around me.

"Here, let me help," he offers.

It only takes him a second to slide the key into the lock and push the door open. I take the keys from him and hang them on the little hook inside the door. We both kick off our shoes, and I give him the grand tour. My place is small, but it's clean and the things inside it are decent, so I'm not embarrassed to show him.

I wonder what Lucky's place looks like. I'm sure it's meticulous and probably as monotone as mine in decoration. The opposite of Heart's chaotic, warm apartment. They're almost like two sides of a coin—Lucky is order and Heart is chaos. Maybe that's why I'm able to like them both so much?

"Do you want a drink?" I offer after the brief tour.

"Water or soda is fine."

I wave toward the couch, and he sits down while I step into the kitchen to grab a couple of water bottles out of the refrigerator. Then I take a few extra seconds out of his line of sight to drag in a few deep breaths and give myself a mental pep talk.

Lucky likes you; he wouldn't be here otherwise. You've pretty much got this kissing thing down after practicing with Heart, and nothing's going to happen that you're not ready for. I nod firmly to myself and then head back into the living room.

Setting both water bottles on my coffee table, I sit down on the opposite end of the couch from Lucky, leaving the middle cushion between us. He raises an eyebrow at me and then crooks a finger at me, beckoning me closer. I scoot a few inches, but he doesn't seem satisfied so I keep going until I'm pressed up against his large, sturdy body.

"That's better," he whispers with a smile.

"Yeah," I agree with a chuckle.

"You mentioned kissing?" His tone is teasing but it's obviously his way of checking that I'm still comfortable with that plan now that he's inside my apartment.

I nod and then move around on the couch, trying to find a good position where we won't have to crane our necks to kiss. A flash of me straddling Heart's lap while we kissed enters my mind, and I decide to throw caution to the wind, climbing onto Lucky's lap. He looks surprised but pleased. Heart would be so proud of me.

I lean forward and press my lips against Lucky's. I'm struck again by how firm and sure his kisses are as we find a rhythm with our mouths. His tongue teases mine, coaxing the kiss deeper. One of Lucky's hands is tangled in my hair, and the other is resting on my waist, his thumb tickling my skin under my shirt ever so slightly.

I remember the way Heart sucked on my tongue, and I do the same to Lucky, drawing a rumbly moan from him that makes my cock throb. For a strange moment, I wish Heart was here too so I could kiss both of them. The thought makes me equal parts anxious and horny. Two guys at once might sound like fun to Troy, but to me it just sounds like twice as much chance I'll screw things up.

Is Lucky enjoying what we're doing now? Maybe he's hoping I'll change my mind about the sex part and the kissing will turn into more? After all, what kind of adult invites a date in just to make out on the couch? God, what am I, twelve?

"Is everything okay?" Lucky asks, his voice huskier than usual, his lips wet from our kisses.

"Yeah. Sorry, I just got in my head for a second."

"Do you want to talk about it?" he offers.

"It's just...it's really weird that I invited you in and we're not going to...you know."

Lucky pulls his hand out of my hair and cups my chin, tugging me close for a slower, more chaste kiss this time. "I was serious when I said I'm not in any rush. We'll take things at our own pace."

I nod and let some of the tension ease from my chest. "Thank you."

"No need to thank me. Can I ask you a question though?"

"Sure."

"I don't want to pry, and you can feel free to tell me if I'm out of line. But have you ever..." Lucky trails off, and I wait for him to finish his sentence. When he doesn't, I think back over his words again, and it hits me what he's trying to ask.

"Oh, yeah," I assure him. "I'm not a virgin. Is that what you were asking?"

Lucky chuckles and runs his thumb over my lips. "Yes, that's what I was trying to ask. With how nervous you are, I thought maybe you didn't have much experience."

"I don't have much experience. I've only, you know, with

two guys. My ex wasn't very nice, I guess, so I'm not very good at *stuff*. You know?"

"That's why your friend is helping you? You needed to gain confidence?" Lucky guesses.

"No, I needed to learn how to be good at kissing and stuff."

"Babe, you are *very* good at kissing, and I'm sure when we get to the *stuff* part, you'll be good at that too."

I blush at the compliment, and my whole body feels warm. I can't believe I didn't know before that this was how someone you're dating is supposed to talk to you.

"The thing is, it's not just about learning to be good at stuff. I really like my friend, but I like you too. It's kind of complicated," I admit.

"That's okay; we'll figure it all out. What I'm more concerned about is the part where you said your ex wasn't nice to you. What happened?" Lucky's expression is dark now. I can't blame him; I'm sure with his line of work, he's seen the worst of the worst.

"He said a lot of things that weren't very nice. That was how I ended up such good friends with Troy. One day he saw Brad berating me at the coffee shop, and Troy stepped in and told him off. It wasn't like Brad hit me or anything like that, he just told me a lot that I was really bad in bed."

My face is on fire as I admit this. Now Lucky won't ever want to have sex with me. "And he hated that I wasn't very good at being social and how nerdy I dressed, things like that."

Lucky's hand, which had been on my waist, is now rubbing soothing circles on my back. I let myself sag forward, resting my head on his shoulder.

"Not everyone loves social situations, and I *love* your whole nerdy look. As far as being bad in bed, in my experience that usually has more to do with a lack of chemistry and comfort than a lack of skill."

That was more or less what Heart said, too. Is it possible it's true? Heart didn't seem disappointed with me when we had sex. If I get that far with Lucky, will he enjoy it too? I'm almost afraid to hope.

"I know I'm not like most people. My mom passed away when I was seven, so it was just me and my dad. My dad was kind of an introvert himself... Actually, I think he might be agoraphobic? Anyway, he home schooled me up until high school so my whole childhood I didn't really interact with anyone but him. When I got to high school, it was really overwhelming, and I had no idea how to act normal and make friends. I guess I never really figured it out," I explain with a self-deprecating laugh.

"I don't think that's true. You have friends—Troy and whoever your other friend is. And I kind of like you," Lucky jokes.

"I kind of like you too," I tell him, feeling a little lighter now that he knows the depths of my awkwardness. "Can we kiss more now?"

Lucky laughs and then tugs me back down to devour my mouth. As the kiss deepens, his broad shoulders and firm chest feel good under my hands, and I start to wonder what it would feel like to have his body covering mine as he fucks me. I moan into his mouth at the thought. I'm nowhere near ready for that, but god, does it sound amazing.

Lucky's hands rest on my waist as our tongues tangle. My hands continue to roam all over the front of his body, appreciating his muscles. As they slide lower, the large bulge forming in the front of his pants becomes difficult to ignore. I haven't had good experiences with giving blowjobs, and I'm not ready to do anything *else* I practiced with Heart yet. But there is one thing I could do; maybe I can manage to do it right?

"Lucky, can I touch you?" I ask breathlessly against his lips, my fingers toying with the button on his jeans mindlessly.

"If you're comfortable, then of course. Feel free to do anything you want," he encourages.

My heart flips with a mixture of excitement and nerves as I pop the button on his jeans open. Am I really doing this? Oh god, it's probably too late to change my mind now that I've unzipped him.

I reach my trembling hands into the open front of his jeans and find his erection, thick and long, trapped in the confines of his black briefs.

I can do this, I can do this, I can do this, I chant to myself as I work the front of his briefs down far enough to gain access.

Lucky groans and drags his lips along my throat, licking and nibbling at my skin while I wrap my hand around his cock. His skin is scorching hot under my palm, and as much as I want to take a few seconds to look and appreciate it, now that I'm touching him I just want to get this over with before I screw it up or chicken out.

I pump his cock steadily, trying different grips and speeds until Lucky's moans become insistent against my skin. On each upstroke, my palm gets sticky with precum, and my confidence grows by a fraction.

Our mouths find each other again, and this time the kiss is frantic and hungry, Lucky's tongue thrusting between my lips in the same way I'm stroking his cock. His grunts and groans vibrate inside my mouth and drive me crazy.

He likes it! I'm doing it right!

I tighten my grip just slightly and tug him faster, adding a little twist each time I reach the head.

"Mason, oh god, I'm...I'm..."

Lucky's body tenses and his cum coats my hand in steady pulses.

"Holy shit, that was hot."

"Uh-huh," Lucky agrees, kissing my cheek once his orgasm has subsided.

"I'm just going to clean up real quick," I say, climbing off his lap, holding my cum-covered hand out in front of me awkwardly. Surely there has to be a sexier way to deal with a mess like this? I'll have to remember to ask Heart next time I get a chance.

I do a little happy dance in the bathroom as I wash my hand. I did it!

24

HEART

For someone who works in porn, my life has become pretty damn predictable. Part of that is because of the restrictions my parole period has placed on me, of course. Even after Lucky loosened the rules, there's still a lot I can't do.

Granted, it's still a hell of a lot more freedom than I had in the three years before that, so I'll take it. I still have nightmares about it, about being locked up. Not as often as the first weeks after my release, when I'd wake up screaming from nightmares about being back inside, but every now and then I get these nasty dreams. I'm sure they'll fade over time, at least, that's what I've read in the online support group for young felons I'm a part of.

The routines I've grown accustomed to may be restrictive, but they're also comforting. I've had enough surprises to last me a lifetime, thank you very much. I appreciate knowing what my day is gonna look like when I get up. Like, today, I'll be working at the senior center again, which I don't nearly hate as much as I had expected to. It's a comfortable routine by now, just like my whole life.

That's why it takes me a few seconds to handle the shock when I see him in the parking lot, hanging against my car, clearly waiting for me.

Terry "Slick" Shaffer.

Also known as my ex, the guy who landed me in prison for three years. I should have known anyone who has "Slick" for a nickname is a no-good motherfucker, but I was sixteen when I met him and so fucking naive.

My blood starts boiling when I see him, and I clench my fists. This is not gonna end well. For him, that is. I'm no longer that naive sixteen-year old I was when I first met him, and if there's one thing I've learned in prison, it's how to defend myself.

"What the fuck are you doing here?" I snap at him.

His face lights up as if I sprouted some declaration of love. "Babe! I missed you..."

He's gotta be kidding me. Three years in prison because of him and *that's* what comes out of his mouth? *Babe?*

"You need to leave," I tell him between clenched teeth. "I don't want you here."

He holds up his hands. "Look, I know things didn't go as planned...and I'm so sorry for that. You have no idea how much it hurt me to know you were suffering in prison... without me."

"You set me up, you piece of shit!"

He manages a look of indignance. "Babe, you know that's not what happened. I'm sorry you got caught, but that was never my intention..."

One of the things I did in those three years—because believe me, time is one thing you have way too much of inside—is try to analyze what happened between Terry and me. How the hell could I have been so fucking dumb? He played me like a fiddle and up till the moment I got sentenced, I somehow believed he would save me. I know, it's pathetic.

I read tons of stuff about relationships like I had with Terry, and it's called gaslighting. He's so fucking good at twisting facts and spinning words, even my own, until the truth becomes a distant memory and you're left with a sense that it's all your fault.

Even now, knowing what a self-centered, pathological liar he is, having recognized the abuse he put me through, a part of me still wants to believe him. More than anything, my heart wants to grasp at straws that he didn't set me up to take the fall for him, that he did love me after all.

And I get so furious with myself, with him for this, so fucking angry that he's standing there as if nothing happened. I feel this rage fill me, this red-hot, bubbling anger that I can barely contain.

"I will never believe another word out of your lying mouth. Now get the fuck away from my car and fuck off to hell."

I'm standing there, fists balled, my body trembling, and Terry looks at me and smiles. "Damn it, Gunny, you're so fucking sexy when you're angry. You always were. I know you must be angry over what happened... It was bad luck you got caught, babe. But you know there was nothing I could do. They had evidence against you, so what could I do? Turning myself in would've solved nothing except land me in prison as well, and I'm sure that's not what you wanted..."

The rage inside me boils over, and before I know it, I've taken a few quick steps forward, and I've pinned him against my car, my arm pressing against his throat. For the first time, his reaction is real, and his gasp of shock fills me with a deep satisfaction.

"That's where you're wrong, asshole. There's nothing more I wanted than for you to be in prison...but it's not too late to get you there. Get the fuck out of my life before I start talking to the cops about what I know about you and your sorry excuse for a criminal operation."

His eyes harden, and with a hard shove, he pushes me off him. "Don't forget that everything you tell them about me incriminates you as well."

"Dude, I just did three years. I served my time. There ain't nothing else you can pin on me."

Terry brushes himself off and takes a step back. "I wouldn't be too sure about that," he says. He turns around and heads over to what I assume is his car. Then he looks over his shoulder and says, "I managed to do it last time."

My legs go weak on me, and I crumble to the ground even before his car flies off the lot. He *did* set me up. I've known it since I had my eyes opened in prison, but to hear him admit it? It's liberating and painful as fuck at the same time.

See? *This* is why I won't ever do relationships again. He fucking betrayed me, and I don't think I'll ever lose the pain inside me over this.

My hands shake as I find my phone, because I need to call this in before I lose the courage, before someone else does and fucks me over. I wouldn't put it past Terry to screw me over like that.

His voice is reassuring, even as he simply answers the phone. "Stone."

I breathe shakily. "It's me...Heart. Gunner, I mean. I need..."

God, why am I crying? This is absurd. I can't be crying in a parking lot just because my asshole ex showed up.

"Heart, are you okay?"

Of course, the concern in his voice breaks my last bit of hold on my emotions. "Could you... I'm sorry. I need... My ex showed up."

The man is a fucking genius for making sense of that, because he asks, "Are you at home?"

"Yeah. Parking lot."

"Okay, Heart. Go back inside. I'll call the senior center to let them know you won't be coming in, and I'll be there in an hour, okay? I need to finish this up and I'll be over."

"Yes. Thank you, Mr. Stone."

If that's not the most ridiculous and pathetic thing ever, to be this comforted my PO is coming over—a man I still address as Mr. Stone—I don't know what is. Yet I know one thing: even if he hadn't been my PO, I would've still called him, simply because he's like a rock. He's solid and dependable, and for some reason, I just know I can lean on him.

25

LUCKY

I make it to Heart's apartment in under fifty minutes, and he opens as soon as I knock. His eyes are red and his face blotchy. It's the first time I've seen him this raw and disheveled, and it does strange things to my stomach.

"What the hell happened?" I ask as he closes the door behind me.

"Terry showed up," he says, spitting out his name with as much venom as a cobra.

I recognize the name, of course, having read Heart's file. Studied it, more like. Terry "Slick" Shaffer is a name I'm all too familiar with.

"What did he want?"

Heart drops himself on his bed. "Reminisce over old times? I don't fucking know."

I lower myself on his couch. "Why don't you start at the beginning," I say gently, sensing Heart is genuinely thrown by the whole encounter.

"He was there when I walked out...leaning against my car as if he fucking owned it." He sits up, then props a pillow in his back and leans against the wall, wrapping his arms around his legs. "I told him to leave, but he wouldn't go. He told me he was sorry I got caught, but that it was an accident...that he had missed me."

I don't speak until I'm confident I have my temper in check. "Do you believe him?"

Heart huffs. "I'll never believe a single word coming out of that motherfucker's mouth."

That is strangely comforting to hear. "Then what happened?"

"He spouted some shit that doesn't bear repeating...so I threatened him I would rat him out to the cops, and then he told me if I did, he'd make sure he'd implicate me as well." Heart meets my inquisitive eyes. "I told him I'd done my time and that he couldn't pin anything else on me; his parting words were that he managed to do so last time."

My head reels with the implications of that last sentence. "He admitted to setting you up?" I ask, my voice filled with disbelief.

Heart, unfortunately, takes it the wrong way. His eyes fire up to blazing. "You don't believe me, do you? You think I'm making it up... God, you think I did it, that I stole that shit."

He gets up from the bed, his body tight with anger. "Get the fuck out," he says, but I hear the slight tremble in his voice, and more than anything, that convinces me.

Still, I have to tread carefully here. I'm not his friend, his bestie. I'm his PO, and I have a responsibility here.

"I'm not leaving," I tell him. "Not until you tell me the whole story and give me a chance to believe you. Tell me the whole story, Heart."

"You've read my file, haven't you? What more do you need to know?"

"Sit down," I tell him, and when he doesn't respond, I

say it with a little more force. "Sit the fuck down. We're not done here."

He throws himself back on his bed, his face mutinous.

"Do you know how many clients I see in a year? You wanna take a guess as to how many of them claim to be innocent?" I ask.

"I'm telling you the truth," Heart says stubbornly.

"And I'm telling you that as much as I want to believe you, I'm gonna need more. Talk to me, tell me the whole story..."

He hesitates, but then the fight seems to leave him, and his shoulders slump. "Never mind. What good is it gonna do anyway? It's not gonna change the past. Hell, it's not even gonna change the future. It is what it is, and I'll have to learn to live with it."

An angry Heart, I can deal with. A sexy Heart is more difficult, but so far, I've managed to resist. But a sad, rejected Heart? A man who looks like he's lost all hope? That, I can't take, and before I know it, I'm on the bed beside him with my arm around him. He doesn't even hesitate but snuggles up against me, and dammit, it feels so right. I want to protect this man, though I have no idea how or why.

"Please, tell me what happened," I all but beg him, needing him to trust me.

He's quiet for maybe a minute before he relents. "I met Terry when I was sixteen. I was...living on the streets, and he took me in."

"You were homeless?" That hadn't been in his file, which only showed how selective that information was.

"Yeah. My dad was killed in Afghanistan, and a year later, my mom died as well. I had no intention of letting the state shove me into foster care or some fucked-up group home, so I took off."

"How did you...?" I start but I realize the answer before I finish my question.

He doesn't look at me when he answers, apparently not needing a full sentence to understand what I was asking about. "I whored myself out. Hand jobs or let them fuck me, mostly. I tried to stay away from blowjobs because sucking with a condom is nasty but without has too many risks. It was good money, considering how young I was and how good I looked. It's how I met Terry."

He says it so factual, but it breaks my fucking heart. Sixteen and prostituting himself to survive. Still, I force myself to hold my reactions back. "He was a client?"

Heart laughs, but it's a bitter sound. "Yeah. He only paid me twice and after that, it was sort of included in the deal of letting me stay at his place, I guess. He's ten years older than me, with a thing for young boys...even younger than I was at the time, though I didn't have the tats back then, and I looked younger. He...collected boys, but I didn't realize it at the time. He reels you in with sweet words and promises, tells you you're different and that he wants to make a life with you..."

"What happened?" I ask softly, keeping him pulled close against me. I shouldn't sit like this with him, but I can't help myself. He needs me...and on some level I can't even pinpoint, I need him.

"I knew that aside from pimping boys out, he was involved in other shit. Not drugs, 'cause I had a strict policy about that. I'm clean, always have been, and I stay away from that shit. Terry did, too, which is why I trusted him, stupid enough. He dealt in fake Louis Vuitton handbags, Ray Bans, Louboutins, stuff like that. I knew it was illegal, but I didn't think it was a biggie. Then he asked me to pick a friend of his up from the airport, and I stupidly did as he asked. Used his car, picked up the guy, and promptly got arrested because the guy had real Prada purses, all stolen from some store...and I had just become an accessory to grand theft. I kept waiting for Terry to come forward, but his partner took a deal and implicated me instead as the mastermind...and I got three years while Terry walked away."

"Did he set you up to be arrested?" I ask.

"I honestly don't know. He must've suspected something, otherwise he wouldn't have asked me to pick his friend up... He'd planned to do it himself, so maybe he was tipped off? I dunno. All I know is that he fucked me over, and he did it intentionally."

"But they must have had evidence against you to get you convicted," I push. I can only hope he doesn't take it the wrong way, like I don't believe him, but I need more facts to make sense of this.

"Yeah," Heart says, and his shoulders drop again. "It didn't look good. He'd put his expensive car in my name for tax reasons, and since I was driving it, it all looked like it really was my car. I had his phone on me because I'd need it to contact that friend I was picking up, but it turned out that phone and the data plan were in my name as well. It showed how everything had gone down with that deal, and they had me. God, I was so stupid, but I never thought he'd fuck me over until he did. Even then, I kept waiting for him to tell the truth, to tell them it was all a misunderstanding, but of course, he never did. He was happy to let me do time for him..."

I let it all run through my mind, the facts he's telling me, the way his ex screwed him over. "But Heart, why didn't your lawyer say anything?"

Heart lifts his head, which has been tucked away against my shoulder that whole time, to look at me, his eyes showing that characteristic mix of deliberate disinterest and fire. "You mean the public defender who spent maybe ten minutes to read my file before advising me to take the plea they offered me?"

"You pled guilty?"

"No, of course, I didn't. I'm not *that* stupid. It didn't earn me any favors from my lawyer though, 'cause it meant more work for him. And for the judge. Neither of which gave a flying fuck about a kid like me and the fact that I kept assuring them I was innocent. Like you said, it's what they all say."

"Except in your case, it's true."

He freezes. "You...you believe me?"

"Yeah, I do. Color me stupid, but I do. I can't explain why other than that your story rings true to me...and it fits with what I know about you, and what you told me about your ex just showing up."

His mouth drops open a little, and then his Adam's apple bobs as he swallows. "I...Thank you. For believing me. I didn't think anybody ever would."

"I'm sorry no one ever did, but I do. Now, I'll need to file a report about your ex showing up, just to make sure you won't get into trouble for being seen with a criminal associate if he ever shows up again, okay?"

He nods. "Yeah. That'd be...that'd be good."

I've just written down all the information—Heart even had the presence of mind to remember Terry's license plate —when there's a knock at the door.

"Do you think he's back?" I ask Heart.

"I dunno..." he clears his throat. "Who is it?" he calls out.

"Erm, it's me."

The voice sounds vaguely familiar, but I can't place him.

Heart visibly relaxes. "It's a friend of mine. Can you not..."

"I won't tell him who I am," I assure him. "No worries."

26

MASON

I don't usually drop by Heart's place without texting first, and standing in the hallway waiting for him to answer my knock, I'm starting to second-guess the wisdom of doing so today. The downstairs door was propped open so I didn't buzz to let Heart know I was here either, so this really is completely unannounced. I was just bored and had nothing better to do.

I was supposed to have lunch with Lucky, but he'd called me an hour ago saying he had a work emergency and that he'd have to take a rain check. I called Troy, but he didn't answer. So I ended up here, outside Heart's apartment like an idiot, hoping he's even home.

There's shuffling on the other side of the door that sounds like two sets of feet, and now I feel like even more of an idiot. He has someone over and here I am interrupting. *Way to go, dumbass.*

Maybe I should bolt before he opens the door. I glance at the stairway leading out of the building and shuffle my feet. *Yeah, it'll be better to just leave.* Just as I turn and step toward the stairs, the door behind me opens.

"Mase? Where are you going?"

I spin around to face Heart with an awkward smile.

"Sorry to stop by without calling. I was just—"

Before I can finish, movement over Heart's shoulder catches my eye. My stomach sinks when I see a stunning man standing by the couch with his thick arms crossed over his broad chest. Not just any stunning man with thick arms and a broad chest...

"Lucky?"

Lucky's head whips up and when his eyes meet mine, they go wide with surprise and something else. He almost looks like a little kid getting caught with his hand in the cookie jar. But why would he...

"Oh," I say, the pieces clicking easily into place.

I look between Heart and Lucky, and it makes a lot of sense. I don't know how they met, but they make a lot more sense together than I could ever make with either of them. They can go through life together, both so beautiful anyone who gazes upon them feels the urge to fling themselves off a bridge.

"You know Lucky?" Heart asks, glancing back at Lucky and then to me in confusion.

"He's...we're...um..."

Heart's eyes go even wider than Lucky's had when he realizes what I'm trying to stutter out. "Lucky is the guy you've been dating?" Heart guesses.

"Uh.... yeah, kind of." My face is hot, and I can't bring myself to look at Lucky again.

"This isn't what it looks like," Heart assures me.

Lucky still isn't saying anything, just standing in the background looking embarrassed. It's not like either of them has to answer to me about who they spend time with or what they do together. We made it clear we weren't exclusive. Hell, *I've* been fooling around with Heart since Lucky and I have been seeing each other.

"Oh, it doesn't matter," I stammer, glancing between Heart and the man a few times. God, they probably are unbelievable in bed together.

"Seriously, Mason, this is...um..." Heart's face pales a little and he glances back at Lucky for help explaining.

"Mason, really, Heart and I are just friends," Lucky assures me, finally finding his voice.

He steps forward with an apologetic smile and his hands shoved into his pockets. It's an entirely different side of him than the confident man I'm used to seeing. Something about it makes my heart flutter a little. It's a more human side, a more relatable side.

"I was just leaving, actually. See you next week," he says to Heart with a pointed look.

Heart seems to shrink slightly under his gaze and then nods in agreement. "Yeah, see you then...*Lucky*." For some reason, a mischievous smile accompanies the name, and I get the feeling there's a lot more to their relationship than just friends.

Lucky moves to stand in front of me, tilting my chin up and trying to smooth some of my wild curls out of my face.

"Sorry I had to cancel lunch; can we plan for tomorrow instead?"

"Uh, yeah," I agree.

"We're good?" he checks, and I nod. Lucky presses a quick kiss to my forehead and then walks out without a backward glance. I can't resist a quick peek at his high, round ass as he heads down the hallway toward the stairs.

"That was awkward, right?" I check, turning back around to find Heart wistfully checking out Lucky's ass as well.

"What?" Heart asks, shaking off his reverie and stepping aside to let me in.

"You know...you and Lucky..." I feel the heat rising in my cheeks.

"Seriously, it's not like that," Heart insists.

"If it's not, then why did he blow off lunch with me, claiming to have a work—" *Oh shit.* "Is he your parole officer? Are you on parole?"

Heart's face goes pale, and I wish I could snatch the words back out of the air. "Sorry. Forget I asked that. I shouldn't have said anything about it; it's none of my business."

"Why don't you come inside? This seems to be the afternoon for confessions, so might as well keep it rolling," Heart waves me in, and I hesitate. "Get your ass inside, please."

I stand awkwardly beside the couch, waiting for Heart to tell me where to go, because honestly, my awkward quotient is off the charts at this point, and I'm not sure I can take much more.

He sits down on the far end of the couch, leaving plenty of place for me to join him. I try to keep my mind off the things we were doing the last time I was here. I thought sex was the most uncomfortable thing two people could experience together, but I clearly underestimated my own ability to create unpleasant situations.

"Please stop looking like a kicked puppy and just sit down?" Heart requests, sounding tired. I notice for the first time that his eyes are slightly red and puffy. Has he been crying?

"You really don't have to tell me anything. It's none of my business," I repeat as I sit down on the opposite end of the couch.

"You're my friend, and I want to tell you. But you have to

promise not to say anything to Troy. Bear knows, since he signs my paychecks, but no one else does."

"I promise I won't say anything."

Heart sighs and tilts his head back against the couch. "I don't really want to get into the whole story, mainly because I've had a shitty day already. But basically, I was a stupid kid who thought he was in love. Turned out the guy was a criminal and a lowlife who ended up landing me in prison for three years. Mr. Stone...Lucky...is my PO."

Heart's words come out in such a rush, it takes me a few seconds to sort them out and figure out what he's saying. He went to prison for something he didn't do? Something his ex set him up for? No wonder he's so against the idea of dating. And here I was thinking he just didn't want to date *me*.

Lucky being Heart's PO doesn't change the vibe I was getting from the two of them though. "But, the way you two were looking at each other...there's something there."

Heart shakes his head. "He would lose his job, and I'm in *no* position to be dating anyone."

Interesting, no denial of the attraction, just of the wisdom of pursuing it. My gut clenches again. Those obstacles will be easy to overcome, and when they do, I certainly won't stand between them.

27

HEART

My heart hammers, and I wipe my sweaty hands on my jeans. I try to think of anything I've done recently that might've pissed Bear or Rebel off and come up blank. I can't think of a reason, aside from getting in trouble, that Bear would've asked me to come by his office after filming today.

Getting in trouble at work is the last thing I need after this god-awful week. First, my ex shows up, then it turns out *Lucky* is the guy Mase has been dating. I'm not sure why that's been under my skin, making me itchy and irritated since I found out, but it has.

I run my hands through my hair, still damp from my post-shoot shower and knock at the door.

"It's open," Bear calls out.

I step inside, and I'm surprised to find only Bear behind the desk. Since Rebel stepped into his new role, they're usually always together at work. Maybe that means I'm not in trouble. Bear gestures to the chair on the opposite side of the desk, and I take a seat. I tug my lip ring between my teeth and wait for Bear to tell me what this is about, while my heart tries to pound out of my chest.

"No need to look like you're facing a firing squad," he assures me with a chuckle. "I just wanted to check in. Your PO called the other day to verify continued employment, and it made me realize I haven't been as proactive as I should be in making sure you're doing well."

My mouth falls open, and I blink a few times, trying to piece his words together. "You don't have to worry about me. I'm used to taking care of myself," I assure him.

"I have no doubt about that. But I like to think I'm more than just the old perv who owns the porn studio. I care about you boys, and I want you to know I'm here for you."

His words hit me right in the center of the chest. I'm not sure I can remember the last time anyone told me they cared about me. It's strange...nice, but strange.

"I really am okay. I love working here, I feel close with the other guys, and I have friends outside of work." *Friend* would be more accurate, but whatever. "Hell, I have enough money to keep a roof over my head and food in my fridge. It's safe to say I've never been better. I appreciate you checking in though; it means a lot." I swallow around the lump in my throat and flick my tongue against my lip ring again.

"I'm glad to hear it." Bear looks me over one more time like he's trying to assure himself that I really am doing okay and then he leans back in his chair. "Listen, while I have you...Pixie has been pushing for a DP scene, and I was thinking I might pair him with you and Campy if you're up for it."

"You know I'm always up for some three-way action," I assure him with a smirk. One of the first scenes I filmed for

Ballsy was a DP scene with Tank and Campy, although that time I was on the receiving end.

"Pixie is delicate. You'd be gentle, right?" The anxious expression on Bear's face isn't one I'm familiar with. He's typically confident and self-assured, so it's a little jarring to see him worrying.

"Of course. You know I love Pix; I'd never do anything to hurt him. And I'm sure Campy feels the same way."

"Love him?" Bear's voice is thick, and if I thought the concerned expression was jarring, I'm not sure what to make of this.

"Not *love* love. He's sweet and has an air about him that I just can't help but want to take care of him. But in a friend way, not a boyfriend way or anything. Is co-stars dating against the rules or something?" I ask, trying to make sense of Bear's odd behavior. "Oh, wait, I guess not since Tank and Brewer just started dating. By the way, don't get me started on what a shock *that* was. I thought those guys hated each other."

Bear gives me a weak smile. "You know what they say about there being a fine line between love and hate."

"Good point. But, back to your original question—I'd love to do a DP scene with Pixie, and I promise to take good care of him."

Bear nods and lets out a long breath. "All right, I'll talk with Rebel about that and see about setting something up."

Sensing the end of our talk, I say goodbye to Bear and let myself out of his office. As soon as the door is shut behind me, I shake my head, trying to figure out what all just happened in there.

"You okay?" Rebel asks as he walks by.

"Oh yeah, just...nothing, yeah I'm fine."

Rebel eyes me suspiciously but doesn't press the issue. "I

was just about to head out to meet Troy for dinner. You want to come? Pixie and Campy are coming, and I think Troy invited Mason."

"Sure, that sounds good."

Rebel pats me on the back and steers me toward the exit, where Pixie and Campy are waiting, while I shake off whatever weirdness is going on with Bear.

We end up at a burger joint down the block from Ballsy and find Troy already waiting for us.

"Hey guys," he greets. "Mason's coming but he's running behind. He lost track of time and had to shower and get dressed."

My stomach flutters happily at the mention of Mason, and I frown. We're just friends. Sure, the fooling around is *a lot* of fun, but we're still only friends. There's no reason to get all swoony at the mention of him. This isn't middle school. Between Mason and Lucky, I'm starting to wonder if I have the stomach flu or something with all this damn fluttering. That would make a hell of a lot more sense than having a crush on both of them.

"So, you and Mason are finally fooling around?" Troy asks with a smirk as soon as we're seated. It's obvious by the way he's waggling his eyebrows that he already knows the answer.

"Yeah. Not really a big deal," I shrug, ignoring the way my heart jumps a little at the mention of Mason again. I've been down *that* road before, and it doesn't lead anywhere good. A little harmless fun is all I'm willing to offer, and Mason knows this.

I'm not even sure what Mason is still doing messing around with me when he has Lucky on the hook. Lucky's the kind of guy anyone would be blessed to be with— dependable, strong, *good* in a way few people are. Not to mention he's hot as fuck. Lucky is the total package and everything Mason deserves.

"Good, good." Troy nods. "I think he probably just needs some confidence, right? I can't imagine Brad the asshole made sex that much fun for him."

"Mmhmm," I agree, not really wanting to talk about Brad or get into details about how *not* boring in bed Mason is.

"Well, thanks for doing this for him."

"He's a sweet kid; trust me, it's no hardship."

"And you're cool that he's seeing someone else, too?" Troy continues his interrogation, and irritation starts to prickle at me.

"He's an adult. He can see whoever he wants. I'm his friend, not his warden."

"Point taken." Troy holds up his hands in surrender. "I just want to see him happy. He deserves something good in his life."

"Couldn't agree more."

Mason shows up two minutes later and trips over his feet, nearly wiping out Pixie in his chair. I stand up to steady him and pull out the empty chair beside mine.

"Why don't you sit down before you break something," I suggest with a smirk, and Mason blushes, his bottom lip between his teeth. The urge to lean forward and kiss him washes over me, and we both shift awkwardly on our feet. A kiss in greeting would definitely be boyfriend territory and should be Lucky's. I need to keep kisses confined to *practice* sessions. Everything will be less complicated that way.

Mason shakes his head and looks down at the chair I've pulled out for him. He gives me a small smile and then plops down. I sit back down too and fall into casual conversation with all the guys, sure to keep Mason engaged. He's prone to fall quiet in large groups. He says it's because he's lost in thought but I can tell by the way he fidgets and blushes that it has more to do with feeling uncomfortable around so many people. I've noticed over the past few months that when I purposefully include him in group conversations by asking him direct questions, it always earns me a grateful smile. I'm not sure why it makes me feel as good as it does, but it's nice to know I'm helping Mason.

On a whim, I reach over and put my hand on his leg under the table. He stills, and his blush deepens just before he nearly knocks his drink over. I smirk, knowing no one will attribute it to anything other than Mason being Mason. I give his leg a squeeze and let my fingers trail upward teasingly. He shivers and casts an anxious look in my direction. I wink at him and pull my hand back before leaning close to whisper in his ear.

"Maybe we should add teasing and flirting to your curriculum," I suggest, letting my lips brush against the shell of his ear and enjoying the second shiver I elicit from him. "Come over and hang out after dinner?"

Mason nods, and I resist the urge to draw his earlobe between my teeth.

"Ew, no flirting at the table. It makes sad, single boys feel bad," Pixie complains.

"Aw, poor Pixie. Do you need some snuggles?" I offer, opening my arms for him and earning a few side-eyes from people at the adjacent tables.

Pixie sticks out his bottom lip in a pout and then throws one of his fries at me. "I'm too cute to be teased; be nice to me."

I chuckle and blow him a kiss.

"I can't see you having trouble finding a man," Troy says,

eyeing Pixie like he's looking for an extra limb or something strange that would scare perspective dates away.

Pixie lets out a long-suffering sigh. "The heart wants what it wants," he says, offering no further explanation after that.

What's up with everyone being so weird today?

28

MASON

I straighten my Pac-Man t-shirt and check my hair in the mirror. Maybe this shirt is a bad idea. I know Lucky has made a point of saying he's into the whole nerd thing, but this feels like it might be pushing it. I fiddle with the hem of the shirt, trying to decide if I should change into a plain white t-shirt instead.

The door buzzer decides it for me. No time to change, Lucky's here.

I hit the intercom button and let him know I'm on my way down, then I slip into my blue Converse and grab my keys before heading out. Since running into Lucky at Heart's the other day, my mind has been turning the situation over and over. There's something between Heart and Lucky, the kind of chemistry that can't be ignored. They'd be good together, even if their situation is complicated. Maybe they need a little push?

I'm still thinking the whole thing over when I hit the bottom step. Lucky's standing in the entrance to the building, a black t-shirt stretched tightly over his muscles, his hair neatly styled, bottom lip a little puffy like he's been chewing on it. My heart stutters, and my stomach flips. He's so hot, it's kind of unfair. But it's easy to see that a man like this was never meant for me. Heart and Lucky make sense. I don't fit.

I pull open the outside door, my heart settled low, my mood spiraling down at the obvious solution to the whole problem.

Lucky looks up and smiles when he sees me. His eyes rake over my body, and his eyes darken, making me shiver. I open my mouth, not sure what I'm planning to say. Before I can figure it out, Lucky is on me, hoisting me against his large body and attacking my lips.

My feet are barely touching the ground as Lucky's hands dig into my ass, holding me close. The front of his shirt is twisted in my fists as his tongue slips into my mouth. His lips move commandingly against mine, making me pant and whimper as I try to keep up. His tongue fucks my mouth, carrying the spearmint taste of gum and the masculine flavor of Lucky.

When he pulls away, I blink my eyes open in a haze to find a bright smile on his kiss-swollen lips.

"Sorry, you just look so hot I couldn't help myself."

"Really?" I ask in a stupor.

"Fuck yes. Although this nerdy t-shirt would look much better on my bedroom floor, I think. Then I could have you in my bed in nothing but your thick rimmed glasses, your curly hair all messy from having my fingers run through it."

I whimper at the image he's painting.

"Uh...di-dinner?" I suggest, taking a step back and quickly adjusting my raging erection. Lucky chuckles at the move and throws his arm over my shoulders.

It's difficult to remember the conclusion I'd been in the process of coming to before Lucky kissed me, but as we walk down the street to my favorite Mexican restaurant, it starts to come back to me.

"Can we talk about the whole thing the other day with Heart?" I ask once we're seated and have complimentary chips and salsa between us.

Lucky stills, and his smile falters. "It's not what you think," he rushes to assure me.

"Oh god, I don't care about that. I'd be a pretty big hypocrite if I was mad at you for fooling around with him."

Lucky's eyes go wide. "You mean...Is Heart the guy you mentioned on our first date?"

I nod, stuffing a chip into my mouth and watching the emotions play over Lucky's face—surprise, interest, *lust*?

"Heart told me that you're his PO, so I know you didn't break our lunch date to have sex with him or anything like that," I explain. "But I did notice the way you two looked at each other."

My gut twists as I say the words. It's epically stupid to push them together and lose not one but both men I really like. But what else am I going to do?

Lucky shakes his head but can't seem to come up with a denial beyond that. I reach across the table and place my hand on his.

"I really like you, Mason."

"I like you too," I admit. "But you and Heart make a lot more sense than you and me or Heart and me."

"Even if you were right, it's not an option. I'm his PO; I'd lose my job," he argues.

"Couldn't you give his case to someone else?"

Lucky shakes his head again, but I can see the dawning in his eyes. He hadn't thought of my suggestion before, but he *does* want Heart.

"I couldn't drop you for him. I *am* attracted to Heart, but

I'm insanely into you too. I don't see how I could possibly—"

"This is *so* not the kind of thing I ever thought I'd say, but...If I'm hooking up with both you and Heart, there's no reason you should have to choose."

Lucky's eyebrows go up and his pupils blow wide. I watch his Adam's apple bob in his throat as he considers my suggestion.

"Who's to say Heart would even be on board for this idea? I'm sure he thinks I'm an asshole."

"I saw the way he was looking at you. Just think about it."

The way Lucky shifts in his seat makes me think he's going to be spending a lot of time *thinking* about the idea. Then it hits me what I proposed. Oh my god, did I really suggest that we have a threesome? No, right? I told him he could fool around with Heart too if that's what they both wanted, not that the three of us would...

"Why do you look so freaked out? Are you already having second thoughts about your idea?"

"No, just, uh...I didn't mean like a threesome or anything." My face heats. God, I have had sex with Heart *once* and Lucky not at all yet. Now I've somehow talked myself into both of them at once? "I mean...maybe like eventually or something, I just meant you and Heart could...you know, do whatever you two want to do. I wasn't trying to—"

Lucky leans over the table and cuts off my rambling with a kiss. "I understood. There's a lot to consider and a number of variables in this scenario. Let's let things rest, think about them, and see where things go," he suggests and I nod, letting out a relieved breath.

Oh god, now all I can think about is Lucky and Heart, writhing naked and sweaty together in bed. Surely they wouldn't want me to be included in that, would they?

29

HEART

I'm staring at the contents of my refrigerator, not really seeing them, not even sure I'm actually hungry, when my door buzzer goes off. I frown and close the refrigerator door. I'm not expecting anyone unless Lucky is making *another* unscheduled visit. You'd think he'd have more interesting clients to check up on. Although I'm starting to think he's checking on me more because he has the hots for me rather than expecting to catch me violating my parole.

The idea of Lucky being into me in any way makes my blood heat and causes a strange longing to bloom in my chest. But he can't want me; it would be illegal as my PO for anything to happen between us. If Lucky is anything, it's moral; he'd never break the law for a hookup. That's what's so great about Lucky: he's reliable and trustworthy like no one else I've ever met. He's a truly good person inside and out.

"Who is it?" I ask into the intercom. I swear to god if it's my ex again, I'm going to flip.

"Mason," the answer crackles back through the speaker.

I smile and hit the button to unlock the outside door, and then I crack my door open so he'll know to walk right in when he gets up here. The melancholy feeling that was weighing me down seconds ago is lifted just by knowing Mason is on his way up. I don't know how the kid does it, but he lights me up.

I plop down on the couch and kick my feet up on the coffee table while I wait.

"Hey, babe," I greet him with a smile as he steps through the door. Mason returns the greeting with a shy smile, his teeth biting into his bottom lip and his posture unsure like he doesn't know if he's really welcome here. How can he be unsure after the months we've spent hanging out?

"Come sit down." I pat the cushion beside me.

Mason toes off his shoes, leaving them neatly by the door and then joins me on the couch. He licks his lips as he sits down, his gaze flicking to my mouth and then to my eyes, a slight pink blush creeping into his cheeks. My body heats at the unasked question in his eyes. I crook my finger, and Mason leans in automatically.

His lips meet mine in a kiss that's at odds with his otherwise shy behavior. His mouth is firm and confident against mine, his tongue licking against mine, drawing me in deeper by the second.

"Nice to see you, too," I smirk against his lips when the kiss ends.

He chuckles and leans back on the couch, visibly more relaxed now than when he first walked in. "Hope I'm not barging in on your day. I finished up my classes and didn't feel like going home yet, so I thought I'd stop over."

"You're always welcome here," I assure him, patting his knee. "Want to play video games? Watch a movie? Go out and grab something for dinner?"

"Um, actually, there's something I wanted to talk to you about. Maybe we could order takeout and talk?"

"Sure," I agree, my mouth going dry. He's going to tell me he doesn't want to fool around anymore. I knew it was coming, what with dating Lucky and all. Mason isn't a multiple partner kind of guy.

I grab my phone and put in an order for Thai food I know Mason likes, and then I look at him expectantly, careful to keep my expression neutral. It's better for him to put an end to things between us now. It was never going to be forever anyway. So why is my heart beating so hard and my stomach in knots as I wait for the hammer to fall?

"It's about Lucky," Mason says after a few painful heartbeats.

"I figured." I give him a wry smile. "You don't want to fool around anymore because you're really into him. I knew it was coming, and I completely understand."

"What? No, that's not it at all." Mason's eyes are wide as his cheeks turn deeper pink and then suddenly pale. "Wait, do *you* not want to fool around anymore?"

"Of course, I do, I just thought that's what you were trying to tell me."

"No, listen." Mason turns his body toward me and reaches for my hand. "You have feelings for Lucky."

"No, I told you he's my PO."

"Okay, but what if he wasn't?" he presses.

"What do you mean?"

"If he wasn't your PO, you'd be into him. Right?"

My heart jolts at the question, and my skin feels hot. Is it that obvious that Mason would notice after seeing Lucky and me together for less than five minutes? Of course, I'm into him; who wouldn't want a man like Lucky? He's strong and confident, he's moral and good in every way. Not to mention, he's sexy as hell. Anyone with a brain would want Lucky.

"It doesn't matter either way because he *is* my PO. And on top of that, he's dating you. I would *never* take someone from you like that," I assure Mason. That has to be what this is about, right? Mason's worried Lucky and I might mess around behind his back or something?

"I don't think I'm explaining this right." He frowns, his eyebrows scrunching together as he tries to get his thoughts together. "Let's say Lucky wasn't your PO and the three of us agreed to date each other. Would that be something you would want? Would that make you happy?"

"The three of us?" It's my turn to frown as I try to figure out what Mason is getting at. Is he seriously proposing a triad?

"Not *together*," he adds while I'm trying to work it all out in my head. "Like, you and Lucky date, and me and Lucky date, and you and I keep messing around."

"Um, why? If all three of us are together, why wouldn't all three of us be *together*?"

Mason shakes his head, his face scarlet now. "I can't... god, can you imagine? I can't keep one man happy in bed; there's no way I can make both of you happy at once. I highly doubt I'll be able to keep one of you happy in bed. Actually, you two dating is kind of perfect because at least I'll know you're both being sexually satisfied."

"Mase." I cup his chin and tilt his face to meet my gaze. "You are more than enough for either of us. When you fucked me, it was *incredible*. If this is some misguided way for you to feel bad about yourself, then I am very much not on board. You can and you will make Lucky very happy in bed. You don't need to outsource the job to me."

"I'm not outsourcing anything. I saw the way you and

Lucky were looking at each other. You're into each other. I tried to tell Lucky he should break up with me and date you, but he wouldn't go for it. Then I realized I certainly don't want to choose between the two of you so why should he have to?"

"You're serious about this? You want me to date Lucky while you also date Lucky?"

"Yes. I think we could make it work."

"There are a few problems though, babe. Lucky *is* my PO. And, on top of that, I don't want a relationship. I like fooling around with you, but I can't be more than that with anyone."

"Don't worry about the PO stuff, seriously. Heart, you keep telling me about all these things you think I deserve, so I'm going to tell you what I think you deserve. You're a good, sweet, wonderful man, and you deserve to let me and Lucky show you that. He's crazy about you and so am I."

I tug my lip ring between my teeth and sigh. "I don't know, Mase. Let me think about it, okay?"

His smile brightens like he's sure I'll give in after I've had time to think it over. Can I really open myself up to be vulnerable again? I know Lucky and Mason would never fuck me over the way my ex did. But can they really accept all of me?

30

LUCKY

Ever since Mason brought it up, I've thought about Heart and how to handle my crazy attraction to him. I've never taken an impulsive decision in my life, and I'm not about to start now.

There's so much to consider. There's my job and my professional integrity, which make it all but impossible for me to build anything personal with a client, let alone someone like Heart who is so much younger...and who works in the porn industry. I can't lose my job, but am I willing to lose Heart? That's a question that isn't so easy to answer, especially considering there's more that complicates things.

Take Mason, who deserves more than to be second choice, though I could argue he's anything but. He intrigues me as much as Heart does, albeit in a completely different way. With Heart, I wanna peel off all his masks, all his layers to see the real him. And with Mason, he's like a caterpillar that's afraid to transform because he's convinced he's never gonna be a butterfly.

I laugh at my own thoughts. Look at me, being all poetic

on a Monday morning on my way to work. But it's been like this all weekend, me trying to figure out the right thing to do.

I want them both, but can I? Could what Mason suggested ever work? I don't see how, even if I somehow were able to date Heart as well. How can I build a relationship with two men at the same time, two men who are dating each other as well? We'd be in a threesome. Mason doesn't realize it, I think, doesn't fully comprehend that there's no way this wouldn't result in a threesome. And is that something I want?

A year ago, I would've answered with an adamant hell, no. Now, I'm not sure anymore. All those things that were so black and white are suddenly not so clear cut and easy anymore. It's messy and complicated, and my heart and head are at war. But the bottom line is that I can't let them go. I just can't.

By the time I walk into my office, I know what to do, but it's not gonna be easy.

"Cynthia, could I have a word, please?" I ask my boss as soon as I'm sure she's had the required two cups of coffee that make her human.

"Sure thing, Lucky. What's up?"

I carefully close the door behind me, and when I turn around, she's studying me with raised eyebrows. "Uh oh," she says. "I'm not gonna like this, am I?"

I try for a reassuring smile but considering the fact that she starts a nervous tap with her fingers, I'm not confident I pulled it off. "I'd like to be taken off Gunner Harris' case."

Cynthia's tapping stops, and she frowns. "Help me out, the name rings a bell, but…"

"He's the young kid who served time for the stolen

designer goods." When she still can't place him, I add, "The one who works as a gay porn star now?"

Her face lights up with recognition. "Right, him. The hottie. He has all the women and half the men drooling when he shows up for an appointment."

It shouldn't bother me, not when I have the exact same reaction to him, but it does. "Yes, him."

"Why?"

Here comes the hard part. "Because I find it impossible to work with him in a professional manner."

It's what I came up with over the weekend, even though I know that shit won't fly. Not with Cynthia who is sharp as a diamond and can be equally ruthless.

She leans forward. "Is that some convoluted way of saying you had sex with him?"

My sexual orientation is not a secret here in the office. I made it clear when I applied that I was gay and out, just to avoid any homophobic shit. Turns out Cynthia is bi, so she couldn't care less, though some of my coworkers are less tolerant. It's more behind-my-back gossip though than outright hostility, so I've learned to live with it.

"Fuck, no. I mean, of course not." I sigh under her stare. 'It's a convoluted way of saying I want to have sex with him."

"Honey, we all do. That's not a reason to be taken off his case."

I can't help but smile at her brutal honesty, but then it's time to confess even more. "No, but I'd like to actively pursue that goal."

"You know what I discovered about you, Lucky?" she says, leaning back in her chair. "You hide behind formal words when you feel the most. It's like the more your heart is involved, the more you force your brain to take control."

As I said, she's sharp. And ruthless, at times. "And that's a bad thing?" I ask.

"Nope, just wanted to point out to you that I have your number. Lucky, you can't sleep with a client, you know that."

I nod. "That's why I want to be taken off his case, so he's no longer my client. And it's why I'm informing you of my intentions since I don't want to go behind your back."

She studies me with narrowed eyes. "You could decide to find another hot piece of ass."

I dig my nails into my hands to keep myself from lashing out. "I could, but I don't want to. You could also try to see him as more than his body...or his current profession."

Her face changes into one I'm well familiar with, and I speak before she has the chance to say anything. "No. Don't tell me I'm stupid and want to reform him, or that I'm naive in believing he's good, or whatever it is you want to say. I don't need you patronizing me. I need you to take me off this case so there's no conflict of interest, and I can see if what I feel for him is real or not."

"Does he feel the same?"

I shrug. "I have no idea. I haven't talked to him about this."

"Are you telling me you don't even know if your feelings are reciprocated?"

"I'm telling you that I'm not even sure what my feelings are, exactly...on my side, on his side, on anyone's side. I'm telling you that I intend to find out, but I can't do that until you relieve me of my damn responsibilities where it comes to him and give me permission to pursue him."

Her lips curve into a smile. "I'm not your mother," she says.

"No, but you're my boss who can make my life hell for

dating a felon who also happens to be a porn star. I'm not stupid, Cynthia. I know what I'm risking here."

She nods, her face serious again. "Good, then I won't need to tell you. I'll allow it for now, but you're treading on dangerously thin ice here, Lucky. You can't allow him to break the rules, not even when he's with you. That means no drinking, no drugs, no associating with criminal contacts..."

She sighs. "Who am I kidding? We both know you'd never get involved in that. I don't think I've ever met someone with your moral standards...asking me for permission to date a porn star..." She gently shakes her head. "Only you could come up with that."

"Thank you?" I say, then smile. "I mean it. Thank you. I don't know where this will lead but thank you for allowing me to explore."

"You're welcome, but weren't you dating some cute nerd? Alicia told me she saw you at a bar with someone."

"Yeah, well, that's another complication I have to find a solution for."

She laughs. "You don't exactly make things easy for yourself, huh? Anyway, you can hand the case over to Patrick since his caseload is the lightest right now."

I nod, forcing myself to not say anything. Patrick is an ass and probably the least competent officer we have, but if I want a chance with Heart, I'll have to let go of my professional involvement in his life.

"I'll sign over the files in the system to him right now."

"Thank you. And Lucky?" She waits to speak until I've made eye contact. "Good luck and keep me posted. You know how much I hate surprises."

She and I are on the same page there, I muse as I walk back to my office to grab Heart's files. It's something I learned in the Marines: surprises are not good and usually end up in someone getting hurt. That's why you learn to do everything you can to consider possible scenarios and then prepare for them, so you can avoid getting caught with your pants down when something takes a different turn than expected.

Heart has a digital file, so all I have to do is sign that over to Patrick so he'll be listed as the responsible case officer for him. Before I do that, I want to take one more look to see if I've updated it with my last notes. I want Patrick to have a positive first impression of him. That, at least, is something I can do for Heart.

My first appointment doesn't come in till eleven, so I take the time to read through Heart's file again.

31

HEART

Mason is bat shit crazy, right? He can't really think it could work with the three of us dating each other. Not a real threesome, as he keeps stressing, because apparently that's freaking him out, whereas dating both Lucky and me is perfectly normal.

I should have said no, of course. I should have bowed out gracefully and leave those two to date together, because they make way more sense than me and Lucky. Or me and Mason, in all fairness. I'm not good enough for either one of them, and that's so fucking obvious, I can't believe neither of them has brought it up. I'm a convicted felon and a porn star—both should have them running in the other direction.

Well, technically, I was innocent, at least on the felon part. Doesn't make my record go away magically, but it's a small consolation to me at least. All I'm guilty of is being monumentally stupid and naive...and that will never happen again.

Which is why I know this three-dating thing or whatever we're gonna call it won't work. I know at some point, I'm gonna get dumped. By both of them. So why the hell am I on my way to hang out with Mason right now?

I'm debating with myself all the way, and even when I park my car and walk up to Mason's door, I'm still telling myself I should turn back and forget about this. Then Mason opens the door, and he's disheveled, his shirt crumpled, his cheeks flushed, and his lips swollen and wet...and my heart breaks.

Not because it's Lucky he's been clearly making out with, because he's a good man and he'll take good care of him, but because I know whatever we had is over. I can't compete with Lucky...and I don't want to. Hell, I couldn't even choose between the two of them if I had to.

Words won't come, and so I merely turn around and leave. I'm already halfway down the stairs when Mason calls after me. "Heart, no! Please, don't go."

I look up, and he's so beautiful like this, all sexy and flustered and looking like he got worked over good. I send him a sad smile. "It's okay, Mase. It really is. You should be with him."

Mason runs down the stairs so fast, I automatically hold out my hands in case he trips. By miracle, he makes it in one piece.

"No," he says with a look more stubborn than I've seen on him so far. "No, you can't leave. We had a date."

"Babe, you're with Lucky..." I plead with him. "There's no room for me in that arrangement and there shouldn't be."

"Don't you like being with me?" he asks, and I swear his bottom lip quivers just a little.

"God, that's not true, and you know it. I've always loved hanging out with you, and messing around with you was... perfect. That has nothing to do with it."

I hear a sound above us, and Lucky slowly descends the stairs. He looks slightly less disheveled than Mason, but someone clearly messed up his hair. Not that it looks bad on him, but then again, I don't think this man could look bad. *Ever.*

"I'll go, Mason," he says, shooting me an apologetic look. "I lost track of time; I'm sorry. I knew he was meeting you, but we got...distracted."

I scoff. "Yeah, clearly."

"I'm sorry, Heart. I didn't mean to make you feel...whatever it is you're feeling."

Something snaps inside me. "How about rejected? 'Cause that's pretty close to how I'm feeling."

"But...but I didn't reject you," Mason says, his eyes wide open.

"No, baby, but you will. Now that you have your confidence back, you don't need me anymore. You and Lucky can build a real relationship."

"Are you saying what we had isn't real?" Mason asks.

How the hell do I answer that one? Of course, it was. It's always been real, just not for him.

"Actually, I should bow out," Lucky says. "You two were together before I showed up, and I don't want to break up your friendship."

"No," Mason says. "I'm the odd one out. You two fit, somehow, and I'm just...me."

"You're perfect," I say at the same time as Lucky says something similar.

Lucky sends me a tight smile. "It seems we're at an impasse, then."

"I'm not discussing this in the stairway," Mason says with uncharacteristic resolve. "We'll talk inside."

Lucky and I both hesitate. "Mason," Lucky says.

"No," Mason says. "No one is leaving right now. We're gonna talk this out like adults...and I cannot believe the words coming out of my mouth right now. When the hell did I become the sensible one?"

I can't help but smile at that statement. "You always were smarter than you give yourself credit for, babe."

"Thank you. Now let's get back inside. We've given my neighbors enough of a show already."

I obediently follow Mason back inside and so does Lucky. Who would have thought Mason would become the voice of reason here?

"You wanted to talk," Lucky says to Mason after we've all found a spot to sit and have been staring at each other for half a minute or so.

"Yeah, but now that we're here, I have no idea about what," Mason says. "Sorry. Temporary brain fart, I guess? I'm not good at this."

"Why do you feel you're the third wheel?" I ask Mason. "I don't get it, because you're what brought us together."

Mason sighs. "Because I think you'd get bored of me real soon...both of you." Lucky inhales sharply as if to say something but then lets Mason continue. "Look, you only started hanging out with me because Troy asked you to...because he thought you could help me improve my...skills. You wouldn't have looked at me twice if he hadn't asked."

I see where he's coming from, but that's not how I feel at all. Somewhere along the way, Mason became much more than a project or even a friend. He brings out a sweeter side of me again, a side I've pushed down ever since Terry fucked me over.

"I don't know if I'd started dating you if Troy hadn't pointed you out," I say. "I'll admit that. But Mase, you're anything but boring, and I really like hanging out with you...the fooling around included."

He shakes his head. "I don't get that last part. You're... you." His cheeks grow red in that way that makes me want to kiss him silly. "You're a porn star...not that I'm judging, because you're really good at it...I heard." He clears his throat.

I grin. "Have you been watching my videos, babe?"

"No..." he says slowly. "Maybe...just a few. They're...good."

I can't help it, and I reach for Mason's wrist and tug until he gets the hint and scoots closer on the couch. Then I move us around until he's on my lap, my hands on his ass. "Which one was your favorite?" I say before teasing his bottom lip with my teeth.

I love making him too flustered to think. When he's turned on, all his defenses come down, and he's this rambling, flustered, adorable man who will answer every question you ask him.

"Of you and Rebel..." He cringes. "I shouldn't have watched it, because he's Troy's boyfriend, but it was so freaking hot, the way he... God, his dick is big, right? But the way you took it was... Yeah, that one's my favorite, I think."

His cheeks are crimson now, and I melt on the inside. I don't care that he's seen my videos. On the contrary, I'm rather proud of them. And I have to admit, the one with me and Rebel was fucking hot. Hell, I watched it a few times myself...primarily to see how I look on camera and how to improve, since it was one of my first scenes, but also because damn, that was really good sex.

"I'm sorry," Mason babbles again. "I shouldn't have watched your videos, not after we became friends, but it was too hard to resist."

"Oh baby, I have no problems with you watching me. It's kinda hot, actually. But I didn't know you had a subscription?"

He looks down. "I've had one for a long time... But Heart, when you get to have sex like that, with men who look like that, how can you like being with me?"

I lift his chin with my finger. "Because that's my job, Mase. It's just sex. I like it, of course I do, but it's about my body, nothing more. Take Pixie, he's super cute, right? But when he and I did a scene the other day, both of us had to work hard at getting in the right mood. He's not my type and even though I like fucking him, he doesn't make me hard instantly..."

I gently take Mason's hand and place it between us on my crotch, where my half-hard cock is paying attention to the conversation, but even more to the feeling of Mason's body against mine. "Unlike you. I like you, both as a friend and to mess around with."

32

LUCKY

It's the first time I'm seeing Heart and Mason together...and it's even better than I had pictured. Mason is skinnier than Heart, who clearly works out regularly and takes good care of his body, but they're about the same height. But Heart's colorful, strong body fits Mason's slender one, like they're contrasts and yet they mesh.

"But you told me you don't want to date," Mason says, slowly removing his hand, though he's still sitting close to Heart.

While that's news to me, it doesn't surprise me. It fits what Heart has shown me of himself so far.

"I don't. I think. The only time I ever dated, it turned out to be a big mistake, you know? He betrayed me, played me for a fool. I don't think I could ever go through that again."

"You know I would never do that to you," I speak up, not able to keep silent when I hear the pain in his voice.

"Me neither," Mason says quickly.

"I know that...or I should say, my head knows that. But it's so hard for me to trust again. And I didn't think it would even come up, since I figured no one would ever want to date me," Heart says softly. "Not once they knew about my job...and my past."

"I don't care," Mason states firmly. "I don't believe you did what you were accused of, and I don't care about your job."

Emotions flash over Heart's expressive face. "Babe... there's more."

I almost hold my breath, knowing what Heart is about to reveal. He looks at me for a second, and I nod, encouraging him to be honest. He's right; Mason needs to know the whole truth.

"There's more?" Mason asks, his voice small.

"Before I met Terry, my ex, I was homeless. I needed to do something to make money, and since I was underage and trying to fly under the radar out of fear of being sent to a group home, I couldn't get a real job. So, I...I did the only thing I could think of. I sold myself."

Mason's gasp is audible, and I'm so tense, awaiting his reaction, that my muscle hurt.

"I'm so sorry you had to do that. That's horrible!" Mason says. "Not horrible that you were horrible, but horrible that you had no other choice. You were a kid!"

I let go of the breath I've been holding, and my body relaxes. Mason hugs Heart tightly, and his eyes are suspiciously watery.

"He's innocent," I say when they look like they've calmed a bit. I rise from the chair across from them and take position on the couch right next to them. "You're right, Mason. He didn't do what he was accused of."

"Thank you...Lucky," Heart says.

I smile at his obvious hesitation over using my first name. "You wanna keep calling me Mr. Stone?" I tease him.

Mason climbs off Heart's lap, settling between us, his body plastered against us both. It's quite fitting, I guess, for him to be in the position he's had all along. "Is Lucky even your real name?" he asks.

"No. It's a nickname I earned in the Marines. I stepped on an IED, and it should have killed me, but it didn't go off. After that, I was known as Lucky and the name stuck."

"What's your real name?" Heart asks, and it hits me how little he asks, how he always keeps himself closed off.

"Jasper," I say. "But you can keep calling me Mr. Stone, if you want."

He grins. "Not a chance. Though the name fits you." Then his face sobers. "Mason told me you're off my case now. Is that true?"

"Yeah. I didn't have a chance to tell you yet, but I requested your case be transferred to a coworker." I won't mention to Heart just yet what an ass Patrick is, but to be honest, I don't feel much loyalty toward him.

"Why?"

"Because as long as I was your PO, I couldn't hang out with you socially. And I want to."

"You want to hang out with me socially," Heart repeats. "Is that some fucked-up code for sex that I'm unaware of?"

"No. It means exactly what it says: hanging out with you socially. Getting to know you. Dating, would be another term, I suppose."

His eyes grow big. "Dude, you don't wanna date me. You want to fuck me. Big difference."

I'm one second away from getting angry at his reaction, when I realize that he means it. He's fully convinced I only want him for sex. And to be fair, I have given him little reason to believe otherwise.

"That's not true," Mason says with indignance. "That's not like Lucky."

His defense of me warms my heart. "Heart's got a point," I admit. "My first attraction to him was sexual. It's grown into more, but I haven't done a good job of expressing that. Granted, I couldn't act on anything until a few days ago, but I haven't given you much indication that I wanted you for more than sex." I aim my last words at Heart, who shrugs.

"I don't care about the sex part. I'm fine with you wanting me... Hell, I'd love to let you fuck me. Just don't bullshit me about it being more than that."

My heart sinks. He doesn't believe me. He doesn't believe I want more than mere sex. "I'm not lying. It's not about sex for me. If that was all I wanted, I could score at any gay club."

Mason cringes at my rather crude assessment, and I mentally shake my head at how badly I'm fucking this up. I've got one guy who doesn't believe I could want him for anything else but sex and another who believes I'd rather have anyone else but him for sex. Talk about a fucked-up situation. How do I prove to both of them that I mean what I say? How do I make Mason believe he's sexually desirable, for lack of a better term, and Heart that I want him for more than his body?

The idea hits me so fast, I mentally stagger. It's the perfect solution, but will they go for it? It's crazy...and yet I believe with all my heart it will be good for all three of us. I don't know what's going on between us, but I want a chance to figure it out. For me, but also for Mason and Heart. We deserve this, all three of us.

"I have an idea," I say. "An idea that will help all three of us navigate whatever this is...whatever we are to each other."

Heart meets my eyes over Mason's puppy eyes, which are full of hope. "I'm listening."

"Heart, you and me, we take sex out of the equation. Until you and I are both convinced what we have is more than sexual attraction, we won't have sex. We can kiss, but all clothes are staying on. At least when it's the two of us."

Heart's eyes widen, but he keeps listening.

"Mason, Heart and I will do our best to make you believe we like you as much for your personality and who you are as for the undeniable sexual attraction. That means we'll make sure you know what you do to us every time we see you."

My words hang in the room as Mason's mouth drops open a little, and Heart looks like he discovered unicorns are real.

"You're serious," he finally manages.

I nod. "Yes. We owe it to ourselves and to each other to explore this, but we can't until we put sex in its proper place."

"You can't tell me who to fuck," Heart sputters, but there's little fire behind it.

"I'm not. You can fuck whoever the hell you want, but I'm telling you, it's not gonna be me...though if it's anyone other than Mason or someone from your job, I suggest you discuss it with us first. It's hard enough to navigate this without being non-exclusive. And no, Heart, your work doesn't count."

Heart looks at me, and I force myself to wait patiently. Mason sucks in a breath, apparently as anxious for Heart's response as I am.

Finally, Heart nods. "Okay. How long?"

I think quickly. What would be a reasonable time to try this out without boxing us in too much? "Two months."

"Done," Heart says. He quirks one eyebrow, and his lips

curve in that crooked smile that shoots straight to my balls. "What will you do for sex?" he asks. "I mean, I can get my rocks off at work, but..."

I grin. "Well, I'm hoping Mason will put out at some point, but if he doesn't, there's always my right hand...with a little help from a certain website, that should work just fine."

His eyebrow shoots even higher. "You watch Ballsy Boys?"

"I was an early adopter. Locked in for life at the opening rate when the website went live. No fucking way am I ever canceling my subscription."

Heart shakes his head, but his lips curve. "The two of you are full of surprises today, bunch of stalker-fans."

"Do you have a problem with us watching your videos?" I check, just to make sure.

"Not at all," he says. "Why would I? Do you have a problem with me doing porn? As my PO, you weren't too fond of it..."

I debate it for a second. "No, I don't. As your PO, it was different, because I didn't want you to get mixed up with the wrong people."

"They're great guys," Mason pipes up.

"So Heart keeps telling me. I hope I get to meet them soon..."

We look at each other, all three of us nervous, I guess, now that we've taken this huge step.

"I think we should go on a date," I propose.

33

HEART

When Lucky did his whole proposal about the sex-rules, I didn't quite get it would mean we'd now be dating with the three of us. At the same time. He sneaked that one in without me noticing, the bastard. That will take some getting used to, I think.

It's Sunday morning, and we're all in Lucky's car, on our way to an outing he has planned. Mason is riding shotgun, and I'm in the back, dozing a little. I'm tired, truth be told. The work at the senior center isn't super taxing physically, but they're long hours, and I already did three shoots this week.

They were all for the same video, a more complicated production involving a few guest stars that Rebel is directing. I wasn't needed in every scene, but Rebel wanted me on set for all three days, so it was tiresome hanging out there for three whole days.

Plus, one of the scenes was a DP, and while I don't mind them, this one was...taxing. Hot damn, my ass can take a lot, but that guy's dick was challenging all by itself, let alone with another crammed in there. To be fair, Rebel checked with me twice to make sure I was okay. And I was, even though my ass is still a little sore. A DP bonus is good money, and I'm not turning that down.

All I can hope is that today will be relaxed, 'cause my body is kinda in need of some rest. Mason and I both have no idea what we're going to do, though Lucky did ask us if we could swim. Turns out, we're both decent enough to stay afloat and that was enough. Maybe we're going to a lake to swim?

My guess is that Lucky is an excellent swimmer, what with being a Marine and all. If Mason manages to get himself overboard—and let's face it, that scenario is quite realistic considering how accident-prone he is—I'm confident Lucky can rescue him.

I doze in that perfect state between being awake and asleep, content to keep my eyes closed while I listen to Lucky and Mason chat. By the time we arrive, I'm already feeling a bit more rested.

"Where are we?" I ask as Lucky turns off the engine.

"The beach," he says.

I smell the ocean as soon as I open the door. It's still early since Lucky wanted to leave at the crack of dawn. I wondered why since we didn't drive for more than an hour.

"We're going to the beach?" Mason asks.

"No," Lucky says with a boyish smile. "We're going sailing."

We follow him onto a path that leads to small harbor, filled with all kinds of boats. "You have a boat?" I ask.

"It's not mine. It's my parents'." He points toward a sleek boat almost at the end of the dock. "That's her."

I know literally nothing about boats, but the boat he points to looks nice enough. Pretty new, as far as I can tell.

Ronja is painted on the side with dark blue, elegant letters. "Is that your mom's name?" I ask.

"No, it's from a children's book she loved and that made her want to become a writer. My mom's an author of children's books."

Just as I want to ask him what his dad does—or did, maybe, since he could be retired—a man pops up on the boat from below deck. He waves as he spots us, and Lucky waves back.

"Who's that?" Mason asks, as usual not bothered by any social norms. I gotta love that about him.

The guy leaps from the boat to the dock with a graceful move, waiting for us to come closer. "Guys," Lucky says. "This is my brother, Ranger. Range, this is Heart and Mason."

His brother? Fucking asshole for not mentioning that. Though one look at Mason clamming up, and I realize he did it on purpose. If Mason had known, his stomach would have been in knots for days, probably.

Mason finally manages to untangle himself and extends a hand to Ranger, who's watching him with quiet patience. "It's so nice to meet you, Mason," he says with a voice that sounds remarkably like Lucky's, even though physically, they're very different. "Lucky's told me good things about you."

Okay, with that, both brothers score major points in my book. Anyone who manages to make Mason feel good about himself is good people.

I extend my hand as well. "Pleasure to meet you," I offer.

His grip is stronger than his thin frame looks. "You too, Heart. Looking forward to getting to know you better."

My eyebrows shoot up before I can hold back my reaction. Getting to *know* me? What the hell is he talking about?

Is this some kind of fucked-up sex reference? Does he really think I'm gonna...?

Lucky's hand clamps down on my shoulder. "Relax," he says quietly in my ear.

Ranger has let go of me by now and is grabbing the bag Mason was wearing, probably to prevent it from ending up in the water.

"He means it literally, getting to know you. Talk to you, chat, nothing more."

"Oh."

Lucky turns me around to face him. "Do you get now why we need these two months without sex? When even an innocent remark like that makes you suspect other motives?"

I nod, feeling like a first-class idiot, but he cups my cheek. "It's okay. I understand where it's coming from."

"I didn't mean to insult him...or you."

He bends over and kisses my cheek with warm, soft lips. "I know. No worries."

"Why is he even here?" I ask, resisting the urge to feel my cheek where Lucky just kissed me. "I thought you wanted to date us. Isn't that kind of hard with your brother there?"

"I can't sail this boat by myself. Technically, I can, but it's not safe since I guessed neither of you has any experience. That was one reason to ask my brother along. Also, his presence will help me keep my hands off you." He shoots me a wicked grin.

I step closer, our bodies almost touching—but not quite. "You struggling with that?" I tease.

He leans in, his mouth hovering a breath away from mine. "You have no idea. But I'm a man of my word, Heart. I will not touch you."

"You said no sex," I remind him. "But kissing was okay, right?"

"True." He cocks his head ever so slightly, his eyes fixated on mine. "But do you really want our first kiss to be here, with strangers watching, while we're in a bit of a hurry to catch the wind?"

"No." My voice is barely more than a whisper. "But we'll kiss at some point, right?"

"Yes. But not before I think we're ready for this. You need to learn to stop using your body to draw me in, babe. You have my attention...now I want to get to know *you*."

I keep pondering his words as Lucky and Ranger do all kinds of things to make the boat ready, and a few minutes later, we leave the harbor. The boat has an engine, too, I discover, which makes complete sense because I imagine it would be hard to always be dependent on the wind.

They wait till we've left the harbor, the Pacific stretching out before us like a calm glistening blue blanket, before hoisting the sails. I've never been on a boat this small, and it's a little scary at first, but then the wind fills the sails and all of a sudden, the engine is turned off and we're sailing. Lucky smiles as he pulls on some ropes, adjusting the sails, and he calls out some sailing lingo to Ranger I have no hope of understanding. But whatever it is, it's like magic, because the sails pull tight in the wind and we're flying.

Mason lets out a little squeak, his cheeks almost as red as the life jacket he's wearing. We're all wearing one per Lucky's orders, even him and Ranger. I wondered why since they both seem excellent swimmers, but Lucky calmly explained even experienced swimmers can drown at sea, especially when there's a chance you can get knocked out cold by something.

Wow, I had not expected us to go this fast. I figured

sailing was more for older people, like a calm, relaxed activity, but Lucky and Ranger are making the boat fly through the water.

"You okay, Mase?" I check.

"We're going really fast," he says.

Lucky makes eye contact with me since Mason is sitting with his back toward him. "Do we need to slow down?"

"Do you wanna go slower?" I ask Mason.

He bites his lip, then shakes his head. "No. It's a little scary, but the good kind of scary, you know?"

Do I ever? I close my eyes and raise my head toward the sun, the wind a welcoming breeze as the sun is still gaining power. No wonder Lucky warned us to put sunblock on. You'll burn alive on the water with the wind masking how fast you're developing sunburn. But what a rush, this sensation of being one with the wind and the water, the sun even.

I don't know how long we've sailed when Ranger calls out. "Ready about?"

Right, this is the part Lucky explained to us in simple terms. We're changing our position relative to the wind, if I understood correctly, which means that big beam is gonna come right over our heads—preferably *over* and not *against*, as Lucky said with a wink to Mason.

"Watch your head, babe," Lucky tells Mason, and I love him for taking that extra precaution. He winks at me when he sees me watching him. "Going about," he calls to Ranger, followed by, "Lee ho!"

That big beam moves fast as it flies over our heads into the opposite direction. It only takes seconds before the wind hits the sails again, slower this time. Lucky does something with the ropes and we're steady again, but at a slower pace. Ranger moves over to where Lucky stands, and then Lucky comes sit between us.

"How are you doing?" he asks me.

"This is magic," I say, a big grin plastered on my face. "Dude, I never thought we could move that fast."

"Yeah, we had the perfect position," Lucky says, returning my smile. "She can go even faster, but I figured this was enough excitement for a couple of newbies like you."

"Thank you," I say. "For taking us out on the water. It's...perfect."

Lucky leans in, and for a second, I think he's gonna kiss me. But his lips find my forehead instead, and somehow, that kiss feels more intimate than any French kiss he could've given me. "So are you," he says. "Perfect, that is."

34

MASON

I'm a little shaky but as we get off the boat, but I'm smiling so much my face hurts. I had no idea sailing would be so much fun. Heart reaches for my hand to steady me on the dock while Lucky and his brother do whatever they need to do to the boat now that we're done with it.

"You guys hungry?" Lucky asks as he climbs off the boat with Ranger behind him.

"Starving," Heart says, and I nod in agreement, my stomach growling at the same moment.

"I'll leave you with your boys; thanks for taking me out with you on the boat," Ranger says, clapping Lucky on the back.

"Thanks for helping me show them a good time." Lucky pulls his brother into a quick hug, and I smile. It must be nice having a sibling, someone who's always there for you, someone to have grown up with.

"Nice to meet you guys; I'm sure I'll be seeing you again." Ranger winks at Heart and me before taking off down the pier.

"Did you guys have fun?" Lucky checks, putting his hand on my lower back and absently rubbing his thumb along a patch of exposed skin. I shiver and lean into his touch, loving the feeling of having both Heart and Lucky so close.

"Yeah, I've never been on a boat before."

"Neither have I," Heart added. "It was cool; thanks for taking us."

"Good, I was hoping to make our first date together something to remember."

I snort a laugh. "I don't think I could ever forget going on a date with two men at the same time. It's a notable event for me to have a date with one."

Heart laughs and kisses my cheek. "You're just too good at keeping your awesome hidden away. Good thing for Lucky and me that we were able to spot it."

A pleasant, warm buzz in my chest accompanies Heart's words, and I feel myself blushing. I can't say I understand any of this, but I'm going to enjoy it as long as I can.

Lucky leans closer and his lips brush my ear. "He's right; you're sweet, sexy, and completely amazing."

My face burns hotter, and I grasp around my brain for any sort of response. Brad's hateful words try to find their way in, but Heart and Lucky's words manage to drown them out. I squeeze Heart's fingers and rest my head on Lucky's shoulder.

"How do you guys feel about pizza?" Lucky asks. "There's a great pizza place just a block over."

"Works for me," Heart says, and I nod in agreement.

I realize as we start to walk off the dock that I should probably stop touching one of them. Not that anyone in LA would likely look twice at three men together, but I'm not sure I'm ready to go there. Lucky's hand falls from my shoulders, and a chill creeps over my skin. I want to reach for him again but I resist.

At the pizza place we get a large pizza to share—half mushrooms and green peppers and half pepperoni. With the three of us seated around the table, Heart shifts uncomfortably in his seat and then gives Lucky a wry smile.

"This is weird as fuck."

"That there's three of us or...?" Lucky tries to guess, and Heart tugs his lip ring between his teeth, looking around the restaurant and avoiding eye contact with either of us. I reach for Heart's hand under the table and give it a squeeze.

"Being around you in a social setting. I feel like I've been called to the principal's office, but instead of getting detention, he took me on a date." Lucky cringes at the analogy, and Heart immediately starts trying to backpedal. "Not that I *don't* want to be on a date with you. I think my brain just needs to catch up with the fact that you're not my PO anymore, if that makes sense?"

Lucky's shoulders relax a little. "It makes sense, and it's a big part of the reason I want us to hold off on sex for the time being. I don't want you thinking of me as your PO when we get to that point."

Heart nods and looks relieved. "Why don't you tell me about what you do for fun," he suggests.

"I game some," Lucky admits, and Heart's face is so full of surprise, I giggle.

"What did you think Lucky and I found to talk about?" I point out.

"That makes sense, I guess. I just can't picture you sitting on your couch playing video games. I figured you'd be all about lifting weights and rock climbing on your free time."

"I do both of those things too. I also enjoy trail running

and hiking. But that doesn't mean I can't enjoy a lazy Saturday with my PlayStation from time to time."

The image pops into my head of the three of us lazing around in our pajamas, playing video games, and cuddling all day. That's my perfect weekend, hands down, and the thought makes me smile. Maybe one day.

The pizza comes and the topics stay in general *getting to know you* territory. Heart makes us laugh with a story about a fan proposing to him recently.

"He just got down on one knee right there in the supermarket, I didn't even know what to do."

"Oh my god, that's hilarious," I say.

"It must be strange having a job that makes strangers think they know you," Lucky comments, and the mood sobers a little.

"Yeah, it's kind of weird. Aside from the nutcases, though, the job is pretty awesome. Who wouldn't want to have sex for a living, right?"

Lucky looks skeptical, opening his mouth and then snapping it closed again without comment. I've never thought twice about Heart's job; it's just part of him. But does Lucky have an issue with it? That possibility sits heavy in the pit of my stomach. If Lucky has a problem with Heart's job, this is never going to work. I'm not sure at what point I became so invested in this whole thing, but it feels as vital as breathing, even if I don't understand yet how it's going to work.

When the bill comes, Lucky snags it in spite of Heart's and my protests. "Tell you what, one of you can pay next time."

"Fine," Heart grumbles.

I'm happy enough to take turns paying, but Heart seems somewhat irritated by the gesture. "Hey, is everything okay?

You never make this big of a deal when I get dinner for us or anything," I ask quietly.

"Yeah, I just don't want Lucky to see me as someone who can't take care of himself."

"There's no way he thinks that. This is a date, not that I've been on a lot, but I know it's typical for one person to pay. He said you could pay next time."

"Yeah," Heart agrees. "Sorry, I'm being stupid. This is weird, that's all."

"Good weird, though. Right?" I check, and Heart smiles and then leans over and presses a quick kiss to my lips.

"Yeah, good weird."

"Is everything okay?" Lucky asks, looking between Heart and me warily.

"Great, just whispering about how hot our date is," Heart flirts with a smirk.

"You two are going to be a handful, aren't you?"

"If you're lucky."

I snort a laugh at the unintended pun, and as we all get up from the table, my hand twitches toward Lucky. With a quick glance around, I decide to just go for it. He looks pleasantly surprised when my hand slips into his, and the three of us head back toward the car we left near the marina.

When we reach Lucky's car, he turns and pins Lucky with a look that's equal parts nerves and lust.

"So...about that kiss?"

Lucky smiles and gives my hand a squeeze before letting it go.

"I'll get in the car," I offer, making a move to skirt around them. Heart's first kiss with Lucky should be special; they don't need me standing here making it weird.

"No," they both say at the same time.

"I want you here. This isn't just about me and Lucky or you and me. I want you to be part of this."

I nod and shuffle my feet, not sure if I should stay standing right next to Heart or give them a little space. Heart makes the decision for me by grabbing my arm and pulling me close. Then he turns his attention back to Lucky and bats his eyes suggestively. Lucky chuckles and cups Heart's face, tilting it up and running his thumb along Heart's bottom lip.

A little jolt of anticipation prickles along my skin as if I'm the one about to be kissed. I smile and hold my breath, my eyes fixed on their faces as they inch closer, both captivated by the moment.

Heart seems to be holding his breath as well, his eyes fluttering closed as Lucky's nose bumps against his. Lucky's lips hover a few inches from Heart's, his descent on hold as he seems to savor the moment. Heart's lips part, and he drags in a ragged breath before fisting the front of Lucky's shirt and dragging him in to close the gap between their mouths. Lucky chuckles but it's muffled against Heart's lips, and it quickly turns to a moan.

Their lips move together, and I can't tell who's leading or if they're battling for control. All I know is it's unbelievably hot to watch their tongues slide together, their lips crashing and parting over and over. Heart's hand squeezes mine tight like he's afraid I'll run away if he lets go. Fat chance I'm going anywhere with a scene like this playing out right in front of me.

When they finally part, they're both dragging in panting breaths, lips damp and swollen, and cheeks pink.

"Wow," Heart mutters, and Lucky smiles smugly. "Do I get a kiss from you too, sweetie?" Heart asks after the daze from Lucky's kiss seems to fade.

"I'm not sure I can follow that." I force a laugh, nerves fluttering in my stomach. I've kissed Heart plenty, but after the way Lucky just kissed him, I'm sure I'll pale in comparison.

"Don't be silly." Heart yanks me forward without giving me further chance to protest.

His lips are just as hot and sweet against mine as they always are, but this time there's the hint of Lucky's flavor on his mouth as well, and it makes my cock harder than it's ever been. Heart coaxes my tongue into his mouth and tangles his fingers in my hair, turning the kiss deep and greedy. When he releases me, Lucky is watching us with heat in his eyes.

"Thanks for a great day." Heart climbs into the passenger seat, and I make a move to get into the back seat. Lucky stops me, and I get my own goodbye kiss from him, just as possessive and heated as all our kisses have been.

When I finally do climb into Lucky's car, I try to think of a more perfect day in my life and come up epically short.

35

LUCKY

I handed over Heart's file to Patrick—but not before I made a print out. For personal use, so to speak. The truth is that ever since Heart's ex showed up, and he told me more about what happened to him, I've been wanting to dig a little deeper. Not that I'm in any way qualified to do said digging, fuck no. I'm a decent PO and a more than decent Marine, but I'm not a cop or a lawyer or a PI.

But I know someone who is.

Once again, I make the hour-and-a-half journey to my brother's ranch. I called him, of course. Showing up unannounced at Ranger's place is not a good idea. Much like me, he's never liked surprises, and I can't blame him. We got enough of those during deployment—he probably even more than me, considering the state he was in when I visited him. He seemed okay when we went sailing, but that was in front of others, so I'm wondering how he's really doing.

The garden looks a lot better than last time, though he's left most of the wildflowers for the bees and the butterflies.

But the grass is nicely cut, and he started growing some herbs in colorful pots. The man always had a green thumb.

"Ranger?" I call out when he doesn't show up as I walk up to the house. He usually hears my car pull up and will be waiting for me.

For two seconds, my blood freezes as I think the unimaginable. He wouldn't...*would he*?

No, not like this. Not without talking to me first. We know each other too well. We're too close.

I carefully try the front door, which is unlocked. "Ranger?" I call out again as I let myself in.

"In here," my brother calls out, and I sigh with relief.

I find him in a spare room he turned into a mini gym, where he's twisted his body into what looks like a mighty uncomfortable yoga position. I wince. "Doesn't that hurt your balls?"

He grins as he slowly unfolds himself. "You get used to it."

He looks better, thank fuck, though still thinner than he should be. "Still practicing to be a pretzel?" I tease.

"Yup and loving it."

Ranger swears by yoga, claims it completely relaxes him. Just the thought of spending two hours torturing yourself by forcing your body into unnatural positions sounds stressful to me, but what the fuck do I know. To each his own and all that.

Ranger pats himself with a towel, then trots to the kitchen with me on his heels. "Soda?" he asks. He knows me well.

"Coke, please."

He hands me a Coke and grabs OJ for himself. "You're drinking Coke? It's that serious?"

"I need your help with something," I say. "Something confidential."

"Okay."

"Can we sit down here?" I gesture toward his kitchen table.

"Sure."

He doesn't say a word as I spread out Heart's file, neatly organized into sections. "I need you to read through this and tell me what you think."

He raises his eyebrows. "You're not gonna give me more than that?"

"I don't want to influence you in any way. And I need you to be honest with me, okay?"

He eyes the stack of papers. "That's gonna take me a while."

"I know. Got anything to do for me in the meantime?"

A few minutes later, I'm outside, cleaning his driveway with the pressure washer. It's not an unpleasant task considering the weather, as the mist coming off the washer cools me down a bit. I'm wearing an old shirt and shorts of Ranger's, not wanting to get my own dirty, as well as a faded Yankees cap I intend to grill him about later. *New York Yankees?* When the hell did he switch allegiance to *them*?

When I'm done, I spend an hour or so cleaning up his garage. He promised he'd come get me if he was done, so I might as well make myself useful. I'm just finishing up when he walks in. He whistles as he looks around. "Nice! I need to ask you over more often," he jokes.

"You're welcome. Now tell me."

"Inside," he gestures, and I follow him back into the kitchen. He hands me a bottle of water and a fresh soda, since I forgot to drink mine before I went outside.

"This is Heart's file," he says.

"You know I can't tell you that."

He nods. "Fair enough."

"Did you see anything strange?"

He leans forward. "Other than a kid who clearly was framed for something he didn't do?"

I can't hold back the gasp that's on my tongue. "You think he's innocent?"

"I know he is. Based on the evidence here, he should have never been convicted. He had the bad luck of getting stuck with a public defender who probably had fifteen minutes to read his file, if that, and spent ten of that trying to convince him to take a plea bargain."

"He rejected the plea, because he refused to plead guilty," I confirm, my head storming with thoughts and emotions I can't even hope to identify. Heart is really innocent. He didn't do it. I believed him when he told me, but to hear my brother confirm it brings it home all over again.

"I figured. It was ballsy, because he could've gotten away with a few months, probably, had he taken the deal."

"Now what? What do we do now?"

"We?"

For once, I drop the mask I usually wear and allow my brother to see inside me. "Mack," I say, using his given name instead of the honorary name he prefers. "He's innocent. And I like him. I really, really like him. Enough to want to see if we have a future…and we can't have one without fixing this. I need to fix this for him."

Ranger looks at me for a few seconds, then nods. "Okay. I can't do this since I have zero experience. But I have a friend who may be able to help. I'll ask him to contact you, okay?"

"Thank you."

"Sure thing."

We sit in silence as we finish our drinks. "You're still dating both of them?" Ranger asks after a bit.

"Yeah. It's proving to be...interesting."

"I bet," he says. He sends me a smile, but it's filled with sadness, so I don't expand on my answer.

"Are you okay?" I ask finally. "I don't need details, but I need to know that I can leave you here by yourself."

For the longest time, Ranger doesn't say anything, but his hands tremble as he puts his glass down. "I lost someone, a friend. My unit got attacked. and he...he didn't make it out. We were...close. I didn't realize how close till it was too late."

He raises his eyes, and the sheer pain on his face is staggering. He loved him, this friend. There's no doubt in my mind. He's grieving for something that never had a chance to be.

"Mack..." I say, my voice breaking.

"So, no, I'm not okay, and I probably won't be for a while. But I will be at some point... I do know that. The fact that I have that hope means you can leave me here."

I reach for his hand and squeeze it. "Promise me you'll tell me if that changes."

"I promise."

36

HEART

For our third date together, Lucky took Mason and me to a minor league baseball game. It clearly wasn't Mason's thing, but I made a game out of flirting and touching him to keep him entertained.

When the game ended, Lucky asked if we wanted to go back to his place for a while or if he should drop us off at home. It was an easy choice, but I'm honestly not sure how a date is supposed to end when sex is off the table. I suppose that's the reason Lucky made the rule in the first place. He thinks I'm going to learn some big lesson about how I'm more than a sex object. Somehow, I find it hard to believe that he's going to convince me of that in two months when all the life experience I've had to this point tells me the opposite.

Lucky opens the door to his apartment, and I follow him and Mason inside. He gives us a quick tour, even though I assume Mason has been here before. The place is spotless, not a single item out of place—his shoes all lined up perfectly, the throw pillows on the couch placed neatly, not a crumb on the counters, and *big surprise,* the bed is made with military corners.

Not to be all *poor me,* but I honestly can't figure out what Lucky sees in me. Mason is just as neat and organized; those two would keep a beautiful home together. Me? I'm just throwing a wrench in the works. I could understand if Lucky was only interested in me for sex, but wanting to date me doesn't compute.

Mason's hand slips into mine, and he gives my fingers a squeeze.

"What's wrong?" he asks, tracing the frown lines in my forehead with his index finger.

I force a smile and lean in to kiss his sweet lips. "I'm good, baby," I assure him, letting myself enjoy the flutter in my chest for just a second. Maybe this will miraculously work out, and I'll get to have both Mason and Lucky permanently. I'm not holding my breath, but a guy can dream.

I turn my head to find Lucky watching us with a heated gaze. At least the sex part of this strange relationship won't likely be a problem when we get to it, *if* we make it that far.

"Hey, you said you and I couldn't have sex," I point out, an idea striking me.

"Yeah," Lucky agrees warily.

"Well, you're here, and Mason's here..." I turn my attention back to Mason and bite my lip suggestively. "You want me to give you some pointers on how to give the best head on the planet? We even have a real-life dick you can practice on while I instruct you."

Mason's mouth falls open, and his cheeks flame red. He looks over at Lucky and then back at me.

"Um...if Lucky wants," Mason agrees in a shaky voice.

I glance back at Lucky and notice a prominent bulge in the front of his jeans. "I'd say Lucky *definitely* wants."

I turn Mason's head and point his gaze at Lucky's pants. Mason's eyes go wide. "I'm not sure if I'll be any good. He's really big."

"You've already seen his dick?" I ask with interest.

Mason nods, his gaze still fixed on the bulge in Lucky's pants. "I gave him a hand job, and it was *huge*."

"All the more fun to play with. Trust me, you're going to love taking that big cock in your mouth and watching a put-together man like Lucky fall apart."

Mason shivers, and his breath hitches, then he nods and sways closer to me.

"Why don't we go to the couch," I suggest, and Lucky leads the way without comment. There's a stiffness to his shoulders, and I can't tell if it's because I'm pushing the bounds of his rules or if he's trying to keep his composure in spite of being turned on.

Lucky sits down in the center of the couch, and I direct Mason to one side while I take the other.

"Is this okay *Mr. Stone*?" I ask playfully. "I don't want to break your rules."

"As you pointed out, this is well within the rules," Lucky concedes.

"In that case, this is going to be fun." I smile wickedly and then lean forward so I can see Mason around Lucky. "Kiss me, sweetie?" I ask Mason.

He nods and leans over so we're directly in front of Lucky's face. I give Lucky a flirty wink before pressing my lips to Mason's. The kiss is slow but hot as hell as I thread my fingers through Mason's curls, our tongues playing, making sloppy noises. Mason whimpers and moans into my mouth, and I can hear Lucky's breathing hitch and become more ragged the longer Mason and I kiss.

"I think poor Lucky is feeling left out; why don't you give

him a kiss," I suggest, giving Mason one more peck before leaning back and letting him go to Lucky.

My cock aches at the sight of their tongues tangling. I can see the way Lucky takes control of the kiss, forcing Mason to slow it down when he gets overly excited. Lucky's hands roam over Mason's upper body, mostly staying over his shirt. It's sweet and sexy at the same time, but I'm ready for a little raunchy. Mason seems unsure what to do with his hands, keeping them on Lucky's chest, so I decide to help him out with that. I take one of his hands and move it down to the substantial erection Lucky has tenting his jeans.

They both moan as I use Mason's hand to gently squeeze Lucky's cock and then rub it a little through his clothes. Mason catches on and starts to do it himself while Lucky deepens their kiss.

When they part, I can't contain the groan that escapes at their kiss-swollen lips and Mason's messy hair.

"Come here," Lucky commands, his gravelly voice sending a pulse of need through me. Lucky's lips meet mine, hot and demanding. Since I'm sure groping Lucky is against the no-sex rules, I reach for Mason instead, running my hand up under his shirt and pinching his peaked nipple. Mason gasps. Lucky pulls away to see what I'm doing to Mason and arches his eyebrows when he sees.

"Mason *loves* having his nipples played with, just as an FYI," I inform Lucky cheekily, and Mason blushes.

"Good to know." Lucky sneaks his free hand up Mason's shirt, and Mason's head falls back on a low moan. "I see what you mean."

"I made him come by just playing with his nipples once; it was so fucking hot."

Lucky grunts and flexes his hips, pressing his cock harder into Mason's hand.

"You're so hard," Mason murmurs in wonder, and then his eyes go wide like he can't believe he said that out loud.

"You made him hard with your hot kisses and the way you're touching him," I tell Mason and enjoy the flicker of pride in his eyes. "You want to make him come, don't you?"

Mason nods eagerly, and Lucky cants his hips again, biting down on his puffy bottom lip. Mason starts to unzip Lucky's pants with shaky fingers, and after several painful seconds, I reach over to help him out, flicking the button open and then helping him with the zipper. Lucky's cock is outlined in his tight, black briefs. The ridge of his head is prominent, and now that it's not being trapped in his tight jeans, it's obvious he's even bigger than I thought.

Mason licks his lips and then glances over at me with a question in his eyes.

"Remember before when we talked about foreplay and how any touch can be erotic?" I ask Mason, and he nods readily. "Teasing the buildup makes an orgasm a lot more intense, so never be afraid to take your time, play around for a while before going in for the kill."

"So maybe I can touch and lick him through his underwear first?" Mason guesses, and Lucky's cock twitches.

"It looks like he likes that idea."

Mason slides off the couch and positions himself on the floor between Lucky's legs. I nibble and lick at Lucky's neck while watching Mason palm the huge erection and take his time stroking from base to tip with the most adorably sexy look of concentration on his face.

"Have you given a blowjob before, babe?" I ask Mason.

"Yeah, but it was awful. Brad would just kind of grab my head and shove his cock in my mouth, and I'd try not to gag too much while he got himself off."

"Okay, well Lucky's not going to do that unless you ask

him to. So, you can take your time and enjoy finding ways to pleasure him."

"That sounds fun," Mason says, leaning forward and flicking his tongue along the head of Lucky's cock through his underwear. Lucky squirms, and his cock flexes again. Mason does it a few more times until Lucky is panting, one hand fisting one of his throw pillows and the other gripping my thigh for dear life.

Mason tugs at Lucky's briefs, finally freeing his cock. He stares at it for a few seconds like it's a work of art. I've seen a lot of cocks, and I have to agree; Lucky's is incredible—fat and long, dark pink with arousal and pulsing with need. The thick mushroom head is glistening with precum.

Mason licks his lips and then leans forward and gathers Lucky's precum onto his tongue. The look of innocent surprise on Mason's face is almost enough all on its own to make me cream my pants. Then he wraps his lips around the head of Lucky's cock, and I moan right along with Lucky.

"That's so good, baby," I praise, and Lucky grunts in agreement, petting Mason's hair as words seem to be lost to him.

Mason bobs his head, taking Lucky deeper. He makes it about halfway down Lucky's length before gagging.

"That's okay," I assure him. "We can work on your gag reflex if you want, but for now, give me your hand."

Mason does as I ask, and I position his hand on Lucky's cock and then show him how to move it in time with the thrusts of his mouth.

"Oh god yeah," Lucky groans as Mason finds a steady rhythm.

The smell of arousal hangs in the air, and the sloppy sounds of Mason sucking Lucky make my cock even harder, my balls getting heavy and tight. I unzip my pants and reach inside to free my cock. Both Mason and Lucky's eyes zero in on my hand as I work it fast up and down my cock. I decide to ham it up a bit for them, moaning and thrusting into my fist. Mason tries to match my pace on Lucky's cock, sucking faster and taking him deeper with each pass.

I turn my head and find Lucky's lips. We're both too close to the edge for anything resembling skill as we haphazardly crash our lips together, panting and licking into each other's mouths.

"Oh shit, I'm going to...ungh," Lucky warns, and the look of determination on Mason's face deepens.

Lucky tenses as Mason sucks his orgasm from him. I thrust into my fist a few more times and then cry out against Lucky's lips as my cum splatters my stomach and chest. Mason is licking the remnants of Lucky's orgasm off his flagging cock, and then he turns and eyes the mess I've made.

"Can I..." His blush deepens, and if I hadn't just blown my load, it would've been hard to resist grabbing Mason and shoving my cock between his swollen, wet lips.

"Lick my cum up and then come kiss me," I instruct. He can't feel self-conscious about it if he's been told to do it, right?

Mason does as I told him, lapping up my release with hungry strokes of his tongue all over my stomach.

"So sexy," Lucky tells Mason, stroking his fingers gently through Mason's hair as we both watch him lick me clean. When he's satisfied he's gotten every drop, Mason climbs onto my lap and thrusts his tongue into my mouth. The combined flavor of Lucky and me in Mason's mouth makes me crazy.

"Tastes so good," I murmur against his lips before reaching blindly for Lucky and then dragging him close. I want him to taste too; I want him to be part of this kiss where he belongs.

When Lucky's lips and tongue join the mix, Mason freezes as he tries to figure out what to do with the addition. After a few seconds, he relaxes and follows our lead, the kiss a hot tangle of tongues, lips seemingly everywhere. It's pure fucking heaven.

Mason whimpers and grinds against me; it's then I realize he hasn't had a chance to come yet.

"Who do you want to suck you off, baby? Me or Lucky?" I ask, and Mason whimpers again.

"Oh god, I don't know," he pants, his whole body trembling as he thrusts his hard cock against my stomach again.

"How about both of us?" I suggest with a wicked grin. Mason moans and nods rapidly.

"Please."

I cock an eyebrow at Lucky to make sure he's okay with the plan, and he nods and smirks at me.

"Get up real quick," I instruct Mason.

He stands on shaky legs, and I make quick work of his pants and underwear. He bites his bottom lip and awkwardly moves his hand like he's considering hiding his erection from view.

"You have such a pretty cock," I praise, and Lucky hums in agreement.

"It's smaller than both of yours," Mason points out as he steps out of his pants and underwear, then kicks them aside.

"Mase, you know I've been with a lot of men, and I can tell you with great confidence that size is not the most important thing."

"Really?"

"Really," I assure him. "Now, where were we?"

Lucky reaches out and tugs Mason closer to us. With the

two of us sitting on the couch and Mason standing in front of us, we're at the perfect height to have some fun with him.

"I think we were right about here," Lucky quips, licking a stripe up the underside of Mason's cock.

"Oh yeah," I agree before swirling my tongue around the head of Mason's cock, gathering up the salty, sweet precum.

Mason sways on his feet and clutches at my hair for balance while Lucky and I run our tongues all over his cock, occasionally sharing hot kisses with Mason's head between us. I use my tongue to trace each vein while Lucky alternates between long slow licks and quick flicks of his tongue along the shaft.

Lucky sneaks a hand under Mason's shirt, and based on the moans he draws from our sweet boy, I'm betting Lucky's playing with his nipples. I wrap my lips around the head of Mason's cock and swallow him down easily. He's right, he is a bit smaller than Lucky or me, but I was being honest when I told him it didn't matter. He may not be huge, but when he topped me, it was exactly the right size to peg my prostate every time in the right position. Lucky doesn't strike me as the type to bottom, but if he is, I don't see him having any complaints about the size of Mason's cock either.

I bob my head over his length, humming and moaning as I take him all the way in over and over while Lucky continues to play with his nipples and suck his tightening sac.

"Oh god, oh...I'm..." Mason wails, and I suck harder until his cock plumps in my mouth and then starts to pulse. Salty release bursts on my tongue, and I swallow it down greedily. When I release him, Lucky laps at his sensitive cock, searching for any drop I might've left behind.

Mason stumbles forward and ends up in Lucky's lap.

The three of us trade lazy, cum-sticky kisses for what feels like hours.

"That was fun," Mason says with a yawn some time later, resting his head against Lucky's shoulder.

"Told you sex was fun," I crow, snuggling close on Lucky's other side and enjoying the way his arm comes around me to keep me there.

"Yeah, that wasn't anything like before."

"I'm glad." I lean over and brush one more kiss against Mason's lips, and Lucky smiles at us.

As crazy as this whole thing may be, it seems like it could actually work. God, I hope it does.

37

MASON

My phone pings, and I find a message from Lucky in our group chat with Heart.

Lucky: Since I planned our last three dates, I think it's someone else's turn to plan our Sunday date this week. You up for it, Mason?

Mason: Uh...I'm not sure you guys want that. If I plan the date, we're going to spend the day on the couch in our pajamas, playing video games, watching movies, and fooling around

Heart: I'm in!

Lucky: sounds good to me

Their easy acceptance of my date idea makes my chest warm.

Mason: If you guys are sure, then come on over any time Sunday. I'll be sure to have snacks and stuff on hand

Heart: Can't wait

Lucky: See you both Sunday XOXO

. . .

The next few days pass quickly, and before I know it, it's Sunday morning, and I'm lying in bed, thinking about Lucky and Heart. That's not surprising; it seems like they're all I think about recently. This whole thing still feels like a crazy dream. I can't believe two men like them would want *me*. I'm sure, sooner or later, they'll realize they don't need me getting in between them, and they'll ride off into the sunset together. But until then, I'll enjoy this crazy mistake the universe made by giving them both to me.

The door buzzer sounds from the front of my apartment, so I drag myself out of bed and hit the button to unlock the outside door. I stifle a yawn as I unlock my door and prop it open so Heart or Lucky can walk right in when they get up here. Then, I shuffle to the kitchen to start coffee.

"Morning, baby," Lucky calls out as he steps inside. "You really shouldn't leave your door open like that, it's not safe."

"I knew you or Heart were on your way up."

"You didn't ask who it was buzzing to come up; what if it wasn't one of us?" Lucky's brow furrowed with worry makes me feel warm and fuzzy again. I press the button to start the coffee maker and then I go to Lucky, burrowing myself into his strong arms.

"I'll be more careful next time."

"I don't mean to be a hard ass; I just worry." He kisses the top of my head, and I melt further into him.

"I know, and I appreciate it."

"Aw, you guys are getting started on the cuddle portion of the day without me?" Heart teases.

"How'd you get in here without buzzing?"

"Some woman was leaving and held the door open for me. Kinda dumb on her part; maybe I was coming in here to rob apartments or something. I *am* a criminal after all."

Lucky raises his eyebrows at me as if to say *I told you so*.

"You're not a criminal," I argue, wiggling out of Lucky's grasp and walking over to Heart.

"Technically, I am."

"Yeah, but you're innocent," I argue, and Heart's eyes soften. He holds his arms open for me, and I step into them, pressing my lips against his as I do.

"Thank you," he murmurs against my lips. I don't think he's thanking me for the kiss.

When we part, I look at both men and realize they came over in pajamas just like I asked. I can only imagine how awkward Lucky felt walking down the street in sweatpants. Meanwhile, Heart has on pajama pants with hotdogs and ice cream cones all over them, and he seems comfortable as can be.

"You guys want coffee or anything? I was going to make breakfast, but chances were high I would burn anything I tried to make, but if you're hungry, I can figure something out."

"No need, I brought donuts," Heart holds up a bag I hadn't realized was in his hand before. Apparently, I've developed a serious one-track mind with these two.

"Perfect. I'll get coffees, and then we can all get comfy on the couch together."

"I'm going to have to be careful with you two; you both manage to seriously undermine my normally strict diet," Lucky complains.

"Undermining strict rules is half the fun of life," Heart teases him with a wink.

"You're not going to get me to break the no-sex rule."

"You're no fun."

"Oh, I'm plenty of fun, and you'll find out exactly how much in two more weeks," Lucky counters. "I'll help with the coffee," he offers, following me to the kitchen while

Heart grabs napkins off the counter and takes the donuts to the couch, grabbing my controller and pulling up something for us to watch.

Spending a day being lazy on the couch has always been my favorite, but with Heart and Lucky, it's a whole new level of awesome.

After our coffee and donuts, we end up in a complicated cuddle pile with me in the middle. We decided to watch *Star Wars*, the original trilogy obviously, and I think I underestimated how much of a geek both Lucky and Heart are on the inside.

"Oh, come on, the Rebels are essentially terrorists. Sure, the Empire is evil, but what government isn't? Just because the government sucks, doesn't mean you get to blow up giant infrastructure projects," Lucky argues.

"Are you seriously siding with the Empire right now?" Heart asks incredulously. "You do realize they're a dictatorship, enslaving the universe and blowing up planets at will."

"I think he's right, though, Heart. What the Rebels are doing won't ultimately lead to a stable government; it's not the right way to go about a resistance."

"I can't believe my ears right now. You're both crazy."

I giggle at Heart's indignation and steal a quick kiss from him.

"Fine, whatever. Next topic is Jar Jar Binks as the Master Sith Lord, so I hope you fools are ready to throw down," Heart warns before climbing off the couch and stretching. "But first, I need to piss."

I settle against Lucky happily. "This is fun," I murmur as he rubs his hand soothingly up and down my back.

"It is," Lucky agrees.

I tilt my head and take his lips in a slow, lazy kiss. He

drags his tongue against mine, his hand still tracing slow circles on my back.

"You two are so hot together," Heart says, and I pull my mouth from Lucky's.

"Please, you should see you two together," I counter with an eye roll. "Frankly, I can't figure out what I'm even still doing here." I try to play it off as a joke, but I can see Lucky and Heart both frown at my comment.

"I'm not sure how many different ways to tell you we like everything about you, just the way you are. But eventually, you'll see we mean it," Lucky says, and Heart nods fervently in agreement.

I reach for Heart and tug him down onto the couch again and sigh with contentment as I'm trapped between the two of them again. I want to believe Lucky; I want it so badly. I don't ever want either of them to leave.

After *The Empire Strikes Back*, we order sandwiches to be delivered and make out while we wait for them.

When the delivery person buzzes, I let him up and wait by the door. I'm sure our recent fooling around is written all over my messy hair and rumpled clothes based on the way the sandwich guy eyes me. He glances over my shoulder, and I follow his gaze to where Heart and Lucky are still kissing on the couch. A sense of possessive pride surges through me when I see the look on his face when I turn back.

"Holy shit, is that *Heart*?" the guy asks, eyes wide. Apparently, he has a Ballsy Boys subscription.

"Yup," I confirm, grabbing the paper bag from him. "He's my boyfriend," I blurt when he continues to stare at Heart and Lucky.

The delivery guy gives himself a shake and then shoots me an apologetic smile.

"I'm your boyfriend, huh?" Heart asks in a teasing tone after I close the door.

My face heats as I realize my mistake. "I didn't mean...it was just because he was staring, and...oh god, I really didn't mean that I think you're my boyfriend..."

Heart gets up from the couch and cuts off my rambling with his lips on mine. "I'm teasing, baby. I like the sound of being boyfriends. If that's what Lucky wants too, of course."

"I want," Lucky chimes in form the couch.

I let out a shaky breath and smile.

"Were you jealous he recognized me?" Heart asks with concern.

"Not exactly. I don't mind if he watches your videos or whatever, but you aren't working right now—you're just my boyfriend in my living room. He doesn't have the right to perv on you when you're not on the clock."

Heart chuckles. "Good point." He kisses my cheek once more and takes the sandwich bag from my hands. "Let's eat; I'm starving."

After lunch, we play *Mario Kart* and eventually order pizza for dinner. All in all, it's the best day ever. I never expected I'd find *one* awesome man, let alone two. But Heart and Lucky? They're sweet to me, always patient...they *get* me. I've never felt this way about anyone before, and it's both scary and exhilarating. I hope like hell they were serious earlier when they said they weren't going anywhere because I'm pretty sure I'm falling in love with both of them.

38

HEART

I guess Lucky decided that subtlety was not the best strategy here, so he told me in no uncertain terms I was responsible for figuring out a date with him. Just him and me, not with Mason. I thought for a minute Mason would be upset about that, would feel left out, but he applauded the idea. He and Lucky have a date planned too, and Mason, the sweetheart, is even trying to figure out something for him and me to do.

When we said we wanted to date with the three of us, it also meant trying to figure out who we are both as couples and as a threesome. It sounds super confusing, but the reality is it that it's all way easier than I could've imagined.

I thought long and hard about what Lucky and I could do together. A movie seemed too easy, almost lazy, and besides, the whole idea is that we get to know each other better. A movie doesn't really accomplish that, unless you combine it with dinner, which makes it even more of a cliché. No, I needed to up my game and come up with something better.

My car is a piece of junk, so I did ask him to pick me up

instead of the other way around. As soon as I get in, he leans in for a chaste kiss on my cheek.

"Seriously?" I scoff. "You're kissing me on the cheek?"

Lucky looks at me for a second as he puts the shift into drive. "With you, it seems the line between chaste and wanting to bury myself inside you is super, super thin. I figured it would be wise to stay on the safe side."

I almost choke on my own breath. Lucky hasn't made a secret of his attraction to me, but this casual admission wasn't what I was expecting. "Uh, thanks, I guess?"

He grins. "Hell, you have no idea how much I need to keep myself in check when it comes to you. Trust me, when our no-sex rule has ended, you and I are gonna create fireworks. Now, where am I driving to?"

It takes me a second to switch gears, and I hand him the address I've written down on a piece of paper. He quickly puts it into the GPS of his car.

"Ah," he says with a happy smile. "We're go-karting. Awesome."

As he drives off, I shoot him a look sideways. "Yeah? You like it? I wasn't sure what to do. I don't have much experience dating."

Yeah, I shouldn't have added that last sentence. Now I come off as a total loser.

Lucky reaches for my hand and quickly squeezes it. "It's gonna sound weird, but that makes me strangely happy. We get to figure this out together. And yes, I love karting."

It's Friday night, so it's a little busy at the karting place, but after fifteen minutes of waiting, it's our turn. We quickly get changed into the required coveralls and safety gear and then endure the equally required explanation of how the equipment works. I haven't done this in a while, so I should probably pay more attention, but I can't drag my eyes off Lucky.

There's maybe twenty of us standing here, only two women amongst us, and something about him draws the attention of all the people in the room. I don't know if it's because he is sexy as fuck, because he is, the coverall he's wearing accentuating his height and build, or if it's because he has this presence about him. He radiates calm and quiet dominance, and he does it in a way that just makes you want to follow him. I can totally see why he thrived in the military. He's the type of man you'd follow into battle.

Once we get seated in our karts, he flashes me a big grin. "Try and keep up."

I grin right back. "Don't choke on my dust."

The race starts, and it's quickly clear that we have a few newbies who have no chance, a few guys who've clearly done this before, and then there is me, Lucky, and four other guys who are taking the lead. Four laps in, I discover something about Lucky I didn't know before. He is competitive as hell.

I don't know if he hates losing in general, or he hates losing to me, but as soon as I've carved out a little lead, I see this concentrated frown on his face as he does everything to catch up with me. He clearly intends not to lose, at least not to me.

The noise of the karts in combination with the helmets we're wearing makes it impossible for us to communicate with each other, but I can almost see the words coming out of his mouth to encourage himself... And to diss me, just a little. And man, I love it.

In the last lap, I manage to increase my gain on him, and we both know there's no chance in hell he'll ever catch up. That doesn't mean he gives up, though. It reinforces my previous conclusion about his competitiveness because he keeps fighting until I cross the finish line. Then he crosses seconds behind me, having managed to gain more than I would've thought possible. We end third and fourth in our group, and I think that's a pretty good result.

I climb out of the kart and take off my helmet, waiting for Lucky to strut over to me, his helmet under his arm.

"Congrats," he says, earning major points in my book with that small word. I love a man who can admit his defeat and be generous toward his competitor. "That was a great race."

"It was," I say.

He steps closer, reaching out with his index finger and gently raising my chin to meet his eyes. Then he leans in and kisses me, a soft, warm kiss that is chaste and incredibly sexy at the same time.

"That was...nice," I say, struggling for words when he lets go of me.

His eyes light up, and the corners of his mouth pull up in a cheeky smile. "Nice? Huh. I guess I have to work on my technique, then."

"Hey, Lucky!" an unfamiliar voice calls out, interrupting us.

Lucky and I turn around at the same time, and a strange guy is walking toward us. He obviously knows Lucky, considering the fact that he called him by his name, but also because his face lights up when he gets closer. He's a wall of muscle, this guy, and he's even taller than Lucky. I wonder how they know each other.

"Dozer," Lucky says with affection, letting go of me and taking a step toward the guy.

A warm and manly embrace follows, one of those hugs straight guys give each other. And suddenly, I know how they know each other, because when his arms come around Lucky, I spot the Semper Fi tattoo on Dozer's arm. He's a Marine, like Lucky.

No wonder he let go of me so quickly. There is no way he's showing this straight as an arrow fellow Marine that first of all, he's gay, and second of all, he's out with a guy like me. His friend may not know I'm a porn star, but even without that, I'm hardly appropriate dating material for a guy like Lucky.

"I haven't seen you in months, man," Dozer says. "How've you been?"

"Good, man. Sorry I missed the last few times you all got together. My life has been pretty crazy."

"Your convicts giving you trouble?" Dozer jokes.

Lucky's face tightens, but it's so subtle that I wonder if his friend even spots it. Then he turns around to face me, and for one second, I think he's going to pretend he doesn't know me, that were not here together. Instead, he reaches out for my hand, and I take it without even thinking about it.

He pulls me forward and turns again to face his friends. "No, I've been busy dating. Dozer, this is my boyfriend..."

There's a pause at the end of a sentence, and it takes me a second to realize it's because he's not sure if he should introduce me as Heart or as Gunner. I'm not sure either. Would he be embarrassed to be seen with a porn star? I only have a split second to decide, and I follow my gut. I don't ever want to have to pretend to be something or someone else than I am. So I reach out my other hand to Dozer.

"I'm Heart," I say, feeling an incredible rush flow through me as Lucky squeezes my other hand, the one he's still holding.

Dozer shakes my hand enthusiastically. "I'm Dozer," he says. "I'm so excited to meet you."

He lets go of my hand and focuses on Lucky again, slapping him on his back. "You lucky bastard; I can't believe you kept this hidden from us. How long have you guys been dating?"

Lucky shrugs. "We've known each other for a while," he says, deftly evading the actual question.

They chat for a little while longer before Dozer rejoins his group. Lucky and I do another round of karting, and he manages to beat me this time. Barely, but he's elated nonetheless.

An hour later, we're hunched over huge burgers in a small, homey diner that's around the corner from the karting place. I've been here a bunch of times before, and their burgers are phenomenal. The whole menu has like ten items on it, but everything is delicious. Lucky seems to think so as well, as he finishes his burger in no time at all.

"Can I ask you something?" he asks me as I'm wiping off my fingers on the napkin.

I shrug. "Sure. Fire away."

"Are you embarrassed to be seen with me?" His eyes never leave mine as his words hang between us.

I frown. "Why would I be embarrassed to be seen with you?"

"Because you thought I would be embarrassed to be seen with you," he says softly, his eyes still trained on me.

He picked up on that, huh? It doesn't surprise me. I've known he was perceptive from the moment I met him. There's not much you can get past him without him noticing.

"Yeah, I thought for a second you were gonna deny you

were there with me," I admit. "You can't really blame me, though, right?"

"Why not?"

"What do you mean, why not?" I ask.

He leans in, his eyes laser sharp. "Why can't I blame you for having that little faith in me? Have I ever given you any indication that I would be ashamed of you?"

Rash words are at the tip of my tongue, but I hold them back. His question deserves my consideration, even if I am tempted to answer it with a quick, heartfelt yes. Of course, I would assume he'd be embarrassed to date me. After all, I am a convicted felon, and he's a parole officer, a Marine, a veteran. He's got this whole...life, friends, family. He's the epitome of a successful man, so what the hell would he want with a former hooker like me?

Then it hits me. Everything I just thought, it's all in my head. He has never mentioned anything like this, has never said that's how he sees me. Other than some hesitations he shared about me doing porn when he was still my parole officer, he has never spoken out against my job. Even though I told him about my past, never brought it up again. Not me whoring myself out, not the stupid things I did for and with Terry, none of it.

"It doesn't bother you, who I am?" I shake my head as I hear my own words. That did not come out right, not the way I had intended it. "No, that's not what I meant. Like, my past... I told you what I did to survive. That doesn't bother you?"

He reaches for my hand, and I let them take it, the coldness inside me thawing a little when his big hand wraps around mine. "Of course, it bothers me," he says softly. "But not for the reason you think. It bothers me to think that was the only option you had. It bothers me to think that you had to do something you didn't want, just to survive. It bothers me to know that no one was there to take care of you. It bothers me that you had so little self-worth and so few other options, that you got trapped into an abusive relationship. That is what bothers me, not you. Never you."

When I look up from the table I've been studying for the last minute or so, Lucky's eyes are still fixed on me, warm, compassionate. Loving. And for the first time, I start to believe that he sees something more in me than just my body.

39

LUCKY

It's dawn when my alarm goes off. Usually, I don't even set an alarm on my day off, but we have something special planned for today. Next to me, Mason groans in protest, a sound that is echoed by Heart on my other side.

A rush warms my blood at the incredible joy of waking up with these two men. I love waking up like this, even at this ungodly hour. They started sleeping over the last few days, and I love it. It's only two weeks till my no-sex period with Heart is up...and I can't wait.

I hope I've shown him how much I care about him. Unlike Mason, he still keeps his emotions close most of the times. I can't blame him, but I long for the day he accepts us into his heart.

"Remind me, why the hell did I agree to this?" Heart grumbles. "Is it even light out? Is the sun even up? Because I refuse to get up before the sun. That's like, inhuman."

I grin as I gather both my boys in my arms and kiss their heads, first Mason, then Heart. "It's a good thing you guys were never in the military. You wouldn't have survived a week."

Mason opens one eye and sighs. "Just the thought of being in the military is enough to make me throw up. Can we please just snooze for half an hour more? I'm with Heart; I really don't think we're supposed to get up before the sun is out."

Excitement about the day I have planned for us has me wide awake, and I can't help but laugh at the protests of these two. "I guess I'll just have to kiss you awake then," I say softly, before rolling over on top of Heart and covering his mouth with mine.

He is pliant in my arms, so much more pliant than usual, his body still half asleep. But his mouth quickly wakes up, and it opens for my intrusion. He lets out a soft little moan as I gently kiss him. Another part of his body is definitely awake as well, his morning wood poking me in the leg.

Mason cuddles up against us, and I take my mouth off Heart and lean over to kiss him as well. After a few minutes of kissing, I'm convinced the both of them are sufficiently awake, so I roll off them and get out of bed.

"Where are you going?" Mason pouts. "We were just getting to the good stuff." He lazily rubs his cock, which is as hard as Heart's...and mine. But we don't have time for that right now because I know once we get started, it's going to take at least half an hour, and I want to get on the road. Plus, our two months of no sex are almost up, and I'm not breaking my rule with Heart this close to the finish line... which would absolutely happen if I don't leave the bed right fucking now.

"You can rub one out in the shower, as long as you hurry the fuck up. Remember, we agreed to be out of the house by five-thirty. That means you each have about fifteen minutes to get ready."

Heart pushes himself up and rolls over on his stomach,

looking at me like a puppy, and I just took away his favorite toy. "You missed your calling in life as a drill sergeant," he says.

I shoot him an amused look as I pull on my boxers. "Dude, my drill sergeant was nowhere near as friendly as I am right now. If he'd ordered you to get out of bed, you would've done so a second after the command, trust me. Now, stop whining and get your ass in gear. I'm heading out at five thirty, with or without you guys."

We all know this is an empty threat, as I would never leave without them. The whole point of today was to spend some more time together. Grumbling, Heart and Mason finally get out of bed and a few minutes later, they're in the shower. Together. I hear them giggling as I make my way to the kitchen to pour the coffee I programmed into the coffee maker yesterday into our travel mugs and put the last things into the cooler. I prepared everything yesterday, so we could get out of here early this morning.

I have little doubt as to what they're up to in the shower, but it's fine with me. I can spare the five minutes it will take them to get each other off, and it will certainly improve their moods. It's what we call a win-win.

We're out the door six minutes after the agreed time, and to me, that's a success. I'm driving, as I usually am, and the roads are blissfully empty this time of day. Well, empty by LA standards anyway. There is always traffic; it's just not as bad as it usually is.

"Wow," Mason says as we get closer to our destination. "I had no idea this was so close to the city."

Heart, who is riding shotgun, looks over his shoulder with an amused smile. "Admit it, baby, you're not exactly the outdoors type."

Mason shrugs, in no way offended. "True, but I guess I'm

just surprised that there's all of this so close to a major metropolitan area in the country."

He gestures out the window at the landscape that has changed into the rugged beauty of Joshua Tree National Park. I've been here many times before, and Heart said he visited once, many years ago, but Mason has never been here.

"I appreciate you leaving your natural city habitat to explore nature with us, baby," I say to him. "I know you were a little apprehensive about this, and I appreciate you giving it a try."

"It's not that I don't like trying new things," Mason says, then he frowns. "Well, maybe I do have a little resistance to trying new things, but it was more that I was scared of all the trouble I could get into here. We all know I'm not the most coordinated person on the planet, so forgive me if the idea of breaking a few bones in some deserted national park didn't really appeal to me."

A smile splits my face open. "You're such a little drama queen," I say.

"Are you still a drama queen if you legit worry about things that could happen?" Heart wonders. "It's not like he's exaggerating about his lack of coordination, you know."

"True," I admit. "Let's just try to not break anything today okay?" I say as I park the car at the entrance of the park.

"That sounds like a plan," Mason says.

He opens the door to get out and promptly trips over his own feet, managing to avoid a fall by holding onto the car door rather inelegantly. I get out of the car as well and look at him, shaking my head. "You were saying?"

Mason's cheeks stain with that adorable blush he gets when he's a little flustered. "Sorry?"

I reach out for his wrist and gently tug until he steps in for a hug. "Some days, I just want to wrap you in bubble wrap to make sure you're safe. Just promise me you'll be careful today, baby."

Once I have picked up an updated park map, we get back into the car to drive farther into the park. I know a few excellent spots for a short, easy hike that's perfect for these two novices.

"It's beautiful here," Heart says with a sense of wonder in his voice as we get out of the car at the first spot I picked.

It's still early, just before eight-thirty, and the park is all but empty. The air smells fresh, energetic, and I inhale deeply, closing my eyes for a second. There's something about nature that calms me, steadies me.

I love the city, and unlike my brother, I could never live as far off the grid as he does. Sure, for a weekend or maybe even a week, but I would go crazy if I had to spend time out of the city for that long. But every now and then, I need to escape. I need to breathe, feel the wide-open spaces around me.

I hand Heart the backpack I packed for him and watch as he puts it on, making sure he tightens it properly. He looks different in his outdoor outfit and the new hiking boots I made him buy. He wore them a few times to break them in, and I think it's enough to prevent blisters, because we're not gonna make that many miles today. Once I'm satisfied he's good, I turn to Mason.

"Your turn, baby. Your backpack is a lot lighter, so I hope it won't bother you."

Mason takes it, testing the weight with one hand. "Why is it lighter than yours? Shouldn't we divide the weight equally?"

I shake my head. "I'm used to it, you're not. You're only

carrying your own water and food, Heart has some added supplies, and I'm carrying the rest."

Mason puts his backpack on, and I tighten the straps until it fits snugly against his back, then adjust the chest and waist band. "How much heavier is yours?" he asks.

I smile, then kiss him on his nose. "Trust me, you don't want to know. A lot heavier than yours, let's just leave it at that."

Heart chuckles. "Was that a subtle version of 'don't you worry your pretty little head about it'?"

Mason sputters as I grin. "That about sums it up. Thanks for ratting me out."

Mason's indignance is quickly forgotten as we start the trail I have picked out. Within minutes, their faces reflect the same sense of wonder I always experience in this place. You can't help but be almost overcome by the desolate beauty of the landscape. You would think that a combination of desert, rocks, and strangely formed trees would not be much to look at, but it's stunning.

It's honestly hard to describe to someone who's never been here, but a friend I once did a long hike here with described it as otherworldly. I think he's right. It does sometimes feel like a different planet, like how a movie director imagined a scene taking place on a strange planet in a science fiction movie.

"Is it my imagination, or is it actually cooler here?" Heart asks me after a while.

"It is. People often associate desert with hot, but the Mojave Desert is actually a bit higher and thus cooler. It's still dry here, but at night, the temperatures can drop pretty low compared to surrounding areas. It's one of the reasons why I always bring extra clothes when hiking here, as well as a warming blanket. Then again, I always bring those, no matter where I hike."

"So, if you go by yourself, what kind of hiking do you do here?" Heart asks. "Because don't deny it, I know we're slowing you down."

"We?" Mason asks with a laugh. "You mean me."

Heart sends him an affectionate smile, then carefully pulls him close and kisses him gently on his lips. "Even if that is true, we don't care. We love you just the way you are."

The three of us freeze in our tracks. Heart just casually dropped the L word, and I don't think either of us knows how to react. Does he mean it?

It's the same word that's been floating in my brain pretty much since the three of us decided to try a relationship together. I'm not there yet, but I'm close...but was that really what Heart meant to say as well?

Heart looks like a frightened animal, and I take pity on him. "He's right, baby. We love you just the way you are."

I see Heart's shoulders relax, and Mason loses that scared look on his face. I guess my words helped normalize Heart's expression and not make it so emotionally heavy, even if that's pretty damn close to how I feel.

40

HEART

Me and my stupid big mouth. My father always warned me that my big mouth would get me in trouble, and as much as I hate the bastard, I think he was right about this one. I learned to be a lot more guarded in prison and not blurt out everything that pops up in my head, but I find myself lowering my defenses when I'm around Lucky and Mason.

They make me feel more relaxed than I've been in a long time, maybe even before I went to prison. Let's face it, the last two years with Terry were anything but relaxing. I knew he was bad news; I just chose to ignore it. It's that head-in-the-sand strategy that got me into so much trouble.

Thank fuck Lucky chose to save my ass by affirming my comment or things could have gotten awkward really fast. What the hell was I thinking, using a word like *love*? And yet it came so naturally...

But I can't be in love with Mason, can I? Not when I'm also seeing Lucky. It doesn't make sense. It's supposed to be fun, relaxed, just fooling around. At some point, Mason and Lucky will realize they're perfect for each other and don't need me for anything else than maybe some kinky sex.

Though if they're only in it for the sex, then why won't Lucky have sex with me? Why is he stubbornly holding onto the two-month thing? And it's not because he doesn't want me, because I know he does. He gets hard every time we make out.

I ponder this as we continue on the trail, Lucky leading the way and me closing our short procession. I've known from the moment we met that Lucky was interested in me. Granted, I had a hard time reading him, and at first, I wasn't convinced he was gay. I'd pegged him as bi-curious, maybe, or a closeted gay. Discovering that he was out and proud surprised me. I don't know why. Maybe it's because he has this vibe about him when you don't know him well, this somewhat aloof and stern appearance.

But even then, I sensed his interest in me. He hid it well, but it was a flicker of interest that caught in his eyes every now and then, the slight reaction of his body to me, to my presence, that gave him away. That's why I thought he wanted me, for sex. Nothing else.

So, his proposal of taking sex out of the equation, it's confusing to me. I just have a hard time imagining what he sees in me other than a body. Someone he wants to fuck. How could he possibly be interested in me any other way? And yet I can't come to any other conclusion than that he is because he's gone out of his way to show me over the last two months.

Like today, this is as far from a sexually loaded date as you could possibly imagine. Look at us, we're more dressed for comfort and convenience than to look our best, although I have to admit Lucky looks hot as fuck in his black shirt and black cargo pants. If you want to seduce someone, if you're serious about ending your date on some kind of sex fest, you don't take them out for a hike in Joshua Tree. You wine and dine them, maybe go to a sappy movie or something. All of it suggests that Lucky was honest when he said he was interested in me as a person and not just my body. Plus, he's not showing any signs of being more interested in Mason than in me.

We've hiked for a good hour when Mason indicates he's ready for a break. I'm amazed he even made it this far, as he's not exactly the sporty type. I have to give him credit for coming along and trying his best. We find a spot in the shade with a few large rocks behind us. Mason wants to sit down, but Lucky stops him.

"Always check before sitting down," he says.

"Check for what?" Mason asks, frowning.

"Anything. Snakes, spiders, scorpions. Vegetation that could hurt you, like poison ivy."

Mason's eyes grow big. "There are scorpions here?" Then he frowns. "You're messing with me. There's no poison ivy here."

Lucky has finished his inspection of the rocks where we intend to sit down and now looks up at Mason with a kind smile. "No, there's not, but it's a good habit to have. No matter where you are, you have to train yourself to check before you sit down anywhere. It could potentially avoid a lot of nasty surprises."

Just to make sure, I double-check the rock I picked to sit on before I lower myself. I carefully take the backpack off my shoulders and grab a water bottle, drinking half of it before I twist the cap back on and put it back. "Let me guess, you were a Boy Scout," I say to Lucky, who has also found a spot to sit.

"I was," he says with a smile. "But my dad taught me

most of this. Both my parents are avid outdoors fans, and they took us hiking plenty of times. My dad had near endless patience teaching Ranger and me this kind of stuff and other survival skills he learned on duty."

"Your dad was in the military, too?" I ask with my mouth full, enjoying the delicious sandwiches Lucky made us.

Lucky nods. "He was a Marine, like me. He served for thirteen years until he sustained an injury to his foot and had to take an honorable discharge. So, he was a civilian from the time when I was ten or so. I do remember him being gone for long periods on his tours as a younger kid, but he took a regular job after his return to civilian life, so I also had a lot of time with him during my teenage years. I lucked out with him. He's an awesome dad."

I can't help the pang of envy inside me. What I wouldn't have given for a dad like that. Maybe my life would've turned out completely different if I'd had someone who was happy to spend time with me, rather than seeing me as a nuisance, a disappointment.

"Do your parents still live here?" Mason asks.

"No, they live in Florida now. My mom's sister developed early Alzheimer's, and they decided to move close to her so she would have family nearby. They're planning on moving back here after she passes away, which they expect to be pretty soon."

"What about your parents, Mason?" I ask Mason.

"My mom passed away when I was young, and I don't remember her. My dad is..." Mason seems to seek for words, his nose crumpled. "My dad is super sweet and nice, just socially anxious, I guess. He decided to homeschool me until high school, to prevent me from getting bullied. I totally get it, and I'm not saying it was the wrong decision, but it didn't keep me from being socially awkward as well.

When I did go to high school, I'd sort of missed out on the chance to learn how to make friends naturally. I wasn't really bullied, more left to myself, but I never made any friends. It's...it's still not easy for me, connecting with others."

He looks at me from between his lashes, a soft blush staining his cheeks. "If Troy hadn't sort of pushed us together, I'm not sure I would've ever found the courage to even talk to you. You have, like, this cool factor that is so way out of my league it's not even funny."

He turns to Lucky. "And the same is true for you. I have literally no idea what the two of you are doing with me unless you were actively looking for a way to drag down your cool quotient."

I never know what to say when Mason says something like this. It's so contrary to my experience with him, that it's hard for me to figure out how to counter it. It's clearly how he feels, but do I deny it? Do I express that I experience it completely differently?

Lucky puts the bottle he was drinking from down, then gestures Mason over. "Come sit with me for a spell, baby," he says.

Mason doesn't hesitate but gets up and moves from the rock he was sitting onto Lucky's leg, nestling against him.

"I don't know what happened to you to make you believe that you are not cool or somehow less cool than we are," Lucky says. "But I want you to know it's not true. We don't see you as less in any way."

"But you can't deny I'm awkward," Mason whispers. "Both socially and literally. I mean, I stumble over my own feet constantly."

"It's endearing," I say. "It doesn't bother me. It doesn't make me see you as less. It's just one of your quirks that makes you who you are, like Lucky only wearing certain colors or the fact that he likes his routines. It's just a part of who you are."

Much to my surprise, Mason's eyes well up. "Then why do I always feel less?"

Lucky pulls him closer, and I can see his arms tighten around Mason. "Maybe because someone used your insecurities against you, fed them," Lucky says.

"You mean my ex," Mason says.

I nod in agreement. "Lucky is right. I think you had these insecurities, and he used them to make you feel even smaller. It's what abusive people do. Anything to take power away from you. Anything to make you feel useless, hopeless, trapped."

I realize I've revealed too much when both Lucky and Mason look at me with compassion in their eyes. "What about your dad, Heart?" Mason asks me.

Lucky cringes, almost imperceptibly, and somehow, that comforts me. He didn't ask the question, because he knows the pain this will trigger. But Mason doesn't know any better, and if I reject him right now, if I in any way show him how much even the question hurts me, I will affirm every negative feeling he has about himself. I can't hurt him, I won't.

"My dad was not a good man...and that's an understatement. He was a Marine, too, but not a good one. At least, not from what I've heard. He started out well, had pretty good career, I guess. I don't know much about it, but he made it to Gunnery Sergeant, and that's a pretty decent rank."

"It is," Lucky confirms. "I never made it that far, but my dad was one, too."

"What happened?" Mason asks.

I shrug. "I don't know exactly. I tried to find out, but my

mom didn't want to talk about it, and the few friends my dad had turned out to be tight-lipped. All I know is that he changed. My mom says it was because of an injury that prevented him from going back to active duty. They didn't discharge him, but he was placed in an administrative position, and apparently, he hated being sidelined. He got... aggressive, at home but also at work. He was written up a few times for disturbances. Finally, he managed to bribe his way back onto active duty, where he was killed in action."

Mason gazes at me with compassion, but it's the look in Lucky's eyes that brings me to my knees. There's this mix of pride and profound sadness that tells me he can read between the lines. He knows what I mean when I say aggressive, and the sadness is for that part, but he's also proud of me for finally opening up. It's just a glimpse I'm showing here because I need to test the waters.

Maybe because I'm not sure how Mason will react. Maybe because I'm worried Lucky will slip back into parole officer mode. Maybe because if this is supposed to be casual, as I keep insisting, I have no business bringing up my dad, or anything in my past. And maybe, just maybe, because I've never told a soul, and even sharing this tidbit feels surprisingly good.

Then Lucky holds out his other hand to me, and I find myself responding. Before I know it, I'm perched on his other leg, leaning against him as well. And that's how we sit for a little bit, Mason on one leg and me on the other, both with a strong arm around us. I've never felt more complete in my life, and it scares the fuck out of me.

41

LUCKY

I'm awake first, as usual. For some reason, I tend to end up in between my two boys, but today Mason and Heart are wrapped in each other's arms as they sleep, which allows me to slip out of the bed unnoticed. It's only six-thirty in the morning, way too early for the both of them to be awake, but I've always been an early riser.

I pick out a fresh pair of boxers from a drawer, closing it softly so I don't wake them, then drag a clean shirt over my head, and head into the hallway, closing the door gently behind me. My guess is I won't see the two of them until eight at the earliest, probably later.

Heart seems to have a thing for sleeping in whenever he's not expected at work early. He told me it had to do with not feeling safe enough to sleep in for a long time, and then being in prison where you had to get up at a certain time. I guess it makes total sense, and I love that he has that freedom now. Plus, he was back home late yesterday after a night out with the boys. Mason joined him as well, and I would've loved to, but I had to work.

Home. When did I start to think of my apartment as home not just for myself but for the three of us?

I stand in the doorway to the living room and look around. The evidence of two extra people in my living space is undeniable. Mason is pretty good about cleaning his stuff up, but Heart is a first-class slob. He tries, and I appreciate that, but despite that, I spot a pair of his boxers, socks, a backpack, a book he was reading, and a trail of crumbs where he ate some cookies two days ago. I've resisted the urge to clean them, hoping Heart would see them and do it himself, but I guess that's a lost cause.

There's some irony in the fact that a structured, organized guy like me who is so set in his routines, got involved in a threesome. And not just any threesome, but one with a guy who would forget to eat if he didn't set his timer and another guy who seems to bring chaos wherever he goes.

Mason has to be the most distracted guy on the planet. Yesterday, he showed up wearing two different socks. And not just any socks, one was black and the other was bright yellow. Aside from the fact that I have never seen bright yellow socks in my life, I honestly wondered how distracted he would have to be to put a black sock and a yellow sock on and not notice they were different. It's classic Mason, and you can't help but be endeared by it. The fact that he's so cute and adorable helps.

I lower myself on the armrest of my couch and study the relative mess in my living room. To most people, it would still look pretty neat, but I've always been rather...I guess you could call it strict, about keeping my house clean and tidy.

My mom says I've always been like that, even as a teen. She suspected it had something to do with us moving a few times, and me needing the comfort that order in my own space would bring me. Obviously, she never protested much. I don't know if she's right, but it sounds as good an explanation as any. Spending time in the military certainly satisfied my need for structure.

By all accounts then, the mess that inevitably follows Heart wherever he goes should bother me, right? And it does a little, but not to the extent I would've expected. When they first stayed over, I was a little anxious about it, knowing it would bring a bit of a mess. But it doesn't bother me nearly as much as I thought it would, and I wonder why.

I do know one thing, Heart is doing the best he can in cleaning up and expecting anything more would be unrealistic. So, I get up from my position on the couch and get the few items he's left on the floor. I don't want to vacuum the crumbs right now, not even with the hand vacuum, certain that it would wake them. Instead, I spray the coffee table and wipe it clean. There, that looks good enough.

I decide to go for a quick run, so I grab my shoes from the hallway closet, happily remembering that I have running clothes on the clothes rack in the laundry room. I never throw them in the dryer. Technically, they should be able to handle it, but they're pretty expensive, and I just don't want to run the risk of them shrinking or getting damaged. I always line dry them, and since I did a round of laundry two days ago, they're still there. Perfect.

I write a quick note so the boys know where I am, then put a key in the little pocket in my running shorts and head out. When I come back an hour later, there's still no sign of them being awake. I guzzle down a bottle of water, and then decide to get started on breakfast. If I'm awake and I can't shower out of fear of waking them up, I might as well make myself useful and prepare us some breakfast.

Lord knows out of the three of us, I'm the only one

who's a decent cook, though Heart is certainly trying to improve his skills and seems open to suggestions. Mason, we're all pretty much in agreement on, should stay out of the kitchen. For his sake as much as ours...and the kitchen's.

I'm not a big bread fan, preferring either eggs or something with yogurt in the morning. But eggs will get cold if I don't know what time they'll wake up, so I decide to prepare us a little healthy granola. I use store-bought granola when I have to, but I prefer to make my own. It's super easy, actually. All you have to do is roast a mix of oatmeal and various seeds and nuts in the oven. To make it crispier and to prevent it from burning, you have to mix it with something liquid. I use a mixture of maple syrup and unsweetened applesauce.

The smell the mixture gives off during roasting makes my mouth water, and I can't wait for it to be done. In the meantime, I cut some fresh strawberries and bananas and mix them with the Greek yogurt. Just as I pull the granola mixture out of the oven to let it cool, I hear movement from the bedroom. Mason's giggle is one of the best sounds you could ever imagine. It's this happy, carefree laughter, and it's infectious.

By the time they stumble into the kitchen, I've set the small table I have in the kitchen with breakfast for the three of us.

"Good morning," I say, smiling at Heart's hair, which is literally sticking up in every direction possible.

Heart stretches, his lean muscles rippling as he lets out a loud yawn. He's only wearing bright blue boxers that fit snugly around that gorgeous butt of his, and I have a hard time dragging my eyes away.

When he's done stretching, he sends me a sweet smile.

"Good morning. I see someone was awake bright and early?"

There is an awkward moment as the three of us hesitate how to greet each other. We haven't found a rhythm yet, I guess, the kind of rhythm that people who have been in a relationship longer have. Those kinds of rituals grow over time, but we're not there yet after only two weeks of sleeping over.

Because I think he needs it the most from me, I step in to greet Heart properly first. His eyes widen in surprise, but then his smile spreads across his face as he offers me his lips. I kiss him, letting myself drown in the sensation of those soft lips on mine. My hands go around him, my right hand specifically cupping his ass, squeezing it gently.

He plasters himself against me, losing himself in the kiss. His hands curl around my neck, pulling me closer. He lets out a soft little moan into my mouth, and the sound shoots straight to my balls. I'm seriously tempted to forget all about breakfast and simply drag down those provocative boxers and feast on his ass instead. God, I want to eat him out. He tastes better than any breakfast I could create. But I won't. A few more days until our time is up...and I won't break my word.

"Mmmm," he says when we finally let go, both slightly panting. "Now that's what I call a good morning kiss."

Mason stands to the side, watching us with a guarded expression. Without letting go of Heart, I reach out my hand to him. "Come join us, honey. I want to kiss you properly too."

"He smells delicious," Heart says. Before I realize what he's planning, his tongue comes out, and he licks my neck, then bites it. "He tastes delicious too, all sweaty."

With a smile, Mason steps into our embrace, and I pull

him toward me as soon as he's within reach. He's still fragile, our boy, so easily feeling left out. I don't think he needs words right now. He needs to feel he's part of us.

So, I sling my left arm around him, still holding on to Heart with my right arm, and pull Mason in for a kiss. He latches onto my mouth with something close to desperation, and I'm happy my instincts were spot on. He needs us, as much as we need him.

I plunge my tongue into his mouth with aggression, needing him to feel how much I want him to. He opens up for me instantly, allowing me access to his sweet mouth. I chase his tongue until he lets himself be caught, and then he does that sucking thing Heart taught him, and I moan.

My cock, which had grown hard during my kiss with Heart and hasn't let up since, is now peeping from under my waistband, trying to escape the tightness of my running underwear. Mason ruts against me, and I don't know if it's an innocent move or if he shares my need for friction, but I push back against him, reveling in the sensation it brings.

Heart's hand is still on my neck, and now he's pulling me off Mason toward him, and I seamlessly switch from one mouth to another. Our heads are close together, and it's a hot, wet mix of mouths and tongues that find each other, chase each other, the three of us pressed against each other with no room to spare.

All thoughts of breakfast are forgotten, and a thundering want storms through my system. I want them. I want them now.

But how do we do this without one of us feeling left out? Mason is so easily hurt, but so is Heart, still not convinced I like him as much as Mason... Or that I like him for anything else but his body, no matter how much he assures me he believes me. And I don't want to break our two-month rule.

"Hey, Mase," Heart whispers against Mason's lips. "Are you up for another lesson?"

Mason nods eagerly, his hair all messed up, and his lips swollen and glistening. "What are we doing today?" he asks, excitement clearly audible in his voice.

Heart's eyes meet mine as he says, "I'm going to introduce you to the joy of rimming. I'm going to show you how to drive Lucky absolutely insane to the point where he'll be begging for release."

In that moment, I realize two things. The first is that I'm about to experience the rimming of a lifetime. The second is that all of a sudden, I know why the little mess that Heart leaves behind in my apartment doesn't bother me.

I love him.

Somehow, somewhere along the way, I have fallen completely, head over heels in love with him as well. He's mine, ours, and we're never going to let him go. Now, all we need to do is convince him of that truth.

42

HEART

Something passes over Lucky's face that I can't identify. Not a bad thing, but it's like he's had some profound realization or something. I don't know, maybe I'm imagining things.

"You game?" I ask, as much to Mason as to Lucky.

Mason looks at Lucky first as if to ask approval. "Hell yes," Lucky says. "As if I'm gonna say no to getting rimmed. Just, let me get myself cleaned up, okay? I want Mason's first experience to be good."

I don't think I've ever met a more considerate man than Lucky Stone. I love how he's always careful with Mason, gentle both with his body and his emotions.

"Sounds good," I say. "We'll be waiting for you, right, Mase?"

Lucky gives us both a last kiss before dashing into the bathroom. It's not till then that I realize he's set out a breakfast for us. I point toward the bowls with yogurt and fruit. "Let me put these in the fridge."

"I'll help," Mason says, then catches himself. "Maybe not. We don't want things to end up on the floor."

I snicker as I quickly put the bowls in the fridge. "Unless it's you. I would totally do you on the floor."

Mason inspects the floor with a serious look on his face. "It doesn't look all that comfortable," he says. "But at least it's clean enough."

I laugh even louder. "Dude, floor sex is about as uncomfortable as it gets. My advice: don't do it, unless you have carpet, in which case you want to be very careful you don't end up with a horrible case of rug burn."

"Rug burn? How do you end up with rug burn?" Mason asks.

I grabbed his hand and tug him toward the bedroom, while I answer him. "For instance, when you kneel on a rug and then get fucked doggy style for, like, twenty minutes. I don't know what the guy's issue was, but he had a hard time coming, and by the time he did, my knees were killing me. I had rug burn for a week, not kidding. Last time I ever did it on a carpet."

Mason is still chuckling, his hand in front of his mouth, when I tackle him onto the bed and settle myself on top of him.

"Hey! I thought you were going to teach me how to rim," he protests.

I move my mouth so close to his our breaths mingle. "I will, but I figured until Lucky gets back, you and I could do a little...warming up."

I wait a second or two to make sure he has no objections, but before I can initiate anything, he drags my mouth down and kisses me. By the time Lucky steps out of the bathroom, Mason is a whimpering mess on the bed, the front of his boxers soaked with precum. Not that mine fare much better, as my cock has been leaking like crazy too.

I notice with satisfaction that Lucky is still rock hard. It's even more visible now, since he's taken off his shorts and is buck naked, his rigid cock sticking out. I love his body. He's not overly bulky like some guys, but you can feel the strength in his muscles when he holds you...and when he fucks you, I'd imagine. God, I can't wait to experience *that*.

"I could watch you two for hours," Lucky says with a mix of lust and happiness in his eyes.

I love that he is not hesitant to join us but instead rolls onto the bed behind me, his hands immediately reaching out for both of us. I roll over him to his other side so he's in the middle, and my heart grows warm as I watch him kiss Mason again gently.

"Did Heart take good care of you when I was in the shower?" he asks. His hands drift to Mason's groin, and he squeezes it. "It looks like you're...excited."

Mason puts his teeth in his bottom lip. "I am, but I'm also a bit scared. I don't know if I'm gonna like it. It looks sexy when I see Heart do it in his videos, but I'm just not sure if it's something I'm gonna like... Or if I'm going to be any good at it."

"Baby, I am fine with whatever you want to do, you know that. If it turns out you don't like it, you stop. Simple as that. There are enough fun things we can do together that you do like, right? I'm proud of you for trying new things and for allowing Heart to teach you stuff," Lucky says, his voice soft and warm.

I can see Mason relax, his shoulders coming down and the tightness around his mouth disappearing. Then Lucky adds, "And remember, baby, you thought you weren't good at kissing and blowjobs, and that turned out to be a lie as well."

"True," Mason admits, and it's the first time I hear him

confirm that what Brad told him was a lie. I'm so happy to see him gain confidence, even if it's in little steps.

Mason gives Lucky one last kiss, then sits up and looks at me with an adorable smile. "Okay, let's do this."

Spontaneity is still a ways off, but I'll take eagerness and honest curiosity over that any day. I give Lucky a wink, and the smile he sends back at me affirms we're on the same page here. We're gonna make this good for Mason, though I certainly intend to make it good for Lucky as well.

I pull Mason down, so the two of us are side to side between Lucky's legs, which he has helpfully spread as wide as possible. It gives us complete access to his ass. "Technically, rimming is focused on your asshole, but let's not get micro-focused here. You can fluidly move from a blowjob into rimming and vice versa, and give the man's balls a little attention in between. If you handle them gently, ball play can be incredibly satisfying. Now, not everyone is equally sensitive here, and not everyone likes the same sensations, so we'll have to figure out what Lucky likes. Fortunately for us, the man is good at communicating what he wants, so we should have no issue gauging his reactions."

Mason sends me a look that has more confidence than I've ever seen from him. "So maybe I start with loving his balls a little?" he asks.

"Excellent suggestion. Use your hands and fingers first to see where his sensitive spots are."

I take Lucky's left testicle into my hand, showing Mason how to gently roll it. He copies my move with Lucky's other nut, and I can feel the man's muscles tense underneath us.

"Let's see if this is a sensitive spot for him," I say, and I wet my index finger thoroughly in my mouth, then slide it slowly from the spot behind Lucky's balls all the way to his hole. His muscles contract as he forces himself to stay still, but a soft moan escapes his lips.

"Oh," Mason says, "I think he likes that. Can I try?"

"He sure does. Go ahead."

Mason repeats my move, and Lucky shows a bit more of a reaction, which elates Mason. He's like a kid in a candy store who discovered a new candy he really loves.

"Next, we're going to use our mouth and tongue. Lucky's balls are pretty big, so I'm not sure they'll fit into your mouth since you've never done this before, so you may want to start with just licking them."

Mason all but dives into it, his tongue peeping out of his mouth, taking a few careful licks. I guess he likes the taste, because his tongue comes out completely, and he laps around Lucky's balls, leaving them tight and glistening. There's no doubt the man loves this, as his hands clench into fists, and a series of low noises flow from his lips.

Inspired, I move my head in as well, and then Mason and I lick him together, our tongues finding each other, then him, then each other again. It's a sloppy, wet kiss that leaves drool all over the place, but it's sexy as fuck.

"Show me how you suck his balls," Mason tells me, and I gladly comply.

I wasn't lying; Lucky's balls are big. But I have a bit more experience with this than Mason. So, I open my mouth wide and take one nut in. As soon as it's enveloped in my mouth, Lucky moans, and that intensifies as I gently suck, then use my tongue to put pressure on various points. By the time I'm done with his other ball, Lucky's cock is almost quivering with tension. Mason notices it too, and without asking, he bends over to lick the pearls of fluid off the tip.

"Oh fuck," Lucky moans. "You two are going to kill me."

We haven't even gotten to the actual rimming yet.

I push Lucky's left leg back a little farther and gesture at Mason to do the same at the right side. It lifts his ass up to us like a buffet, and I'm almost sad I can't claim the sole privilege of eating him out.

I show Mason how to lick a trail from Lucky's balls back to his hole, which by the time Mason gets there, is actually quivering. Lucky is still fisting the sheets with both hands, and it looks like he's fighting hard to let us have our way with him.

"Now what?" Mason asks.

I smile. "Now, you dig in."

43

MASON

A few months ago, I would've been endlessly intimidated by the sight of a man like Lucky, ass up with his cheeks spread, waiting for me to give him pleasure. But with Heart at my side I'm more determined than intimidated.

I lean in and tentatively swipe my tongue against Lucky's pucker. He moans, and I do it again, this time a little more slowly.

"That's right; don't be shy," Heart encourages. "God, I want to suck him while you do that," he laments.

Lucky lets out a strangled whimper at Heart's declaration.

"We're so close to the two months," Lucky argues, with a desperate edge in his voice.

Spurred on by the noises Lucky is making, I spread his cheeks wider and lick deeper until my tongue is inside him, fucking him. I want to make him feel so good he loses his mind.

"Please let him, Lucky. I want this to be the best rimming you've ever had, and I know Heart's mouth on you will only make it better. Please?" I beg, grazing my teeth along the curve of his ass cheek.

Lucky groans in defeat and clenches the sheets in his fists. "Okay. Yes."

Heart smiles widely and scrambles onto his back and then wiggles his way under Lucky while I return to licking his hole.

Lucky curses and bucks his hips, and I look down to see Heart has managed to maneuver his way under Lucky, and I assume he's sucking him as promised. I run my hands over the taut muscles of Lucky's back and ass, squeezing the firm globes in my hands while continuing to lick as deep inside him as my tongue can reach. His hole is so tight around my tongue, I have to wonder if he's ever bottomed.

The distinct popping sound of a cock being released from the tight confines of a mouth makes my own cock throb.

"Use a finger too, Mase," Heart instructs, and then sloppy sucking can be heard again.

Lucky's hole is dripping with my saliva so I don't bother to go in search of any lube. I work my index finger in alongside my tongue, and Lucky's fists twist his sheets. Curses and incoherent babbling from Lucky join the symphony of noises in the bedroom.

I add a second finger and angle it in search of his prostate.

"Oh god, right there, I'm...oh fuck." Hearing a man like Lucky—typically completely in control—fall apart from our mouths is a heady feeling, and it has my cock leaking and my balls aching for release.

Lucky's already tight channel clamps down around my fingers and tongue, his hips flexing as he empties himself into Heart's mouth. With my free hand, I shove my underwear down and grasp my cock. It only takes two strokes to follow Lucky over the edge, shooting my release all over the back of his thighs as pleasure rages through me.

Heart's satisfied cry joins the fray moments later and then we all collapse in a sweaty, sticky heap.

"I liked that, can we do that again?" I say after I catch my breath.

"Yes, please," Lucky mumbles, sounding like he's about ready to fall back asleep.

"I call middle man next time," Heart quips.

"Yeah, if three of us in bed is going to work we're going to need to set up some sort of rotation." I surprise myself with the joke, but it feels so good to blurt something like that without worrying that either of them will like me less.

We lie in heap for a while, kissing and talking occasionally until Heart's stomach growls.

"I guess that protein shake wasn't enough," he jokes, and Lucky gives him a pinch on the ass that makes Heart squeal.

"Let's get you boys fed, then we can figure out the rest of the day."

∼

I GRAB my laptop and settle onto the couch. I've always loved the quiet solitude of my apartment, but after spending the weekend with Lucky and Heart, it's not as appealing in here as it usually is. But both of them have work today, and I have some coding and other classwork to finish up on.

With my second to last semester wrapping up, I know I should get my resume together and start applying to jobs as well. But the thought is overwhelming as hell. Troy started looking months ago and hasn't landed anything yet; why would it be any different for me? Everyone thinks going into anything tech related is a no-brainer these days, but the industry is competitive, and there is no shortage of people trying to become the next Steve Wozniak or Neil Druckmann.

I pull up my email and immediately delete a bunch of junk. Then one catches my eye.

MR. MASON REDMAN,

I'm reaching out from Blue Star Games. We're a small, indie developer located in Escondido, California. Quite by chance I stumbled upon a game I understand you helped to design, Breakup Artist? *The reason I'm contacting you is because that game is brilliant, well put together, and genius in its simplicity. I don't know if you are currently seeking a position, but I'd love to speak with you further. I've contacted your co-developer as well. We feel that the two of you would make an incredible addition to our team. I look forward to hearing from you.*

Marsha Fontaine, Senior Developer

I READ the email several times to be sure I'm not imagining things. Then, I google the company to make sure it's legit. As described, Blue Star is a small—as in ten employees—indie developer, but they've been making waves recently with a few unique titles. It's no Bethesda or Rockstar, but it seems like the perfect place to get my foot in the door. And it's likely the kind of developer where I'd have the chance to pitch my own ideas rather than just working on things other people come up with.

I respond to the email, telling Marsha I'd love to meet to discuss the position further, then I send a message to the group chat between Lucky, Heart, and me telling them I have potentially exciting news next time I see them. Before I can set my phone down, a call from Troy comes in.

"Dude, did you get an email from Blue Star Games?" he asks as soon as I answer.

"I did, and I agreed to a meeting. What about you?"

"Same. This is wild. I can't believe they saw our game."

"I know, it's crazy. Oh god, a job interview, I hope I don't fuck it up." Nerves squirm in my stomach, but not nearly as badly as I would've expected. Maybe it's the fact that this company sought *me* out? Or maybe it's knowing that no matter if I fuck up or not, Heart and Lucky will still be there cheering me on. Nothing can go too badly with the two of them in my corner.

When they get my texts, Lucky suggests we come by his place for dinner so I can tell them my news, and he says he has something to tell Heart too.

When I get to Lucky's a few hours later, he greets me with a long, deep kiss. "How was your day, baby?"

"Mostly boring, until the afternoon. But I want to wait until Heart gets here to tell you what happened."

He nods and gives me one more peck on the lips. "Of course. Why don't you go relax on the couch while I finish up dinner? Heart should be here any minute."

Less than five minutes later, Heart knocks on the door, and I let him in. I get another kiss, this one slow and sweet. How is this my life? It's unbelievable and amazing and a million other adjectives I never thought I'd be able to apply to my life.

"You look tired, did you have a hard day?" I ask.

"You could say that," Heart jokes with a wink.

"Dinner's about ready," Lucky calls from the kitchen.

Once everything is on the table and our plates are full, both men look at me expectantly.

"I'm not sure if this is anything yet, but I'm really hopeful and excited so I wanted to tell you guys, even though nothing may come of it."

"Tell us," Heart encourages, practically bouncing in his seat.

"I got an email, inviting me to apply for a job at an indie game developer. It's just an interview, and I obviously wouldn't start until after I graduate in six months, but it seems like it would be the perfect starting position."

"That's so great. They'd be stupid not to hire you," Heart declares.

"Where is it?" Lucky asks, a hint of reservation in his tone.

"In Escondido, so not very far. And jobs like this, you usually don't have to go into the office five days a week or anything. So, the commute would be a pain in the ass, but still doable," I assure him, and his guarded posture relaxes, giving way to a smile.

"That's amazing, baby. We're so proud of you."

"Thank you, it means a lot."

"You said you had news too, Lucky?" Heart asks after the *congratulations* stuff dies down.

Lucky clears his throat and sets his fork down.

"I've been looking into options about how to clear your record, get things set straight. I had Ranger help me out, and he introduced me to a friend of his who's a really great defense lawyer. He's agreed to take your case. His paralegal should be contacting you sometime this week to conduct an interview so he can start building a case to get your record expunged."

"What?" Heart's mouth hangs open, his eyes wide. "What are you talking about?"

"Having your name cleared once and for all. Nothing is for sure yet, but this is our best shot."

"Are you serious? You did this for me?" Heart's tone is filled with vulnerability. I reach for his hand. "How much does this cost?"

"He's doing it pro bono, so it won't cost a thing."

Heart looks skeptical but doesn't argue. Instead, he gets up and goes around the table to climb onto Lucky's lap. They whisper and kiss, and the whole scene makes my heart feel so full it could burst. I love them both so much.

44

MASON

Unlike the last few weekends, Heart isn't able to spend Sunday with Lucky and me because he has to work.

"I wonder what he's filming today," I muse as I lie on Lucky's couch, my feet in his lap and a movie playing in the background. Lucky raises an eyebrow at my question and smirks.

"Trying to picture him at work?"

Heat creeps into my cheeks as I realize how that sounded. "Maybe," I mutter.

"I think under that shy exterior is a seriously filthy man just waiting to get out."

"I don't know about that," I chuckle. "Does Heart's job bother you?"

I know it's a bit of a non sequitur, but Lucky is so straight laced, I have to wonder if it's weird to him that one of his boyfriends is a porn star.

Lucky's quiet for a minute, seeming to think through the question, rubbing his hands absently over my feet. "I think he can have better; I don't want him to settle," he finally answers.

"It makes him happy."

"You think so? I've worried that he's putting on a façade, like he *wants* everyone to think he's happy doing porn."

I shake my head. "I don't think so. I'm not sure he wants to do porn forever or anything, but I think he enjoys it. As long as he's happy, I'm happy for him."

Lucky nods and squeezes my foot but doesn't say any more about it. His attention seems to drift back to the movie, but mine is stuck on something I've been thinking about for over a week now. I want to have sex with Lucky, but I'm terrified. Terrified I'll disappoint him, terrified he'll realize I can't be enough for him. Sex with Heart is great, but that doesn't mean I won't manage to mess it up with Lucky.

"What are you thinking about so hard over there?"

My face heats, and I bite down on my bottom lip, trying to decide if I should tell him the truth.

"Sex," I blurt.

"Do you always look so nauseous when you think about sex?" Lucky asks, his eyebrows furrowed.

"Generally, yeah," I admit with an awkward laugh. "We should have sex."

"Mason, baby, come here." He pats his lap, and I scramble up and straddle his legs. "I told you before, there's no rush. We can do things at whatever pace you're comfortable with."

"But I *want* to have sex with you. I can't stop thinking about it. I want you so badly."

"I want you too." He puts a hand on the back of my head and guides me in for a kiss. His lips are as firm and commanding as always, dragging a moan from my chest as he parts my lips with his tongue.

My cock is hard and straining, and I can feel his erection against my ass. The memory of his long, thick cock in my mouth makes me ache and squirm against him. I want to taste Lucky, feel him inside me, make him fall apart again. But can I do it without Heart here to give me confidence and cheer me on?

"Promise me something?" I beg against his lips.

"Anything, baby. What do you need?" Lucky's voice is rough with arousal and restraint, his hands grasping my ass and the light stubble on his chin scratching against mine. It's sensation overload in the best possible way.

"If I'm not doing something well, will you tell me? Please just tell me, and I can do it better. I swear, I can learn how to do it better. Just don't leave me." My voice cracks at the end; I'm too anxious to be embarrassed about my pathetic plea.

"Shh," he soothes, moving his hands from my ass to my back and rubbing comforting circles. "I'm not going to leave you, certainly not over sex. All couples have a learning curve with each other, figuring out what they each like and how they fit together sexually. That can be a really fun part of the relationship, and I swear to you it's nothing I would ever look down on you for. I want to learn how to please you and teach you about what I like."

I nod rapidly, burying my face in the crook of Lucky's neck and taking comfort in his steady warmth.

"That sounds nice, learning together."

"It'll be more than *nice*," he flirts, moving his hands back to my ass and massaging my cheeks. "Let's take this one step at a time."

"No," I pull away and shake my head.

"No?"

"I don't want to go slow anymore; I want you inside me."

"You're sure?" He searches my face, and he must not find

any reservation because the next thing I know, he's lifting me off the couch with a playful smile. "Let's take this to the bedroom then."

My anxiety takes a backseat to the need thrumming through my veins as Lucky drops me onto his bed. Obviously, it's not the first time I've been in this bed, but it's the first time Lucky is going to fuck me, so it takes on a whole new meaning.

I unbutton my pants with shaking fingers and shove them down while Lucky does the same. My shirt follows, and then I take a second to fully appreciate how unbelievably hot Lucky is—ripped muscles, tan skin, just the barest dusting of hair over his chest, his huge cock stretching the front of his briefs.

I palm my own erection through my underwear and squeeze at the base to slow my overexcitement. *That's* certainly not a problem I ever had with Brad. If anything, it was difficult to get into it much at all—first due to nerves and later because I knew it was inevitable I'd disappoint him. I don't have to be nervous with Lucky.

"You'd never hurt me," I say with certainty as Lucky tosses a bottle of lube and a condom on the bed.

"Of course, I wouldn't," he assures me, crawling over me, forcing me to lie back as his large body blankets mine. "I love you, Mason."

I gasp, and my heart breaks out into a gallop. I don't know why, but my throat clogs with emotion, so thick I can't manage to form a response. I don't realize I'm crying until Lucky starts to wipe the moisture from my cheeks and then kisses each one.

"You love me?" I whisper once I can manage it.

"I really do."

"Do you love Heart?" This question feels just as important to me as the previous.

"Yes, but he's not ready to hear it."

I nod in agreement. Heart isn't ready to know how we both feel; it would only scare him.

"I love you, too."

Lucky smiles more brightly than I've ever seen, and then his lips are on mine again. My hands roam greedily over his body as our tongues tangle, his cock grinding against mine through our underwear.

"Want these off," I murmur against his mouth, tugging at his underwear. Lucky pulls his lips away and rids himself of his last stitch of clothing while I do the same.

I reach for his cock and wrap my hand around the weighty girth. He returns to the kiss while I stroke him in long, slow tugs. Lucky moans against my lips, and pleasure rushes through my body. Just knowing *I* got him to make that sound is like an orgasm in and of itself. I tighten my grip and stroke faster.

"If you don't slow down, this is going to be over faster than either of us wants," Lucky warns in a strained voice. "Let me get you ready."

I reluctantly release his cock and nod, spreading my legs wider and bending my knees to give him access.

I close my eyes and drag in a deep breath, forcing myself to relax for the next step. The snick of the lube cap is followed by the squelch of Lucky coating his fingers.

"Ready?" he checks, and I nod again, drawing my knees up farther.

I manage not to jump when his slicked finger slides into my crease and glides over my hole. He takes his time, circling my pucker, wrapping his free hand around my cock. Heat pools in the pit of my stomach, and it doesn't take long before I'm whimpering and begging Lucky to put a finger inside me already.

When he finally breaches me, the painful burn I've come to expect from penetration isn't there—or at least not to the extent I'm used to.

"Oh god," I groan, flexing my hips, unable to decide if I'm trying to thrust up into his hand or down onto his finger. "Please, more."

Lucky obliges, adding a second finger. There are a few seconds of discomfort this time, but it quickly turns to hot, all-consuming need to be stretched, filled, fucked. I don't know who this person is right now, but it's not me...at least not typical me when it comes to sex. It's incredible and addictive; it's everything I always thought sex was supposed to be.

My cock throbs in his hand, and my legs shake with every uneven thrust I manage.

"Please, please, please."

"Okay, baby, I've got you," Lucky assures me.

His fingers slip out, leaving me feeling empty and desperate. The sound of the condom package being torn open keeps me from protesting, and within moments, the thick head of Lucky's cock is resting at my entrance.

"Ready for me?" Lucky asks. I nod, holding my breath and waiting for the invasion, equal parts anxious and terrified for it. "Okay, deep breath for me and try to relax."

I blow out the lungful of air I was holding and slowly inhale fresh, focusing on relaxing my muscles and opening for him. As I'm letting out my second full breath, Lucky pushes inside, breaching the tight ring of muscles and making me gasp. I tense, and my asshole burns from the invasion.

"Fuck, ow, shit, I forgot how much that hurts."

"I'm sorry, baby, try to relax. Keep taking deep breaths, and if you want me to pull out after you've given it a second, I will."

"No." I clutch at Lucky's firm ass. "Don't stop; I just need a second."

Lucky's lips find mine, coaxing a slow kiss, making it easy to forget the pain from only a few seconds before and melt against his body. His cock slides deeper, and this time I moan with pleasure as he presses against my prostate.

I wrap my legs around his waist and pull him deeper, not content to go at the slow pace he's setting. I want Lucky to pound into me, claim me, make me feel it for a week.

Lucky buries his face in my neck as he fucks his cock into me, deep and fast. The friction of my cock against his stomach and the way he pegs my prostate on every pass has me on edge within a few minutes.

He licks and sucks along my neck and down my collar bone while I dig my fingers into his biceps and let out unintelligible cries. When his teeth graze my nipple, a strangled wail escapes my throat, and I thrust myself harder against him, precum coating my cock and my ass tightening around him.

"I'm close, I'm close, Lucky, oh god."

Lucky grunts and fucks harder into me. He throws his head back and groans, the sound settling in the pit of my stomach and making my blood heat. He likes it; he likes fucking me.

"Come, Mase. Please come," he growls, and that's all it takes for my balls to draw up tight and white-hot pleasure to pulse through me as I spray our stomachs with my release. My ass pulses hard around his cock as my orgasm rages through me, and I can feel the moment he falls apart as well, thickening and then throbbing deep inside. I can feel the heat of his cum through the condom, and I somehow manage to come harder, until I'm sure I'll pass out.

Lucky twitches and gives a few more lazy thrusts as he rides out the aftershocks. Then he pulls out and discards the condom onto the floor beside his bed.

"That was amazing," he murmurs in my ear as he pulls me close. "You were so good."

I nearly sob with relief. "I love you," I whisper, still unable to believe any of this is real.

"Love you too, baby."

My body feels sated and heavy as I cuddle against Lucky.

"Let's take a nap and then it'll be time for dinner," he suggests, and I yawn, snuggling closer and closing my eyes.

When we wake up, the sun is starting to go down, and my stomach is growling. I can't stop smiling as I stretch and rub my eyes. There's only one thing missing from this perfect moment.

"Can we take a picture to send to Heart?"

"Sure, tell him we miss him."

I slide off the bed and go in search of my phone in the living room. When I return, I put my head on Lucky's shoulder and hold the phone above us to snap the picture, then I send it to Heart with the message *We're both missing you.*

My phone pings with a response seconds later.

Heart: Looks like you two are having a fun afternoon ;)

Mason: Very fun

Heart: I'd ask how it went, but that smile on your face tells me everything

Mason: It was amazing. Lucky has a magic cock I think, just wait until it's your turn

Heart: No fair teasing. Ugh, I just got fucked six ways to

Sunday, and I'm already hard again thinking about being between you and Lucky

Mason: I can't wait until the three of us are together

I SURPRISE myself with that response. The thought of being in bed with both Heart and Lucky has been a major source of anxiety for me, but now I can't wait. It's amazing how much great sex can change your perspective.

"I think your cock is better than any therapist I ever could've seen," I tell Lucky, setting my phone aside and running my hand along the hard planes of his chest and stomach.

He snorts a laugh and kisses the top of my head.

"I'm glad to hear that. Now, how about dinner?"

45

HEART

I've been nervous since the moment I got out of bed. It's a strange sensation for me, first of all because I'm rarely nervous about anything and second of all, because I'm nervous about sex. I'm a freaking porn star. Why the hell would I be nervous about sex? And yet here I am, my stomach all tight and twisted, and my hands sweaty at the thought of having sex.

Of course, it's not just sex with anyone. Today, our two months of no sex are up, and that means that hopefully, me and Lucky will have sex. He hasn't said anything about it, so I'm not even sure if it is going to happen today, but just the thought is enough to send me into a frenzy. How weird is that?

I can't deny it's been good for us, these two months. We've had dates with the three of us, but I've also been spending time with Lucky and Mason separately, and the two of them have done the same. I loved hearing how well their first time having sex went, a couple of days ago. It's been good to get to know each other better, but also to grow closer together as a threesome.

Because there's no denying anymore that that's what we are, a threesome. We spend more time together now than apart, and usually we sleep over together as well. Lucky's apartment has become our favorite, which makes sense because it's the biggest.

I only have a full-size bed in my studio, and that doesn't even fit the three of us, and in Mason's queen, it's still a tight fit. Lucky, of course, has a king-size, so we're plenty comfortable there. To be honest, I'm a little worried about us spending so much time in his place. Not because I think he doesn't like having us around, but there's no denying his place is a lot less...pristine than it was before.

Hell, the first time I saw his apartment, it looked like a freaking show apartment, one of those apartments you see on TV in those home decorating shows. Or in pictures on realtor sites where they try to convince you to buy or rent a certain apartment. It was almost scary, how empty it was.

Well, I guess we solved that problem for him. I really try to not make too much of a mess, and Mason regularly reminds me to clean up my shit as well. Still, I must be getting on Lucky's nerves, I fear.

Now that our two months of no sex is up, he basically has a choice to make. Does he want to continue his relationship with me and venture into sexual territory? Or has he discovered that he really was only interested in my body after all?

I can't imagine the latter is the case, no matter what my fear tries to tell me. As hard as it was to believe at first, I really do think Lucky likes me for way more than just sex. If it was just sex he was interested in, why would he even hang out with Mason, who clearly has some sexual hang-ups? Hell, I'm pretty sure those two are in love with each other... and yet they still want me there as well.

And secondly, sure, I'm a porn star, but I'm not the only one who will put out with him. He could walk into any gay bar or any gay club and score someone willing to be fucked by him. He doesn't need me for that. The fact that he was willing to wait for two whole months, all the time he has invested in getting to know me and Mason, all the emotional energy he's put into the three of us, it all points toward him telling the truth.

He *really* wants me, us.

It's exhilarating and scary as fuck at the same time. I honestly don't know how I feel about it. Ever since Terry, I've always said I never wanted to be in another relationship again. You don't need to be a psychologist to figure that one out. I got fucked over good and had no intention of repeating that experience. Naturally, I was reluctant to even start dating.

Then Mason came along, and without even realizing it, I opened my heart for him. How could I not, when he never even intended to be in a relationship with me as well? It just...happened. For both of us. With Lucky's arrival on the scene, things got complicated even more. Here was a man who from the start was honest that all he wanted was a relationship. And he's proven it to us, time and again.

So where does that leave me? How can I continue this with the two of them if I insist on not wanting to be in a relationship? It doesn't make sense. I either need to get the fuck out before all of us get invested even more, or I need to decide that I *do* want to be in a relationship after all.

I wish I knew which choice to make. The first, walking away, I'm not even sure I can do it. Just the thought of not seeing them again is...painful. As a matter of fact, even thinking about that option now makes it hard to breathe.

My phone rings, interrupting me and my thoughts. It's Rebel, and I pick up quickly. "Hey man," I say. "What's up?"

"Hey, Heart. Quick question. We had a shoot planned for this afternoon with Pixie and Campy, but Campy had a family emergency. Is there any chance you could take over for him? It's another boyfriend scene, so no extensive preparation or scripts, just a lazy Sunday afternoon fuck."

My first instinct is to say yes, but then I hesitate. If I do a scene today, chances are I won't be in the mood tonight to do something with Lucky. Boyfriend scenes especially wear me out, not so much physically as emotionally. Maybe it's different now that I'm with Mason and Lucky, I don't know, but am I willing to run the risk?

I run the idea again through my head. I've always liked doing scenes with Pixie, but now I find myself hesitating. I frown. Why am I feeling different about this shoot? It's not Pixie; the kid is cute as a button, and I would love to do a shoot with him any day. We may not have the same sexual spark that he had with Rebel for instance, but we're a good match, and I love hanging out with him.

Then it hits me. It's not Pixie. It's the concept of the boyfriend scene.

"Heart? You still there?" Rebel says.

"Yeah," I say quickly. "Sorry, lost in thought for a second. Erm, is it going to be a big problem for you if I say no?"

"Of course not," Rebel quickly assures me.

I have to tell him why, though. "You know I've been kind of dating Mason, right? Well, I'm also dating this other guy, Lucky. I guess the three of us are dating each other? Like, a threesome?"

Rebel whistles through his teeth. "Wow, that's awesome. Go you! But I'm not quite sure what that has to do with today's shoot. Does either of them not want you to do porn anymore? Is that what you're telling me?"

I sigh. In for a penny, in for the whole thing, right? "No, that's not it. Lucky and I are supposed to have sex for the first time today, so I really don't want to do a shoot just before that."

"Oh, okay. That's understandable. How long have you guys been dating?"

"Two months. He thought it would be best if we didn't have sex for a while to make sure it wasn't just about that."

Rebel's voice is warm as he replies. "That's sweet, Heart. He sounds like a good guy who has your best interests at heart."

I let Rebel's words sink in. He's right; Lucky does have my best interest at heart. Mine and Mason's.

"I'm not sure I want to do the boyfriend scenes anymore," I blurt out. "Mason and Lucky have no problem with me doing porn, but I think I would feel dishonest pretending to be someone else's boyfriend, even in a scene. So, could you maybe schedule me for different type of scenes? I don't mind acting a little, but the boyfriend scenes are just...too intimate, I guess. Does that make sense?"

"Absolutely," Rebel says, not a trace of hesitation in his voice. "And Heart, if you ever do decide that porn is no longer working for you, no hard feelings. We don't want you to do anything you're not comfortable with."

I let out a sigh of relief. "Thank you. I really appreciate that."

"You're welcome. I'll see if I can find someone else for today, and if not, we'll cancel the shoot. No problem. You go and have a sexy time with your boyfriend, okay? Or I should say boyfriends..."

I disconnect the call, and then I sit for a little bit,

wondering what the hell is happening to me. And suddenly I realize it's not the sex with Lucky I'm worried about. It's the feelings that it will inevitably bring. I'm kidding myself if I think I can walk away from him, from them. I'm already in way over my head. And to be honest, it doesn't scare me nearly as much as it should.

46

HEART

By the time I get a text from Lucky around noon, I'm a ball of nerves. The text comes to our group message like usual. Even one-on-one dates are arranged in our group messages typically.

Lucky: You both want to come over for dinner tonight? I thought I'd make something special...

Something special? Does that mean he's thinking what I'm thinking about tonight? I wasn't sure if Lucky would want our first time together to include Mason or not, but I hope it does. Just like I told Mason when I had my first kiss with Lucky, he's part of us. It's not me and Lucky or Lucky and Mason. It's the three of us, always. Even when it's not.

Mason: I'm in! Why something special though?

Heart: Because he's finally going to fuck me tonight

I attempt humor to hide my mounting nerves at the thought. Seriously, how can I be nervous about this? I've lost track of how many men I've been with in my life, the first one being when I was fifteen years old and most of them blurring together over time. Between my time on the streets and my porn career, sex is no big deal to me. But with Lucky, it feels different. Maybe with Lucky I want it to be a big deal.

Mason: Oh! You don't want me there then, right?
Heart: I want you there
Lucky: Of course, we want you, baby
Lucky: See you both at seven?
Heart: Yup!
Mason: Sounds good

I SET my phone down and take a deep breath. If I'm getting fucked later, I should jump in the shower and make sure I'm all squeaky clean. Plus, a hot shower should help dispel some of these ridiculous nerves.

∼

WHEN I GET to Lucky's just after seven, Mason is already there, relaxing on the couch while Lucky finishes up dinner.

"Hey, babe," I greet Mason with a kiss, and when he clings to me, I linger for a few minutes, nibbling his lips and devouring the little sounds he makes when my tongue plays with his.

"Mmmm, I think that's officially my favorite sight in the world," Lucky says from the living room doorway, his deep voice even huskier than usual.

"Why don't you get over here and join us," I suggest.

"As much of a temptation as that is, I don't want dinner to get cold while you both distract me. So, come eat, and then we'll get back to the distractions."

I lace my fingers with Mason's and tug him off the couch with me. We round the corner to the kitchen, and I stop in my tracks, my heart pounding so hard I'm sure it will shatter my ribs.

There are candles lighting the table. I've never had someone go to the trouble of a candle-lit dinner. In truth, I always thought it sounded a little sappy and cliché, so why are my eyes leaking now at the sight of it?

Mason's hand squeezes mine, and Lucky steps in front of us. He cups my chin and tilts my face up toward his.

"Our no-sex rule is up, but I wanted to show you that doesn't mean everything changes. Sex or no sex, I intend to continue showing you that you're more to me than just a hole to stick my dick in. You're smart and funny. You have confidence even I envy. You're an incredible person, and I'm lucky to be with you."

My mouth falls open, and I flounder for words as even more tears leak from my eyes.

"He's right, Heart. You're amazing." Mason kisses my cheek.

"Come on, sit down," Lucky urges, saving me from having to form a response to either of them.

I pile my plate high with all sorts of healthy food Lucky cooked for us, grateful for an excuse not to talk while I process everything. Mason and Lucky talk but I don't bother to pay attention, my focus instead on everything that's gone on between the three of us over the past two months. And I circle back to my earlier thoughts about whether or not I can commit to Mason and Lucky or if I need to let them go.

I shovel food into my mouth, not paying attention to what it is or even really tasting it. Lucky made a candle-lit dinner for me. In two months together, he's proven to be exactly what I thought he was—steadfast, trustworthy, moral, and *good*. Better than I deserve without a doubt, but everything I didn't realize I was longing for. And then there's Mason, my sweet, wonderful, perfect Mason. How could I give these two up?

"You okay, Heart?" Mason asks, reaching under the table and putting a hand on my knee. "You're really quiet."

"I'm good, baby," I assure him. "I was just thinking, and there's something I want to tell you both." They look up from their meals, expectant but patient. I clear my throat and put my hand on Mason's for the comfort and reassurance. "I was hesitant when we started this. I didn't think I could ever trust anyone again after what Terry did, and I didn't want another relationship ever again. But you both proved me wrong; you showed me what I was missing, and I want you both to know I'm all in."

Mason smiles more widely than I've ever seen before, and the look of happiness and relief in Lucky's eyes warms my chest.

"Your trust means a lot; I'll never take it for granted," Lucky promises, and I know without a doubt he's telling the truth.

When we finish dinner, Mason and I do the dishes while Lucky puts away leftovers, and nerves start to flutter in my stomach again.

"God, I don't know why, but I'm kind of nervous to have sex with Lucky for some reason," I confess quietly to Mason with a laugh.

"Welcome to my life," he jokes and then bumps his shoulder against mine. "It's going to be great; you'll see."

When the kitchen is clean, Lucky leads us to the bedroom and the three of us get undressed. I snort a small laugh as Lucky folds his clothes as he takes them off. That's just so him I can't help but find it amusing.

Mason is the first one to crawl onto the bed, his expression as eager and sweet as always. I follow him and blanket him with my body, my lips finding his in a kiss that helps me to relax a fraction.

The bed shifts under Lucky's weight, and I hear him rummage in the drawer beside the bed for a few seconds, presumably getting supplies. I keep kissing Mason, sliding our hard cocks together between our bodies.

Lucky's first touch is so gentle I almost don't register it. His hands ghost over my back, and his lips trail along the back of my shoulder. His hard cock brushes against the curve of my ass, and I shiver in anticipation as I kiss Mason deeper.

Lucky takes his time kissing and touching me, and by the time one of his slicked fingers finds its way between my cheeks, I'm relaxed and so ready to feel him inside me.

"You don't have to take long prepping me," I assure him, reaching between Mason and me to run my finger through the precum gathering on the tip of his cock and then my own.

"Tell me if I'm going too fast," Lucky requests, and I nod, licking and kissing my way down Mason's throat.

He goes right for two fingers, and I moan at the burning stretch of being filled. I squirm against his fingers and whimper against Mason's skin.

"You look so hot," Mason groans, wrapping his hand around both of our cocks.

"Please fuck me, Lucky," I beg as a third finger joins the first two.

He thrusts his fingers in and out a few more times, likely making sure I'm really ready for him. And then he eases them out, and I make a disgruntled noise at the loss. Mason's hand on our cocks is a slow rhythm, nowhere close to getting either of us off, just enough to make me desperate and insane.

The sound of Lucky tearing open the condom makes me sigh with relief, and seconds later, the blunt pressure of his cock is at my entrance. I take Mason's mouth again, letting my body relax and accept Lucky as he pushes in steadily. When I feel his hairy thighs against the back of mine, I turn my head, and he leans forward to kiss me.

I'm not sure if it's the fullness of his cock inside me or the emotions of the kiss that leave me breathless, but either way, my chest heaves against Mason's.

Lucky's powerful thrusts cause my cock to drag against Mason's in the confines of his grip. If I had any brainpower left, I'd suggest pausing for a second so I could be inside Mason, but I can't form words let alone coherent thoughts as Lucky fucks me hard and deep.

On the porn set, I can last for a good forty-five minutes to an hour if I need to. But surrounded by Lucky and Mason, smelling, feeling, and tasting them both has me ready to blow within minutes.

"I'm close, I'm so close," I warn them as I turn back to Mason, resting my forehead against his and closing my eyes to let the sensations wash over me.

Lucky's grip on my hips tightens, and he somehow manages to fuck me deeper, hitting my prostate with each stroke. Mason cries out beneath me, and his cock pulses against mine. The feeling of his hot cum coating my cock, along with Lucky inside me, sends me careening over the edge with a harsh wail as my orgasm rips through me violently, shooting my seed all over Mason.

Lucky fucks me through the pleasure and then lets out a deep groan, stilling with his cock deep inside me.

We end up in a sweaty, sticky heap, all too tired to bother

cleaning up. Lucky spoons around me from behind, and I lay my head on Mason's chest.

"Thank you for trusting us," Mason whispers just after Lucky's breathing evens out signaling sleep.

"Thank you for giving me the time to learn to trust you." I press a kiss to the middle of Mason's chest and close my eyes.

47

HEART

I haven't told Lucky and Mason anything about what I have planned for tonight at the Ballsy Boys social potluck. I can't exactly explain to myself why. Sure, I could argue that Mason is already nervous enough as it is, even though he has met all of the boys already. It's just how he's wired.

Social situations freak him out, especially when there's pressure on him, or he *feels* that there's pressure on him, to make a good impression. He feels like he could potentially embarrass me and Lucky, and that's enough to send him into a fit of nerves. It's sweet and adorable and completely Mason, and I see Lucky reacting with the same patient acceptance as me, and that warms my heart.

"Do they always hold these types of events at the studio?" Lucky asks me as we get dressed.

I shake my head. "No, before I joined, they would meet in bars or restaurants, but Bear knows I have to be careful visiting places like that. I don't know how he explained it to the others, but nobody has ever asked a question about it. I'm not even sure they know it's for my benefit."

Lucky sends me a warm smile. "That's super nice of Bear, to accommodate you like that."

"He's a good guy," I affirm. "I didn't know it, but I surely chose the best studio."

"How...how do I look?" Mason asks as he turns around to face us.

I love that he's embracing his nerd identity more and more. His relationship with me and Lucky is making him feel more confident about himself; there's no denying that. He used to be super worried about every little detail about himself, but lately I sense he's more at peace with who he is and more confident of the fact that we genuinely like him.

Like now, he's wearing a black Minecraft shirt that looks adorable as fuck on him and a pair of tight jeans that make me want to keep my eyes glued to his ass all night. Well, it would be a competition between his and Lucky's, because that man's ass in the tight cargo pants he's wearing is not exactly a hardship to look at either.

"You look perfect, baby," Lucky tells Mason in that super sweet tone he uses for him.

It's funny, how Lucky seems to have a different voice for me and Mason, like, I can tell which one of us he is addressing even without him mentioning our name, simply by the tone of his voice. He's always a tad more sweet and soft toward Mason, as if he fears even the slightest bit of anger would hurt Mason—and it probably would.

With me, there's always a bit more sexy in there, a touch more bossiness, and a dash of that masculine authority he has that pushes buttons I never even realized I had. He's sweet and spicy at the same time, and while I never thought it would work out with the three of us, I'm amazed to see how well we fit together.

Because it's not just Lucky who is slightly different with

me than with Mason. It's the same for me. With Mason, I'm softer, somehow, probably for the same reason Lucky is. He triggers that in us, this protective instinct. But with Lucky, I can be as sexy, bratty, and loud as I want to, and he gives back as much as I dole out.

He's good for me, pushing back where I need it, not putting up with my bullshit. And I guess I do the same for him. Lucky tends to hide behind a mask when it gets personal for him or when he gets emotional. So I get on his case and keep nagging him until he opens up.

As I said, it shouldn't work, this weird combination of the three of us, but it totally does. And slowly, I'm starting to wonder if maybe, just maybe I was wrong about not being suited for a relationship.

"What do you think, Heart?" Mason asks me, then bites his lip as if expecting me to criticize him. No wonder, I must've been staring off in space for quite a bit.

I send him a dashing smile. "I love it, baby. That color really makes your eyes pop. And you know how much we love it when you go all nerd on us."

Mason lets out a sigh of relief.

"You look pretty epic too," he tells me, letting his eyes slowly wander over my leather pants with the tight black tank top that shows off all my tattoos.

Lucky slaps my ass with a hearty smack. "He's one of the few men I know that can actually pull off leather pants, especially pants that tight. You know what we should do?" he says as he walks over to Mason. "We should tease him until he comes in his pants. He's going commando, and those things are a bitch to take off when they're wet."

My eyes widen, and I point a threatening finger in his direction. "Don't you dare."

"Oh," Mason says as he snuggles up to Lucky, looking at

me with a cheeky smile. "That sounds like a wonderful plan."

I make a few more threatening gestures that we all know mean absolutely zero. "Don't even think about it. I will not put out for a month if you guys do that."

We keep joking and teasing as we get in the car, and Lucky drives us to the studio. The bundle of nerves in my stomach tightens. Am I doing the smart thing, revealing my past to everyone? I don't know what the outcome will be, but I do know that I've reached a point where it feels disingenuous to continue working with these men without revealing to them who I really am.

I was as shocked as anyone when Tank and Brewer revealed that they hadn't just fallen in love, but that the two of them were actually working hard to get their college degrees. Who would've thought? And even as I thought it at that moment, I realized they would experience the same shock if they knew about me. We all wear a mask, we all pretend to be someone and something we're really not, we all hide our past and our shame and pain. I guess I'm ready to reveal a little more of myself, at least with these men who have become my friends.

Once we're inside, Mason quickly loses his nerves as Troy takes him under his wing and starts chatting with him. Those two are a funny combination for sure, but you can't deny they work well together. I love seeing Mason being successful professionally. Their game is doing really well, and I have every faith he's gonna nail his job interview with that game developer.

I introduce Lucky to each of the boys, and they all react as I knew they would, with warmth and genuine interest in him. After about half an hour of chitchat, Lucky grabs my hand and gently pulls me aside.

"What is up with you tonight?" he asks. "You seem nervous for some reason. Is there anything going on I should know about?"

My stomach sours. "Are you asking as my boyfriend or as my PO?"

I regret the question as soon as it leaves my mouth, but it's too late to take it back. Lucky's face tightens. "I don't think I've done anything to deserve that," he says, his voice controlled but tense.

I reach out and put my hand on his arm. "You're right. I'm sorry. It was a gut reaction to your distrust. Maybe you didn't mean it that way?"

Lucky hesitates for a second, then puts those strong hands on my shoulders and pulls me in to hug me. We stand there for a little bit, me taking comfort from the warmth and strength of his arms.

"It wasn't distrust," he whispers in my ear. "I'm worried about you. Something is going on, and you're tense. I'm worried, that is all."

I leaned back so he can see my face, and everything in his eyes tells me he's telling the truth. I lean in for a soft, slow kiss. "I'm sorry," I say again. I take a deep breath. "I'm going to tell them about my past tonight."

Lucky's face relaxes, and then a broad smile curves his lips. "I'm so freaking proud of you, baby," he says. "That is such a big step for you; I'm so happy to see you starting to trust other people."

I nod. "They're good guys."

He looks at me with tenderness. Then he leans in, grabbing my face with both his hands and moving his mouth an inch away from mine. When he speaks, I can feel his words dance on my lips, almost as a kiss. "So are you."

Then he kisses me, not a hot, passionate kiss, but a slow,

deliberate lovemaking to my mouth, him claiming every single inch of me. I melt against him, giving him everything he asks for and more, until our mouths and bodies are plastered together everywhere.

We don't stop until loud wolf whistles from behind us alert us to the fact that we have an audience. Brewer—who else? —is doing the whistling, while Troy, Campy, and Pixie are joining in with cheers and appraisal as well.

"Hot damn, what a kiss," Pixie says, a wistful look on his face. "That almost set the room on fire."

My eyes seek out Mason, wanting to make sure he doesn't feel left out, but he's watching us with an expression that looks a hell of a lot like pride. Plus, the bulge in his jeans is unmistakable, even from this distance. I guess he liked our little show as well.

"You should see the three of us," I say with a big smile on my face. "Ain't no porn video as hot as that."

Troy gives Mason a little shove. "You should join them... Give us a little demonstration."

Mason shakes his head. "No way, dude. Unlike most of you here, I like to keep sex to myself, thank you very much."

I'm proud of him for managing to stand up to Troy, even if he does look a little flustered. He's grown so much, my sweet nerd. "He's right," I say with all the love in my voice I feel for him. "The three of us, we're better in private."

Lucky gives me a last kiss, and just as I want to let him go, he casually strokes my half-hard cock with his index finger. "I haven't forgotten about this, you know," he says softly, his voice low and sexy. "I fully intend to make you jizz your pants before this night is over."

I push my dick into his hand, then lean in to tug his earlobe between my front teeth, knowing how much that drives him wild. "What happens if you lose?" I whisper after I let go of his ear. "What do I win?"

The absolutely devastatingly sexy smile he flashes me is enough to make me regret challenging him. This is not a man who expects to lose.

"If I lose, I will wear the leather pants next time we go out."

Oh, this is *so* on.

48

LUCKY

An hour later, I have no idea which one of us is going to win this bet. I had forgotten one tiny little detail when I confidently decided I would make Heart come in his pants. The guy is a freaking porn star. He is well trained in coming on command...or in this case, in not coming.

He's told me his secret once, because I was genuinely interested in how he managed to keep from coming too soon during a scene. He explained to me his mind is in a different place when he does a scene than when he is with me or Mason or both of us.

Doing a scene, even though he enjoys it, is for the most part work for him, and he treats it as such. He said that sometimes, he even has to work at getting hard, because the sex doesn't always do much for him. Being with us, obviously, is completely different. He allows himself to let go with us, and that made perfect sense when he described it.

Of course, as soon as he knew about our bet, he somehow switched into porn star mode. I can't explain how I can tell that he's different with me than usual, but I see it and I feel it. And I'm not upset about it in any way; I'm more in awe of his smarts. He's sure found a way to endure my sexual teasing without reacting too much. That being said, he's dishing it back to me as much as I hand it out, so if he continues this, I may be the one who ends up coming in my pants.

"You two are crazy," Mason whispers as we're seated at the table to start dinner.

It's potluck style, so we all brought something to share. It's an eclectic mix of dishes, but I'm sure there's enough for everyone to fill their stomachs.

"What do you mean, crazy?" Heart asks as his hand slips under the table and starts rubbing the inside of my thigh. He is so damn good at this. Why the hell did I ever think I could win a sexual contest against a porn star?

Mason sighs. "Are you telling me your hand is not on his dick right now under the table?"

Heart grins. "It's not. Granted, it's pretty close, but it's not on his dick."

"I give up," Mason says, but he's still smiling, so I know he's not upset.

Heart and I keep teasing each other through dinner. Initially, I started this little wager to help him get rid of his nerves, but it looks like it might backfire on me. If he keeps this up, I'll be forced to wear super uncomfortable leather pants. There's no way I can pull those off. I have to figure out a way to make him come. How do I trigger him to switch from work mode to private Heart?

As dinner comes to a close, Heart's teasing of me subsides a little, and my guess is he's getting himself ready for his big revelation. I wish I could help him, but this is something he needs to do on his own. At least Mason and I will be here to support him. Not that I think these men will react in the wrong way. From everything Heart and Mason have told me about them, they seem like genuinely good guys.

I spent a little time talking to Bear, the owner. I've only spoken to him on the phone so far, but as Heart has assured me, he's a friendly, reliable man, not at all what I had expected the owner of a porn studio to be like. Then again, that probably had a lot to do with my prejudice and biases and not a lot with reality. After all, there are a lot of negative rumors and preconceptions about the porn industry in general.

When the conversation at the table comes to a natural lull, I notice Heart sitting up straight, and I grab his hand just to assure him I'm right here next to him. He sends me a quick look of gratitude, then takes a deep breath.

"I have to tell you guys something," he says, his voice a little shaky. All heads at the table turn toward him, but my eyes are on Mason. I just hope he doesn't feel left out that I knew what Heart was planning, and he didn't. Mason frowns with that adorable gesture he has that crumples his nose, and then I can see the light bulb in his head switch on, and he reaches out for Heart's other hand. And that's how he does his story, seated between the two of us, holding both our hands.

"I made some stupid decisions as a teen and got involved with the wrong crowd. I'll save you guys all the nasty details, but the end result was that I was sentenced to three years in prison for grand theft. A few weeks after I was released, Bear hired me for Ballsy Boys. So, technically I am a convicted felon on parole... And this is why I couldn't join you guys when you flew to New York, because I wasn't allowed to leave the state yet. It's also why he has graciously organized all the trips and events that we've had in establishments that

I can visit as well, since under the conditions of my parole, for the first six months, I couldn't visit any places where they sold alcohol. So...that's what I wanted to tell you, because I didn't want to lie to you guys anymore."

I squeeze his hand as we wait for the others to react. Rebel is the first to process. "Wow, that's quite the story, Heart. Thank you for trusting us with this. All I can say is that I'm sorry life got that shitty for you. Doesn't change how I see you, though."

It hasn't registered with me until then that Heart never said he was innocent. Did he leave it out on purpose? Did he want to make sure they would accept him no matter if he was guilty or innocent? Or maybe he did it because he was scared they wouldn't believe him if he said he was innocent. I'm not sure, but something tells me this was not a coincidence.

The others in the room echo Rebel's sentiments. Not one of them responds negatively, not even nonverbally. And I would damn well know, because I am watching them all like a hawk.

Troy is the first to make the connection. "Didn't you say Lucky is a parole officer?" he asks Mason, then looks at me. "Are you? Is that how you met Heart?"

His question isn't accusatory, merely curious. Still, I check with Heart if he's okay with me revealing this. After all, these are his coworkers and friends, not mine. He gives me a nod. "Yes, I am, and that's how I met Heart. He was my client when we met, but I asked to be taken off his case. It's illegal to date a client."

"That's so romantic," Pixie gushes. I swear, if the kid was a cartoon character, he'd have little pink and red hearts dancing around his head, probably with a few butterflies and pixies thrown in.

"I agree," I tell him with a soft smile, squeezing Heart's hand again. "And I don't regret it for a single moment."

"Is that also why you are never available on Saturdays?" Rebel asks.

"Yeah, I work as a volunteer in Senior Center each Saturday," Heart says. "It's part of my community service."

Brewer leans forward. "That's such an interesting place to volunteer," he says. "I love working with elderly people. They have such amazing stories to tell."

Heart nods enthusiastically, and I can see he's lost all of his tension. "I feel the same way. I've been thinking about going back to school and getting a certification as a nurse's aide, but I'm not sure they would accept me with my record."

My head whips around at those words. He's never told me anything about this, and I see my surprise mirrored on Mason's face. "That's a wonderful idea." I say. "I didn't know you were looking into that."

"I told Patrick about it," Heart says, shrugging and avoiding my eyes. "He didn't seem to think it was a very attainable goal, said he couldn't think of a school that would accept me with my felony record."

And then I blurt it out, because I can't stand to see him this sad over something he never did in the first place. "But baby, you're innocent. You shouldn't be punished for something you never did in the first place."

Heart's head shoots up as he meets my eyes, a slight blush staining his cheeks. "Sweet of you to say that," he says after a slight hesitation. "But it doesn't change the reality that I am a felon, no matter if I did it or not. The judge sentenced me, and it's on my record, unless that lawyer manages to get the case reopened and we win."

"He will," I say with confidence. "You have to believe

that, baby. I will make sure your record gets cleaned, even if it's gonna take me years to accomplish."

Heart stares at me, his beautiful eyes filling with tears. I don't think I've ever seen him this emotional, let alone cry. "Why would you do that for me?" he asks, his voice thick.

And then the other truth stumbles out because I don't care anymore that it's the worst timing with so many people watching or that Heart may not be ready to hear this. None of it matters, except for the truth that has to be said.

"I love you," I tell him, and watch his eyes freeze wide open in absolute shock. "There's little I wouldn't do for you, baby."

Heart gasps, his hand flying to his mouth, and for a few seconds, he just stares at me. Behind him, Mason's eyes fill with tears, but they're the good kind of tears, tears of joy for what he sees happening right in front of him.

"But...but you love Mason," Heart finally manages. "I can tell."

"My heart is big enough for the two of you, baby. I know it's hard to understand, because if someone had told me I would fall in love with two men at the same time, I would've declared them nuts. But here we are, and my love for you is just as big and a special and as wonderful as my love for Mason. You know we work well together, baby. We fit, the three of us."

"We do," Mason whispers, then clears his throat. "I don't understand how it works either, but he's right."

Heart just stares at me, blinking every now and then, and I can almost see the gears in his head turn, trying to process everything. I get it. From what I've read in his file, I doubt that he's ever even heard these words before. And I'm not expecting him to say them back. For me, the simple joy of expressing how I feel about him is enough.

He opens and closes his mouth a few times before he finds the words. "I don't know what to say. Thank you, maybe? Um... Shocked, I guess. I... Never knew you felt this way about me."

And in that moment, this bad ass guy looks so vulnerable that I simply drag him toward me, take him on my lap, and hug him tight. He allows himself to melt against me, and his arms come around me in a strong grip. I bend in, kissing his head, looking up when I feel Mason's presence beside us. He maneuvers himself on my other knee, and before I know it, both my arms are filled with my men, my boys. God, I love them.

I'm so thrown off my game by my spontaneous declaration that I completely forget about our bet...right until we walk outside afterward, and Heart pins me against the car, kissing me and rutting against me until I can't hold back the orgasm that thunders through me. Mason is giggling, and Heart smiles at me with a grin that drips with satisfaction. Honestly, seeing the two of them so happy will be totally worth wearing leather pants.

I think.

49

HEART

When Lucky told me he'd approached someone to try and clear my name, I was blown away. I knew he believed me when I told him I was innocent, but there's a big difference between believing someone is innocent and actively trying to make right what's been done to them. For me, knowing that Mason and Lucky believed in my innocence was enough.

I honestly never even considered the possibility of clearing my name. Sure, when I had just been sent to prison, I thought about it. Fleetingly. A few conversations with fellow inmates who had tried to do just that quickly made me realize the futility of that idea. I'm not a fatalistic type, but I am a realist, and the reality is that you need either connections, deep pockets, or a very long breath to win against a legal system that's set against you.

And I can't blame it all on the legal system. A lot of it is on my shoulders for being so stupidly naive. Up until the point the judge sentenced me, I somehow still believed Terry would speak up and save me. Yeah, I know. Dumbass.

Lucky is different. He's a realist too, but one who still has hope and optimism that justice will prevail. Maybe that's because his background is a little more privileged than mine, I don't know. Maybe it's just his character, because the man has an unwavering faith in systems, procedures, rules. Even though he knows as well as I do that they don't always work out, he still believes that if you fight hard and long enough, you will get the justice you deserve. I can only hope he's right.

We're on our way to meet his brother's friend who is a criminal attorney, and from the little research I've done online, he's a really good one. There is no way I'm able to afford him, but Lucky assured me he's taking on my case pro bono. I'll double-check that, because there is no way Lucky is paying for this. Justice may come at a price, but it doesn't mean my boyfriend has to pay it.

David Klein isn't the slick, corporate type I was expecting. Sure, his office certainly exudes the big money he must be making defending clients, but the man himself is very down to earth. He must know what I do for a living, but his handshake is warm and his demeanor friendly as he greets us and welcomes us into his office.

"Do you prefer I call you Gunner or Heart?" he asks after greeting Lucky and me, immediately scoring points in my book.

"Heart, please. Thank you."

He nods, then points toward a small conference table in his office. "Grab a seat. Let me get something to write on, and we'll get started."

His secretary pops in to bring us the water we requested, and then David sits down, a legal pad in front of them. "Okay, I've studied your file, and I think we have a good chance here. But I'm going to be honest with you. There are no guarantees in a case like yours. I hate to say it, but a lot depends on the judge presiding over your case, and his or her willingness to reopen it. I just wanted to make that clear to you before we start proceedings, so you don't set your hopes too high and get disappointed."

I nod. "I get it, and it's kind of what I expected. I appreciate you even trying, to be honest." I shoot Lucky a quick look sideways, then decide to get the money topic out of the way first. "Lucky said you decided to take this case on pro bono, is that correct? I just want to make sure, because I don't want him paying for it. If you charge a fee, I will do my best to pay you."

David shakes his head, a smile on his face. "No, there's no need to pay me. This is pro bono, both as a favor to Ranger and to you. I'd love to claim it's because your case is special or challenging, but I'd be lying. The sad truth is that I see a lot of cases like yours, and nine out of ten times pro bono lawyers reject them because there is not much glory and fame to be made. I try to do as many of them as I can fit into my schedule, because I happen to think justice shouldn't be exclusive to those who can afford a good lawyer. So, we're good."

"Thank you," I say, and I don't think I've ever meant the words more.

Lucky takes my hand, a simple gesture that means more to me than he could possibly understand. The fact that he's sitting here with me, it means everything to me.

"As I said, I've read your file, and I think the case is pretty clear. Your...ex-boyfriend or whatever you want to call him set you up to take the fall. I'm not sure if he had planned this specific case, or if it was more of a coincidence that you got caught on this one, but the fact is that he set precautions in place that would make sure he could walk away free and you would get blamed."

Lucky speaks up for the first time. "How did his lawyer miss this? I mean, if it's this clear to you."

David sighs. "Look, it's easy to blame his lawyer, but the reality is that those public defenders, they're not only rookies trying to get enough experience to be hired by a reputable firm, but they're also horribly overworked. They're court-appointed and get paid little to work an impossible amount of cases. I've seen some statistics that on general, they have less than half an hour to prepare a case, sometimes even as little as ten to fifteen minutes. So yeah, his lawyer fucked up, but it wouldn't be fair to just blame him. The system behind him bears guilt as well."

I'm not surprised by his explanation since it's kind of what I came up with myself. The young guy who defended me wasn't a bad guy. Okay, he could've shown more interest in me, both as a person and for my case. But even I could see he was at the end of his rope, probably on the verge of a burnout. It doesn't make it okay, but it does help to understand how it happened.

"What we need to reopen your case is new evidence of your innocence," David says. "Obviously, the period to appeal the initial ruling has long passed, so this is our only option. The good news is that we have found enough evidence to request a judge to reopen the case."

I sit up straight. "You have? What kind of evidence?"

"You spoke to one of my paralegals a week or two ago, right?" David asks.

"Yeah. She asked me a ton of questions about what happened, and I tried to give her as much information as I could. It was hard to remember all the details, but I told her as much as I could remember."

"Correct. Based on the information you gave us, we decided to focus on what we think was the weakest element in the case against you. You told us that the car you were driving was put in your name by Terry, arguably to protect this asset from either the IRS or litigation of some kind. The insurance, however, was in his name, which made sense because he would've paid an insurance premium for you, considering your age. You were under twenty-five, after all, so a young driver premium on an expensive car like that would've been hefty. That's a definite argument that the car was, in fact, his. We've further established this by doing a little research into the history of the car and who was driving it. One of the mistakes he made, is that he put a toll pass in it, again in his name. We requested the files from the transport authority since they so helpfully take pictures regularly when people pass through the toll gates. Every single picture shows Terry as the driver, not you. He also got pulled over twice for speeding in that car, and in both cases, he was listed as the driver on the ticket. We feel we have enough evidence to suggest that the car was in fact his, not yours."

Lucky squeezes my hand, and I look over to meet his eyes; I can see my own excitement reflected in his.

David checks some printed papers in front of him, before continuing. "But there's more. You also told us that you couldn't remember signing for both the purchase and the contract of the phone that was supposedly yours. Plus, you claimed you never used it before that day, that it was in fact Terry's phone. That was pretty easy for us to check, and we found the contract he signed with the cell phone provider. Yes, it has your signature on it, but it's clear it's a forgery when we compared it to the signatures you provided us with. It shows he impersonated you without your permission."

I'm suddenly lightheaded. I know Lucky believed me.

And I've heard David say he knew I was innocent as well. But to hear him lay out this evidence that clearly shows I was set up, it does something to me. I can't explain it, but it kind of feels like something is loosening inside me. Something that had been tied up, chained, maybe. It rushes through me, this sense of exhilaration, of joy.

"Do you need a moment, baby?" Lucky asks, looking at me with a worried look on his face.

I shake my head. "No, I'm good. Better than I've ever been. Thank you so much, David. I can't believe how much you've been able to dig up already."

David sends me a kind smile. "This is just a small sample of all the facts we've gathered in your defense. As I said, I want to warn against declaring victory just yet. We still have to convince the judge to reopen your case, but I'm confident that once this happens, you will be exonerated. There is no denying the evidence we've found."

"If the judge reverses the verdict, then what?" Lucky asks.

"In that case, his criminal record will be cleared, and he could receive a monetary award for each day he spent in prison. In cases like this, it's not a lot of money."

I shrug. "I couldn't care less about the money. I just want to clear my name."

"With your permission," David says, "I would also like to contact the district attorney. I think that with the evidence we've gathered, he might be interested in prosecuting Terry for a number of offenses, identity theft being one of them. But his first question will be if you would be willing to testify against him. You shared a lot of information with my paralegal about the criminal activities Terry is involved in and your knowledge thereof, and I'm sure the DA would love to hear more. The question is, are you willing?"

I don't even have to think about it. "Yes, absolutely."

"Heart, I would be remiss if I didn't inform you this could have repercussions. Terry is not a guy with a lot of reach, but he could make things unpleasant for you if you testify against him. He may drag your past into this, your work as a prostitute, and also your present job working in porn. Both things could be used against you, and it could get ugly. I just want you to be aware before you make your final decision."

"I know, but I'm willing to anyway. I should've come clean when I got arrested instead of protecting him. I should've never felt this loyalty toward him because he clearly wasn't worth it. He fucked me over, causing me to spend three years of my life that I'll never get back in prison. The very least I can do in return is to talk to the DA or anyone else about everything I know about his operation."

David smiles. "Good. My office will prepare all the paperwork to file a motion with the judge, and we'll keep you posted as that develops. Don't expect quick results. This might take a while."

I all but dance as we leave his office, the joy inside me barely containable. I know David warned me not to get my hopes up, and I realize there's still a chance I will get fucked over again. But the truth is that it doesn't matter anymore. There is evidence that I'm innocent, that I was set up. That's all that matters to me. I'm not gonna deny getting my name cleared would be the icing on the cake, but for now, this is enough.

Lucky hasn't let go of my hand, and I turn to him as soon as were outside, launching myself in his arms. He catches me, as I knew he would, and his strong arms come around me.

"Thank you so much," I manage. "You have no idea how much this means to me, to see you believe in me this much."

He kisses my head first, then my forehead, then finally, his lips settle on mine for a long, deep kiss. I pour all my emotions and all my gratitude...and all my love. If there has ever been any doubt in me that I'm in love with Lucky, it's all gone now.

"I love you," I whisper against his lips. "I love you so fucking much. I'm sorry you had to wait so long for me to say that. I was so scared of getting hurt again."

Lucky's face breaks open in a smile, and my heart stumbles. "It was worth the wait, every minute of it. I love you so much. Loving you and Mason, it's made me the luckiest man on the planet."

50

LUCKY

I'm lying in bed, waiting for Heart and Mason to get out of the shower. We spent a few hours on the beach and got all sticky and messy from playing an impromptu beach volleyball game against some guys we ran into on the beach.

Mason was a little apprehensive about playing at first, obviously since he considers himself not the most athletic type in the bunch. But the other guys did a great job assuring him that it was for fun alone, and it only took a few minutes before he joined us. It was a lot of fun, the three of us against those three, even though we lost miserably.

That wasn't Mason's fault, by the way, as it turns out Heart sucks at beach volleyball as well. Not that it bothered him; whenever he spectacularly missed a ball, he was the first one to laugh about it. I admire that about him, the ability to be spontaneous and allow himself to fail at things. It's something both Mason and I can learn a lot from.

Obviously, when we got home, we all wanted to shower. My shower is pretty roomy, but not big enough for three. So, I went first and then sent in Mason and Heart to shower together. I know how much Mason loves it when he gets to shower with one of us. It's not even always sexual. For some reason, he just enjoys the intimacy of that simple act. I guess he still has a lot of affection to catch up on, courtesy of his asshole ex-boyfriend. I swear, if I ever run into that guy…

I'm naked, hoping to entice those two in a little fooling around after their shower. We've had a busy couple of days with me working overtime three days in a row, and Heart doing a double shift at the senior center because one of his coworkers fell ill.

Mason on his part has been pretty busy with Troy, trying to get more funding for the game and take it to the next level. I am so freaking proud of him for the steps he's taking. He's told me about a few ideas he and Troy have for their next game, and I'm sure it's gonna be a big success. They're also preparing for their job interview next week.

But with being so busy, we've had little time to spend together, especially for sex. Now obviously, that's not the most important thing, but I have to admit I do miss it. So here I am, lying naked on the covers, my cock already hard at even the thought of spending quality time with my boys. My heart speeds up when I hear the shower being turned off, and then Mason's cute giggle as Heart teases him about something.

When they walk in, I am propped up against the headboard, my legs spread wide to give them a good view of my erection. Heart is the first to notice me, and a sexy smile spreads across his lips.

"That's a pretty picture," he says, his voice a little husky. "Don't you agree, baby?" he says to Mason.

"Mmm," Mason says, as he usually does when he can't find words that quickly. His appreciative look at my body makes me even harder.

"I think he's trying to tell us something, don't you think? Like, maybe he wants us to...do something." Heart's voice is teasing, and his eyes twinkle.

Mason clears his throat. "What...what do you think he would want us to do?" he says, playing along.

Heart tugs at the towel that is wrapped around Mason's waist, causing it to drop to the floor. Of course, he himself walked in naked in the first place, comfortable as always with his body. He reaches out and grabs Mason's neck, then pulls him in gently to bring their mouths together. Just before he kisses him, his eyes find mine as he says, "I don't know, but let's find out..."

I watch, my body hardening and my heart warming, as Heart seduces Mason into one of his toe-curling kisses. I love the way he drags Mason out of the shell of insecurity that's still there. It's not as bad as it was, not by far, but it always takes a few seconds before Mason lets go of it. And no one can make him lose it faster than Heart. Then again, when he kisses you, the world could pretty much explode, and you wouldn't notice.

The kiss intensifies, and I can see Heart's tongue plunging into Mason's mouth again and again, until all Mason can do is hang on for the ride. He starts rutting against Heart, his cock seeking friction, and it's a wonderful sight to see his slender body next to Heart's toned one. They're such a study in contrasts, and yet they both have my heart.

I fist my cock, slowly, not because I have any intention of jerking off for real, but more because I need to do something with this building desire inside of me. I love watching them, but it's the sweetest torture to be able to only *watch*. I need them, but it seems I'm on Heart's schedule now, and he's intent on making me wait a little longer.

He takes his time kissing Mason, and I think minutes have passed before he finally breaks off the kiss, leaving both of them with their lips wet and swollen. They're beautiful, and my heart does a little tumble.

"Do you think that's what he had in mind?" Heart asks Mason.

Mason looks at me, my fist still wrapped around my cock. "I think he may want a little more," he says.

Heart smiles. "I think he does. So, let's give him a little more, shall we?"

He gently pushes against Mason until he gets the hint, and then he walks him backward till Mason hits the bed and lets himself fall backward on the bed with Heart on top of him. They're at the foot end of the bed, just too far from me to reach.

Heart gestures at Mason to scoot up the bed a little higher, and after giving him a last kiss, much sweeter than the passionate kiss before, he starts a trail of kisses from his mouth downward. This is private Heart, not porn Heart, and the difference is so clear to me that I feel honored and warm inside at the same time that I get to witness this.

He is so sweet, so attentive, so wonderfully loving toward Mason, peppering his chest with little licks and bites and kisses until Mason is squirming on the bed. Heart takes his right nipple between his thumb and forefinger and gently twists and rolls, causing Mason to let out a loud moan.

Heart smiles. "I love how you respond to my touch," he says, then does the same to Mason's left nipple.

His tongue soothes the pert little buds with a lick, and then he does it all over again. Mason bucks off the bed, begging Heart for more.

Heart continues his slow, torturous descent of Mason's body, and I note with interest that Mason's cock is leaking as much as mine. Then Heart's tongue peeks out to lick the few droplets of fluid that pearl at the tip. Mason and I moan at the same time. This is sheer torture, watching the two of them play with each other. But what a sweet torture it is, observing how Heart makes Mason soar.

Mason's body is trembling now in anticipation of Heart's next move, and I can't imagine him making the boy wait much longer. Mason is so unfiltered in his reactions that you can't help but give him what he wants. It's intoxicating, the way he responds to your every touch, your every word, every little thing you do to him.

Heart sends Mason one last sweet smile, and then his mouth descends, and he swallows Mason's cock in one big gulp, taking him to the root. Mason's eyes cross, and the pleasure on his face is so intense, I can feel my own balls respond.

Heart has serious oral skills, and it only takes a minute or so before Mason starts to tremble, grabbing Heart's head with both hands. Heart lets him, allows Mason to buck upward into his mouth. Seconds later, Mason lets out a loud grunt, and his body twitches and jerks as he comes down Heart's throat.

Heart licks him clean before letting him go, and he cuddles up with Mason on the bed. Mason's body is completely slack in Heart's arms, wiped out by his orgasm.

"You're so beautiful when you come," Heart tells Mason.

"That was…" Mason lets out a long sigh. "Epic."

His head suddenly jerks to the side as he looks at me. "What about Lucky? We completely forgot about him."

Heart chuckles. "I didn't forget about him at all. I just figured he would appreciate a little show before he got involved."

He meets my eyes, and I smile at him. "Oh, I did appreciate it. What did you have in mind next?"

Heart kisses Mason on his lips, then rolls over to cuddle with me. I pull him close, reveling in his swollen, warm lips against my cooler ones. Mason snuggles against him from the back, and Heart is tucked between us with both of us curled around him. His face is softer than I've ever seen it, devoid of the weariness he so often shows. He's lost his mask, and it's a gift I vow to never betray.

"What do you want, baby?" I whisper against his lips.

Heart takes a deep breath, reaching for Mason's hand and lacing his fingers through it as he meets my eyes. "I want you guys to DP me."

51

HEART

I wait anxiously for Mason's and Lucky's answer. I honestly don't know how they will react. I've wanted this for a long time, but up until now, I didn't know how to say it. Or maybe I wasn't ready yet. Hell, maybe we weren't ready yet, as a threesome.

Double penetration is not for beginners, no matter how sexy it may look on a porn video. It takes serious experience on the part of the bottom, and good prep is an absolute requirement. Obviously, I have done it plenty of times, and it is something I truly love. I'm vers, and I love being fucked as much as I love topping, but if a DP is on the table, I will happily bottom anytime.

That being said, doing it with these two men will be a completely different experience, and I can't wait to share this with them. It takes a lot of trust for me to do this with them, but they've shown they're worthy of my trust every step of the way. I want to share this with them, to show them how much they mean to me. I just hope they want to, that they don't think this is too kinky or too...I don't know, *out there*.

Mason and Lucky look at each other before Lucky refocuses on me. "I would love to," Lucky says. "But baby, are you sure this is something you want to do? You don't have to. We don't expect you to do anything with us that you don't really want to."

I sit up so I can see both of them, but I make sure to stay physically connected to both. I never thought I'd come to crave this intimacy, but I do.

"I really want to. I love doing this in a scene, so I can't even imagine how wonderful it will feel with the two of you. It's hard to explain since neither of you have any experience with this, but I really love it. And I think it would be an amazing experience for you as well. I mean, I have done DPs where I was topping as well, and the sensation of your cock being squeezed tight against another man's cock is a unique experience."

Lucky extends his hand to Mason, and when Mason accepts its, he pulls him close so he sits next to him. "What do you think, sweetheart? Is this something you want to do?"

I worry my bottom lip as I see the doubt flash over Mason's face. Maybe this was a stupid idea. Not everybody is into things like this. I guess I shouldn't have pushed my luck.

"I'm scared we will hurt you," Mason whispers. He gently shakes his head as if talking to himself. "No, I'm scared I will hurt you. You know I'm not the most coordinated guy on the planet, and I'm afraid I'll do something clumsy and inadvertently hurt you. I would never forgive myself if that happened."

The worry in my stomach dissolves. "Is that what you worried about?" I ask. "You're so sweet to think of me first, baby. But you don't have to worry. We will do this together, and I won't let you hurt me. I will tell you exactly how to do it, okay? And it's not like Lucky has ever done this before, so I can teach you both. I just... I want to experience this with you."

Mason nods, still a little hesitant, but I can see the determination on his face. "Okay. If you promise me you'll tell us when we're doing something wrong."

"I promise," I say. "Lucky?"

He flashes me a big smile. "Oh, I'm in. I'm *so* in."

For a second, we stare at each other, a tangible zing of excitement in the air.

"Wanna help me prep our man?" Lucky asks Mason, who nods after a short hesitation.

Lucky gently pushes me on my stomach, and seconds later, I hear the familiar sound of lube being opened. Two hands touch my ass, one hesitant and one quite sure, and it's easy to tell who is who.

"Look at him, all beautiful on display for us, baby," Lucky tells Mason.

"I love his ass," Mason sighs with a little more confidence in his voice.

"Me too," Lucky chuckles. "But yours is pretty sweet too, baby."

Sucking sounds inform me they're sharing a kiss, but Lucky is a good multitasker, because he finds my hole and slips a finger in at the same time, starting to stretch me. Seconds later, Mason's finger joins him, and I love that they're doing this together as well.

"I think this is going to feel so good, sweetheart," Lucky says, his voice low and sexy. "Not just for the two of us, but for Heart as well. I can't wait to bring him pleasure, can you?"

Mason hums his approval, and Lucky adds a third finger.

I welcome the burn of the stretch, impatient to get ready for this. I can't wait to share this with them, to offer myself to my men like this.

Mason drops a wet kiss between my shoulder blades, then another one. "You're so beautiful," he sighs, his voice soft with emotion.

Lucky mumbles something, and then I'm stretched even wider, and I breathe in deeply to relax. It's Mason's finger, I'm sure, and even the thought of their fingers inside me is sexy as hell.

"Feel how tight our fingers are squeezed together?" Lucky whispers to Mason. "Imagine how that's gonna feel on our cocks."

I have to clear my throat before I'm able to speak. "I'm ready," I say. "I'm more than ready."

They pull out, and Lucky turns me over. "You can tell us to stop at any time," he assures me before kissing me softly. "Thank you for trusting us with this, baby."

Lucky rolls a condom around Mason's cock, while I sheathe him up. I'd love to go bareback someday, but that's not gonna happen as long as I'm in porn.

With a little maneuvering, my men position themselves, facing each other and their asses pressed against each other, Mason's legs on top of Lucky's, so I can bring their cocks together. Lucky is still propped up against the headboard, and I've put a few pillows behind Mason's back so he can continue to see what's happening.

Lucky grabs both their cocks in his big fist. "Mmm, look at how beautiful this is, our two cocks squeezed together. It's gonna be even tighter when we're inside Heart..."

Mason lets out soft little moan, and I send Lucky a smile of appreciation for helping me to relax Mason and get him ready for this. I position myself above their cocks, my knees on either side of my men as I face Lucky. Lucky's hand stays wrapped around their cocks, holding them straight so I can guide them in.

"Now watch, baby," Lucky says. "Watch our beautiful boy swallow us whole."

I focus on my breathing as their cock heads press against me. No matter how much experience you have, a DP is never easy. It takes skill to stay relaxed at an intrusion like that, and I pause a second as they breach me, stretching me with a burn that's as much pain as it is pleasure.

"Holy crap," Mason gasps. "He's really doing it."

"Hold absolutely still," I warn, grateful for Lucky's strong hand that's able to prevent Mason from moving too much. In this phase, that could potentially hurt me.

I frown with concentration as I lower myself, taking them in another inch. It's slow going now, with me focusing on my breathing and on relaxing. I love this part, the burn that spreads from my entrance all the way deep inside, and I can't wait to feel them completely inside me. There's nothing to describe the sensation of being that full.

Sweat beads on my forehead as I take them in another inch, and then another, until I feel Lucky remove his hands, and I can bring them home. They're inside me, filling me deeper than I ever thought possible. My eyes well up, and it's not because of any pain.

"We're in," Lucky says, and the look on his face is pure joy. "Are you okay?"

"I'm good," I whisper. "More than good."

Carefully, I raise myself a few inches and then lower my ass again. Holy crap, it thunders through me, this fullness and burn and sensation of being stretched beyond my limits. It's everything I thought it would be and then some.

"How does it feel for you, sweetheart?" Lucky asks Mason.

It's like he knows I don't have words right now. I can't focus on anything else but the incredible fullness inside of me. It's like it pushes everything else out, and all that's left is to feel. And right now, all I feel is pleasure.

My body is on fire, sensations assaulting me from every side. Even the tiniest move causes one of their dicks to tag my prostate, and the feeling is indescribable, sending flares of delight deep inside me, then radiating back outward to my balls and my dick.

But I don't want to come. I want to stay like this for a long time, stay connected to them...forever.

52

MASON

I've never felt anything like this in my life. My cock trapped against Lucky's, surrounded by Heart's hot, tight channel. I drag in ragged breaths and will myself not to blow it too soon, a task made all the more difficult by the way Heart is carefully riding us, his head thrown back and desperate moans falling from his lips.

"So good, ungh, fuck," he whimpers, clutching Lucky's shoulders. My cock throbs, and in the confined space, it sends shockwaves through me, every sensation feeling like it's amplified a million times.

Careful not to move too much and accidentally slip out, I reach for Heart's waist, desperate for more points of contact with him, with both of them. Lucky's hand lands on top of mine and our eyes meet over Heart's shoulder. There's a smoldering heat in his gaze that tightens my balls and sets my body on fire. How is this my life?

Heart turns his head toward me, his face distorted with pleasure so intense you'd swear it's killing him.

"Kiss, please, Mase," he begs.

"Anything, always," I assure him, shifting slightly,

causing a strangled cry to fall from Heart's lips and a gasp from Lucky's.

My lips meet Heart's. I expected a hard, hungry kiss since that's what Heart seems to favor when he's close to coming. Instead, he licks lazily into my mouth, teasing and playing with my tongue, the kiss completely incongruent with the desperate way he's riding our cocks.

The feeling of Lucky's cock sliding against mine is enough to drive me out of my mind all on its own. But when Heart's channel tightens, the breath is punched from my lungs, my body trembling with my effort to hold back my threatening orgasm.

"I'm close," I warn against Heart's lips, my hands tightening on his hips.

"Me too, make me come, sweetheart. Please, I need your hand," Heart pleads.

Lucky and I move our hands to Heart's cock at the same time, and Heart grunts and whimpers as we jerk him off together.

"Oh god, oh fuck, I'm coming, I'm...ungh," Heart gasps and cries, and this time his channel squeezes so tight around our cocks it's almost painful. With one last deep moan, his warm seed spills over our fists.

I can't hold back any longer, the pulsing of his hole dragging me over the edge. My balls draw up tight, and the heat in the pit of my stomach explodes through my body as I come deep inside him, spilling into the condom. Every throb of my orgasm is amplified not only by Heart's muscles squeezing tight in return, but by every hard pulse of Lucky's cock against mine. It feels like our orgasms go on forever, drawn out by each other's pleasure, until we end up in a sticky, sweaty heap of bodies, all panting for breath.

Eventually, Lucky and I manage to remove our condoms

and throw them away, and Heart grabs a stray article of clothing to wipe himself off, and then tosses it to me to wipe the cum off my hand, and Lucky does the same.

When we lie back down, I somehow end up between Lucky and Heart. The feeling of both men surrounding me is almost more perfect than my heart can handle. Lucky spoons against me from behind, trailing lazy kisses along my shoulder and the back of my neck as he reaches out for Heart as well. Heart scoots close to me and puts his arms around both me and Lucky. Lucky's hand rests on Heart's hip to connect all three of us together.

Sex always wears Lucky out, so I'm not surprised when his breath evens out and his arm gets heavy. Heart's eyelids flutter open and closed like he's trying to keep them closed but can't seem to manage it yet.

"Was that good for you?" I whisper, not wanting to disturb Lucky's sleep.

Heart gives me a sweet smile and leans forward to kiss the tip of my nose. "It was amazing. My ass is going to be feeling that for a week."

A little ripple of pleasure goes through me knowing Heart will be feeling me and Lucky long after we were inside him. I'm surprised to realize a primal part of me likes that thought.

We fall silent for a few minutes, both of us still awake but neither bothering to break the peaceful moment with words. My mind wanders, and before I know it, it's dug up an issue I had put aside to worry about later. I guess my brain has decided it's later now.

"Can I talk to you about something?"

"Of course, baby. What's up?" Heart asks, concern in his eyes.

"When the three of us were first talking about trying

things, and Lucky told you he wanted to hold off on sex with you, he said something about wanting you to know that not everyone is only after sex from you."

"Yeah, I remember," he agrees.

"I want you to know, I wasn't only after sex from you. I know I asked you to help me with my bedroom skills, but I never meant to make you feel like I only saw you as a sex object or anything like that."

"Oh, sweetheart." He brushes his lips against mine, sweet and slow until my heart feels like it's going to burst. "I never thought you only wanted me for sex. You're the best friend I've had in my whole life. Before I met you, everyone I've known either looked down on me or saw me as a means to an end. I was never just a person to anyone. Then you came along, all sweetness and pink cheeks, and you just wanted to hang out, talk, joke around. All you wanted was to be with *me*. By the time the sex stuff came up between us, I was happy for an excuse to have an outlet for all the things you'd made me feel, even though I wasn't ready to feel them."

I lick my dry lips, my stomach in knots as I try to parse out what Heart's trying to say.

"What did I make you feel?" I ask.

Heart's quiet for so long I start to think he's not going to answer. Then he tilts my chin up, and his eyes bore into mine. There's so much emotion spilling from his gaze that I almost can't breathe, but I can't look away.

"You made me feel special and seen. You made me feel loved, and you made me fall in love with you."

I gasp at his words. It was one thing to hear Lucky tell me he loves me, still surprising and surreal, but it made sense in a way. But Heart? I don't understand how he can love me. How I can possibly have two amazing men who are all mine?

"I love you," I choke out, pressing my lips to his again and letting all my emotions flow into the kiss. I don't care how crazy it is, these men are mine, and I'm never letting them go.

53

MASON

I'm still shaking when we step out of the conference room.

"I did it," I say with awe. "I really did it. I didn't drop or break anything, and I got through my whole presentation without messing up."

"I know; you did awesome, man." Troy claps me on the back. "And we officially have a sponsor."

I resist the urge to do a little dance. With my luck, all the fancy people in the conference room would come out right at that moment to see me dancing like an idiot.

"We did it," I say again in a bit of a daze.

"We did," Troy agrees. "This calls for a celebration. Call your men, and I'll call Rebel; let's get everyone to come out to the club tonight to celebrate with us."

My men. I'm not sure I'll ever get over the little thrill that goes through me at that.

We head out of the building to catch our Uber, both making our calls to set up our little celebration. And for once, I'm actually excited to go to the club. I don't even care that I'll look a little dorky dancing with Heart and

Lucky. I'll still have the hottest boyfriends in the whole club.

We get everyone to agree to meet at the club in a few hours, except Lucky who tells me he'll be a little late but will make it as soon as he can. And then we both get dropped off at our places to drop our notes and get ready to go out later.

I whistle as I get dressed, no longer stressing over what to wear. I know Lucky loves my nerdy clothes, so I pick a t-shirt with an N64 cartridge and the words *blow me* on it. Heart will like the crude joke, and Lucky will enjoy the reference, win-win. I pair it with a pair of my tighter jeans that, according to Heart, make my ass look fantastic, finger-comb my hair and slip on my Converse and then grab my keys and head out.

When I get to Bottoms Up, the guys are all waiting outside. Rebel and Troy are hand in hand, Brewer and Tank are alternating between bickering and kissing, Campy has his new roommate Jackson with him looking uncomfortable as hell, making me think he's never been to a gay club before, and Pixie is flirting with Bear to no avail. Heart smiles as I approach and pulls me in for a kiss as soon as I'm within arm's reach.

"You look sexy as fuck," he murmurs against my lips, copping a feel of my ass and making me giggle.

"You two are disgustingly adorable," Troy declares.

"Just wait until Lucky gets here." I wink, and Troy laughs.

There's a lightness in my heart I'm starting to get used to. I feel like for the first time in my life I'm free to really be myself without anyone judging or rejecting me, and at the core of it, I have Troy to thank. If he hadn't stepped in when Brad was being so horrible, who knows where I'd be? Not to mention, introducing me to Heart, dragging me to the club the night I ended up meeting Lucky. He really is the best friend a guy could have.

The bouncer, Greg, greets us and groans when he spots Heart's hand in mine.

"You boys keep pairing off, and I'm going to die of heartbreak," he jokes.

"Aw poor thing. I get the feeling you get plenty of action with all the cute boys who come here," Pixie says, patting Greg's broad shoulder.

"There are plenty of cute boys," Greg agrees. "But I'm still looking for Mr. Right. Maybe one day," he says wistfully before waving us inside.

"Dance or drinks first?" Heart asks.

"One dance and then drinks until Lucky gets here."

Heart nods in agreement and pulls me toward the dance floor. The thought of dancing in the crowded club used to give me hives, Brad would drag me out here and then get mad when I'd get away as quickly as possible. But with Heart's chest pressed to my back, my ass snug against him, our bodies moving to the music…yeah, this isn't so bad.

I tilt my head back against Heart's shoulder, and his lips trail along my exposed neck. My moan is swallowed up by the pounding music, but I know Heart felt it. His hard cock pressed against my ass gives me all kinds of ideas about how we can continue this celebration after the club tonight.

After twenty minutes or so on the dance floor, I'm in desperate need of something to drink.

"I'm going to grab a drink; I'll be back," I say into Heart's ear, and he nods, kissing me hard and then smacking my ass as I walk away.

I grumble a little to myself as I push my way up to the bar. I don't care how many boyfriends or how much confidence I have, some things will always be hell on earth.

I ask for a couple of water bottles and then lean against the bar to wait.

"You still haven't improved your shitty fashion sense."

I cringe at the familiar, snide voice. I accept the water bottles from the bartender and then gather my courage to turn around and face him.

"Brad," I say blandly, giving him a simple nod in greeting before making a move to step past him.

"Hold on a second," he says, grabbing my arm. "It's been awhile, you don't want to catch up?"

"Not particularly. I have to get back to my boyfriend," I inform him, feeling smug.

Brad snorts and gives me a pitying look. "Your *boyfriend*? You mean that guy you were dancing with who started making out with some other guy the second you walked away?"

I crane my neck to see what Brad's talking about. Just as I suspected, Lucky showed up while I was getting waters, and the two of them are putting on quite the show—grinding and making out on the dance floor like the world's about to end.

"Yeah, those are my boyfriends," I confirm with a smirk.

"Yeah, okay," Brad responds sarcastically. "You're a geek who doesn't like sex, and you're dating the two hottest guys in the club?"

"I like sex, Brad. I just didn't like the artless way you used to shove your tiny dick inside me and writhe around like a dying fish." I kind of wish Troy was here to hear that zinger and laugh at how purple Brad's face turns. "Now, if you'll excuse me."

I make my way through the crowd toward my men. When I reach them, they part and tug me in between their sweaty bodies. I hand each of them a water bottle, and then

I grab the back of Lucky's neck and kiss him hard, before turning my head and doing the same to Heart.

"Someone's in a good mood," Heart notes, wrapping an arm around me and trailing it up my chest, under my shirt.

"It's a good night. But I have a feeling it'll be even better after we get out of here."

"Mmmm, I like the sound of that," Lucky murmurs, licking and nibbling at my throat.

"Dance a little longer, then home for sex," Heart declares.

"Good plan," I agree, letting myself get lost in the rhythm of Heart and Lucky's bodies sandwiching me between them.

I have no idea if Brad stayed to watch or not, and I don't care. The Mason who let himself be berated and degraded by his boyfriend is gone, and he's never coming back. No need to dwell on the past because my future is looking damn good.

EPILOGUE (HEART)

One Year Later

"I just realized something really stupid. I've known you over a year and we've been dating for more than six months, and I've *never* asked your real name." Mason looks horrified by his realization.

I lean forward and give him a sweet kiss, because that's just *so* Mason.

"My birth name isn't really me. I *am* Heart. Even after my porn career ends, I'll be Heart."

"Okay," he says simply, perfectly content with that answer, and that's why I love him so fucking much.

The front door opens and Lucky steps into his apartment—no, *our* apartment. I still can't get used to the idea that I live with Lucky and Mason, that they love every ugly and beautiful part of me, and that I get to keep them forever. It's surreal and amazing.

Lucky greets each of us with a kiss before settling in beside me on the couch, with Mason on my other side.

"All set for your first day of classes tomorrow?" Lucky checks with me, and I nod.

It didn't take as long as I thought for the defense lawyer to get my record expunged, and the best part about it is now that I don't have a criminal record, I can go to nursing school. Well, not nursing school quite yet, I still have a lot of prerequisites to do before I can apply, but I'm taking the first step toward a career where I'll be able to help people every day. On the bright side, I finished my GED while I was behind bars, so at least that's out of the way.

"I'm a little nervous because I never liked school that much, but I'm excited to take this next step in my life."

"It's different when you're learning stuff you're interested in," Mason assures me. "And I have it on good authority that one of your boyfriends is a total nerd who can likely help you with just about any class...except public speaking."

I snort a laugh and reach for Mason's hand.

"What's your work schedule like this week?" Lucky asks Mason.

"I have to go into the office Tuesday and Wednesday, then I'll be working from home the rest of the week."

Lucky and I weren't surprised when Mason was offered the job at Blue Star games, and shortly after he started, they even got on board with developing one of *his* game ideas. He's been over the moon about it and having to spend a night or two a week out of town isn't as bad as any of us feared when he accepted the position. As he predicted when he told us about the interview, most of his work can be done from home, so he normally only has to go to Escondido for meetings and aspects of the project that require work with other team members.

Troy accepted the job as well, and I have a feeling the two of them together are going to continue to create gaming magic.

"I talked to my dad yesterday, and I was thinking maybe the three of us could go out there in a few months for Thanksgiving? I've talked so much about you guys he's actually curious to meet you," Mason chuckles. He's told us a lot about his dad, and it explains so much about how Mason was when I first met him. He's still socially awkward and anxious at times, but the confidence I've seen shining through him in the past year has been astounding.

"Works for me," I agree.

"I'm up for that," Lucky adds.

"Love you guys," Mason says as he crawls into my lap and then reaches for Lucky's hand. "Let's have sex."

I snort a laugh. Did I mention Mason's confidence has grown exponentially?

"You know I never turn down sex," I agree, sneaking my hand under Mason's shirt and pinching his nipple.

"Hey, do you still have that sexy dice game?" he asks, his eyes lighting up.

"Sexy dice game?" Lucky asks.

"It's something Heart and I played when we first started fooling around," Mason explains to Lucky.

"I think I do have it. Why don't we go to the bedroom and look," I suggest with a lecherous grin. I have no fucking clue if I kept those dice in the move or not, but as long as the three of us are together, I have no doubt we'll manage to entertain each other.

The End

KEEP AN EYE OUT FOR MORE BALLSY BOYS!

Sexy porn stars looking for real love! Expect plenty of steam, but all the feels as well. They can be read as standalones, but are more fun when read in order.

Rebel is the star of Ballsy Boys, but will he find a man to call his own? Why is Campy being so secretive? And will Pixie get his daddy? And don't miss the sizzling enemies to lovers story from Tank and Brewer!

- Ballsy (free prequel)
- Rebel
- Tank
- Heart
- Campy
- Pixie

MORE ABOUT K.M. NEUHOLD

Author K.M.Neuhold is a complete romance junkie, a total sap in every way. She started her journey as an author in new adult, MF romance, but after a chance reading of an MM book she was completely hooked on everything about lovely- and sometimes damaged- men finding their Happily Ever After together.

She has a strong passion for writing characters with a lot of heart and soul, and a bit of humor as well. And she fully admits that her OCD tendencies of making sure every side character has a full backstory will likely always lead to every book having a spin-off or series.

When she's not writing she's a lion tamer, an astronaut, and a superhero...just kidding, she's likely watching Netflix and snuggling with her husky while her amazing husband brings her coffee.

Stalk Me
Website: www.authorkmneuhold.com
Email: kmneuhold@gmail.com
Instagram: @KMNeuhold

Twitter: @KMNeuhold

Bookbub: https://goo.gl/MV6UXp

Join my mailing list for special bonus scenes and teasers: https://landing.mailerlite.com/webforms/landing/m4p6v2

Facebook Reader Group Neuhold's Nerds: You want to be here, we have crazy amounts of fun: http://facebook.com/groups/kmneuhold

MORE ABOUT NORA PHOENIX

Would you like the long or the short version of my bio? The short? You got it.

I write steamy gay romance books and I love it. I also love reading books. Books are everything.

How was that? A little more detail? Gotcha.

I started writing my first stories when I was a teen...on a freaking typewriter. I still have these, and they're adorably romantic. And bad, haha. Fear of failing kept me from following my dream to become a romance author, so you can imagine how proud and ecstatic I am that I finally overcame my fears and self doubt and did it. I adore my genre because I love writing and reading about flawed, strong men who are just a tad broken..but find their happy ever after anyway.

My favorite books to read are pretty much all MM/gay romances as long as it has a happy end. Kink is a plus... Aside from that, I also read a lot of nonfiction and not just books on writing. Popular psychology is a favorite topic of mine and so are self help and sociology.

Hobbies? Ain't nobody got time for that. Just kidding. I

love traveling, spending time near the ocean, and hiking. But I love books more.

Come hang out with me in my Facebook Group Nora's Nook where I share previews, sneak peeks, freebies, fun stuff, and much more:
https://www.facebook.com/groups/norasnook/

Wanna get first dibs on freebies, updates, sales, and more? Sign up for my newsletter (no spamming your inbox full... promise!) here:
http://www.noraphoenix.com/newsletter/

You can also stalk me on Twitter:
https://twitter.com/NoraFromBHR
On Instagram:
https://www.instagram.com/nora.phoenix/
On Bookbub:
https://www.bookbub.com/profile/nora-phoenix

BOOKS BY K.M. NEUHOLD

Stand Alones
Change of Heart

Heathens Ink
Rescue Me
Going Commando
From Ashes
Shattered Pieces
Inked in Vegas
Flash Me

Inked (AKA Heathens Ink Spin-off stories)
Unraveled
Uncomplicated

Replay
Face the Music
Play it by Ear
Beat of Their Own Drum
Strike a Chord

Ballsy Boys
    Rebel
    Tank
    Heart
    Campy
    Pixie
    Don't Miss The Kinky Boys Coming Soon

Working Out The Kinks
    Stay
    Heel

Short Stand Alones
    That One Summer (YA)
    Always You
    Kiss and Run (Valentine's Inc Book 4)

BOOKS BY NORA PHOENIX

Perfect Hands Series

Raw, emotional, both sweet and sexy, with a solid dash of kink, that's the Perfect Hands series. All books can be read as standalones.

- **Firm Hand** (daddy care with a younger daddy and an older boy)
- **Gentle Hand** (sweet daddy care with age play)

No Shame Series

If you love steamy MM romance with a little twist, you'll love the No Shame series. Sexy, emotional, with a bit of suspense and all the feels. Make sure to read in order, as this is a series with a continuing storyline.

- **No Filter**
- **No Limits**
- **No Fear**
- **No Shame**

- **No Angel**

And for all the fun, grab the **No Shame box set** which includes all five books plus exclusive bonus chapters and deleted scenes.

Irresistible Omegas Series

An mpreg series with all the heat, epic world building, poly romances (the first two books are MMMM and the rest of the series is MMM), a bit of suspense, and characters that will stay with you for a long time. This is a continuing series, so read in order.

- **Alpha's Sacrifice**
- **Alpha's Submission**
- **Beta's Surrender**
- **Alpha's Pride**
- **Beta's Strength**
- **Omega's Protector**

Ballsy Boys Series

Sexy porn stars looking for real love! Expect plenty of steam, but all the feels as well. They can be read as standalones, but are more fun when read in order.

- **Ballsy** (free prequel available through my website)
- **Rebel**
- **Tank**
- **Heart**
- **Campy**

- **Pixie**

Ignite Series

An epic dystopian sci-fi trilogy (one book out, two more to follow) where three men have to not only escape a government that wants to jail them for being gay but aliens as well. Slow burn MMM romance.

- **Ignite**

Stand Alones

I also have a few stand alone, so check these out!

- **Kissing the Teacher** (sexy daddy kink)
- **The Time of My Life** (two men meet at a TV singing contest)
- **Shipping the Captain** (falling for the boss on a cruise ship)

Printed in Great Britain
by Amazon